CROWN
of the
WARRIOR
KING

THE SONG OF PROPHETS AND KINGS

CROWN
of the
WARRIOR KING

HENRY O. ARNOLD

WhiteFire
— PUBLISHING —

CROWN OF THE WARRIOR KING

Copyright © 2021, Henry O. Arnold

All rights reserved. Reproduction in part or in whole is strictly forbidden without the express written consent of the publisher, with the exception of a brief quotation for review purposes.

Cover design and typesetting by Roseanna White Designs
Cover images from Shutterstock

Author photo by Ben Pearson

Published in association with the literary agency, WTA Media, LLC, Franklin, TN

WhiteFire Publishing
13607 Bedford Rd NE
Cumberland, MD 21502

ISBN: 978-1-941720-75-2 (print)
       978-1-941720-76-9 (digital)

To my daughters, Kristin and Lauren,
whom I love beyond measure.

PART ONE

PART ONE

Prologue

SAUL SLIPPED ON HIS ROBE OVER HIS UNDERGARMENTS—A RUS-
tic's garments. He was not ready to put on royal attire. He watched Ahinoam to see if his dressing awakened her before he bent over to pick up his
sandals. She did not move, her breathing soft and constant.

Ahinoam had not been feeling well. She became easily fatigued and
would experience unexpected waves of nausea. They both agreed that the
daily demands from their world turning upside down and the sweeping
changes of their lives was taking a physical toll on both of them. Becoming
a king and a queen of a nation, when they had always lived a simple farm
life, had not been an easy adjustment. Saul tucked his sandals under his
arm and tiptoed over to Ahinoam's side of the bed. He gently lifted the
lamb's wool blanket over her bare shoulder and then crept out of their
room.

Saul listened for any stirring in the children's rooms on the second
floor. Not a sound. It amazed Saul how his children had matured and
adapted into becoming a royal family much easier than he and Ahinoam
had. Jonathan was now a captain in the growing ranks of the national
army, the twins, Malki and Ishvi, were still too young to be soldiers, but
Abner was supervising their training, and their aspirations were high. And

his daughters, Merab and Mikal, had made the transformation from farm girls to princesses seem effortless.

Saul had not known what to expect in his role as king. It was a new way of life for him, his family, and the nation of Israel. But the new course was set and there was no going back to the old ways.

The first significant changes that were made were the compound walls. The interior of the house had not undergone any expansion. That was the last thing Saul wanted on his agenda. But the compound walls had been fortified and the builders had attached a flight of stairs on the east and west exteriors of the house. Abner had insisted this be done so the soldiers could have access to their guard posts on the roof without going inside to climb the ladder each time there was a changing of the guard. Ahinoam especially appreciated this attention to detail. That would have been too much disruption on his family.

Saul drank a few swallows of water from a goblet and splashed the remainder onto his face to clear the fog of exhaustion. Hours of sleep had been few—too much to be done, too many details to consider, too many tasks, and too few qualified people for delegating responsibilities. These were not farm chores or common trades. A new system of governing was being created and set in motion, which meant experts were needed to handle different tasks, and a thousand questions were brought to him each day, requiring a thousand decisions. Success or failure would be credited to him alone, which was enough to banish sleep. Slumber was a commodity that kept tightfisted accounts.

A splash of cold water in the face, a gargle of strong wine, and a few bites of flatbread and honey were not enough to ward off the constant weight of weariness he felt in his bones. He gave one final glance at the interior rooms of his house, whispered a prayer for Yahweh to make His face shine upon his sleeping family, and picked up a small torch to light his way to the prophet's tent before exiting.

He thrust the head of the torch into the flame attached to the exterior wall beside his doorway and then stepped into the chilly morning air, licking the honeyed breadcrumbs off his fingers. He held his robe tightly around his body as he marched toward the new entrance of his compound. The high wooden archway had been completed recently with the carved head of a wolf snarling down on all who entered ensconced in the center of the arch. Jeush, the chieftain of the tribe of Benjamin who Abner had elevated to the rank of general in the new army, had insisted upon the wolf head carving, identifying Saul's tribe of origin. Saul was the first king of Israel from the smallest tribe of all the twelve tribes, and the insignia of a wolf was the sign of Jacob's blessing and thus a point of pride. The lettering above the wolf's head read: "TRIBE OF BENJAMIN. HOUSE OF SAUL. KING OF ISRAEL."

The walls of the compound would eventually be built up and encase the arch with stone. Saul dreaded the day when he would no longer be able to walk out his front door, stand in his courtyard, and look over the wall into the forest surrounding his property. The view would be blocked by a rampart of stone with planked staircases and scaffolding running along the fortification like veins beneath the skin. But he had no choice. He and his family had to be protected. The enclosure was gradual, and with it, Saul began to feel as if he were a prisoner; that he had to be protected from enemies real and imagined. He had never been a prisoner. He had never made an enemy. But the compound walls were rising daily, and Saul felt a creeping sense of unease.

All this fortifying of his property was financed by the tribute from the tribes given in support of the chosen king. The fact that Saul had done nothing to earn this bounty was difficult for him to accept. But he had not asked to be a king, had not sought it, had done everything to avoid it, so if he was to be king by the will of Yahweh and the people of Israel, then someone must cover the expenses. The tribal leaders had come to Mizpah prepared to offer their allegiance and payment.

In the months following Saul's being crowned king, eight of the tribes had sent delegations to Gibeah to deliver the tribal tribute and began to build permanent structures outside the compound walls of Saul's home. These became the dwellings for ambassadors and dignitaries who came to petition and advise Saul and offer their assistance in helping him govern the country. The four richest tribes gave no tribute on the day he was crowned, had not sent a delegation to Gibeah since that day, nor given any explanation for this disgraceful rebellion.

Abner and Jeush argued for sending a contingent of soldiers to the four tribal leaders and their wealthy chieftains to exact payment, but Saul would not allow such strong-arm tactics, believing it wiser to give them more time to accept his leadership as Israel's first king.

The two guards posted at the entrance of the compound snapped to attention when Saul marched out of the opening. The king had established a daily routine, and the sentries knew when to anticipate him each morning. Abner demanded discipline in his military, and he expected the guards to be at attention every time the king passed before them. Saul considered his best decision so far as king was his first one: appoint his cousin Abner as commander of a new army.

Abner embraced his new position with unequaled passion, and he immediately began to recruit young men from all over the nation to form a standing army. After all, this was the main reason why the tribal leaders wanted a king. They wanted someone to fight their battles against the enemies of Israel. Saul and Abner devised a demanding military training program that quickly gained a reputation around the country. So many young men wanted to be a part of this elite fighting force that Abner had no trouble filling the quota of three thousand soldiers as the core of the first professional army financed by the nation.

Abner had impressed upon Saul the importance of a loyal military. "You treat those who protect you and are willing to die for you better than anyone else," he had told him. "A warrior's devotion is to the man not to a kingdom. Never take a soldier's loyalty for granted."

Saul bade the guards good morning and made his way across the front of the compound to the prophet's tent. So much of the landscape had changed around his home and compound that it was difficult to remember how it had been before becoming king. If this pace of construction and steady influx of people continued at its present rate, there would be no empty space between his farm and the city of Gibeah. Forest and field were giving way to a rapidly growing sprawl of new residents and complexes for military and Levitical needs. It was hard for him to come to grips with this unrelenting shift in his new reality.

He crept up to the front of the tent and pulled back the flaps, sticking his head inside. Gad and Nathan were both asleep, but the table had been set in the center of the tent with one of the chests full of scrolls beneath it and two oil lamps on either side.

Saul was envious of the indulgence of the sleep of young men. He would love a few extra hours for himself, but that was impossible. He moved quietly around the table; his tall frame bent over so as not to scrape his head along the top of the tent. After lighting the two oil lamps, he extinguished the torch in the clay receptacle beside the table, sat down on a stool, and took a moment for his eyes to adjust.

He did not pretend to be a scholar. Saul could read and write well enough, but burying his head inside sacred, historical scrolls and studying hours at a time or listening to lengthy instruction was not a practice that could keep him tied to his seat. He wanted knowledge and understanding of the ways of Yahweh to aid him in ruling. He would encourage the rituals and the offering of the sacrifices and saying the prayers and keeping the Sabbaths, but he accepted the fact that he did not have the type of relationship the prophet Samuel had with Yahweh, so he thought it was best to keep a respectful distance.

Yet deep within, Saul desired to see if it were possible for him to make his own connection with Yahweh. If, indeed, he had been chosen to be king there seemed to be some mysterious link between the Almighty and this choice of him to lead Yahweh's chosen people. Was it possible to step outside the traditional ways of engaging with the Almighty and form an individual alliance? Was this the exclusive sphere of prophet and priest or did a king or even a commoner have an opportunity to form such a bond with the Almighty on their own?

There were examples of such divine-to-human contacts in the ancient stories of Israel's past. But Samuel had not encouraged such hopes in Saul. The prophet seemed to want to remain as mediator between Yahweh and himself and had not encouraged Saul to seek out his own individual path. Perhaps the scrolls Gad and Nathan had brought with them could shed light upon these secrets.

Saul lifted the lid off the chest and removed the Scroll of Blessings. He loosened the ribbon around the scroll and smoothed out the record of blessings Moses pronounced upon each of the twelve tribes before Israel entered the land of promise. He read the prologue citing how Yahweh had instructed Moses to speak to a rock and water would come forth, but Moses chose instead to strike the rock in an outburst of temper because the people of Israel had driven him to distraction with their quarrelsome natures. In that instance, Moses had not upheld the holiness of Yahweh before the people, and the consequence for Moses was for him to die on Mount Nebo, never to enter the land of promise.

Yahweh's reaction to Moses's minor infraction of disobedience mystified and frightened Saul. If the punishment for a moment of human weakness—for the prophet of prophets no less—was this harsh, then what kind of reaction might Yahweh give to a king or anyone else who might evoke the Almighty's displeasure? Yahweh's holiness was not a trifling matter. Close association with the Creator of heaven and earth was not to be entered into lightly. Such kinship was unfathomable to Saul, incomprehensible.

Saul eyed the list of tribal blessings until he found the one Moses pronounced upon the tribe of Benjamin, last of the twelve sons of Jacob, Saul's tribe, the tribe of his fathers and his children: "'Let the beloved of Yahweh rest secure in him, for he shields him all day long, and the one Yahweh loves dwells between his shoulders.'"

Saul set the scroll back upon the table and rubbed his eyes. The image of a father carrying his child upon his back came to mind. He had borne all his children at one time or another on his back when they were small. When Jonathan was a boy and could be perched between his father's shoulders, he would ask Saul to "Jump, Abba…touch the sky."

Each child had felt the safety and protection from the strength their father provided when resting upon his back. Dwelling between the shoulders of Yahweh had to imply a similar truth of being carried, protected, sheltered; but how to dwell within the shoulders of the Almighty?

Saul felt the table begin to vibrate and a tingling surged into his feet and legs. He heard voices from outside the tent and knew whatever the cause of the commotion it would require his attention, so he rolled up the scroll and retied the ribbon around it. He lifted the lid of the chest to return the scroll, and saw Abner stick his head through the tent flaps, the morning light seeping in around him. His cousin's expression indicated an unpleasant reaction to whatever was taking place in the courtyard.

"You will not believe who is riding into the compound," Abner grumbled.

Saul knew it was impossible for Abner to conceal his emotions, favorable or disgruntled, and his cousin was obviously irritable this morning.

"Who, Cousin?" Saul raised his finger to his mouth for Abner to lower his voice and pointed to the two young prophets asleep on their cots.

"Leaders from the four lost tribes, dressed in finery and empty-handed."

Saul and his inner circle had come to refer to the four tribes who had scorned Saul when he was crowned king—and disdainfully ignored him since by refusing to pay tribute or send a delegation to Gibeah—as the "lost tribes." Saul had almost given up winning them over.

Abner held the tent flaps open for the king to make his exit.

Gad raised his head, and when he saw the king, sprang up in bed. "My lord, forgive me. You should have awakened me."

Gad rubbed the sleep from his eyes as he swung his legs off the bed. He patted Nathan on his back. When Nathan began to stir, Gad returned his attention to the king.

"My lord, I need a moment to relieve myself, and we can begin our lesson."

"No time this morning, Gad." Saul rose from the stool and his head almost disappeared into the fabric folds of the ceiling. He had to scrunch down like a turtle retreating into its shell. "We have company."

Through the tent opening, Saul could see a dozen riders perched atop their mounts in the courtyard. He took a deep breath and looked back at Gad.

"Gad, go to the tent of Ahiah and Eleazar and rouse them. Tell them to come straight. I need the high priest and the guardian of the Ark standing with me."

"Yes, my lord."

Saul stepped outside the tent and took his sword from Abner, strapping it around his waist. Saul had agreed with Abner to always wear his sword when he went out in public. He had no crown. He carried no scepter.

There was no signet ring to leave his royal mark. He wore no splendid attire. Such trappings made Saul uncomfortable. A sword, however, was something he wore with ease. Though its use in mortal combat had not been tested, it was a symbol of power. Perception was all Saul had in these early days of his kingship, and this modest display of strength encouraged respect.

Chapter 1

SAUL AND ABNER MARCHED ACROSS THE COURTYARD TO GREET the tribal delegations. All twelve riders did not bother to dismount but remained in their saddles as Saul drew near. Everyone had been caught by surprise. Jeush was hastily organizing the ambassadors and officials from the other tribes positioning each group beneath their tribal banners. Saul smiled as these representatives scrambled from their encampments to gather at the entrance of the compound to greet these new arrivals.

Saul looked over the wall inside the compound and saw Ahinoam burst out of the door of their house and scurry toward the front gate to meet him. One by one, the children followed their mother. Saul was so proud of his family, and he wanted to show them off even if their faces were still red and creased from sleep. He waved to them as he walked along the compound wall. The laborers, assembled to begin the day's work, paused to bow as he passed while the company of soldiers, whom Abner had pulled together as an honor guard to impress the new arrivals snapped to attention.

Jeush had situated the clan chieftains from the tribe of Benjamin behind the royal family. Saul's tribe deserved the honor of proximity to him. All the members of his tribe were the first to honor Saul with a bent knee when he approached. The other tribes followed this example.

Once Saul was in place, his family gathered around him. Ahinoam stood on one side of Saul and Abner on the other. Jeush stepped forward to announce the king to the four tribal representatives each with an escort of two additional riders. Before Jeush could open his mouth, the tribal leaders swung around to their respective banner bearers mounted behind them and took the wooden rod with their tribal banner tied to the top.

"Carmi, son of the tribe of Judah!" Carmi shouted, driving the rod into the ground, its banner bearing the image of a lion rearing on hind legs, the claws of its two front paws glistening with blood.

"Hammuel, son of the tribe of Simeon!" Hammuel did the same as his kinsmen, planting his banner in the ground with its image of crossed swords.

"Allon, son of the tribe of Dan!" he barked, plunging a pole into the earth, its banner displaying a coiled serpent, head raised preparing to strike.

The fourth horseman eased his steed forward a few steps, separating from the other leaders before he drove his shaft into the ground. "Beerah, son of the tribe of Reuben, the firstborn of the twelve sons of our father Jacob, the first sign of Jacob's strength." He leaned forward in his saddle and glared down at the king.

Saul saw it as a dare to refute Beerah's claim of progeny, his disdainful scowl that of an older brother to the younger. The banner of Reuben bore the insignia of a warrior standing in turbulent waters.

Saul was impressed as he observed all four leaders dressed in ornate robes with jeweled headbands tied around their heads and breastplates of gold and silver. By position of tribal rank as the eldest son of Jacob's loins, Beerah marked himself the spokesman of the four tribes. His white and gray hair hung over his broad shoulders in braided tails tied in scarlet ribbon. The sleeves of his robe were trimmed in gold and cut at the top of his shoulders so the chiseled muscles in his arms exposed intimidating strength. His ashen beard was short and groomed to a tapered smoothness around the jutting rock of his jaw. Saul had no inkling what these leaders wanted except to flaunt their superiority over him.

The four banners flapped in the breeze. All were silent, no one sure who should speak after so bold a self-inflated introduction. Neither Beerah nor the others in the party made a motion to dismount, which should have been the next thing to happen. Saul looked to Jeush who appeared to be tongue-tied, so the king extended his greeting.

"Beerah, Allon, Hammuel, Carmi, sons and kinsmen of Israel, my brothers, I welcome you to Gibeah and my family compound."

Saul paused, thinking there might be a comment or even a question from Beerah regarding the health of Saul and his family or just the progress on the building projects, but there was none.

Saul placed his hand upon his wife's shoulder before waving it over the rest of his family. "This is Ahinoam my wife, the queen. My children. And my cousin Abner, commander of the army of Israel."

The four tribal leaders and their escorts did not respond. They did nothing to acknowledge Saul's introduction. They sat motionless in their saddles.

"How long has it been since you were crowned king in Mizpah?" Jeush barked loudly. This was not a question that needed answering. Jeush had addressed the tribal leaders as equals, tribal leader to tribal leader. "It took you longer to come to Gibeah than for our forefathers to wander out of the wilderness. Did your mapmakers fail to give you the proper location of Gibeah?"

Beerah smirked at Jeush's verbal gibes, but he did not bother to look at him.

"Do you not dismount and bend the knee in honor of your king?" Abner added.

Saul could see Abner's angry assertion at this display of flagrant arrogance had finally been the magic words to spark a hostile reaction, but not one that should elicit a proper obeisance from loyal subjects.

"We do not dismount because we do not recognize this man as king." Beerah's scornful manner astounded the crowd. His disrespect was indefensible, but no one moved to vindicate Saul's honor. No one could comprehend the words just spoken, nor were they even sure of what they had heard. Faces fell. Hands and arms dropped at everyone's side. A sense of powerlessness was let loose like a cloudburst upon all—all except the twelve who had ridden that morning from their private camp hidden in the forested outskirts just south of Gibeah.

"How dare you speak thus to the king." Abner was the first within the crowd to regain his senses after Beerah's affront.

Abner's remark unleashed a rolling grumble in the crowd, a vocal disapproval of Beerah's unwarranted comment. Soon fists began to pound the air and the clapping sound of the soldiers' swords slamming against shields resounded. But as quickly as the din rose, it lost strength as Gad and Nathan began clearing a path through the crowd, forcing the people to step aside, making way for Eleazar and Ahiah. The guardian of the Ark and the high priest stopped between the royal family and the mounted delegation.

Ahiah stepped forward and raised his hand to speak. Without prodding, Beerah's horse backed away, giving ground to the high priest.

"You delay coming to pay homage to the king. Your hands are empty of tribute. Unlike our other kinsmen, you offer no gift. Instead of congratulating the king, you insult Yahweh's chosen. You do not even show the courtesy of dismounting from your horses to bend the knee."

Saul could tell that the high priest's rebuke had some effect as he watched Beerah's stern face begin to crack and erode.

Eleazar continued to upbraid the four tribal leaders, pointing at each of them.

"You, Beerah; you, Allon; you, Carmi and Hammuel were the most insistent of all the tribal elders for a change in leadership, hounding us to confront the prophet Samuel and evoke the right of kings. We agreed and faced down the prophet on your behalf. Am I right in this, Beerah?"

Beerah did not respond to Eleazar's public reproach.

"Your intentions seem clear, Beerah. All you and the others want is to announce the casting off the yoke of the new government before it has had even a firm chance to be established. Am I right, Beerah?" Eleazar demanded.

Beerah uttered a harsh, disdainful growl before he responded to Eleazar's question. "You are right, my lord. We did come to you expressing our desire for a king to lead us, but for a king of noble birth, one of fortune who was well-bred, one who could lead us in all things civil and military, not…not this commoner plucked from obscurity."

Jeush was the first to react in defense of his king—a hail of curses, a voice of violence, a sword drawn ready to shed blood. Were it not for the hands of his fellow Benjamite chiefs clasped on his shoulders and arms, Jeush would have rushed upon Beerah to remove his head.

Saul waited for the clamor of the mob sparked by Jeush's threats to peak. He did not want it to collapse altogether. He wanted Beerah and the three other tribal chieftains to think that the loyalists' outcry had a bite to accompany their bark. Saul did not mind the hostile noise the crowd created; its unsettling effect on the steeds carrying these haughty chieftains forced them to firmly grip their bridles and stroke their necks. Saul was the only one who could keep this from spilling over into bloodshed. He did not want this to become an inner-tribal brawl marring the advent of his kingdom.

Saul saw the tide had turned against this delegation. Yet, when he noticed Ahinoam beginning to tuck their children under her arms, he knew it was time for a calming voice. By gathering her brood together, Saul knew she was expecting a potential breakout of hostilities. The muscles on the side of his face twitched. His arms dangled to his sides, and he shook his hands as though casting off water after a scrub.

Saul stepped in front of his wife and children, reached out his long arm, and placed a hand upon the back of Jonathan's neck. His son had not cowered in front of the arrogant contingent, but Saul felt his firm touch relax the tense muscles in his son's neck, bringing a measure of calm to him as well. Saul raised his other hand. This simple gesture reduced a threatened rupture down to a smoldering tension. Yet Saul knew this crowd was on the knife's edge, that a massacre could play out in his own front yard that could incite civil war and possibly bring his kingship to a swift end.

"My lord, Beerah, since we had no advanced knowledge of your mission, it must have been secret. You wanted to catch everyone off guard with your surprise visit, state your business, and depart, leaving us properly chastised and humiliated. So, Lord Beerah, in all things you have spoken the truth. You will get no argument from me. Would the prophet had chosen another, one more suitable to your liking, but the choice was made."

Beerah had not yet looked in Saul's direction until this moment, and Saul could sense the man's contempt of someone he thought unqualified for such a high position and thought him no more than an impostor. Saul was forcing Beerah to address him, but the chieftain still refused to engage his eyes and looked just above Saul's head. He suspected nothing he could do or say would make Beerah change his mind on the fact that he considered Saul a commoner who had no business being king.

"Two questions I ask, Saul, son of Kish, before all assembled here: on the day of your ascension, while we watched the prophet and the high priest cast the lots eliminating each tribe, clan, and family head until the lot fell upon you, is it true that when the prophet called your name, you were hiding in your wagon beneath your baggage?"

It was an appalling question, one that created a vibrative murmuring. Beerah's description of the facts was true, but Saul did not realize the incident at Mizpah of such unrefined behavior had been circulated, proving in the minds of many, his unqualified ascent to the throne. He had forgotten all about the episode when Ahinoam had to coax him out of the wagon like a frightened child. In the euphoria of that day and in all the time that followed, the sting of that moment seemed to be swallowed up by the more pressing matters involved in becoming king.

Until Beerah's question, he thought he had tucked away the memory altogether. Now it rushed back into his mind and a knot began to form in the pit of his stomach. Yet Saul disguised his anxiety with a broad smile.

"I will be forever grateful to my wife that day, Lord Beerah." Saul looked back at Ahinoam and gave her a wink. "I could sense which way the wind was blowing, and it did frighten me. 'Plucked from obscurity' as you rightly say, can be overwhelming for someone like me, and I took refuge in my family's wagon, hoping the Almighty might decide on a different outcome. Alas, for your sake and mine, it did not happen, and my wife inspired me with the courage to accept Yahweh's choice."

Beerah allowed Saul's answer to resonate with the crowd before asking his second question. He could tell from his elevated perch that the impostor's admission of fear had created a rustle of consternation. Some exchanged questioning glances, some whispered into cocked ears, while others were more vocal in expressing disappointment with unacceptable kingly behavior. The mission of Beerah and his group had been simply to declare themselves free of the yoke of this fledgling monarchy and be on their way. He and the others had not come to Gibeah specifically to dethrone the king; however, Beerah could sense the tide turning in his favor. Perhaps they could install someone more suited to their liking—someone from a much larger tribe, someone of wealth and property, someone of a more noble family line—and not one of such low estate; someone, anyone, who was the exact opposite of the man who stood before him claiming the title.

If, by chance, the gathered crowd on this day was prepared to shift their loyalties, then Beerah and the others would gladly suggest proper alternatives, which would include Beerah himself. He adjusted his position on his horse, elevating his lordly stature. He did not dignify the king by addressing him with his given name, rather the title of his begotten lineage.

"Then, son of Kish, I ask my second question: since you have admitted to your lack of qualifications to be a king, why should we, why should any of us, bend the knee or swear an oath of loyalty or pay tribute to someone who runs and hides like a flushed rabbit when he is called upon to rule our nation and lead us against our enemies?"

Beerah used his first direct eye contact with Saul for his second question, holding his dark glare upon him as if to paralyze Saul. Beerah sensed his comment had given him the upper hand. He would unseat this man before his royal rump could leave an indelible impression upon the throne.

Saul stood like a conspicuous victim of Beerah's accusation, but strangely the knot inside his gut began to unravel, replaced by a calm submission to the truth of his character and a clear understanding of his place in the world around him. Saul knew that whatever answer he might give, Beerah and the other tribal leaders would never accept him as their king, but still he chose to strike a blow against their locked opinions.

"Lord Beerah, you and the other tribal chieftains place great importance on one's privileged station in life. I make no superior claim to wealth or family or the size of our tribe. It seemed Yahweh chose to overlook such deficiencies in my case. And as for strength and bravery to lead our people, I admit the prospect causes me to feel afraid. But I cannot claim to be brave until I first admit to feelings of being a coward. I stand before you for one reason: the choice of Yahweh, the God of Israel. Your argument is with the Almighty.

"And since you have enjoyed pointing out how common I am—a simple herdsman and tiller of the soil—I admit to you and to all that I am more comfortable behind a plow than in a scholar's study or a nobleman's fortress. So, if you will excuse me, I would rather get behind a plow and look at the dung-caked, hind ends of my oxen than to spend another moment in this debate. May Yahweh be with you on your journey home."

Saul touched Ahinoam's shoulder as he passed her and gave her a sly wink. He did not wait for Beerah to respond. He did not wait for anyone to react. He turned his back on everyone the second he finished speaking and began walking toward the stables behind the house. What he did hear by the time he was halfway around the compound wall was the raw, unison chant of "Glory to the king!" repeated with growing intensity and added numbers of voices each time it was uttered.

Saul did not glance over his shoulder but continued marching to the stables. He loosened the knots of the belt around his robe as he quickened his pace, anxious to get into clothes more suitable for plowing. He had been king long enough for one morning. The rest of the day, he would plow the fallow field behind his house. He could start and finish that job with no one's assistance, no one's disapproval, no one's advice. Cut a clean row and be satisfied with what he accomplished for that day. The purity of that uncomplicated task caused him to shiver with delight.

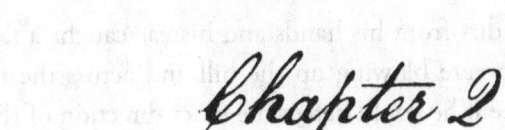

Chapter 2

SAUL SAT ON A ROCK ON THE NORTHERN EDGE OF HIS FIELD beneath the shade of a giant oak and surveyed the plot of earth he had just finished turning. The oxen were lapping the rainwater collected in the trough next to the rock. This ground had been worked year after year, generation after generation. Man and ox and plow had driven over and cut through and planted and harvested this section of earth since the family of Kish settled on the outskirts of Gibeah.

It was quiet, and Saul loved quiet. He was far enough away from both the tumult and the rapid population spurt that had turned his agrarian life and land into a burgeoning city. The distance proved a buffer against the sounds of expansion. This was a place where he could escape.

After draining his skin of water, he slipped off the rock and walked out into the plowed earth, his footsteps leaving impressions in the soft ground. He squatted down and dug his hand into the dirt. After all these years of plowing and planting it was still fertile. The ground seemed inexhaustible; a miraculous process concealed from human eyes that amazed him. This ground did one unique thing: a mysterious cycle of incubation that took life and gave it back. It was always at work receiving the seeds planted beneath its loamy crust, nurturing them, and giving back to the Sower a bountiful yield. For as long as he had lived, the land never failed to produce. Saul crushed the small clods of dirt between his fingers then stretched out his arm and sprinkled the fine-grain soil back to its place. One more pass over this field with a deeper cut blade and it would be ready for planting.

Saul brushed the dirt from his hands and his ear caught a faint, odd sound carried on a breeze blowing up the hill and across the field. He cocked his head to see if he could detect the exact direction of the sound but did not hear it again. He walked back to the storage shed beside the trough and dragged the plow and yoke inside with the other equipment. He grabbed some rope lying on the ground and shut the gate of the shed. He stripped off his tunic as he walked around the oxen to the opposite side of the trough.

Saul put a hand on the head of each beast and pushed them aside. He plunged his head and shoulders into the water, then stood up and rubbed his face and neck and chest, scrubbing the dirt and sweat from his body. He dropped his tunic into the trough then pulled it out, wringing the water from the material back into the trough. He moved to the side and shook the tunic into the wind, snapping off the last droplets of water. Just as he was about to put it back on, he heard the sound again, a human sound, a shout or a wail.

One of the oxen began to bellow, and Saul smacked its snout to silence the animal. He moved away from the oxen and listened. In a moment he heard it again, distinctly human and coming from the direction of his compound. He could not imagine the crowd might still be praising him as they had done earlier that day. Saul stuck his arms through his tunic and brought the collar over his head. He grabbed his sword propped against the shed and strapped it around his waist. He then took the rope and strung it through the rings clamped into the septum of each ox and began leading them around the edge of the field toward home.

Saul could see the guards posted on the roof of his house waving to him and calling as he came into view. They had seen him coming down the path toward the backside of the compound and were waving for him to hurry. Saul yanked the rope, which caused both bulls to bawl from the pain to their tender snouts, but they responded to the quickened pace and began to trot behind him. Saul did not pause at the stables to leave the oxen but circled around the wall of the compound and came into the clearing. Except for the absence of the four tribal leaders and their escorts, who had long since departed, it was the same collection of people who had gathered that morning, only now they were not chanting praises to their king. Instead, it was a great lamentation, with priests beating their chests and raising their arms to the heavens and soldiers throwing dust into the air above their heads. This was the cry he had heard from the field, but he still did not know the cause.

Saul rushed toward the group, leading the oxen by the tethered rope. Ishvi and Malki were being pushed to the outside of the writhing human circle and forced to watch what was happening in the center through waving arms and gyrating bodies in a cloud of dust created by the commotion. He shouted to the twins, and the boys spun around when they caught sight of their father and raced toward him, their faces shiny with helpless wonder at what they had witnessed.

"Abba! Abba!" Ishvi cried. He won the footrace to his father's side. "Three messengers have just arrived from Jabesh Gilead."

"They had their eyes cut out!" Malki shouted breathlessly as he stumbled next to his father's other side. "And Mikal and Merab got sick when they saw them." Malki was happy to make that announcement.

"What are you talking about, Son? What has happened?"

"Come, Abba." Ishvi grabbed Saul's arm, pulling him forward.

"What is it, Ishvi? Why do these people cry out with such grief?"

"Come and see. Just come and see." Ishvi's insistent tugging on the sleeve of his father's damp garment forced Saul to lengthen his strides.

Malki took the rope from Saul's hand and tried to get the oxen to follow but they resisted, yanking their heads from side to side, refusing to budge. Not till a soldier rushed over to take charge of the oxen was Malki free to join his father and brother.

"Make way for the king!" Ishvi shouted, pulling Saul through the path created by the crowd as they disentangled and parted on either side. "Make way for my father!"

Malki dashed behind them and grabbed onto the back of Saul's clothing, allowing his father's momentum to carry him into the center of the circle.

The ring of people widened to accept the king, and Saul caught a glimpse of Ahinoam standing behind the wall of the compound with their daughters' faces buried inside her robes, the girls too frightened to view the scene. Saul lost sight of them as he approached the three men kneeling on the ground, and once he stopped in front of them, the round human shape immediately encircled them.

The emissaries from Jabesh Gilead beat their chests and would not raise their heads before the king. The fronts of their rent garments were streaked with dirt and blood. Their heads were bare. Their beards were matted with grime; the longer strands plastered with sweat to the skin of their necks and exposed chests. Saul scanned the surrounding throng of faces and bodies now pressed in, reforming into one circle of shuddering grief. Then he lowered his eyes to look upon the men crouched on the ground, but he did not move closer, nor did he call for them to rise. He stood in dumb amazement at the grief-stricken trio and the distressful scene their presence created.

"Their eyes! Look at their eyes!"

Saul was jolted out of this trance when Abner shouted and grabbed his shoulders.

"Look at their eyes!" Abner repeated.

Saul instead looked into his cousin's weeping eyes streaked in a red, latticed pattern of anger. He placed his hands upon Abner's arms and the commander released his grip on Saul's shoulders. The wailing of the crowd was reduced to whimpers and moans when Saul bent over and touched the top of the first man's trembling head.

"Be at peace, my son. Look at me."

"I am too ashamed, my lord." The man burst into a fresh round of weeping.

Saul patted his head, and then ran his fingers down the side of the man's face, scooping his chin into his palm. He lifted it, tilting the man's head back until the afternoon sun shone on his disfigured face. Saul's first instinct was to release the clenched hold he had on the man's chin as if he had touched a hot coal, but he resisted the urge to recoil and dug his fingers into the scruff of the man's beard.

"Forgive me, my lord. You should not look upon my wretched state." He was a young man though the violent damage done to him gave his face the effect of melted flesh frozen into a mask of premature aging.

"There is nothing to forgive, my son." Saul kept a tender hold on the young man's jaw, allowing him to speak and weep.

Saul looked around the huddled crowd for Jonathan. He found him standing beside Jeush looking at him horror-stricken. Saul had to look away for he would have burst into tears. This could have been his firstborn. Jonathan could be the one kneeling here in front of him filthy, bloody and humiliated, sobbing, the tears streaming from his one good eye.

"Nothing to forgive." It was only one eye, the right one, which had been brutally gouged from its socket, but the plum-red blood that had gushed from the wound had hardened on his cheek before disappearing into the encrusted hair of his beard.

Saul lifted the heads of the other two men, both of similar age, both with their right eyes removed, both with angry wounds and tarnished faces. He returned to the first young man and spoke to him.

"What is your name, my son?" Saul placed his large hands on either side of the young man's face. Saul knew there was a dreadful story to be told and he wanted this young man to feel his strength pressed into his head.

"Jarib, my lord. We come from Jabesh Gilead. We are under siege and are lost unless the king comes to our rescue."

Saul could see Jarib flinch from the pressure he had placed on his skull, but not from fear. He sensed the spirit of the young man was revived as he latched on to Saul's stalwart arms, digging his fingers into skin and muscle—flesh bound with flesh, the pain of the wounded channeling its suffering into a prospective savior.

"The right eye of Israel has been hollowed out!"

Saul raised his head to see Eleazar, guardian of the Ark, standing before him, his right hand covering his right eye, his left raised to heaven. Ahiah stood next to Eleazar, crying the name of Yahweh over and over while clawing at his priestly robes as if to rip them from his body.

Saul looked back down upon Jarib. "Who has done this to you, Jarib?"

"Nahash, king of Ammon." Jarib and his two companions wailed at the mention of their oppressor. "Two days ago, the city of Jabesh awoke to find the battering rams and the catapults of the Ammonites encamped around our walls. We could not defend ourselves nor could we survive a long siege, so the city council offered King Nahash a treaty if only they would spare us."

Saul looked at Gad as he pulled a scroll from the clay jar Nathan clutched in his arms and stepped forward. Gad pointed to the writing on the scroll.

"It is an old grudge, my lord. The Ammonites allege Israel took their land when our fathers crossed the Jordan River."

Nathan raised the jar of scrolls aloft for the gathering to look upon the divine historical content as recorded by the prophet Moses and shouted, "The sons of the Ammonites are the progeny of incest from a drunken old man!"

Wails of sorrow from the crowd over the tale of the messengers and the grisly insult they suffered swelled into howls for vengeance.

"Lust and wine! Lust and wine!" Ahiah cried, and he took the scroll from Gad and began to read from it.

"And Lot's two daughters gave him wine to drink and lay with their father. And from Lot's seed came Moab, son of the older daughter, father of the Moabites, and from his younger daughter came Ben-Ammi, father of the Ammonites."

Gad raised his arms into the air and spoke in support of the divine word. "The prophet of prophets wrote that the Ammonite and the Moabite should never enter the congregation of the Lord."

Saul continued to interrogate Jarib. "What was King Nahash's response to the offer of your councilors?"

"He grabbed the chief councilor at the Council House by the throat, dragged him into the street, and drew his knife, holding the blade just above his right eye." Jarib broke down again, overcome by the memory.

"Stay with me, my son. Who is the chief councilor of Jabesh Gilead?"

"My father. I am the son of Azriel."

"And did King Nahash harm your father in any way?"

"No, my lord. I bore the wrath of King Nahash. I and my fellow emissaries."

Saul drew Jarib's face into his side, stroking the back of the young man's head. He looked at Jonathan and imagined his son's right eye missing, the blood streaming down the side of his face. The surprise vision filled him with disgust and rage.

Jeush drew his sword and waved it above his head. "The Ammonites have been a thorn in the side of Israel since the beginning."

Saul pushed Jarib's face away from his side and back into the sun. "And what were the conditions of the treaty offered by Nahash to Azriel?"

"Only two conditions, my lord: to spare our lives, the citizens of Jabesh Gilead would become slaves of King Nahash; and every male in the city would have their right eye gouged out, down to the smallest boy child."

Abner raised his arm to keep the crowd from erupting into another round of vocal ferocity at Jarib's report. He leaned in close to his cousin but raised his voice so all could hear.

"This is his signature: every tribal village he raids on our eastern borders, from Manasseh to Reuben, Nahash carries the banner of the bloody eye. He leaves behind an empty socket of every male in every town and village he sacks, making them unfit for war and of no use except as slaves. This cannot stand, Cousin."

Saul viewed the seething mob, who cried out once again, loud enough to raise a cold corpse. He felt within his limbs, his organs, his glands, a scorching flush of blood racing in his veins, burning through the last balk of fear that might keep him from action. The whole world seemed to pour through him. His body was no longer molded flesh and bone but clear, vibrant air and light. His eyes were no longer human. His eyes were the eyes of Yahweh.

Jarib grabbed Saul's arms within his trembling grasp. "My father begged for a time of seven days, my lord. Seven days he asked of King Nahash to find rescue, to find a rescuer. We traveled all night to come to you."

"This petty despot is testing our resolve." Jeush's sword cut through the air contaminated with dust, heat, sweat, tears, and the sounds of wailing.

Eleazar gripped Saul's arm. "He is testing our courage. King Nahash shows his contempt of Israel by giving the poor souls of Jabesh Gilead a week to find rescue."

Even Abner was caught up in the frenzy and would make his case for Saul to prepare for war. "It is true, Cousin. We have been intimidated by the Philistines for decades, unable to fight them effectively. The Ammonites have raided our northern borders without fear of retaliation. Now Nahash knows we have a king, one untested with only a small force and little time to assemble a larger one. He insults us with this seven-day waiting period, believing we are timid and in such disarray that we will do nothing."

Saul had not yet released his grasp of Jarib's head but cradled it in his hands like a precious gift given in his honor, one that spoke, one that would become an oracle and recite the accounts of this day for all time to any who would listen.

Ahiah stepped out of the bumping and jostling bodies surrounding him and laid his hand upon the shoulder of the king. The resolute face of the high priest inspired Saul. "This is the first test of your leadership, my lord. The cry of this man—the anguish of the citizens of Jabesh—is the cry of all Israel. It is even the cry of the prophet Samuel who said, 'To whom is all the desire of Israel turned if not to you?' You are the man of Yahweh's choosing. There is no one like you in all Israel."

Saul brushed his hand over the face of Jarib and then leaned over and kissed the raw crater that once contained the young man's eye. He let go of Jarib's head and spun around and moved toward the oxen. Saul could see the puzzled reactions from the people who could not believe their king was marching away from the pleas for rescue and chose to ignore them. He heard the cries for reckoning against the haughty bravado of King Nahash, and he was about to demonstrate his resolve.

Saul drew closer to his team of oxen and waved aside the soldier who dropped the guide rope and cleared the way for him to maneuver between the two beasts. There was no time for the dumb animals to bellow or bolt. Saul withdrew his sword, and with both hands gripping the hilt, brought it down upon the neck of the first, severing head from neck in one powerful stroke. The eyes of the second beast bulged from its sockets when it registered the approaching danger of the blade. Another swift blow, and Saul had removed its head from its body.

Saul had no trouble being heard when he spoke. The throng had been silenced, faces rendered inert from shock, voices muted by terror. Saul lifted himself to his full height and stood between the lifeless carcasses. Blood pooled so thick around his feet he could have splashed in the puddles like a child after a hard rain. He raised his sword, its blade a blood-red torch reflecting the light from the fading, western sun.

"See that each beast is cut up and a bloody portion sent to the leaders of the other tribes of Israel with this message from their king: 'This will be the fate of the oxen of anyone who does not follow Saul...'"

Then he paused, his breath quickened, his thought process cut short, his directive sliced as clean as the necks of these dead beasts lying on either side of him. *Do not forget the prophet,* he thought. *In all things include him.*

"Who does not follow Saul and Samuel."

In the quiet moment it took for the crowd to come to consciousness, Ahiah raised his voice. "The Spirit of Yahweh has fallen upon the king! The Spirit of Yahweh has fallen upon the king!"

Saul's action and his proclamation had taken the people by such surprise that they could not believe what they had just witnessed. Ahiah had to repeat the phrase several times before the others began to realize the high priest was calling them to recognize the king of Yahweh's favor. It was not until Saul moved back into the widened circle, blood-soaked and breathing heavy, and stood before the three kneeling messengers from Jabesh Gilead, that the crowd found a unified voice and could join the high priest's chant.

Saul wiped the blade of his sword across the sleeve of his garment before returning it to its scabbard. He turned in a circle, eyes closed, listening to the rhythmic chanting of the frenzied crowd, absorbing Yahweh's Spirit as it descended upon him. Then he threw up his arms for silence so he could address them. No one moved, all eyes and ears directed toward him.

"Sons of Israel, listen to me. The flame of the tribe of Benjamin would be extinguished were it not for the citizens of Jabesh Gilead. After the days of the great civil wars between our tribes when only six hundred sons of Benjamin were left, Jabesh Gilead kept us from extinction. The mothers of their mothers gave us their daughters, and our line has survived to this day. And from the smallest tribe of the twelve sons of our father Jacob has now come the first king of Israel."

Eleazar raised his hands to the heavens and shouted his affirmation, "Let the guardian of the Ark proclaim, the Almighty has raised up a deliverer in Israel!"

"And on this day, on this day I, your king, have heard the cry of Jabesh Gilead. The king has seen the bloody tears flow from the empty sockets of his kinsmen. In his own heart, I have felt the humiliation of his brothers. So too, this day, the eye of the king has been plucked out."

Ahiah echoed a proclamation of his own. "Let the high priest of Yahweh exalt, 'Yahweh has chosen His deliverer. There is no one like him in all Israel.'"

Saul stepped forward, his voice a syllabic thunder of cadence and power. "So, on this day there is one message. There is one message for all the sons of Israel. The oxen of any man who does not follow Saul and Samuel shall suffer the same fate as the dead beasts you see before you. Send the message throughout Israel: drop your plows; let your livestock graze in the fields; leave your shops and vineyards; let the ranks of Israel swell with her sons and gather with the king to avenge the shame of Jabesh Gilead."

Jeush climbed upon the shoulders of the man standing next to him that gave him the advantage of extra height and yelled at the top of his voice, "As the wolf rises up hungry for prey…as the wolf rises up hungry for prey, the king rises up to deliver his people!"

The eruption from the courtyard came as the voice of one man, an earth-born thunder thrown back to heaven, an echoed answer in response to the downpour of Yahweh's Spirit. There would be no more oxen slaughtered in Israel. The message of the king was clear: tradesman and merchant, scholar and priest, farmer and field hand, every able-bodied son of Israel would rally to the king's side.

Saul looked over at the corner of the common room and saw his children huddled together silent and anxious, their eyes wide open watching the comings and goings of military personnel, prophets and priests, tribal leaders and clan chieftains. Ahinoam had given them each a plate of food for supper and then rejoined Saul. She had remained at Saul's side throughout the evening. When Saul noticed that his children had not touched the food their mother had given them, rather, the full plates sat uneaten at their feet, he realized he had forgotten his offspring. Jonathan alone was engaged in the military planning ready to carry out any order or request that Abner, the commander of the army, made of him. It was thrilling for Saul to see all this activity going on inside his house even though he knew how frightening it might be for his daughters and the twins. Nothing like this had ever happened inside the house. Saul knew that what had been a normal and routine childhood for his offspring, even after he had become king, now in one day had turned into the striking world of adult circumstances leaving them bewildered observers.

The house was ablaze with torchlight. There was no going to bed. There was no going to sleep. The night was well into its first hours, but the house, courtyard, and compound were so bright from the light of fires and torches that it could be mistaken for the early light of dawn. His children had never seen him behave in such an uncharacteristic fashion.

Even now he paced throughout the house, his clothes caked with dried blood, his sword strapped around his waist, and he knew the firm and steady and loving father they had known all their lives had transformed into something they did not recognize. He would speak to them before the night was over, for he knew they would not go to bed until he had done so.

Meanwhile, Saul returned his attention to Jarib and the other two messengers who stood before the interior wall at the front doorway. They gave detailed descriptions of the layout of the city of Jabesh Gilead and surrounding landscape, and they pointed out where the king of the Ammonites had set his battlements and the camps of his army. As the men spoke, artists drew and redrew every detail of this report on the wall with sticks of charcoal worn down to nubs.

Once everyone was pleased with the artist's results, Jarib and the emissaries were sent to Abner's house inside the compound to get a few hours of sleep before they returned to Jabesh Gilead. Then Saul, Abner,

Jonathan, Jeush, and the tribal leaders moved back and forth in front of the mural, debating strategy and forming battle plans with their imaginary army. The light from the torches cast dancing gray shadows over the wall like giant inhabitants of the etched city they were plotting to liberate. Gad and Nathan sat to the side, recording the conversations as fast as they could write. Ahinoam moved around a table filling sacks and leather pouches with food and clothing. None felt fatigued. Exhaustion had been deferred.

Saul turned from his deliberations and took Ahinoam by the hand. "Be sure to pack the ram horn of the prophet. I do not want to forget that."

Saul squeezed her hand, and then, once more, he caught sight of the wide, probing eyes of his children staring at him. He looked over his shoulder at the others studying the wall and decided he could step away from the discussions for a moment. When he approached the twins, they both leapt to their feet and embraced him, paying no regard to the dried blood on his clothes or the sweet, musty smell of his garments.

"We want to go with you," Ishvi said. "We will stay out of the way."

"We can help," Malki said. "I know we can."

Saul held the head of each boy in the grip of his hand. He could not help but be impressed with his sons' eagerness to be part of this event, and he could not bring himself to deny them. "I agree. You will be great help to me. Pack your things. Then go to bed. I do not want sleepyheads in the morning when I call for you."

The boys bolted from their father's grip and dashed for the ladder to their rooftop sleeping quarters. Saul knew that the boys and the girls had different reactions about his altered nature. The twins' boyish excitement of getting to go to war would banish their uncertainties. Their battles had always been fought with make-believe enemies. Now their father would give them the chance to put their skills to the test and create the legends that would make their names live in glory.

But his daughters' qualms were not so easily diverted. He caught a glimpse of Ahinoam standing beside the table, her balled-up fists planted against her sides, her arms and elbows stuck out like bent bows. Though she had not heard the simple details of the conversation between father and sons, she saw the result. The boys had nearly come to blows trying to be the first to climb the ladder, and she knew her twin sons would accompany their father.

"They can stay with the cooks and the baggage. No harm will come to them." Saul knew he must counter his wife's rigid posture with his own confident stance.

Ahinoam said nothing, her fixed body language belied any satisfaction she might have felt about his answer, but Saul would have to consult with her later regarding the matter. He needed a moment with his daughters before rejoining his war council.

Merab and Mikal sat so close together they merged into one form. Their arms were intertwined, and their fingers interlaced. In a room full of men and with their mother preoccupied, Saul knew they felt helpless and lost. He got down on his knees in front of them. He started to reach out and take their hands, then thought better of it. They were still crusty with blood and dirt, his clothes still caked and smelly. He did not want to cause any more trauma than what they had already experienced.

"You saw what happened today. You saw everything I did...what I said."

The girls nodded in unison, their lips pulled inward and tucked between their teeth.

"It is a difficult thing to explain. I do not fully understand what happened...what came over me."

"The high priest said it was the Spirit of Yahweh that made you do what you did." Merab's lips trembled at the possible explanation of her father's shocking behavior. "Why would Yahweh make you act in such a strange and cruel fashion?"

"The high priest did say that. I cannot refute him. A powerful feeling came over me. I was angry at what King Nahash did to the men from Jabesh Gilead, and I felt I had to make a point, but I do not have a full understanding of what happened to me."

"But to slaughter our oxen, Abba." Merab was near tears. Saul could tell she was disoriented by the memory only a few hours old.

"I think it was Yahweh, Abba. I do." Mikal blurted her certainty as if to blunt her sister's doubts and her own.

Saul smiled at Mikal's eagerness that the Almighty could be so actively engaged in the life of her father. But Merab's fear was not so easily assuaged by some trouble-free explanation for the alteration of the father she had known all her life.

"Is it that simple, Abba? Can Yahweh change you like that?"

Saul could only answer out of his own wonder. "I do not know."

"Are you changed, Abba? Are you a different person?" Merab's awe at such a prospect pierced Saul's heart.

"We might all be different now that I am king. Time will make it clearer." Saul reached out a hand toward each daughter yet did not touch them. "But know this, I am not changed toward you or your brothers or your mother. You are safe, and you need not be afraid of anything."

Saul winced at the sound of his knees popping and cracking as he rose.

Merab reached out and touched his leg as he turned. It was what he wanted. He wanted to touch, to embrace his daughters, but for them to initiate the contact.

"You are coming back." Merab spoke with such tenderness and unease of the possible response it almost brought Saul to tears.

Ahinoam slipped beside Saul just as he was about to speak.

"Your Ima would be very upset with me if I did not come back." Saul spoke with confidence, exposing a broad grin. "And bring your brothers back as well. You will not get rid of them that easily."

Saul gave his daughter his winning smile and comforting words. It was all Merab needed. Saul gave her the father she knew, not the one she witnessed earlier. Saul knew Merab was easily terrified, and the father she saw in the afternoon must go back to the father she had always known, the father that made her feel safe. He did not understand Yahweh and could not explain to Merab what did not make sense to him. It was wiser to return to familiar patterns of behavior and personality, and when he tickled her under her chin, the contact brought a magical relief in tears and laughter.

"Now girls, time for bed. Go to your room." Ahinoam waved the girls out of their corner and motioned toward the ladder to the second floor. They obeyed without complaint.

Ahinoam brought out her hand, holding the empty ram's horn that had contained the oil Samuel used to anoint Saul.

He plucked it from her palm. "Pack this in my bag so I will be sure to see it."

"I never thought of you as sentimental, my love."

"Perhaps it is superstition. Just see that it gets packed."

He lay the horn back inside her palm, then folded her fingers over it and kissed her hand.

Saul heard a rapping sound and turned to see Abner tapping the wall with his knife, drawing his attention back to the task at hand. "The plans are drawn, Cousin. We shall assemble in Bezek with whatever number of men answer the call."

Abner then pointed to Gad and Nathan. "Our two prophets made us copies so we can revise the plans as we travel."

Saul saw that the room had cleared of all the tribal leaders. Only Gad and Nathan remained. They put their writing utensils inside their lap desks, and then stood at attention as he approached, their faces weary with fatigue.

"I trust you had enough parchment for tonight." Saul pointed toward the drawings on the wall.

"Yes, my lord. I drew maps of the city, and Gad wrote down what was discussed."

A look of apprehension came over Gad. "Well, not everything, my lord. Everyone was talking so fast and at the same time. It was difficult to preserve it all."

Saul tried to calm the young prophet's apprehension. "I am sure you heard enough. Make extra copies of what you recorded tonight. Gad, I want you to travel with me. Nathan, when we leave in the morning, you are to ride straight to Ramah to inform the prophet of our plans. Humbly request his presence when we muster in Bezek before crossing the Jordan River to surround Jabesh Gilead."

"Yes, my lord," the young prophets said and then bowed before exiting the house.

Abner stopped them when they reached the door. "Nathan, take nothing with you but food and water. All the documents travel with the king."

"But what if the prophet wishes to see the battle plans?" Nathan looked puzzled.

"Then he must join us in Bezek." Abner offered no more explanation, and Nathan looked to the king for any alteration in Abner's order, but the king sided with his cousin.

"It is best to do as the commander says."

Once the young men departed, Saul gave Abner an inquisitive look. He did not understand why he insisted Nathan not take a copy of the battle plans for the prophet.

As usual, Abner did not soften his words. "I will not risk our plans falling into the wrong hands. It is dangerous to even send him to Ramah. The young man already has enough of our battle strategies rattling around in his head. I will not risk the actual scrolls taken by enemy spies."

"But what if he is followed? What if he is captured before meeting us in Bezek?"

"Then let us hope Yahweh will give him the strength not to break under torture."

"That is a forthright answer…and harsh."

"It is a harsh world in which we live, Cousin. We need to placate the prophet. He is a man of Yahweh. This I understand, but I am the commander of your army. I will stand by your side and defend you to my death. The prophet's allegiance is in doubt."

"Abner, do not say such things." Saul felt a twinge of apprehension at his cousin's bluntness.

"What happened out there today, Cousin? What came over you?"

Saul shrugged, giving his wife and son an unsettled glance then lowered his eyes.

Abner stepped toward Saul and firmly gripped his cousin's broad shoulders. "Do not be ashamed, Cousin. Do not be ashamed by your bold action today. Never have I seen anything like it. That was your true self, a fire within your soul. It is the king the people have begged for. It is the king I wish to follow. I cannot say how many will join us in the coming days, but I predict that after word spreads of your call to arms, every able-bodied man in Israel will meet at us Bezek. I could not have devised a better act for recruiting more men."

"I agree, Abba." Jonathan's loyalty and pride were expressed in his bright face and firm voice.

Ahinoam put her arm around her husband's side and pinched his muscled flesh. Her gesture of support required no spoken word.

"Thank you, Commander. But it was no act," Saul whispered, appreciative of Abner's singleness of thought and purpose.

"And that is why I believe we will raise an overwhelming force to save Jabesh Gilead."

"Can you get an hour's sleep before we leave, Commander?"

Abner just snorted and shook his head before slapping Saul's arms and exiting through the door.

"Abba, may I have your sword? I should clean and sharpen it before we go."

Saul untied the knots in the leather strap that secured the sheath and sword around his waist and handed them to his son. Father and son exchanged a smile before Jonathan followed Abner out the front entrance.

Saul moved over to the enlarged drawing on the wall. He vigorously rubbed his face and eyes to remove the fatigue that was causing them to droop.

"What do you think?" he asked.

"I think you need some fresh clothes. I will burn what you are wearing."

"No, no. I mean about this…all of this…all of these drawn plans?" Saul thoughtfully waved his hand across the wall to include the scope of the drawing. His time as king had not been long, and he was just beginning to understand the responsibility of his role. At once he was like every man, but now set apart, and facing a trial. His first. The world was moving faster than it ever had; faster than he could ever imagine. How would he prove himself?

"Do these plans include my sons coming home in one piece?"

Saul fixed his eyes upon his wife. He would calm her heart. "Yes. What of me?"

"You bring my sons home safely, and the queen will reward the king." Her stern face dissolved into a sultry grin. She helped remove the bloodstained tunic over his arms, and then relaxed inside his warm embrace and kissed his lips.

"Abner is right about you…what you did today. There was a power I had never seen before. I will never forget it. No one will."

"I fear what I might have done to my children. It may have scarred their minds for life." He contemplated the long-term effects his actions could have on his children.

She pressed her body closer into the strength of his embrace. "Your children will remember a father emboldened to defend those unable to defend themselves."

"I do not know what came over me, but when I saw those three young men, a power flowed into me…a measure of the same divine rush I felt when dancing with the prophets after I had returned from meeting with Samuel. It cut right through me."

They became aware of giggling coming from above and turned to see two pairs of faces: one pair peeping from around the curtains of their bedroom and the second pair looking down upon them from the opening onto the rooftop. Ahinoam wiggled out of Saul's arms and faced her audience, simulating a stern countenance. She clapped her hands together with one sharp blow and the four faces vanished from sight. Then she turned back to her husband.

"You are not the only one with power."

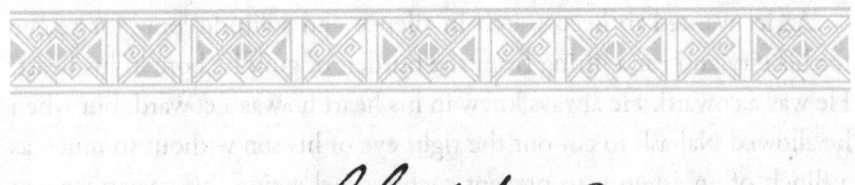

Chapter 3

AZRIEL PACED THE CIRCUMFERENCE OF THE CITY WALL. EACH day he climbed the stairs to the timbered platform built into the wall and surveyed the land from the city gate. Then he began his slow march around the high wall to the opposite side of the central gate. It was a day-long ritual he had to keep. He ignored the smirking glances and verbal harassment from the enemy sentries stationed along the wall as he continued his steady plod to the opposite side, then turned around and make his way back.

His eyes never stopped roving over the landscape for any signs of his son. There was only one road leading into Jabesh Gilead from the southern direction. On either side of the road were the encampments of the enemy, thousands of soldiers biding their time until their king gave the order to pillage and occupy the city. If his son returned, he would have to walk through this gauntlet of scorn and ridicule before entering the city gates.

Since Jarib and his fellow emissaries had been commissioned to seek help from the clutches of King Nahash, Azriel had spent his days pacing the city walls. He hardly slept. He neither bathed nor changed his clothes. He drank just enough water and ate just enough food to maintain the necessary strength to keep up his vigil of pacing and prayer. He did not want to speak with anyone, not any citizen, not his fellow city councilors, not anyone in his family.

Azriel wanted to keep watch in silence and solitude, pray for rescue for his city and for a lifting from the burden of guilt he bore in his heart. He was a coward. He always knew in his heart he was a coward, but when he allowed Nahash to cut out the right eye of his son without so much as a flinch of an attempt to prevent such a cruel action, his cowardice was confirmed to the entire world.

He wished Yahweh would strike him blind. He was an old man, after all. How many more years did he have left to live? And what good was his sight especially now when he would spend the rest of his days looking at the face of his son and the reddened, empty hole where his eye used to be? It would be a mercy if Yahweh struck him blind. It would give his heart some relief from guilt. For such cowardice, Jabesh Gilead did not deserve rescue. Her citizens should suffer the same fate as his son and his companions. It was what they deserved.

It was nearing sunset on the seventh day and his son had not returned. Nor had any advance word come during this time to indicate any progress in the effort to find a liberator. Azriel watched the sun sink behind the western mountains. His fractured heart began to sink, and with it any hope of success. He felt some relief when he did not see his son.

According to the terms stipulated in the treaty, every male citizen of Jabesh Gilead would have their right eye removed in exchange for their lives. If his son was still alive and returned home, at least father and son would be half-blind together. But, if Jarib and the others chose not to return, how could he blame them? They might have lost their right eye, but they would not live as slaves alongside the other cowardly citizens. They would be free.

Now the last thing he would see with his two good eyes in the late afternoon sun was his city surrounded by the Ammonite army. Tomorrow the brutal assault would begin, and he would be the first in line.

"Azriel! Azriel! Any rescuer in sight? Where are the sons of Israel? Cowering in their homes? Hiding behind the skirts of their women and children?"

Every day, several times a day, Azriel would endure taunting and curses. It was never directed at anyone else—only him, only the chief of councilors. For the entire week, the rest of the population of Jabesh Gilead had remained out of sight. When they were not forced to perform some service for Nahash and his military commanders, they remained hidden inside their homes. Any citizen who tried to escape was killed on the spot, their carcass thrown over the north wall, a feast now for vultures and jackals to serve as a visible deterrent to anyone else who foolishly tried to slip out of the city.

"You know what I hear, Azriel? Nothing. I hear nothing. I hear only silence."

On the first day of the siege, Azriel was forced to watch King Nahash and his commanders set up their headquarters in the Council House in the center of the city. Documents and trade records of the city were taken out and burned at the entrance of the Council House.

Instead of spending the next seven days devising battle strategies against the potential threat of attack, they turned the two-story structure into a brothel, forcing those female citizens unfortunate enough to catch the eye of an Ammonite general into becoming a slave to their deviant whims. Why waste time planning for a battle that would never come when they could be indulging in more fleshly pursuits?

"What day is it, Azriel?"

Azriel would not answer the question. He never acknowledged their taunts. Each day, King Nahash emerged from the Council House with his generals, propped up by women of the city taken as hostages and forced to pander to the depraved bents of their captors. Nahash would shout at Azriel on each successive day to the delight of his generals and the sentries posted all along the wall, mocking the chief councilor with fake tears, lamenting each day that had passed without the arrival of a rescuer. And now day seven was ending and nothing could be seen on the horizon but the Ammonite encampment besieging the city suffused in the glow of sunset.

"I do believe it is the end of the seventh day."

Nahash's voice was raw and hoarse from seven days of consuming nothing but wine and screaming curses at Azriel as he paced the ramparts.

"Turn around and face me, old man."

But Azriel stood his ground. He would not face his enemy. He would not willingly turn and look into the eyes of his tormentor. Azriel would have to be forced to turn away from the horizon and gaze upon his enemy. The Ammonite guards were more than happy to make the old man obey once their king had given the order. Two sentries spun Azriel around and forced him to his knees, holding him in place with the strength of their hands upon his shoulders. Azriel looked down upon Nahash and his drunken generals with half-naked women held fast in their clutches.

Nahash swayed atop two hairy, sticklike legs. He wore only a foul breechcloth, his great tanned and weathered paunch hanging over it. His pocked complexion radiated from the effects of the week-long orgy. When his silver crown fell from his bald head, he threw one of his female consorts to the ground and propped his foot on her back as she tried to retrieve it for him.

"So, old man, how many pairs of sandals have you worn out walking the battlements looking for your phantom rescuers?"

Azriel did not reply. All such communication was about to come to an end, so why waste the effort dignifying this pagan with his answer.

"If no army has come to save you, do you at least see any sign of your pathetic son or the other poor, one-eyed dogs sent with him?" Nahash stepped upon the poor woman lying flat on the ground, causing her crushed lungs to gasp in pain from the immense weight upon her back. Ammonite laughter filled the city square, echoing from the sentries all around the walls. Then Nahash knelt, digging his knees into the woman's back, and snatched his crown off the ground.

"Your son has left you in the lurch, old man." Nahash crawled off the woman's back, staggered to his feet, and violently began to swing his arms from side to side. "I could have gouged out both his eyes and sent him wandering in the desert for all the good he has done you."

But then a cry came from the sentry in the south turret. He cupped his hands over his mouth and direct the startling news from the lofty perch of the wooden tower to Nahash and his generals below huddled in front of the Council House.

"Riders approaching, escorting a military transport with three passengers inside!"

With renewed strength, Azriel sprang to his feet, casting off the pressure of the two burly sentries who had been pressing their weight upon his shoulders, and rushed to the edge of the wall. The information was true. And, as the contingent drew near, Azriel could see his son and two others inside the wagon. He ran for the stairs. No guard tried to stop him. They were staring in amazement at the party arriving at the city gate.

Azriel raced past Nahash and the generals who tossed aside the women they had abused and followed Azriel toward the entrance of the city. Once free of their captors, the poor women scattered in every direction like frightened pigeons.

Azriel rushed over to the wagon as it came to a stop inside the city. He could tell from the expression on his son's face that this seven-day excursion had been futile. Azriel moved to the back of the wagon as the three emissaries climbed out.

Nahash waved his crown before Jarib, taunting him with the symbol of power.

"You come back with empty hands along with your empty eye socket."

"No rescuer could be found." Jarib held out his empty hands.

Nahash marched into the center of the city, his arms raised into the air. "Jabesh Gilead is ours."

The battlements erupted with cheers from the sentries as the generals crowded around their king, slapping his shoulders and back.

"I have added another city to my kingdom without hurling a single spear or loosening arrow. Not one Hebrew man could be found to rescue the city of their brothers. No son of Israel has the man-sized parts of the king of the Ammonites."

Nahash placed his crown upon his head, ripped off his loincloth, and began to dance in the square while his generals applauded and chanted the name of their king.

Azriel grabbed his son and led him and the others toward one of the side streets off the square. There was no reason to be a silent audience to this obscene spectacle.

"Hold, Azriel. Hold where you stand." Nahash's command stopped the chief councilor and his emissaries from slipping out of the square unnoticed. "We have one final bit of business."

Azriel stepped in front of the others, fully expecting Nahash to call for a knife to cut out his right eye right then and there.

"Azriel, you are not worthy to be chief councilor." Nahash stumbled toward Azriel. He wore nothing except his crown, poised at a jaunty angle on the side of his head. The exuberant dancing and heavy consumption of wine made Nahash breathless and his speech impaired.

"You are but a craven, like all the male dogs of Israel. Tonight, my generals and I will celebrate our victory, but come morning prepare yourself. Prepare to be my private slave, and you shall be the first to see the world cut in half." Nahash took his thumb, held it above his right eye, and began to rotate it as if he were digging out the eyeball.

Azriel lowered his eyes so as not to look upon Nahash's tottery, naked form.

"The terms of our treaty have been met," Azriel replied solemnly. "Tomorrow we will give ourselves up to you, and you can do with us as you wish."

Azriel did not wait to be dismissed by Nahash. He was not yet his slave. That fate would be sealed in the morning. He spun around and began to shepherd the trio of emissaries down the side street off the square. It would be a mercy if he could lose his hearing along with half his vision so as never to hear the voice and laughter of Nahash again.

When the four men arrived at Azriel's home, Jarib told his companions to go in ahead of them. Once the two were inside the house, Jarib turned to Azriel.

"Abba, did anyone follow us? Anyone looking in our direction now?"

Azriel glanced up and down the street. All windows were shuttered, all doors were locked. No citizen in the street. No Ammonite sentry on the wall above or patrolling the street below. These marauders had acquired an effortless victory over Jabesh Gilead, and the Ammonite soldiers abandoned their posts, caring more about their all-night revelries with their king and his generals than keeping lookout for a nonexistent enemy.

"There is no one, my son. We are alone."

"Abba, this is all for show," whispered Jarib. "We are saved."

"What are you saying?" Azriel was so startled by this news that he hastily looked again in all directions for the eyes and ears of anyone he might have overlooked and could have overheard his son's news.

"Before dawn this morning we were deposited on the western banks of the Jordan River by soldiers in the army of King Saul. We crossed the river and walked until midday when we came to the main road and the first Ammonite guard post."

"What are you saying, my son? How can this be? What does it mean?"

"There is an army, a mighty army. The moment King Saul gave the command to muster they began to arrive by the thousands, tens of thousands. They joined us as we marched from Gibeah, and once in Bezek, the ranks swelled beyond counting."

"Bezek. There is an army in Bezek?"

"Yes, Abba. From every tribe in Israel. Farmers, merchants, and tradesmen—with crude weapons of mallets, rakes, and clubs—are now camped at Bezek. There is enough force to crush the Ammonite army three times its size. The king instructed me to give you this message: Say to the men of Jabesh Gilead, 'By the time the sun is hot tomorrow, you will be delivered.'"

At this news, Azriel began to collapse, and Jarib grabbed his arms to support him and lifted him to his face.

"We are saved, Abba," Jarib said. "Yahweh has sent us one who will rescue."

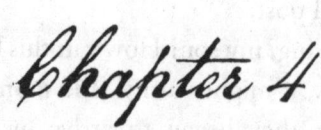

Chapter 4

SAUL STOOD ON A HILL LOOKING OUT OVER A VALLEY ON THE western outskirts of Bezek. He had instructed Abner to have the citizens of Bezek stay inside their walls; located in such proximity to Jabesh Gilead, they had to take every precaution to avoid being discovered. Sentries were posted around the walls to be sure no one slipped out of the village to warn the Ammonites of Saul's assembled army.

Under the glow of the half-moon and a sky full of stars, Saul could see the shadowy swarm of his military forces. The movement was minimal— the voices kept low. At last count three hundred and thirty thousand men had joined the original ranks that set out from Gibeah seven days ago. Saul was amazed by the number, amazed at how rapidly they had rallied to his call, and most amazed to find himself their king. Perhaps Abner had been right, the distribution of severed body parts of his oxen among the tribes had been a compelling recruiting ploy. Saul's rallying cry had provided him with an overwhelming force.

This was their final bivouac before tomorrow's attack. There was no tent staked out for him, no tents for the tribal leaders, no tents for the men. There was no time for such comforts. Saul had ordered a forced march. They were under the constraints of a treaty deadline and taking the time each day to set up and strike shelters was a luxury they could not afford.

Saul considered briefly having Eleazar bring the Ark from his father's home in Kiriath Jearim, but the time and care required to transport so holy an object would have slowed their progress. In future battles, Saul might request the Ark have its place in his camp, a well-protected place of honor for the Presence of the Almighty. But he did not want to be the first king of Israel to lose the Ark to his enemies and endure the humiliation inflicted by the Philistines when they had captured the Ark in Shiloh. He would die before enduring such shame. On this night, Saul would invoke Yahweh's favor with whatever offerings and prayers the high priest would perform on Israel's behalf.

Twelve stations were set up in an expansive circle at the base of the hill: one for every tribe. In the daylight hours of the seventh day, Abner had instructed the fighting men to find the banner of their tribe and gather behind their respective stations so they could be divided into smaller units. Each tribal leader was considered a general over the men in his tribe and the clan chieftains were then appointed captains of the smaller divisions.

Saul was about to make his rounds to each tribal leader before the final push to cross the Jordan River and surround Jabesh Gilead, but he kept waiting for the arrival of the prophet. The hour was drawing near for them to set out and there was still no sign of Samuel. He had wanted Samuel to stand next to him when he addressed the troops.

"Why has he not come? Why has he not shown himself?" Saul muttered as he bounced the empty ram's horn in his hand.

"We must not waste any more time." Abner looked over at Jonathan who stood on the opposite side of his father.

"It is not a waste of time," Saul responded. "I know you wish I would cease fretting over whether or not the prophet would make an appearance."

"I do not wish to dissuade you from your desire to have the prophet nearby, only the time it will take to move the army under cover of darkness is limited and we need to make the rounds one last time."

Saul clasped the ram's horn tightly in his hand and looked at Abner. "Very well, Commander."

When the three men reached the bottom of the hill, Saul waited for

Abner and Jonathan to light their torches from the embers of a small fire. This was the only fire Abner had allowed. Too much concentrated firelight would raise suspicions among the smaller villages and hamlets in the area, and spies could take word back to the Ammonites, ruining the element of surprise.

One by one, Saul visited the tribal leaders standing beneath their banner: Asher and its banner with a golden bowl overflowing with luscious fruit and vegetables; Zebulum with its banner displaying a sailing ship; Isschar's banner with a wild ass kicking out its hind legs; Manasseh with its banner of a fierce bull, its head and sharp horns proudly erect; Ephraim's banner of a bountiful chest of precious stones silhouetted by a blazing sun; Naphtali with its banner of a great horned stag; Gad with its banner of a bloody foot breaking the blade of a sword; the banner of the wolf, the Benjamite insignia of his tribe; the coiled serpent of the banner of Dan; the roaring lion of Judah; the crossed swords of Simeon. All these tribal leaders and the men behind them bent their knee in deference to the king.

The tribal leaders from Dan, Judah, and Simeon had experienced a change of heart and come to accept Saul when they each received a body part of slaughtered oxen, courtesy of the king with the order to join his army to liberate Jabesh Gilead or suffer the consequences. Bending the knee was the wiser choice even if done begrudgingly. The only exception to this demonstration of respect was the tribe of Reuben and its leader. Beerah was not so easily intimidated. He and his clan chieftains remained standing when Saul approached his station with Abner and Jonathan at his side.

Saul had avoided any contact with Beerah during the journey from Gibeah to Bezek. By the second day on the march to Bezek, word had come to him that Beerah and his company had joined the ranks, but Saul kept his distance.

Saul took the torch from Jonathan and raised it for a better view of the banner of Reuben with its proud warrior standing in turbulent waters. "Beerah, you and your chieftains stand proudly under your banner."

"I do." Beerah looked over his shoulder at his chieftains standing behind him, a show of allegiance to their tribal leader. "We all do. I had not expected to see you, son of Kish. I did not know if we would speak before the battle, or if you would lead us or give your commander the honor."

"Do you intend to fight with us, then, Beerah, or will you stay behind to protect the baggage?" Abner blurted.

Saul appreciated Abner coming to his defense with his acerbic remark, but he wanted to reflect a more conciliatory demeanor.

The clan chieftains standing behind Beerah grumbled at the insult. But Saul remained calm as he looked into the eyes of Beerah. He wanted Beerah to feel no threat from him.

"It is enough that you came, Beerah. I am grateful you have joined us." Saul tilted his head toward Beerah as he handed the torch back to Jonathan.

"I am curious to see how the son of Kish will fight tomorrow." Beerah's lips formed a slant smile, his voice coated with disdain. "It is one thing to display your swordsmanship upon defenseless oxen; quite another against an enemy who fights back."

"So true. So true." Saul's quiet amusement at Beerah's remark defused what could turn into a scene of drawn swords, brother upon brother. "May Yahweh be with you, Beerah, and your tribe. May Yahweh be with us all."

Saul wasted no more time with Beerah. He turned and walked between Jonathan and Abner, heading toward the station of the priests where Ahiah and Eleazar awaited. Saul did not want the other tribal leaders, who had only observed this brief exchange from a distance and not heard the caustic remarks between Abner and Beerah, to be disheartened in any way.

Saul spoke under his breath as the three of them walked abreast toward the Levite's station. "I am curious, Abner. What part of the ox did you send to Beerah?"

"The dung-caked rump," Abner said with quiet pleasure.

"Well, that explains the extra portion of Beerah's surliness."

"Do not be surprised, Cousin, if Beerah might suffer an injury tomorrow."

"Now, now, Commander." Saul waved an admonishing finger at his cousin.

As Saul got closer to the Levite's station, Malki and Ishvi dashed to meet him in the middle of the great circle. Saul wrapped an arm around each boy, playfully locking their heads in the crook of his arms.

"Abba, why will you not let us go to Jabesh Gilead with you?" Malki protested while struggling inside the curl of Saul's muscular arm.

"Your mother. Blame it all on your mother."

Ishvi had wiggled his head out of Saul's grip before he asked his question. "But how will we ever learn to fight?"

Saul stopped scuffling with his sons the moment he saw Gad speaking with Nathan as they stood beneath the Levitical banner with the Ark insignia. He pulled his boys in front of him, and though he addressed his sons, Saul looked at the two prophets standing beside the high priest and the guardian of the Ark.

"There is time enough to learn to fight. Abner is training you, and when he says you are ready, only then will you fight at my side. Till such time, you remain with the Levites." He patted his sons' heads before approaching the station of the Levites.

Prophets and priests alike took a knee when Saul entered their station.

"Nathan, why was I not informed of your arrival?"

"My lord, I have just come into the camp." Nathan remained on his knee while the others rose to their feet.

"And where is he? Did he not come with you?" Saul looked about the station, hoping to spot the imposing shadow of Samuel somewhere in the crowd of Levites.

"My lord, the prophet awaits you on the northern plain outside of Gilgal. He said to tell you that if you are victorious—and the prophet prays that you are—he will meet you there and will confirm the kingship of my lord on that occasion."

The words took Saul's breath away. The ram's horn he had carried with him slipped through his fingers. He bent down to retrieve it, and he quickly stuffed it into the leather side pouch belted around his waist before anyone took notice of the object.

No one spoke. Everyone waited for him to respond to this news. Saul had to take a breath to gather his wits as he tried to think of something constructive to come from this disappointment.

"At least the prophet has journeyed partway," he said, though Saul felt little encouragement from his own words. "That is something."

"What happened? Did his mule go lame?" Abner could not contain his scorn. "He could travel no farther than Gilgal? He had seven days to get here."

"It was a quick march, Commander." Saul held up his hand for Abner to stop his accusations. "Our speed could have been a deterrent."

"He comes halfway with his halfhearted endorsement."

"We shall take what we can get." Saul was becoming perturbed at having to calm his cousin's complaints.

"Why do you even need the prophet's approval?"

Saul was having difficulty deterring Abner's annoyance who was making no attempt to hide it. "It is wise to seek the prophet's approval and assurances."

"The prophet will never give it to you."

"Then we win it, Commander. We win it."

"Since when do you have to win the approval of anyone? You are the king. You raised this army all by yourself. You are too accommodating of that old man."

Saul could hear the gasp from those close enough to hear this conversation. He saw gazes drop and bodies become frozen from their shock at Abner's brazen reproach. Saul yanked Abner's arm with a suddenness that caused him to drop his torch as Saul pulled him out of the Levite's station and back into the center of the circle. The torch remained burning on the ground.

Saul dropped his voice to a low swelter that only Abner could hear.

"I have one goal in mind tonight, Commander. Victory. That is my goal. Not winning over Beerah's loyalty, nor winning favor from the prophet, nor trying to stifle your constant abrasions. None of this will distract me from that goal. I do not have the patience to argue with you in public. We have a battle to fight, and I do not expect you to debate me about something over which I have no control. Understood?"

Saul had never confronted his cousin like this. He had never confronted anyone like this. Saul knew his cousin well enough that should anyone else ever make the miscalculation to speak to him in this manner they would have found themselves in one-on-one combat. But Saul knew he had moved beyond being Abner's first cousin. Saul was someone else entirely.

He was the man who, seven days ago, lopped off the heads of two oxen. He was the one who sent out a call for the men of Israel to leave home and gather at Bezek, and by the hundreds of thousands they came to his side. Saul was the man who was prepared to lead that army into battle. Not since the days of the Judges had such men arisen to unify the people against a common foe. Saul would never again be the man Abner had known since they were children growing up together.

"Whether you like it or not, Commander, whether or not you understood it, you must grasp the importance of the occasion and see that you have a simple choice in this matter." Saul was patient, though he was aiming all his ire at Abner. He kept smiling, but Saul would not move one stride toward the battle or take his burning eyes off his cousin until he had backed down from this affront.

Saul watched Abner take a deep breath that seemed to deflate his entire body.

Abner spoke in a quiet, humble rasp. "Cousin, forgive me for speaking bluntly. I was mistaken."

"And one more thing, Commander. While in public, I am no longer to be addressed as 'Cousin.' That endearment may be used only in private. Is that understood?"

Saul needed to dispel any lingering doubts Abner may have had regarding their relationship. Tonight, in this moment, Saul needed to solidify that their bond had changed forever. They were no longer cousins connected by blood; no longer farm boys; no longer unknown in the world and unremarkable to their people. Saul was king and Abner his commander, exalted positions, yet Abner must accept as fact that his was the lesser rank.

It was not easy for Saul to say these words to Abner, and he knew it was not easy for his cousin to accept them. But if addressing him as "my lord" or "your majesty," was a requirement, then Saul knew Abner would make this adjustment, though it would not be something his heart and mind would easily embrace. Saul hoped that in time, this new address might trip from his tongue more easily, but tonight Saul's command would be obeyed, like it or not.

Abner took a hard swallow. "Yes, my lord." Then he bowed his head in a sign of compliance.

Saul exhaled the remaining voltage of fury held in reserve should his cousin put up more of a fight. "Now call the tribal leaders into the circle. I wish to address them before we depart for Jabesh Gilead."

Abner spun around and marched back to where Jonathan stood among the Levites at their station. Saul was relieved that this verbal lashing was over, and he hoped that Abner was appreciative that he had chosen not to contend with him in front of the others, but instead, had pulled him aside. Saul thought this was a display of wisdom, something he hoped Abner would come to see. Perhaps in the future Abner could refer to him as "my lord" without the words getting caught in his throat. And perhaps sooner than he might expect. Saul could only hope for such.

Abner signaled for Jonathan to follow him, and Saul watched as they began making the rounds, ordering the tribal leaders to gather in the circle around him.

Emboldened by his assertiveness with Abner, Saul felt he could address these men with confidence, many of whom resented his selection as Israel's first king and doubted his abilities to lead them into battle. But that no longer mattered to Saul. His mind and heart were focused on the liberation of Jabesh Gilead, and though he felt he could liberate the city with a much smaller number of brave warriors, Saul was grateful that so many men had answered his call to arms.

Whether they had joined him through intimidation or loyalty, Saul did not care. They were here, by the thousands. Samuel may be absent, but the men of Israel were here in Bezek and would fight with him. Abner might be correct about one thing. With the men of Israel at his side, perhaps he did not need to be so accommodating of Samuel. Tomorrow's victory might just give him cause to trust in himself.

Jonathan carried a torch and stood beside his father until the last of the tribal leaders and chieftains assembled around the king. Saul took his headband from his pouch with the wolf's head stitched in the center and tied it around his forehead. He then took the torch from Jonathan and began to move about inside the circle of the men, raising it before their faces, the flames ruffling in the air. He spoke in a low voice, not a halting flow, but a steady and fervent incantation.

"The eye of Israel has been gouged from its socket. We have heard the cry of our brothers, and we are of one heart and mind that those who have inflicted this shame on the citizens of Jabesh Gilead have inflicted shame upon us all. We gathered in haste. We marched at a swift pace. We have come together in a disorderly manner. We are not fully trained or proficient and skilled in the art of war. We are not well equipped. We wear little or no armor. Most fight with crude farm tools or clubs and limbs made from tree branches.

"We are young and old and in between. We come from the four winds that blow over our nation. We descend from the twelve sons of our forebearer, each tribe stands beneath the banner with its symbol of the blessing our ancestor Jacob spoke to each of his sons before he was gathered to the fathers. But on this day, we are all sons of one ancestor, and we are all under one banner, the banner of Yahweh.

"The plan is simple: we cross the Jordan River as one army then break into three columns, four tribes in each column; the commander has set which tribe goes into each column; my column will attack from the south toward the city's main entrance; the commander will lead his column from the north; Jonathan along with Jeush leading the tribe of Benjamin, will attack from the east.

"We will be in place by the start of the third watch. I shall strike first at the main encampment outside the city. Once the sounds of battle are heard, the commander and captain know to sweep down to encompass the city. When we take the city there should only be Ammonite soldiers fighting from within the walls. The citizens of Jabesh Gilead know to remain in their homes until our victory. If they do not heed the warning, their blood is on their own heads. We are free of guilt should they be mistaken for the enemy.

"On this day, we are sons of the Almighty. When Yahweh gives us the victory, word shall go out to all our enemies that there is an army in Israel, an army of valiant warriors who fight as one man, an army that fears no threat from other nations, any army that rises to protect its people and will yield to death before yielding to the yoke of slavery."

Saul turned full circle for one last look into the faces of those who were prepared to follow him. He extended his arm with the torch high above his head. "When the cry of battle is heard, let the mouth of Sheol open to swallow the dead we leave in our wake. And now, for the love of Israel. For the glory of Yahweh, let there be victory."

There was silence when he finished his last words. Saul expected as much. He had not asked for any to speak or thought it necessary for a response, but one by one the tribal leaders began to repeat his last phrase until everyone who had been summoned to join this gathering was repeating it as one man with one voice.

"For the love of Israel. For the glory of Yahweh."

Saul would have been satisfied if the group simply nodded in agreement, but when he handed the torch back to his son, a voice broke above the others.

"For the love of Israel. For the glory of Yahweh. For the honor of the king."

Saul turned to Abner and saw his cousin, his commander, his sword raised. It was Abner who had spoken this third phrase calling for honor upon him, his cousin, the king and sovereign of Israel. Saul felt a surge of love for Abner, and he pulled Abner into his chest, wrapping his arms around him just as the others in the group gave voice to the three-fold chant of praise.

Chapter 5

IT WAS THE SCREAMING THAT AWOKE NAHASH FROM HIS INE-briated slumber. He lay on his back on some hard surface. It pained him to open his eyes, so he clamped them in tight slits and gradually let his sight adjust to the torchlight in the room. When he tried to lift his head, he felt a shooting pain, so he let it fall back onto the hard surface with a soft thud. He rolled his head to one side, and through the window saw a strange vision in the darkness—torches racing back and forth along the platform battlements as if they were floating in blackness.

Something pressed on top of him, making it difficult to breathe. Nahash tried to move his arms and realized that a body lay across his chest. He pushed the sleeping woman off, watching as she tumbled from the table and bounced onto the floor. She moaned from the rough disturbance to her sleep, but it was not enough to revive her.

Nahash looked about the room at the aftereffects of a night of revelry. Humans lay slumbering in a contorted sprawl, discarded clumps of flesh on the floor as if tossed there by a violent wind. Dogs were fighting over scraps of food, and Nahash grabbed an empty goblet on the table and flung it at the animals, then cursed the dagger of pain that shot through his brain caused by the action. He scooted his bare buttocks across the table until his legs dangled off the end, and then he dropped his feet onto the floor.

When his hearing and sight began to improve, the screaming from outside became clearer. Nahash wobbled over to the window. Torches were still racing across the platform along the battlements. The darkness of the night had started to recede, and he could see his men pouring into the city through the entrance so fast the guards were unable to shut the gate. Many wounded soldiers were brought inside only to be deposited onto the ground bleeding and dying so those able-bodied men could defend the city.

Nahash stumbled backward and tripped over a mound of prone bodies, causing him to fall onto the floor. He began screaming at the top of his voice as he got back onto his feet. His tongue and lips were too inflamed to shape intelligible sounds. All he could do was bellow and stumble about the large room, kicking any form that looked recognizable and scream into their distorted, engorged faces.

When he realized he wore nothing, Nahash stripped a goat-hair vest from one of his generals too drunk to be roused by his screams. The vest was too small for his corpulent torso. He yanked the general's sandals from his feet as well and, shod with footwear for a man half his size, he then found a discarded animal-skin apron and tied it around his waist as he stumbled outside the Council House and into the city center. In his panic, he had given no thought to finding his silver crown.

More and more of his men rushed through the gate, fleeing something he could not identify. Nahash saw his archers firing down from the battlements on those attacking the city, and his guards engaged in hand-to-hand combat with those who had succeeded in scaling the walls. It was too chaotic around the gate; too many of his men lay dead or dying on the ground at the entrance, so Nahash rushed over to the stairs to join the fight on the southern wall.

When he reached the stairs, his head began to spin, and he retched. The shock to his system after a week of debauchery forced him onto his hands and knees. The only way he could climb the steps to the top of the platform attached to the wall was on all fours. When he reached the top, he crawled across the platform and plastered himself against the wall, catching his breath and trying to get his head to stop spinning before he dared look over the wall for a view of the landscape.

By now the sun had fully risen, but when Nahash looked up all he could see was smoke filling the sky above him. When enemy soldiers began running in his direction, stepping on the bodies of his men lying dead on the platform, Nahash draped his body over the corpse of an Ammonite guard and feigned death until the soldiers passed and rushed down the stairs to engage with those Ammonites still fighting in the city center.

Once the soldiers had descended the stairs, Nahash lifted his head to see who they were, but with the smoke clouding the morning light and his eyes burning and watery from the consumption of so much wine, he could not get a clear vision. Where had they come from? Who were they?

Nahash glanced down at his feet and saw he had lost one of the sandals while the other dangled from the top of his right foot. He kicked it off and began to inch his way up the wall until he was able to peek over the edge. The horrible screaming forced him off his knees and onto his feet. An updraft of wind blew the billowing smoke out of his field of vision, and he beheld the murderous landscape below.

Thousands upon thousands of dead and dying Ammonite soldiers covered the ground, their tents roiling in the fires set by the force that had decimated his army. Men were crawling over the bodies of the dead like insects, stripping them of their armor and weapons and dumping them in great stockpiles. Nahash began to tremble, not from cold or delirium tremors or even the sight of mass death. His body began a feverish quaking at the premonition that this bloody landscape would be the last great scene his eyes would ever behold.

A contingent of men marched up the road toward the south entrance, led by what Nahash assumed was the leader of this army standing a head taller than all the others. Nahash turned his back on the vision of horror, crept across to the edge of the platform, and looked down from his high position upon the battlements as the enemy soldiers dragged his generals out of the Council House.

They were forced to lie facedown, all in a long row, with two enemy soldiers propping their feet upon the back of the head and neck of each general. Once the leader of the enemy army entered the city gate, he was conducted to the front of the Council House and the prostrate Ammonite generals.

From his position on the battlements, Nahash watched the statuesque leader of the enemy host nod to a man with wild, flaxen hair and blood and dirt splattered across his brawny chest whom Nahash assumed was the commander of this army. The man stepped up to the first Ammonite general. The soldiers who held him jerked the general onto his knees and yanked his head back.

The enemy commander stooped down and spoke to the first Ammonite general. Nahash did not hear the answer he gave, but it must have displeased this enemy commander for when he moved to the next general, the one left behind had his throat cut and was slammed to the ground with the soldier's feet propped upon his back while he bled to death.

When the flaxen-haired commander got to the last Ammonite general in the line, Nahash watched as the commander once again bent down to speak to the general. His answer seemed to please the enemy commander for he ordered the general to rise. The two enemy soldiers helped the general to his feet, and to Nahash's alarm, he saw the general raise his arm and point in his direction and identify him as the Ammonite king. Everyone turned to see Nahash standing on the battlements surrounded by his fallen soldiers, but instead of being set upon, the enemy commander and all his soldiers, burst into laughter.

Nahash stood upon the battlements, a large hairy creature except for his bald head, dressed in an ill-fitted vest and an animal skin apron barely covering his loins, barefoot and trembling. He looked like a king's fool, not a king. Everyone laughed except the tall leader; his face was somber. He pointed toward Nahash and gave a command, and instantly a handful of men rushed to the steps while archers drew back their bows, aiming their shafts at him.

Nahash was not treated like his generals, all but one now lying prone and bleeding out the last moments of their lives into the earth. He was escorted down the stairs and brought before his vanquisher. He was not manhandled by the soldiers or tossed to the ground or held at sword point. He stood face-to-face with his equal. No one laughed at him. No one smiled; his comical appearance no longer amusing.

"Do you know who you stand before today?" asked the flaxen-haired commander.

"No, my lord," Nahash replied, the first words he had uttered since he was roused by the screams of his men. He looked at the commander, expecting him to identify who he was, but instead, he pointed to the tallest man in the group.

"You stand before Saul, son of Kish, from the tribe of Benjamin, under the banner of the wolf, and the first king of Israel, the chosen people of Yahweh the Almighty."

Nahash squinted as he looked at Saul with the bright sun beaming around his head.

"My lord, king of Israel, I have heard of your greatness and your recent rise to the throne." Nahash lowered his eyes. In a sudden rush of shame at the overexposure of his body, he tried to cover himself with his arms and hands.

"I have no throne." The king of Israel corrected Nahash, and then continued, "The people of Israel cried out for a king because of men like you, and so Yahweh gave them a king."

"The God of Israel chose well, my lord." Nahash repeatedly nodded his bowed head. "I yield myself and my kingdom to your great mercy. I beseech your mercy for myself and my men."

"What few men survived have fled. There are no two of them left together."

Nahash was stunned to hear such news from the new king of Israel. If this were true, he and his general were the last two Ammonites taken from the field of battle. He looked at his general kneeling off to the side surrounded by enemy soldiers, a knife blade poised beneath his throat, his eyes wide with terror. Nahash decided now was a perfect time to show deference to his conqueror and began to go to his knees but was forcibly prevented.

"Do not kneel to me." At the victorious king's command, Nahash was held upright on his legs and feet. "Jarib, stand forth."

Nahash was surprised to see Azriel and Jarib standing amid Saul's men. He had not seen them until now, nor had he noticed that many of the citizens of Jabesh Gilead had emerged from hiding once the army of Israel liberated the city. When Jarib moved beside the king, Nahash looked into Jarib's empty eye socket. He felt a sharp pain behind his eyes, and a foreboding of retribution caused his spine to curl in on itself.

"You are responsible for this, yes?" The victorious king directed Nahash's eyes to the empty eye socket in Jarib's face. "You had this man mutilated?"

Were Nahash not kept vertical by the king's men, his legs would have given out.

"Yes, my lord." Nahash's voice waned in strength. He hoped his truthful answer would stand him in good stead.

"Now you may kneel. Kneel before this man. Beg for his mercy."

The soldiers released their hold of Nahash, and he crumpled to the ground. He crawled over to Jarib, laid his head upon his feet, and began to wheeze out his appeal for leniency and forgiveness. Nahash hoped his act of contrition would move Jarib's heart toward mercy, but when the feet his tears fell upon began to move away, Nahash wrapped his beefy arms around Jarib's legs, making it impossible for him to move.

"Commander, your knife!" The king of Israel had barked out his command.

Nahash climbed up Jarib's legs and wrapped his arms around Jarib's waist for dear life.

The king of Israel held out his hand and the flaxen-haired man yanked the knife from his belt and placed it into the king's hand.

Nahash bellowed like a bull, and it took several tries for the soldiers to peel his arms away from his stranglehold on Jarib's legs. Nahash remained on his knees, but his head was pulled back exposing his neck and face.

"Take your revenge, Jarib." Saul offered Jarib the handle of the knife.

Jarib looked at the blade in Saul's hand, but he did not take it. His good eye widened in dismay as he beheld the knife in the palm of Saul's hand.

"My lord, I cannot. Forgive me, but I cannot."

Nahash watched as Saul patted Jarib on the shoulder. A hope began to spark in the heart of Nahash. This young man's pity might influence the heart of the victorious king if he was unwilling to do something so inhumane. The son of Azriel returned to stand next to his father.

Nahash would gladly become their slave if he could avoid the torture he expected to receive and would have inflicted on others had he been victorious. But he had been defeated, and the victorious king pointed for the last Ammonite general to be brought forward. The general was pushed toward the king who held out the knife to him. The offer required no explanation. Nahash and the general knew what was expected.

A dozen swords were drawn, the blade points held inches away from the general's chest and neck in case he took the knife and tried to use it for any other purpose than for what was intended. But the general sneered at the knife, spat on the ground at Saul's feet, and then spun around and drove his thumbs into Nahash's eyes until the blood began to stream down the sides of his face.

The last image Nahash beheld was the enraged face of his general plunging his thumbs into his eyes before everything went black. Nahash covered his face with his hands and fell forward onto the ground, roaring in shock and pain. All he heard above his own screams was the scream of his general begging for pardon followed by the weight of the general's body falling on top of him, bleeding out the last of his life.

The victorious king ordered an empty cart brought to the Council House and for it to be loaded with the bodies of the dead generals. Then he instructed that Nahash be placed on the back of the cart. Nahash was forcefully lifted off the ground and tossed on top of the pile of dead generals. The team of oxen was driven to the front entrance when Nahash heard the victorious king order it to stop before departing the city.

"Nahash, blind king of Ammon." Nahash felt the king's fingers clamp down upon the top of his bald head, and he instantly gripped the wooden edges of the wagon, fearful of having his throat slit. "This wagon is driverless, pointing east toward Ammon, the way you came with your army. Your passengers are the dead generals who rode with you to Jabesh Gilead intent on enslaving innocent people.

"If you make it back to your city alive, tell your people that I, Saul, king of Israel, defeated you and turned you into the blind king of the

Ammonites. Let your people know that this is what happens to those foolish enough to attack the people of Israel."

Nahash's thick cry created a threshold of silence from all who surrounded the cart.

Over the sound of his weeping, Nahash heard someone step forward.

"My lord, may I speak to Nahash?"

It was Azriel, and the king gave his consent.

In a moment, Nahash felt the hands of Azriel grip his head. He then felt Azriel's warm breath flowing into his ear.

"Nahash, it is I, Azriel."

These words were for Nahash alone. His sense of hearing was quickly becoming fine-tuned, compensating for the loss of sight.

"Azriel." Nahash moaned. He knew he had one last gasp for mercy. "I will die."

"Yes, Nahash, you could die before reaching your city." Azriel's voice was dry but kind. "It is a fitting end for the pain you caused my city. You ride a death wagon with the smell of death around you. But you have been given a mercy. You do not have to look upon the means of your death. It may be wild beasts or the hands of bandits or you may give out in dark exhaustion from the heat and cold of the desert. But here is one last mercy. I forgive you for what you have done to my city and my son."

Nahash heard the rustling of clothing as a robe was removed and draped over his exposed body. Then a spout of a skin of water was brought to Nahash's quivering lips.

"Drink."

Nahash clamped his teeth on the spout and guzzled the warm liquid. After a few swallows, the spout was pulled from Nahash's lips, and the water skin was placed in Nahash's hands. Nahash waited for an explanation of this action he could not understand. He could only surmise that Azriel had been inspired by his son's mercy not to invoke an "eye for an eye" when he was given the opportunity.

The order to release the oxen was given, the rumps of the beasts were whipped, and the cart jolted forward.

Nahash, the blind king of the Ammonites, gripped the bodies of his dead generals, hoping to prevent a fall from the death wagon as it rumbled down the road into the fields of slaughter. The spontaneous celebrations of the victorious army filled the air as the howls of the blind king evaporated into the radiant heat of the noonday sun.

Chapter 6

SAUL AND AHINOAM SAT SIDE BY SIDE IN THE FRONT OF THEIR family wagon with their children riding in the back waving to the exuberant crowds around them.

"This was like when you were made king, Abba." Mikal stuck her head between the shoulders of her parents, her giddy excitement manifested by bouncing up and down. "Will they give you a crown to wear?"

"Your ima is all the crown I need," Saul replied, and Ahinoam placed her hand on Saul's knee and squeezed it. "Now go wave to the people like a true princess."

Mikal did not have to be told a second time to assume the duties of a princess.

Ahinoam looked back at her children standing in the wagon holding onto the slats and waving to the people.

"It comes natural to that one." Ahinoam nodded toward Mikal.

Saul laughed and then snapped the reins on the rumps of the mules while Jonathan and Abner rode in front of the wagon, shouting for the people to move off the road and clear the way for the king, the victorious king, the king of Israel.

"You would have been proud of your son." Saul nodded toward

Jonathan; his face unable to conceal his pride. "He led his men well. He was fearless in battle."

"Proud of him, yes, but do not speak of battles." Ahinoam covered her ears with her hands, her face more somber than her husband's. "I am his ima, remember."

"He was made a captain in the army before the liberation of Jabesh Gilead. Now he has earned the rank, and I want him recognized as such." Saul not only wanted to groom his son to be the first prince of Israel and successor to the throne, but to have him build an impressive reputation as a proven valiant warrior. "I want our son to become a true prince. This is a firm beginning as a leader. The people will see him not as pampered, but as a royal scion."

At that moment, Jonathan happened to look back at his parents and smile. Saul nodded his head toward the first prince of Israel. "He will be an uncommon prince, and someday, a great king. I will see to it."

There was barely room along the road for Saul to drive the wagon. Were it not for Jonathan and Abner clearing the way, the cheering people would have swarmed Saul and his clan. But there was very little room for the people to go. They were forced to squeeze between the wagons parked on either side of the road heading into Gilgal. Wagon after wagon after wagon was filled with the plunder of battle. It had taken days to inventory the weaponry, armor and military provisions gathered from the defeated Ammonite forces and dozens of wagons to haul the spoils. This had given the time necessary for Saul to rush home and give his family the news of his triumph and travel back with them to the plain north of Gilgal for a victory celebration.

On the outskirts of Gilgal, stations of the twelve tribes of Israel, their banners flying, formed a large circle with the tribe of Benjamin at the head. Encompassed in this great tribal ring were those warriors who had chosen not to go straight home after the battle but had stayed for Saul's confirmation as king and the celebration of his first victory. There were rumors of a crowning, rumors of vengeance exacted upon those who first rejected Saul as king, rumors of Samuel's permanent retirement. Saul did nothing to dispel these rumors. Time would exhaust the erroneous and elevate the truth.

Once Saul and Ahinoam had taken their places at the front of the roped-in area for the Benjamite tribe, their children and the clan chieftains filled the empty space behind. All eyes were directed toward the center of the great circle as the priests threw their torches upon the altar, engulfing the sacrificial offering in a burst of flames. A ring of priests around the altar blew their trumpets while a second ring raised their shofars to join the blast of praise to Yahweh for this victory over the Ammonite army. Ahiah and Eleazar led a procession of the Honor Guard around the altar as the smoke rose into the sky above the fields of wheat and the desert plains.

Saul kept darting his gaze from the worship taking place in the center of the circle to Samuel and his entourage positioned on his right. The prophet sat in a great chair, his wife seated on one side of him, his two sons standing on the other, and his student prophets huddled behind him including Gad and Nathan. From the way Samuel looked, stationary and humorless, Saul could not tell if the prophet was annoyed or about to fall asleep, but he never bothered to look in his direction.

Saul felt a tugging on his left arm and turned to see Ahinoam's beaming face. This was a much better vision to look upon than a grim-faced old man. He took his wife's hand and brought it to his lips.

After leading their procession around the altar, Ahiah and Eleazar paused before the Levitical station and took items from a table. The high priest and guardian of the Ark, each bearing their gift, moved solemnly toward Saul and knelt before him.

"May the seven lights of Yahweh, the Divine Light of all light, keep darkness from the house of the king," Ahiah said, holding out to Saul a solid gold, seven-stemmed candelabra, each arm fashioned like a branch with a budding flowered end.

"May the sound of the trumpet call forth the king and may he stand in strength over the Mercy Seat of Yahweh," Eleazar intoned, and offered Saul a silver trumpet and a golden spear.

The high priest and guardian rose to their feet so the twelve tribal leaders could approach Saul. They lined up in three columns, four to a column, each tribal leader carrying a gift. One at a time, the tribal leaders announced themselves, knelt before Saul with a gift, and pronounced their blessings.

"Heber, son of the tribe of Asher: May the bowls on the table of the king always be filled with the bounty of the soil," Heber said, setting a bowl of solid gold filled with fruits and vegetables before the king.

"Salma, son of the tribe of Zebulun: May the borders of the king extend beyond the Great Sea and may his ships return full of riches." Salma presented him with a beautiful gold and silver fish.

"Tola, son of the tribe of Issachar: May the burdens of the king always be light wherever he travels," Tola said, proffering a set of beautifully tooled leather saddlebags.

"Barzillai, son of the tribe of Manasseh: May the yoke of the king fit perfectly on the broad shoulders of his oxen that plow his fields and harvest his rich crops." Barzillai extended a yoke of solid silver.

Each of the tribal leaders remained kneeling before Saul until the last in the column of four had pronounced his blessing. Then all four men rose and placed their forearm and clenched fist across their chest before speaking their oath of loyalty in unison, an oath all twelve leaders had composed and agreed upon:

"This is the day of the wolf rising from the tribe of Benjamin. Our pledge is to Saul, son of Kish, known from this day onward as the first king of the chosen, the first king of Israel. We declare our steadfast loyalty of the fortunes and blood of our tribes; we shall be vigilant from generation to generation to serve the king in peace and in war; we shall keep the covenant of Abraham and uphold the Law of Moses; we will raise our sons and daughters to honor the king and to glorify Yahweh, the Almighty forever and ever."

When they finished their pledge, they slapped their arms against their chests and dropped their heads as one man.

"Hear, O Israel, the Lord our God, the Lord is One!" cried Ahiah, and the first of the tribal leaders stepped to the side to make way for the next group of four.

Saul released Ahinoam's hand and rose from his seat, crossing his chest with both of his arms and bowing. He was so moved by the pronouncement of blessing and the words of their vow he did not notice if the prophet was watching and whether he approved of these proceedings. This was an exhilarating moment of liberation for Saul, one requiring his full attention and appreciation. When he raised his head the next column of four leaders approached him, and Saul sat back down.

"Resheph, son of the tribe of Ephraim: May the storehouses of the king be filled with treasures," Resheph said, kneeling and laying a silver chest filled with precious stones before the king.

"Jezer, son of the tribe of Naphtali: May the game in the king's forests be abundant," Jezer spoke, and laid on the ground a large hand-woven carpet with a magnificent stag head sewn with silver thread in the center.

"Ahi, son of the tribe of Gad: May the shield of our tribe protect the king." Ahi presented a shield of gold with a sword blade embossed on its front.

"Jeush, son of the tribe of Benjamin: May the pelt of the wolf, the skin of the lion, and the coat of the bear, clothe the king and his family," Jeush said, laying the elegantly embroidered garments of each animal before the king.

Like the column before them, they all four rose and voiced their oath of loyalty to Saul, then they slapped their right arm across their chest and bowed.

"Hear, O Israel, the Lord our God, the Lord is One," Ahiah said.

Saul again rose to his feet and crossed his arms over his chest, bowing in thanks for their oath to him. But as the third and last column approached Saul, the clan chieftains of Benjamin drew their swords and surrounded the last four tribal leaders.

Saul looked at Abner for an explanation as to what was happening, but Abner looked just as confused as Saul. How could this ceremonial occasion be disrupted by such a violent threat, and instigated from his own tribe? Saul glared at Jeush who he suspected was behind this outrageous plot.

"What is the meaning of this, my brother?" Saul growled. His use of "my brother" in referring to Jeush did nothing to soften the enmity in his voice.

Jeush approached Saul. "My lord, it was not long ago when these four tribal lords came to your home in Gibeah, refused to dismount from their steeds and bend the knee. They insulted the king and offered no gift. They scoffed saying, 'Shall Saul reign over us?' We cannot ignore this affront. I say these men should be put to death and new leaders appointed to these four tribes. I say remove each of the four tribal banners from their spikes and mount their heads on each one."

Jeush drew his sword and pointed the blade toward Beerah. If he was expecting the crowd to roar its approval, he was disappointed. There was no cry of support from the people. The throng was silent, immobile in its collective shock.

Saul could not believe what Jeush and the others of his tribe had done or what they were proposing. In the blink of an eye this beautiful ceremony to honor Yahweh and his first victory had become an occasion for vengeance against the sons of their fathers; an occasion to exact blood for a personal slight to Saul's honor.

Saul glanced at Samuel and saw him squirm in his seat. It looked as though the prophet was about to get out of his throne and assert control over this tense situation, but Saul was not going to allow that to happen. This misuse of justice was being done on his behalf by his own tribe, and he would see to its proper resolution. Just before Saul was about to order Jeush to put away his sword, Beerah approached the king and knelt at his feet.

"Lord Jeush speaks the truth, my sovereign," Beerah spoke with humility, a tone Saul had not heard from this tribal chieftain. "I and my fellow lords deserve to be held accountable for our words and our actions against Yahweh and the anointed king. I yield my life to the king and only beg that my head will appease your judgment and that your mercy would extend to my brother lords."

Saul looked down upon the bowed head of Beerah awaiting his fate. Then Carmi, Hammuel, and Allon, the lords of the last tribes in the third column, set down their gifts and approached Saul only to kneel beside Beerah, empty-handed, prepared to tender their lives to his verdict. The heads of the leaders from the tribes of Reuben, Judah, Simeon, and Dan were offered in submission. What greater gift would Saul receive today than the chance to exert his power over these troublemakers whose blatant prejudice and public display of scorn for his leadership had marred the early days of his rule?

Tribal leaders would come and go; an abundance of good men could fill the spot left vacant in each tribe. This was a perfect opportunity to set a tone of leadership. He had removed heads before. When he lopped off the heads of his oxen, the action had inspired a nation to rally to his side. He could make the same argument for this moment.

Saul took the sword from the hand of Jeush and examined the fine edge of the blade. "Is this what you want, Jeush? You want me to turn this gathering from one of celebration into a court of law? A heavy sentence you demand—the shedding of blood for a few harsh words spoken at my expense."

Saul raised the sword in the air with his left arm and stepped to the side of the four kneeling men. From that position, if he brought it down, he could take off two heads with one swing, reposition his footing and remove the other two. When he brought his right hand beside the sword the people held their breaths, the more delicate in the crowd turning their heads away. Ahinoam nestle the heads of their daughters into her side, shielding them from seeing their father take his revenge.

Saul instead swiped the palm of his hand over the sharp blade, drawing his own blood with a swift cut, and then he hurled the sword at Jeush where the blade stuck in the ground at his feet. He lifted his hand to Jeush and pointed to the blood flowing down his palm and wrist.

"If it is blood you want, bear witness to this." Saul pointed to the red stream staining the cuff of his sleeve. "That is all the blood to be shed on this day, for this day no one shall be put to death. This day shall be remembered as the day the Almighty rescued Israel."

There was no thought given to his response, no pause to deliberate a choice of actions. Jeush fell onto his knees and scrambled to where Saul stood and began to lavish his kisses upon his feet. "May this day be remembered as the day of the king's mercy. May Israel remember the mercy of her king forever."

The reaction from the people was an eruption that rose in waves of volume from one throat, one mouth, one nation.

Saul looked at Samuel seated in his prophet's chair. Enclosed by students and family, the prophet appeared to shrink inside his great throne, leaving only his implacable, wrinkled visage. Saul would not gloat. He would not exult. This was not the time. His heart could not afford to feast on such a bitter indulgence. He suspected Samuel would always gauge him by a standard no man could endure. He distrusted the prophet would ever be a full ally or devoted mentor, but he also knew he must never purposely make him his enemy, and to take pride in this moment could secure the prophet as a permanent adversary.

The waves of adulation continued until Ahinoam stepped over to Saul, took a laced cloth from the sleeve of her chiton, and wrapped it around Saul's self-inflicted wound. As she led him back to their thrones, Jeush helped the four tribal leaders to their feet. They each picked up their gift, and one by one made their offering to the king.

"Carmi, son of the tribe of Judah: May the enemies of my lord the king be scattered to the four winds." Carmi held a scepter carved with the names of the twelve tribes with the head of a wolf on top. He laid it at Saul's feet.

"Hammuel, son of the tribe of Simeon: May this breastplate protect the heart of the king," Hammuel said, presenting Saul with a breastplate of bronze with crossed swords embossed in its center.

"Allon, son of the tribe of Dan: May the king be clothed in splendor all the days of his life," Allon said, holding a beautiful linen robe of purple and scarlet.

Beerah drew near the king, a lambent joy playing over the surface of his face.

"Beerah, son of the tribe of Reuben: May the mercy of the king be rendered to him a hundredfold. May the strength of his horn give the nation of Israel her kings for generations to come. May this crown of glory be borne proudly on the head of our king reflecting a sound mind and shining heart. May our brother Saul, son of Kish, of the clan of Matri, the wolf of the tribe of Benjamin, the first king of Israel, live forever."

"Hear, O Israel, the Lord our God, the Lord is One!" shouted Ahiah.

Beerah held the silver crown of metal cords with a front plate of gold bearing the embossed face of a wolf aloft for everyone to see before placing it upon Saul's head, and then he knelt once again at the feet of his sovereign.

Samuel watched Saul rise from his throne, the sun glinting off the silver crown atop his head, the rough-cut emerald a radiant green heat. Saul beckoned Beerah to rise and was immediately enfolded into his arms. That was all the incentive Samuel needed. He catapulted out of the chair, energized by the rapturous ovations of the people, but instead of crossing to the king, Samuel headed to the center of the great circle and stood beside the altar now smoldering with disintegrated ash of beast and kindling.

Samuel raised his arms for silence, but it did not come. The sounds of fervor kept rising from the tribal chieftains, the priests and Levites, the warriors gathered beneath their tribal banners, anyone with voice to shout and hands to applaud. The only station not swept into the ecstatic moment was the section for the prophet and his faction. Shira, his sons, and his students were mute and fixed. Samuel's arms slowly descended to his side. This was the clearest sign yet that all of Israel had given their collective heart to the king.

Samuel waited. He waited for the exuberance of the crowd to pass; waiting was not something he was used to. He pointed to Nathan to bring his footstool, so the young prophet scooped up the footstool and ran out into the circle, setting it down in front of his master. Samuel braced his hand upon Nathan's shoulder to steady himself as he stepped upon the stool. Then Nathan rejoined his fellow student prophets.

The elevation helped. When he raised his arms again, Samuel was more visible, and the turbulent sound of human praise dissipated into the bright sky. Samuel made a full turn on the footstool, scanning the vast crowd fanned out in every direction, securing their complete attention as if casting a silent spell.

"I have listened to everything you said to me and have set a king over you. In the future it is the king who will lead you." Samuel's voice was grating and reedy. He coughed before continuing.

"As for me, I am old and gray, and my…my…sons are here with you." Samuel raised an arm toward his sons. He could not hide his age or the fact that his physical vigor had diminished. That was obvious for all to see. But his sons. What of them?

He looked at their faces and wondered at that moment why he had even summoned them to Gilgal. Their mere presence was a blatant reminder to all of Israel of their miscreant reputation as judges. Why would he mention the sons as if he were offering them to the people as men who should follow in his footsteps? Perhaps he held an unspoken hope that if he publicly identified them as his sons, their hearts might be quickened to turn from their wickedness.

In part, it was his sons' dishonest nature that forced Samuel's hand to listen to Israel's cry for a king and then to Yahweh's response for him to move forward and appoint one. Were he honest with himself, the offer of his sons was lukewarm at best. He looked at Joel and Ahijah standing beside their father's empty chair, a chair he knew in his heart of hearts that neither man had the character to fill. He watched their faces sinking in humiliation by the extended silence from the crowd after his offer of them as his successors. He saw Shira scoot forward in her seat, her held breath and the look of painful concern for his well-being marking her features, forced him to not burden his family with any more humiliation.

"I have been your leader from my youth until this day. Here I stand." It was time to redirect the attention of the crowd away from his sons and on to his public farewell, but this did not seem to bring his wife an expression of relief. Shira remained on the edge of her seat.

"Testify against me before Yahweh and before His anointed!" he cried, directing his attention toward Saul, forcing him to separate from the tribal leaders and move toward him. "Have I taken anyone's ox? Have I taken anyone's donkey? Have I cheated anyone? Have I oppressed anyone? Have I taken a bribe and shut my eyes to justice? Accuse me now if I have done any of these things and I will make it right."

Saul was dumbfounded. He rose out of his chair, wondering why this litany of questions? Why this assertion of his character and integrity? No one would ever dream of accusing him of any of these crimes. He wanted to rush out to him and stop his mouth, cover his lips with his hand, guide him gently away from this center stage.

Saul took it upon himself to answer the prophet; everyone else was muted by fear.

"You have not cheated or oppressed us," Saul said, his voice a bold rejection to what he perceived as the prophet's ominous intimidation. "You have not taken anything from anyone's hand."

"There, Yahweh is witness against you!" Samuel cried, waving his arm over the crowd, his hand finally settling in Saul's direction. "Yahweh is witness against you, and also His anointed is witness today that you have found nothing in my hands."

Saul sucked into his lungs a frantic breath. The fingers of the prophet pointed at him. He could see where Samuel was leading this dialogue. Someone had to give witness that Samuel had given the people no cause to be weary of centuries of divine leadership provided by prophet and judge. That a demand to change the order of things was a fault they, the chosen, alone had to bear.

"Yahweh is witness!" Saul shouted, accepting liability for Samuel's need for a witness. But there came an echo of response from the high priest, the guardian of the Ark, the tribal leaders, his sons, his daughters, his wife, from the whole body of the people, who all cried, "Yahweh is witness!"

It was a shout of unity, a verbal commitment to break from the past; the acknowledgment that Israel would stand with her king and back his honor and character as he led them into the future.

"Since the days of Moses and Aaron the people of Israel have sinned and forsaken Yahweh to follow other gods," Samuel stated this reminder to the crowd of the history of their unfaithfulness. "Once again, Israel has proven faithless by demanding a king. But Yahweh has granted your wish. If you revere and serve Yahweh, obey His voice and do not rebel against His order, and if you and your king follow Yahweh your God, then all will be well. If you do not, then the hand of Yahweh will be against you and your king."

It was the hand of his wife that Saul felt. Ahinoam moved in beside her husband and clasped her hands around Saul's wounded one.

"What is the old buzzard doing?" she whispered, but Saul gently shushed her. He patted her arm, hoping to distract Ahinoam from the trembling beginning to take hold within him as if a chill were coming upon him. But he knew she would not be so easily fooled, and he stepped forward, breaking free of her clasp.

"Now, watch and see." Samuel lifted his arms to heaven. "Yahweh will do a great thing. It is the harvest time, the dry season. I call upon Yahweh to send thunder and rain this day to show you what an evil thing you have done by asking for a king."

Saul never took his eyes off the prophet. He had hoped he was winning him over, but his chances appeared bleak. By accepting this role as king, did that then make Saul evil? Was he fated to continually look over his shoulder for the dreadful punishments sure to fall on him if he disobeyed Yahweh? The weight of his crown suddenly felt beyond his ability to support.

Saul raised his head as did everyone else around him and looked up into the clear, blue sky. There was no threatening weather looming in any direction. The prophet had overstepped his bounds. Surely, he had lost his mind.

Shira could no longer remain in her seat. She resisted the urge to rush to her husband's side and yank him off his footstool. That would declare to all her husband's instability. Instead, she walked slowly into the open circle. They had had very little conversation in the preceding days, which she had dismissed as preoccupation, a silence she was accustomed to when Samuel might be listening for the inner voice of Yahweh.

He had hardly spoken from the time they had arrived in Gilgal the day before the king liberated Jabesh Gilead. And when word came of Saul's victory, Samuel became mute, barely offering a nod of the head or a faint smile when she or another addressed him. He went outside the camp and wandered in the desert.

Shira assumed her husband was in conversation with Yahweh, but he had not told her of any communication between them. Shira prayed this calling down of thunder and rain was not a sign of a fractured mind. At the very least, it did seem like a sudden attack of a bad conscience on the part of her husband. Was he imagining the hostility of the people? Why must he have this unwarranted amount of validation from Yahweh? Did he not know how to gracefully make his exit? She wanted only to spirit him away, back to the quiet shadows of their hearth.

She stepped closer to him and saw in her husband's face the fragile visage of his mortality, and in her heart, recognized her own. When she reached out to take his hand, she heard the crack of thunder above her. A gust of wind caused her to lose her balance. She felt the hands of the prophet—her prophet—grasp her arms and hold her steady. And when the sudden appearance of the clouds released its deluge upon the plain of Gilgal, those who did not scatter fell on their faces.

Shira did not know whether to laugh or cry. She did not know whether to flee or remain. She would have fallen to the ground along with hundreds of others were it not for the strength of her husband's grip upon her arms, strength she could not remember feeling from him in a long time.

Both were drenched, their clothes soaked through, their hair plastered to their faces. Shira took Samuel's hands. How had this happened? There had been the display of Yahweh's power at Mizpah when the Philistines were preparing to attack and the thunder of Yahweh had caused them to panic, but that was not at the request of her husband. She had never known Samuel to ask Yahweh for a miraculous sign of power. Conversations with the Almighty were one thing. Prophetic insight into someone's soul or second sight into future events, she had accepted from the beginning. She had long since become accustomed to such phenomena as the infrequent and unexpected visitations from his God. But altering the weather patterns was something new, something she never anticipated or thought possible.

Shira turned to see the king and queen standing beside them soaked to the bone like she and the prophet. Around them huddled the tribal leaders and high priest and guardian of the Ark. She saw the fear in their eyes, the panic in their cowed postures, and heard the anguish in their voices as they implored her husband for protection, for intercession with Yahweh, for mercy for themselves and for their king.

Samuel's face was directed to the sky, allowing the rain to pelt his skin until it burned. He was oblivious to the people jumbled around him. Not until he felt his wife's hands cup his face, did he look down at her. He was surprised by what he saw. He had forgotten where he was and whom he had been addressing. He was too enraptured by the response of Yahweh to his summons.

"Do not be afraid for the evil you have done," he said. Any accusatory blast now absent in his voice, and the glint of judgment in his eye, was washed away by the rain and replaced with a vein of pity and kindness. He looked back into the sky to see the torrent of rain beginning to subside. "Do not turn away from Yahweh. Serve Yahweh with all your heart. Do not run after idols. They are useless things. They cannot rescue you."

Samuel lowered his gaze and looked into his wife's face. He cupped his hands against her cheeks, bent over, and kissed her forehead. Then he stepped off his footstool and looked at the king and queen and his royal court.

"For the sake of His great name, Yahweh will not reject His people, for it pleased the Almighty to make you His own." Samuel's gentle tone was an implication of a softening heart. "It would be a sin against Yahweh should I fail to pray for you. I will teach you the way that is good and right."

"That is all I have ever wanted, my lord." Saul dropped to one knee, removed his crown, and bowed his head. His wife and royal court followed his example.

Samuel extended his hand above Saul's kneeling form, but something prevented him from placing it upon the head of the king, of extending the mantle of power and promise by corporal touch. It was difficult enough for him to even contemplate such a transfer of authority or speak it. Dare he pass it from flesh to flesh?

"Be sure to revere the Almighty," Samuel continued, his indecisive hand floating inches above Saul's head; a spontaneous touch would offer hope. "Serve Yahweh faithfully with all your heart, for you have seen the great wonder Yahweh has done among you. Do not persist in doing evil or the nation and her king will be swept away."

Samuel had anointed Saul's head with the oil from the ram's horn as instructed by Yahweh as a sign of the favor of the Almighty. Samuel had kissed the cheeks of the king as a sign of affection and fealty, a kiss to equip Saul with strength. It might not have been a complete act of his will, but Samuel yielded to the power that was pulling his hand down to rest upon the king's drenched head to grace the royal head with an affirming touch. He bent over and kissed the top of Saul's head, then positioned his mouth just above the king's ear.

"I will never cease to pray for you. I will teach you the way that is good and right. Serve Yahweh faithfully with all your heart and remember the great things He has done for you." Then he withdrew his hand and allowed Shira to lead him out of the circle.

Samuel and Shira left the imprints of their soggy footsteps on the wet earth as they made their departure. Samuel glanced back over his shoulder and saw that the king and the others still remained on their knees. He then looked at the stone altar. The fire had been extinguished by the rain. The sacrificial remains of flesh and bone and wood now flowed down the rocky crevices in gray streams forming muddy ponds around its base.

Ahinoam looked inside the lavish transport with its rooftop and windows, floor covered in exotic rugs, cushioned benches, a fur covered mattress, and storage cases of food and wine. Beerah insisted the king and queen take his personal wagon back home to Gibeah. Saul was not easily persuaded to accept the offer from this reformed subject until Ahinoam secretly pinched her husband's backside, and he ceased his protests. By midday, the caravan of wagons and the king's escort of soldiers and servants pulled out of Gilgal, heading south for Gibeah.

Ahinoam stretched out on the mattress and watched her husband move from one cushioned bench to another, trying to get comfortable. As well-appointed as it was, the configuration of the wagon was not designed for a man his size.

"I struggle with this type of trappings that come with being king," Saul said. "It will take time to get used to something like this, maybe never."

Ahinoam rubbed her hand over the soft fur on the mattress. "I may adjust quickly," she sighed, then beckoned to her husband. "Now come and lie next to me."

"I want to see the landscape." Saul pulled back one of the curtains covering a window. "I feel trapped."

Ahinoam took the curtain out of her husband's fingers and tied it onto a corner rod. She did the same with the other curtain on the other side, then extended her arms in both directions. "Now you can see the plains to the west and the mountains to the east."

When her husband stuck his head out the window next to her, she stretched up beside him. They both looked at a military transport wagon ahead of them. Soldiers bounced up and down on the hard benches installed in the interior of the wagon. Then she pulled him back inside and pointed to the luxuries they could enjoy on the way home.

"Perhaps this is not so bad, compared to them." Saul pointed to the military wagon in front of them. He seemed less skeptical and more appreciative, so he climbed onto the mattress next to Ahinoam.

"It did not feel like a complete endorsement of my being king, but it was something." Saul draped his arm over Ahinoam's shoulder. "But after the miracle of rain and thunder, and it being the beginning of the dry season, after something like that, it would be difficult to hand over the reins of power and make a quiet exit."

"I have something I need to tell you," she said, resting her head upon his chest.

"He said he would pray for me. You heard him say that."

"I did. It is a good step toward reconciliation, but you too should make the effort to receive the prophet's instruction."

"He said it would be a sin if he did not pray for me. That's no small thing."

"No, but I think—"

"He said he would teach me the way that is good and right. You heard that too."

"He did say that, and I hope there will be no repercussions if—"

"If I can turn an enemy like Beerah into a loyal friend, then I have a chance; there is a chance we can make this work—the prophet and king. Why should it not work?"

"It should. You are correct, my love." Ahinoam sat up and took Saul's wounded hand and placed it upon her stomach. "I have delayed in telling you, but soon I will no longer be able to hide the truth."

"What are you talking about?" Saul at last became aware that Ahinoam had been trying to get him to pay attention to her.

"You cannot see it yet, or feel it," she whispered, a smile forming on her lips. "But there is life inside me…a second life."

Saul removed his crown, placing it on the spot where his hand had been. He leaned over and kissed her belly protruding slightly through the silver circle. Ahinoam had succeeded in fully engaging his mind in this present moment.

"Be safe, my child. Grow strong in the coming months. Come to us whole and prepare yourself for a royal welcome."

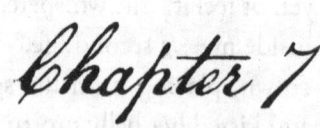

Chapter 7

SABA STOOD ON THE ROOF OF HIS SHOP, STUDYING EVERY lightning bolt that burst out of the dark clouds. The rain assailed his bare body. He had stripped to his undergarments the moment he heard the rumble of thunder and dashed up the interior ladder, through the trapdoor, and onto his rooftop. The image of a lightning bolt was the last thing he needed to carve before turning in his latest commission.

Saba had received the contract to carve a sacred pillar. It was to be used as a territorial marker bordering central Canaan and Israel and erected at some Philistine military garrison along the foothills of the central mountain range. Carving images of a god on a column whose final destination was a roadside border crossing was not what Saba considered a noble commission.

Over the last years his designs for sculptures for the Hall of Lords or the Temples of Mot and Astarte had all been rejected. Those contracts went to other artists more favored by the Philistine elite and politically powerful. He had once been in demand, winning many of the top commissions. His work was recognized all over the city of Aphek. Now he could not even get the job of sculpting the bust of a minor politician or carving a few decorative pieces for a meeting hall in some minor state building. Such was the life of an artist.

His efforts at spying for his country had also met with failure. When Saba had been returning from a circuit of craft fairs in the villages near Mizpah, he had noticed an unusual number of Israel's tribal leaders and their military cohorts all traveling toward Mizpah. He was able to discover where they were gathering on the plains of Mizpah for some type of religious revival, and he reported his findings to Lord Namal. Saba was promised a large commission by Lord Namal for this intelligence as soon as the Fifth Lord returned from his quick and easy victory against their enemies.

But the Philistine attack turned into a rout and the slaughter of many Philistine soldiers. Lord Namal was in no mood to grant any commissions to Saba after such a resounding defeat. Such was the life of a spy. Had Lord Namal been victorious, Saba might have had more work than he could have handled, but it seemed that Saba was bearing the blame, as if his intelligence report had been flawed. Saba thought time enough had passed for him to have been forgiven, but still there were no commissions.

Saba not only could not procure a state commission, but he had also fallen out of fashion with the city art commissioners and wealthy patrons. For an artist of his skill and talent, it was difficult to understand the dearth of creative projects. Lord Namal must have poisoned the well for Saba after his humiliating defeat. There was no other explanation.

In the end, Saba accepted this as Fate, plain and simple, contemptible Fate—indiscriminate in its distribution of rewards and punishments. It was the only way he could come to terms with what he could not control, and it gave him the peace he needed to just keep occupied regardless of the work or status a job might provide. What was the point in complaining? Just keep chiseling.

He was proud of all his creations, but the most important commission he ever received had long since been forgotten. His design for the golden rat and tumor offered by the Five Lords of the Seren at the return of the Ark of the Covenant were more than just objects of beauty. Those pieces held some magical power directly influencing the Hebrew god. He could not point to any work of his hands that had such a profound outcome on god or man.

Saba believed his work of art appeased a god's wrath and helped rescue his people from certain extinction. The commissions he received once the plague lifted from the country was more than he could accept. But that was long ago, and who remembered? He often wondered what had become of that chest of five rats and tumors once the Ark had safely crossed the border into Israel.

When another streak of lightning flashed across the dark clouds, he thought that if he could carve the perfect lightning bolt in the hand of Baal, the god of rain and thunder and fertility would be impressed enough to extend his favor and raise Saba out of this long famine of employment.

The rain came down so hard now it was difficult for him to continue. He was drenched to the bone and shivering. He opened the trapdoor in the roof and descended the ladder into his shop below. To warm his body, he paced around the four-sided column of limestone, which was three times the height of a man, and now stretched out on wooden braces set every few feet to support the great weight of the pillar.

Each time he had finished carving one side, he had to hire a handful of beggars to help him turn the pillar onto a blank side before chiseling the next image. The four sides were bas-relief images of Baal: Baal standing between two lions, his hands gripping their throats; Baal accepting the sacrifice of a bull; Baal studying sacred tablets; Baal holding a whip in one hand, and in the other hand, a soon-to-be chiseled bolt of lightning.

Sweat and rainwater dripped off his body as Saba took his laps around the column, his sandals squishing liquid footprints in the limestone dust on the shop floor. All the images of Baal were life-size. This may be only a marker for a border crossing stuck in the farthest wastelands of Philistia, but Saba had made it an object of beauty. He was an artist. He would never compromise one of his creations no matter how small or demeaning the job or how underappreciated. When he felt he could move his fingers well enough to hold a chisel and mallet, he set oil lamps on the column where he needed to carve and delicately began to chisel a lightning bolt worthy for a god to hurl against his enemies.

Saba wanted to make the best possible impression. The day he finished the work, chiseling an inscription across the capital of the monument and his signature beneath the foot of the Baal that held the lightning bolt, he sent word to the art commissioners that the pillar was ready for transport. A message was sent that priests from the Temple of Baal, commissioners from the arts council, military officers, possibly Lord Namal himself would arrive in two days to accept the column and give the balance of payment.

On the morning of the second day, he hired beggars to help him lift the column from the wooden braces and set it in front of the shop. The citizens of Aphek marveled as they gazed upon the column and its intricate carved images, praising the work and its artist. Many in the crowd pointed out the unique quality of Baal's lightning bolt with its speared beam aimed toward the earth and its fiery, feathered tail. The impromptu exhibition would be the most public exposure his handiwork would enjoy. For who would see it in the hinterland; who would appreciate and admire it; and who would seek out the artist to extol him for this creation? He would enjoy this acclamation for as long as he could.

The veneration by the public was short-lived, and Saba's elation turned to shock and disillusionment the moment the wagon with a single commissioner from the council stopped in front of his shop, followed by a decrepit transport wagon pulled by a team of mules. Where were the priests from the Temple of Baal, the dignitaries of the city, the military commanders, and Lord Namal? Just one commissioner and a female companion, both puffy-faced, red-eyed, clothes disheveled as if they had slept in their garments and abruptly roused. When Saba inquired after the others, the commissioner sighed and groaned and pinched his forehead with his fingers as if to staunch a thriving headache.

"What did you expect?" he quipped. "Do you think the Fifth Lord and his entourage would turn out just for a marker at a border crossing?" He did not even bother to get out of his wagon or take in a full-scale view of the work, but dropped the pouch of coins into Saba's hand, and then barked for the driver to get them out of this part of the city as fast as possible.

Saba watched in disbelief as the wagon sped away. The crack of the whip snapped him back into reality, and Saba stepped aside to allow the wagon to ease in front of the shop. Two low-ranking soldiers sat in the driver's seat. One soldier held up an official-looking document which authorized him to collect, transport, and erect the border marker to the garrison outpost at Geba.

While Saba read the document, the other soldier commanded the same beggars loitering in front of the shop hoping for more employment to load the column into the wagon. But a Philistine soldier, no matter how lowly his rank, does not pay for services rendered, he gives an order and backs up the order with a whip, and so the beggars were forced into service.

The wagon itself did not appear stable enough to carry the size of its load for that long distance to its final destination. Something was sure to break. No one thought to bring any padding or cushions to cover and protect the engravings on the column or rope to tie it off and keep it from rolling side to side in the wagon bed. And the bed itself was not long enough. A third of the pillar would protrude out of the back for the entire journey.

"This is unacceptable!" Saba stepped back and held out his arms stopping the beggars from approaching his monument. His body was vibrating with rage.

It did not take long into the argument with the soldiers for Saba to realize he was dealing with the personnel least equipped physically and intellectually for the demands of this job. His decision was easy and immediate. Saba kept the official document. He would see that the orders were carried out and not depend upon these two soldiers. He would spend his own coin, coin he could ill afford, to see a safe delivery of his work of art.

He used his cushions to pad the wagon bed and every foot of rope he could find in the shop to tie the column down once it had been carefully loaded onto the wagon. Then he informed the two soldiers that he would accompany them on this journey to ensure the monument's safe arrival and oversee its placement into the ground. This was no job for such incompetence. His announcement was met with smirked indifference.

Saba had nothing else to do, no new commissions, nor patrons clamoring for his work. As far as he knew this was his last job, so he was determined to see it through to the bitter end. He packed extra clothing and filled his leather case with tools.

After closing up his shop, he went to the marketplace and bought food, then to the public stables to rent a horse. Before meeting up with the wagon, he stopped at the public well and filled three skins of water. He bounced the coin purse in his hand, the one given him by the commissioner that morning, and could not help but notice its diminished weight.

By the time the sun had reached its highest point in the sky, Saba had caught up with the wagon lumbering its way along the southeastern road toward Geba. At least the mule team looked stout enough to make the trip, lugging his creation over miles of desert, but he had his doubts about the wagon. He prayed to the god of his pillar that there would be no mishap in this journey. Baal should be attentive and merciful. After all, each side of Saba's monument was devoted to him.

Two pigs were roasting on a fire when Saba and company arrived the afternoon of the second day. What should have taken less than a day took two. One wagon wheel had cracked; Saba insisted they travel slower after repairing it, especially when they had to leave the main highway and take lesser-traveled roads to the Philistine garrison. Saba was surprised when they passed signs pointing toward Mizpah and Ramah. They were well inside occupied territory. He had not realized the extent to which the domination of the Five Lords of the Philistines had forced Israel to accept their sovereignty.

The outpost was situated at the edge of a cliff in the foothills of Canaan's central mountain range. Just beyond the garrison the road began a sharp descent, cutting a steep pass through the hills. Saba sat up in his saddle, shielded his eyes from the sun, and saw that the road leveled out at the base of the cliff and led to a small village on the next hill below. What an insulting location for his monument, more like a burial ground.

"Hebrews!" shouted the sergeant who poked the roasting swine with his sword. "You are looking at the great city of Geba full of dreadful Hebrews."

Saba could see that Geba was nothing more than an outpost of rustic huts with a handful of people scurrying about the perimeter, nothing imposing or dreadful.

"We are the only thing keeping the Hebrew hordes from invading us," the sergeant said, then guffawed at his own joke before guzzling some wine.

Saba dismounted and led his horse over to the fire. The soldiers driving the wagon pulled off the road, then hopped down and stretched their legs.

The sergeant was clothed in a helmet, the leather straps dangling loosely on each side, and a tattered and soiled gray robe latched around his neck with the linked chain and insignia of his military rank. No breastplate, no buckler, no cloth skirt or protective covering over his loins, no shin guards, no sandals. Saba was embarrassed at the sight of the sergeant's slovenly appearance and loss of dignity.

"You should feel safe knowing we are the guardians of Philistia," the sergeant said, waving his sword over the landscape. Only he found this amusing. "The last line of defense between you and the Hebrews."

He lost his balance when he tried to step back, his feet tangled inside the hem of his robe which caused him to tumble to the ground. His fall did not put a stop to his laughter, quite the opposite. The sergeant's antics inspired the other soldiers under his command who milled about the grounds to echo the hilarity of their intoxicated leader.

Saba found no humor in what he saw. The ramshackle barracks were for a small company of soldiers. Makeshift, exposed stables provided inadequate shelter for their horses. A few cramped shacks had been poorly constructed and used as privies for the wives who came to visit or the women hired from the nearest city to provide a few days of distraction. Trash, clothing, and equipment were scattered along the grounds. The pungent smell of human and animal waste—and decaying carcasses mixed with the aroma of sizzling pork—hung in the air like an invisible, poisonous cloud.

Even the two soldiers who had traveled with Saba appeared chagrined by the squalid conditions of the garrison and the frowzy appearance of their comrades.

This was what became of a place when abandoned and forgotten. This was where his monument was to stand for all time.

"Who might you be?" asked the sergeant, gaining control of his laughter as he rolled over on his side and faced Saba. He did not bother to cover himself with his robe.

"Saba, artisan and creator of this monument." Saba pointed to his handiwork hanging off the back of the wagon with a measure of pride. "We have delivered it and intend to see it properly mounted as the new sign for our borders."

"Well, Saba, artisan and creator of whatever you wish to call that object," the sergeant said with a sardonic tone as he rose to his feet. "Your monument will mark the entrance into the bowels of the earth."

Saba turned his back on the cackling sergeant and his company of men and faced to the west. The sun was on the downward slope in the sky. Saba turned back to the sergeant and removed the official papers of the military commission from his pouch, which detailed the purpose for this trip, and held them out to the sergeant, whom he dismissed with a listless wave of his hand. Saba chose to read a sentence from the document to the sergeant. "From your superior officers: once this monument to our god Baal is placed in your care, you are instructed to find a proper location on the border for its placement."

Again, he offered the document to the sergeant and again it was refused.

"Put it up wherever you like along the road." The sergeant pointed to the road where it began its steep descent into the land of Israel.

Saba looked in the direction the sergeant was pointing. He knew he would need assistance digging a hole to place the monument inside. Since the sergeant was disinterested in reading the document, Saba thought he would pretend that such instructions were included. He pointed to the document as though such a directive had been written. "A hole needs to be dug deep enough to install and secure the monument in the ground."

The sergeant appeared to think about that last instruction before he answered. "It matters not to me what the instructions are or who signed this document. Digging a hole for the base of a pillar of limestone—orders or not, sacred stone or not, carved with the engravings of Baal or not—is menial labor unsuited for a soldier. They should have sent slaves to do the job."

If the military leaders in Aphek knew the quality of soldiers stationed in this spot assigned to protect Philistia's border were this undisciplined and indifferent to orders, Saba knew heads would roll, beginning with the sergeant. He turned to both military drivers, handed them a coin each from his shrinking coin purse, and told them to start digging.

Once satisfied with the depth and width of the hole, Saba had the driver round up a few soldiers to lift the monument off the wagon and place it into the hole. Dirt and rock were packed around the base, then water was drawn from the trough and poured on top to settle the contents before a second layer of rock and dirt were shoveled on top of the base.

He stepped back to eyeball the monument to be sure it was level. Once satisfied, he nodded his approval to the soldiers. They began to pile the heavy rocks around the base, securing it in place. Though this monument was a far cry from the prestigious halls and galleries of Aphek, for Saba, it represented a pride in his people and in his work.

When this outpost had decayed and crumbled into the earth and all of them here today had turned to dust and been forgotten, this monument would still be standing. Saba did not need a priest's blessing or the accolades of the commissioners. They would all vanish, but his creation would withstand the weathering of the centuries and tell future generations of his existence on this earth.

Saba stepped back and offered his own prayer, "Lo, thine enemies, O Baal. Lo, thine enemies wilt thou smite. Lo, thou wilt vanquish thy foes with lightning from thy hands. And the peoples of the world will tremble and sing of thy great power."

He had just finished his prayer when the sergeant stumbled across the road clutching his wineskin to his chest and looked up at the monument.

"Impressive. What god is that?"

"Baal." Saba was amazed he had to identify the main god of the Philistines.

"Oh." The sergeant nodded indifferently. "What did you write at the top?" he asked, pointing to the words chiseled across the capital.

Saba shook his head in disbelief. Not only did the sergeant not know the all-powerful god of his nation, but he was also illiterate as well. No wonder this outpost was his assignment. "It says, 'May Baal make thee one-eyed from now unto eternity.'"

The sergeant erupted with laughter, uncorked his wineskin, and poured a libation from it onto the ground as an offering. This was all the religious accolade the monument would receive at its dedication.

Before departing, Saba filled his water containers from the trough. He then cut some strips of pork off the remains of the swine carcasses that were cooling beside the fire pit and packed them inside his food pouch. Against the admonitions of the sergeant and the two soldiers who had driven his monument to its final destination not to travel at night and expose himself to the dangers of the highway, Saba mounted his horse and departed the garrison.

He did not care about the risks. He did not care if he died along the way. His obligation was fulfilled, and he just wanted to be alone, have his soul enveloped by the darkness of night. If he made it home, he would keep the doors and windows of his shop closed and drink himself into oblivion. He would not regret it were he never to awaken.

PART TWO

PART TWO

Chapter 8

MIKAL HAD KEPT A WATCHFUL EYE ON HER MOTHER ALL MORN-
ing as she went quietly about her chores. When Mikal heard a low hissing, she looked up to see her sister gesturing with folded hands against the side of her face that their mother was asleep. Then Merab pointed toward the upstairs ladder.

Mikal quietly set the wooden bowl she was cleaning on the table, and Merab placed the blanket at the foot of her parents' mattress where their mother lay fast asleep. Mikal tiptoed over to the ladder. She gave one last look at her mother before she began to climb. Merab followed right behind her.

Once on the second floor, Mikal leaned over the edge to listen for any signs their ascent might have awakened their mother, but all was quiet, so they climbed the second ladder leading from the boys' room to the roof. When Mikal reached the top, she lifted the removable plank in the ceiling and climbed out onto the roof. Once they both were on the rooftop, Merab was about to put the panel back in place, but Mikal stopped her.

"We need to leave the trapdoor open in case mother wakes and calls for us," Mikal said.

Mikal led the way as she crawled on her hands and knees over to the four-foot ledge around the circumference of the house facing the back of the compound and the new and ongoing construction below. Where the stables had once stood, construction on the new officer housing and a military headquarters was underway. The sweeping changes to the family estate and the rapid pace of the family's altered lifestyle had caused an overnight maturity in Mikal, and to a lesser degree, in her older sister.

Mikal quickly embraced her rise in status from simple farm girl to a young woman of royalty. Her sister had been hesitant in the new role of princess, but Mikal led by example. She determined to push Merab in this royal direction, and it included watching the military training of the young men who had come from all over Israel to be a part of their father's army, even if they had to sneak off to do it.

When Merab had shared her pleasure at watching the young men, Mikal was pleased. But when Merab secretly told Mikal that she had her eye on one young soldier in particular, Mikal knew her sister would never go back to being just a farm girl. The transition to princess was happening and there was no going back.

The roof of the house was the perfect location for Mikal and Merab to spy on the brawny recruits during their daily martial exercises. The wheat field and olive grove behind the house had been transformed: the olive grove had been cut down and made into an encampment for the army; and the wheat field had been plowed under and turned into a military training ground.

Abner had chosen to recruit sons of the tribal leaders to make the first officer corps of Israel's standing army, consisting of three thousand elite soldiers. After the victory at Jabesh Gilead, Abner had dismissed the majority of the troops, but these three thousand remained in Gibeah. For Mikal, it was as though she had three thousand potential candidates to choose from who might be her future prince. She saw herself worth of such bounty.

Merab and Mikal used the height of the protective ledge around the perimeter of the roof to make their spying less conspicuous. The raised ledge was over three cubits, and all these new additions had turned their home into a citadel. Mikal had enjoyed these renovations and improvements to the outside of the home to meet the physical needs of the ever-expanding personnel coming from all over the country to serve the royal family. She felt herself deserving of such abundance. But her mother had insisted that nothing was to be done to the interior of her house until after the baby arrived. And Mikal, along with Merab, had become very protective of their mother.

No one was allowed inside the house but family and the midwives who made regular visits to monitor the queen's health. Taking on such responsibility had hastened Mikal's entrance into adulthood. Mikal and Merab had assumed domestic duties beyond household chores. Before now, Mikal had been too self-absorbed. She was much more conscientious in her attention to the needs of her mother, and even though she was the younger of the two girls, Mikal had become an example for Merab to follow. It was Mikal who had instigated these daily escapes to the roof to watch the soldiers practice their skills at combat, but Merab never refused, never tried to talk Mikal out of this escape to the roof. And when Mikal learned that her sister had her eye on the armor-bearer of their older brother, that was all Mikal needed to maintain this secret pleasure they both enjoyed.

Mikal leaned her back against the ledge. Merab crawled up beside her. They needed to catch their breath from climbing the ladders and crawling over the rooftop. Mikal curled her arm around her sister's neck; then she looked over toward the only outside entrance onto the roof from the outside stairway built into the side of the house.

Two guards stood at attention facing away from the roof. Her father and his aide had not yet arrived to observe the exercises. With the inside of the house off limits, only her father came to the roof to hold private counsel with Abner and his officers, entertain tribal ambassadors, or occasionally study sacred writings with priests and prophets. Her mother could no longer climb the outside stairs. It took too much of her strength, and she would not suffer the indignity of being carried by servants up and down the outside stairs.

Midmorning was the best time of day for Mikal and Merab to do their covert observation. Their mother was usually sound asleep at this time, and it was not too hot, and the risk was slight of getting caught. Mikal went first inching her way up the side of the wall until she was able to peer over the ledge using the potted plants for additional cover. The wide ledge was covered with potted plants that helped provide some extra privacy for the family. From this vantage point, there was a wide view of the training fields beyond the compound wall, and they were able to watch Abner and his captains and generals put hundreds of men through their paces.

Merab looked up at Mikal, and when she did not look back, Merab yanked the hem of Mikal's robe. Mikal waved that it was safe for Merab to join her, so she slowly raised herself up beside her sister. Merab lifted one of the potted plants off the ledge and placed it on the roof where she stood. She signaled Mikal to squeeze in beside her between the other plants. Merab pointed to their twin brothers, Malki and Ishvi, as they scampered out of the officers' quarters, wooden swords in their hands threatening mayhem to all phantom enemies. The young soldier she was looking for emerged a moment later with her older brother.

"There he is. There he is." Merab pointed in the direction of the officers' quarters. She kept her voice low, but her excitement was barely under control.

"It is only just Jonathan." Mikal waved in mock dismissal of their brother.

Jonathan and his armor bearer emerged from the walled compound and together walked briskly into the field where Abner stood observing his military instructors putting a company of soldiers through their martial drills.

"He is beautiful." Merab sighed. "He is beautiful, is he not?"

"Jonathan beautiful?" Mikal uttered. "Our stupid, big brother... beautiful?"

"Hush!" Merab slapped the arm of her younger sister.

Merab's slap was more playful than scolding, and both girls could not help themselves and started giggling. But when they saw Jonathan and the young man beside him look toward the rooftop, they panicked and ducked behind the safety of the ledge.

Merab first laid eyes on Adriel at the confirmation of her father's monarchy in Gilgal after his victory over the Ammonites. Adriel stood behind his father Barzillai, leader of the tribe of Manasseh and carried the banner when it was time for Barzillai to kneel before the king and pledge the loyalty of his tribe. When Merab heard her brother tell the story of how Adriel had saved his life in the battle to liberate Jabesh Gilead, her head became filled with fantasies of the young man.

Adriel fought by Jonathan's side when Saul's army surprised the Ammonite camp outside Jabesh Gilead. All he had for a weapon was a farm implement, a pitchfork used for piling hay, that Adriel brought from his home in Meholah situated along the western bank of the Jordan River. Because of the scarcity of sword and spear, there was only enough professional weaponry for Adriel's father and the elder clan chieftains. But in Adriel's hands a pitchfork proved quite lethal.

During the battle, an Ammonite warrior leapt from behind a burning wagon with his sword raised, charging Jonathan. The prince was so surprised, he stumbled as he turned to face the enemy. The Ammonite warrior was equally surprised to see the sharp tines of the pitchfork protruding through his chest where Adriel struck him from behind. Adriel kept the sword of his first slain enemy and had worn it strapped to his side ever since. And in the imagination of Merab, she carefully crafted stories of being rescued by the brave Adriel.

Adriel had a litheness that would turn any young woman's head. Flowing locks of auburn hair cascaded down his muscled shoulders, a soft-spoken voice that was never intrusive and never demanded attention except when Merab was present, which was not often. When she did hear him speak, every word had a heightened quality, every nuance of tone and inflection piqued.

She lived in jittery infatuation for days, repeating a hundred times in her head or whispering the words on her lips the simple phrase Adriel might use in greeting, "Good morning, my lady," or "Have you seen your brother today, my lady?"

He always referred to her as "my lady," an expression she never tired of hearing. A convulsive glee raced through her body each time he spoke. Any verbal response on her part was impossible in such moments; the gift of language had vanished. They had yet to have a conversation beyond a passing greeting. But when they did have an encounter, Merab felt her face brighten as if it were a cool glow of light reflecting off the water.

"Did you see his leg muscles in his warrior's skirt?" Merab fanned her flush cheeks with both hands. "I think I might die."

"Good. Die. Then I will become the only princess in the kingdom," Mikal replied.

Merab knew this was spoken only half in jest, and this time, her reaction was anything but playful. She surprised herself and her sister. Neither of them expected such a reaction. Merab balled up her fist and struck Mikal's upper arm hard enough that it just might leave a bruise. Merab's physical response established a clear "do not touch, he is mine" boundary; cross at one's own peril. Sister or not, Merab claimed ownership, her line had been drawn.

After clearly expressing her mind with the forceful blow to her sister's upper arm, Merab hoisted herself back above the ledge. From her side view, Merab saw Mikal rubbing her arm. She felt a slight twinge of guilt and reached out her hand to lift Mikal to her feet. Mikal accepted, and Merab pulled her to her feet. But Mikal moved a few steps out of range. Merab suspected that her younger sister was apprehensive in case she had not spent all her pent-up violence.

"I do not understand how you could limit yourself to just one." Mikal marveled at the sight of hundreds of men scattered over the landscape below them. "There are so many to choose from."

"Someday you might understand." Merab knew that her fanciful thoughts of a future domestic bliss with Adriel might be something out of reach for Mikal. "Then again, perhaps not."

Mikal did not appreciate her big sister's insinuation that she was incapable of understanding the mystery of single devotion to one person. Mikal heard Merab's emphatic remark as if it exposed a character flaw within her, a blemish on her soul, and she was surprised by the deep wounding she felt. It hurt so much she quite forgot the blow to her arm she had just suffered.

"Girls, what are you doing?" The gruff question came in the direction of the gate as it swung open onto the roof.

They both yelped in surprise and spun around to see their father and his personal assistant, Jarib, standing on the landing at the top of the outside staircase. Even though Mikal knew that her and her sister's presence on the rooftop might incur the wrath of their father, she was prepared to defend their right to be there.

Mikal watched as Jarib pushed open the gate for the king to enter the rooftop. She had been caught off guard by the blow to her arm and heart from her older sister and so had anticipated the arrival of her father and his aide.

Saul had taken Jarib into his service after the liberation of Jabesh Gilead. Her father needed help to coordinate his schedule, set appointments, and prepare records and documents. Of the three messengers who had lost their right eye to the cruelty of King Nahash, Jarib was the only one who accepted Saul's offer to leave Jabesh Gilead and come work for the king.

Mikal tried to be pleasant around her father's secretary, but it was his one good eye, the glare of which she could not escape, and the empty socket of the other eye, that evoked a constant revulsion within her. This man had become a second shadow of the king. Her father found it impossible to start or finish his day without consulting Jarib.

When first entering her father's service, Mikal could tell that Jarib felt self-conscious about the red, scarified indention in his face. And she was mildly relieved when her father had a brown leather eye patch made for him to wear. But she could never quite get over her memory of Jarib's bloody face when he and the other two from Jabesh Gilead came to their home begging for rescue. She wanted to have pity on Jarib, but when she was in his presence, she only saw the empty socket, and no eye patch—even one with a wolf face etched in the center—could erase that image.

"I thought I told you both that I did not want your mother left alone." Saul pointed a reproachful finger at each daughter as he moved toward them.

"She is asleep, and we needed to get some air and sunshine." Mikal spoke boldly.

"But on the rooftop?" Saul asked. "Why not the garden at the front door? Plenty of sunshine and fresh air in that location, and you can still keep an eye on your mother."

"I suggested that, but Mikal insisted on the roof," Merab blurted.

Her sister's fresh lie, deepening the level of her pain, struck against her heart.

"We will go down at once, Abba." Merab grabbed Mikal's arm and started pulling her toward the trapdoor in the roof.

Mikal yanked her arm from Merab's grip. She clamped her fingers upon the edge of the ledge and stood firm. She would defy her father's wishes and space herself from her sister. Perhaps the distraction of the exercises would give her heart and arm time to recover.

She watched Jarib gesture for her father to make his way to the ledge. "My lord, I think they are about to begin."

Her father took three quick strides across the rooftop to the ledge. Mikal knew that there was no need to go back down the ladder and remain inside the house. She knew her father had forgotten about them, forgot his frustration, forgot they were even present. She watched her father and Jarib remove the pots of plants obstructing his view and place them on the floor of the roof out of the way.

Mikal turned around and saw Merab standing at the trapdoor about to descend the ladder. Merab could go alone, but Mikal knew she would miss seeing Adriel and their brother perform their military game. That would be a cruelty Mikal might enjoy seeing Merab suffer. It would be fitting after what Merab had said to her. But she could not quite bring herself to such retribution. She looked back at her father who was stretched over the ledge unaware of the little rebellion about to take place behind his back.

Mikal put a finger to her lips for Merab to be quiet and waved for Merab to join her at the ledge. Despite the rivalry between them and their typical sibling squabbles, Merab was still her sister, and they were both princesses, the only princesses in Israel. Mikal would continue to lead the way by being magnanimous in bridging this small divide. It was what a princess would do.

Abner stood halfway up the hill and ordered all soldiers to stop their individual training exercise and direct their attention toward the firing range. Six life-sized straw men were strategically positioned across the top of a small hill attached to stakes driven into the ground. Archers and spearmen moved back and forth between the straw mannequins; their faces hardened with intent, one bouncing a spear in his hand, another testing the stretch of the line in his bow, no one conversing.

Abner had set the rules of this exercise and appointed Jeush arbiter of the contest. Abner ordered Jeush to stand at the top of the hill, holding two arrow shafts, one with a red banner attached to the end, the other with a yellow banner. If a straw man was hit, Jeush would pronounce the verdict: a kill or mortal wound got a red flag; a miss received a yellow flag. If a human was hit, the verdict would be obvious.

Abner looked down at Jonathan at the base of the hill. He smiled as Jonathan stretched his arms and legs, his expression as hard as the stones he would use in this game. Abner knew this would be a true test of teamwork between Jonathan and Adriel.

The course had been Abner's design. The landscape between Jonathan and Adriel and the animate and inanimate men situated at the top of the hill was entirely open, no protective cover of tree or bush or boulder, no little depression in the earth to dive into to avoid a deadly missile fired in their direction.

Abner had approved of this war game, though he did not know the duo's scheme as to how they would get to the top without injury. What Abner did know was that his cousin would have his head if Jonathan got hurt, or worse, but it was a risk Abner was willing to take. He uttered a quiet prayer for his kinsman's safety.

Abner looked toward Jeush and then checked that the soldiers were lined up along the perimeters of the firing range in position. Once everyone's position was established, Abner stepped into the middle of the range. All talking among the ranks ceased. All eyes focused on Abner as he addressed the troops.

"It is one thing to go up against a target that does not move. It is altogether different when your opponent is trying to kill you."

Abner looked in Jonathan's direction. He nodded once and Jonathan responded in kind, so Abner raised his sword and began to walk backward out of the field of harm.

Jonathan had a sling draped over each shoulder with the ends of the leather strings dangling over his chest. He shook his arms, loosening his muscles. Jonathan did not want the burden of carrying a satchel full of stones that would be too cumbersome for the mobility he needed to use the double firepower of two slings.

Adriel rose to his feet next to Jonathan. He took two stones out of his pouch and began to bounce them in his hands.

Jonathan looked to the top of the hill and saw each archer pull back his bowstring, notching an arrow in place. He ground his sandals into the earth to secure his footing.

"Meet you at the top," Jonathan said, and spat in his hand.

"Meet you at the top," Adriel replied, and spat in his hand.

They slapped their two hands together and then held very still—both pairs of eyes focused on the objective to reach the top of the hill.

When Abner plunged his sword into the earth, the line of men on either side of the range erupted into a cheering pandemonium.

Jonathan yanked the strings of his slings off his shoulders, as both he and Adriel broke into a run, each in a different direction just as the archers on the top of the hill released two arrows that flew between them. Had they remained in place, the war game would have ended before it began.

Without either one breaking their stride, his armor bearer lobbed the two stones in the air just over Jonathan's head. He caught the stones, one in each sling pouch, and then spun the slings while on the run, releasing the stones, left hand first, followed by the right. The first stone smashed into the head of the straw dummy on the far right of the enemy line. The straw exploded into the air.

"First kill!" Jeush screamed, vigorously waving his red flag, and the archer beside the shattered straw man dropped his bow in disgust and lay on his stomach.

The second stone, the one hurled from Jonathan's right hand, flew into the chest of the straw dummy on the far left of the line.

"Second kill!" shouted Jeush as the straw man disintegrated all over the ground, and the archer had to yield the same as the first. Within seconds, Jonathan had dispatched two enemy soldiers before anyone else could hurl a spear or launch an arrow.

The four remaining soldiers sprang into action and began firing down upon Jonathan and Adriel as they zigzagged their way up the hill.

With no cover to hide behind speed was everything, momentum was life. Jonathan and Adriel tumbled and raced their way up the hill, dodging spear and arrow aimed in their direction.

Mikal looked at her father, his body extended over the ledge, his knees pressed into the wall to keep him from tumbling to the ground.

"What are they doing?" Saul cried. "Are they trying to kill my son? Has Abner lost his mind?"

The surface of her father's face was fraught with horror and incomprehension at Abner's audacity to put her brother's life in such peril. Mikal turned to Merab on her other side, and saw her breathing heavily, rocking back and forth. As Merab bounced on her feet, she gasped out Adriel's name and nearly swooned every time he dodged a spear or arrow.

Her father and sister were engulfed in the life and death contest. She was surprised by her own impartiality as she watched; she could observe the players and the spectators with minimal emotional investment in spite of the mortal hazard to her brother and his armor bearer. She found it more intriguing to watch the reactions of her father and sister, even the soldiers cheering from the sidelines, than to watch the game itself.

When Jonathan heard Adriel blow a sharp whistle through his teeth, he pivoted back in his direction to catch the stones he had lobbed into the air. As soon as Adriel threw the stones, he cut diagonally across the center of the barren field, trying to draw fire away from Jonathan.

Jonathan caught one stone in the sling of his left hand, and missed the second, but he did not stop. He kept moving, spinning the sling above his head and dodging two spears hurled at him one after another. When Jonathan released the stone, he destroyed the right shoulder and arm of another straw man.

Jeush determined the stone had sufficiently mangled the target to pronounce a third kill, and he waved the red flag. That spearman dropped to the ground.

When Jonathan reached a halfway point, he did not pause to catch his breath but continued to race up the hill. Three straw mannequins down, three remained with two spearmen and one archer still posing lethal threats. The soldiers on the sidelines started to chant Jonathan's and his armor bearer's names as the two of them crisscrossed the open range, dodging every lethal missile.

Jonathan heard Adriel whistle again and saw him move toward the top of the hill at an angle, a stone in each hand. Jonathan cut to the middle of the field, and Adriel leapt into the air just as a spear flew beneath his tucked legs. In mid-flight, he tossed the stones over his shoulders, and then landed back on the earth with a forward somersault, which created a minor dust storm on the loose ground.

Jonathan snatched the stones from the air, dropped them into his slings, and spun them in both hands, powering up the force needed before release.

"The spearmen!" Adriel shouted, and he bolted off the ground, dashing for the archer drawing down upon him.

For a split-second Jonathan thought he should take out the archer but chose to do as Adriel said and dispense with the two spearmen. From the corner of his eye, Jonathan had just enough time to see Adriel dive to the ground before an arrow whizzed over his head, and then he released both stones at the same time.

The two spearmen did not even attempt to throw their spears, but fell to the ground, terrified by the stones flying in their direction. They buried their faces in the dirt and covered their heads. As clouds of straw flew out of the destroyed mannequins, hundreds of soldiers began to scream in a frenzy of celebration.

Adriel slammed his body into the final combatant, knocking the archer to the ground, and then drew his sword and lopped off the head of the last straw man.

The moment Adriel thrust his sword into the air signaling their victory, Merab uttered a groan of ecstatic joy, and flung her body across the ledge, sending two potted plants hurtling to the ground. Mikal had to grab her sister's robe to keep her from falling like the potted plants. She yanked her back from the ledge, and they both collapsed onto the floor of the roof. Mikal braced Merab's back against the wall. She was drenched in sweat, panting as if she had just finished a footrace. Mikal had never seen her sister in such a physical state, her eyes glazed with confusion.

"Merab. Merab, speak to me." Panic struck Mikal's heart as she wiped her sister's face with the sleeve of her garment.

"Mark me; someone is going to answer for this!"

Her father's voice drew Mikal's attention away from her sister, and she watched him storm across the roof toward the gate with Jarib scurrying behind him.

"Someone is going to be punished!" her father cried as he kicked open the gate. "Has Abner lost his mind? My son could have been killed!"

Mikal watched her father and Jarib disappear from sight as they descended the outside stairs. It was a great relief to Mikal that neither her father nor Jarib noticed her and her sister slumped on the roof floor. She did not want to receive the brunt of her father's outburst of rage.

"We need to get downstairs," Mikal said, jumping to her feet. She gripped her sister under her arms and yanked her onto her wobbly legs.

Mikal looked over the ledge and saw Adriel and Jonathan riding upon a broiling sea of frenzied soldiers set off by this stunning display of teamwork. The exhilarated warriors shouting the names of her brother and his armor bearer thundered in her ears.

When Merab was told Adriel would be a guest at the evening meal, she barely restrained the impulse to scream. Mikal screamed for the both of them. Merab showed no visible sign of panic, though she did brace her hand upon the food preparation table to help stabilize the sudden dizziness she felt when her brother stuck his head inside the front door and informed them an extra place around the family circle would be needed for his armor bearer.

It was only minutes after the girls had climbed down the ladders, and Mikal had poured her a drink to help settle her nerves before Jonathan appeared in the doorway covered in sweat and grime and still panting from the excitement. Merab tried to act surprised and a little indignant that her brother should invite his lowly armor bearer to the evening meal with the royal family.

"Stop pretending." His scold was playful. He pointed a reproachful finger in her direction. "I know you both were watching from the roof."

Merab opened her mouth to deny the accusation, but Jonathan raised his hand to stop her from embarrassing herself.

"Prepare an extra lamb. Adriel and I both will have big appetites tonight." Then Jonathan disappeared from sight, but instantly reappeared. "And be sure to cook it in that garlic and onion sauce mother always makes."

"Yes, my lord." Merab added a quick curtsy to her sarcastic tone, which only made her brother laugh.

"Must fly now." Jonathan vanished so quickly it was like he had evaporated.

Merab looked at the front door to be sure Jonathan would not surprise them and reappear again. When she faced her sister, she watched Mikal lose herself in mock excitement. She began running in place, pounding the floor with her feet. Her knees slapped against the inside of her robe and created a sound of muffled thunder while she squealed into the hands clamped over her mouth. Merab waved for her to be quiet, but there was too much commotion.

"Girls, what is going on out there?" Their mother's strained voice came from behind the curtain.

"Nothing, Ima." Merab rushed over and grabbed Mikal, pulling her away from the drawn curtain of their parents' bedroom. She raised a threatening fist to Mikal to get her to stop making fun of her before she pushed her toward the table piled with raw vegetables waiting to be cleaned and prepared for the evening meal.

"What are you two doing out there?" Ahinoam sat propped up in her bed, her face, arms, and hands bloated, her belly was a rising hillock beneath the blanket, her hair a tangled mess.

"We are to have a guest tonight for dinner," Merab informed her. "Jonathan is bringing his armor bearer."

"No, no, no, please, no." Ahinoam buried her face in her hands and burst into tears. "No one should see me like this. I look like a hag."

Her daughters pushed back the curtain and rushed around either side of the mattress and knelt down, each taking one of Ahinoam's hands and began consoling her.

Ahinoam had been confined to bed for the last month. The midwives had seen these symptoms before—swelling extremities, racing heartbeat, headaches, blurred vision, back pain, appetite extremes—and had instructed Ahinoam that bed rest was the only option to conserve her strength and increase the odds of a safe delivery.

She had not experienced this severe physical reaction with her other pregnancies and intuitively she knew something was not right. She felt lethargic much of the time as though the child inside required more of her life just to sustain its own.

Saul had taken to sleeping on the roof or in the common room so they both could get the rest they needed—a reality they accepted with reluctance and disappointment. Her husband had been understanding and attentive. He checked on her regularly, brought her trays of food, bathed her, massaged her aching muscles, and would stroll around the compound inside the walls with her at night after everyone had gone to bed. In spite of the acute consequences to her body, another addition would soon be welcomed into the family and life would return to normal. But this birth could not happen swiftly enough for her.

It took some cajoling from her daughters to reassure her that all would be well, and that tonight's guest was a singular request from Jonathan. Ahinoam was still reluctant until her daughters committed to make it a special evening. Her spirits brightened when promised a bath, fresh clothes, perfumes, cosmetics, and her hair cleaned and combed. Mikal would devote her time in preparing her mother and Merab would see to the details of the evening meal. Ahinoam knew that each daughter was suited for their separate tasks and that each would require their full attention for the rest of the day.

Jeush stood at attention before the king as he paced back and forth in front of an empty stall inside the royal stables. Jeush knew it would be wise to keep his head lowered. He could endure the king's wrath if he remained honest and lowly.

"Where is the commander? His horse is gone." Saul kept looking at the empty stall as if somehow horse and rider might mysteriously appear.

"A scouting mission, my lord."

"Scouting mission…to where?"

"To the Philistine outpost in Geba, my lord. They will not return until dark."

Jeush glanced up at the king and could see the light dawn in his dark eyes. He then quickly glanced over to Jarib who offered him a helpless shrug. Jeush was on his own, and he knew the berating was about to be unleashed. The commander and the prince and Adriel had avoided Saul after the war games. The three of them did not need to be told of the king's displeasure. They all expected it and had purposefully not informed him of what he would be watching that morning.

Jeush had been assigned to tell Saul to observe the exercise from the roof of the house; the height of the roof would give him the advantage of seeing the whole field of play, Jeush had said. It was a deliberate ploy to keep him from interfering once he realized the dangerous game that was unfolding before his eyes. Should the outcome be as they all hoped—no mortal wounds, no bones broken, no loss of life—commander, prince, and Jeush knew the moment the exercise was over, they should take flight to avoid the irate summons that was sure to come.

To help Jeush, who would be left behind to suffer the coming fury due them, the decision was made for the guilty party to leave on a quick scouting mission right after the games. At least Jeush would not have to lie about that part of their plot.

"A scouting mission to the outpost in Geba. And the reason for this mission might be what, Jeush? Why this urgency for a scouting mission?"

"My lord, we suspected that—" Jeush was not allowed to finish his answer.

"You suspected nothing except to anticipate my wrath." Saul spun around in frustration and then opened wide his arms. "This whole incident has been calculated right down to their escape. You plotted in this scheme, colluded behind my back. Did you not see the folly? You could have exerted your influence with the commander and the prince. Or at least, you could have come to me and shared their plans."

Jeush was silent, waiting for the king's anger to abate. He had only one rebuttal to make and he wanted to be sure it was heard.

"The prince could have been mortally injured, Jeush." Foam from the king's mouth sprayed from his lips, misting over Jeush's drawn face. "My son could have died."

That was the king's final point: his spleen vented; his words exhausted.

"And yet, he did not die, my lord." Jeush kept a mollifying tone in his voice. "He and Adriel defeated their opponents. They are champions. Your son is a champion. The prince has shown the king's army that he is worthy to be the future king when it is his time to wear the crown. Father and son are an inspiration. The army will follow both of you into the maw of Sheol."

Jeush lowered his head. He knew better than to look into the king's face. He had spoken the truth and those words, once allowed to settle, should help calm Saul's fury. After a moment, all Jeush heard was a deep growl, which dissipated into a deep intake of air, and ended with a disgusted muttering, "The queen better not hear of this."

When Jeush raised his eyes, he saw the king marching out of the stables with Jarib at his side.

Chapter 9

MERAB DID NOT SIT WITH THE REST OF THE FAMILY. SHE STOOD behind the preparation table, watching to see that the servants followed her instructions—a wine cup was never to be empty, a plate or bowl should be removed once the contents were devoured. Servants flowed back and forth from the preparation table to the royal family lounging on a circle of cushions in the middle of the room. Her mother alone sat in a chair with her father stretched out by her side.

In the center of the circle, trays of roasted goat and sheep—prepared exactly as Jonathan had requested, simmering in onion and garlic broth, and garnished in wild herbs with a border of dandelion greens—were set for the family to plunder. Each member of the dinner party helped themselves from the smaller trays of roasted vegetables, fresh cucumbers, fruits and nuts, and pomegranates. Two large baskets of barley and wheat bread were passed around the circle.

Merab had seen that a stool was set outside the family circle for Uncle Ner. He was unable to feed himself, and Abner had assumed that responsibility at the family meals. It was the only time in the day he could spend with his father, and he wanted to maintain this small level of filial connection. Until the family became the royal family, the duties for caring for Uncle Ner were shared, though Merab found that she spent more time with her uncle than the rest of the family. Now servants had taken over the duties of care for Uncle Ner's health.

Everyone knew his end was near. He rarely spoke, and except for his brother Kish and Abner, he no longer recognized the faces of his family. During the course of the meal, Uncle Ner's lips might flinch with a curled smile at a voice recognized or detail of a shared story, but most of the time the sparkle in his eyes barely registered.

Merab was conscious that the conversation was subdued, not its usual free-for-all of jibes and tales, and it was not just because everyone was enjoying the delicious meal she had prepared. Abner and Jonathan were not very talkative. They just kept eyeing each other or looking at her father and then looking away as if they shared a secret they must keep from everyone.

Then there was the presence of her mother. No one wanted to vex her with the family's usual boisterous behavior. Her pregnancy was at a precarious stage, and Merab usually brought her meals to her bedroom to avoid undo excitement and stress.

The true focus of her attention was Adriel, and the significance of his added presence raised the tension in her heart. She wanted everything to be perfect for him alone, and it thrilled her heart to see him enjoying the meal. When he caught her eye and subtlety raised his goblet in salute for the quality of the food she had prepared, her knees almost buckled. The twins were all together another matter. Merab could not control their behavior, and the excitement of the feat performed by their brother and his armor bearer that morning was too much to contain.

"Did you see how that arrow just missed your head, Jonathan?" Malki mimed the near-miss of the arrow over his brother's head. "If you had not dropped to the ground—"

"Hush, Malki." Merab signaled that Malki needed to stop at once, nodding in the direction of their parents.

But Malki paid no attention to Merab, and then Ishvi jumped beside his twin brother. The level of pride and excitement expressed on the faces of her two brothers was beyond their control. Merab knew today's feat should be the sole topic of conversation, how Jonathan and Adriel had defied injury and death, but she did not want the twins to take over. She looked at Jonathan for help, but he just shrugged. Both twins would speak of this moment like grand oracles.

"Yes, but it was the spear Adriel jumped over that was the best." Ishvi's legs spread awkwardly as he demonstrated Adriel's defiance of gravity. "You sprang higher than my head…higher than a gazelle."

"Malki, you need to sit down and hush." Merab tried to keep her voice lowered, but it was not low enough for her mother.

"What is all this about spears and arrows?" she asked, handing her half-finished plate to Saul.

"It is nothing, my dear." Saul took her plate and handed it to a servant.

It was clear to Merab that her father had not told her mother what had happened that morning, nor did her father realize that she and Mikal had watched the whole incident.

"We had a little battle demonstration today, nothing more." Saul broke off a cluster of grapes on the tray in front of him and offered them to Ahinoam.

"Fighting." Ahinoam sighed. She ignored Saul's offer of grapes and gently patted her belly. "Always fighting."

Silence ensued. Merab sensed that disaster loomed. All eyes were avoiding direct contact with her mother. Merab prayed she would drop the subject and not make any further inquiry about her son's brush with death that morning. Merab gave her sister a stern look, pleading for her to think of something to divert their mother's curiosity, and Mikal seemed to understand the silent cry for help.

"Ima, would you comb my hair?" Mikal leapt up from her cushion.

She saw Merab's bemused look as if to say, could you not have thought of something else, but Mikal shrugged and tapped the side of her head, indicating it was the first thing that came to her mind.

Mikal turned her attention back to her mother who had not heard the request.

"I…what did you ask?" Her face was a mask of bewilderment.

"My hair." Mikal stepped over her cushion and rushed behind the curtain of her parents' bedroom to fetch the comb she had used to prepare her mother for the evening mealtime. "It needs combing." Mikal emerged from behind the curtain holding the comb in her hand and advanced toward her mother.

"At mealtime? No, Mikal, not now. At bedtime perhaps." Ahinoam looked annoyed by the abrupt request and let out a weary sigh.

"Ima, please, it feels so good when you comb my hair."

"I will comb your hair." Saul tossed his half-eaten grape cluster back onto the tray and reached out his hand to take the comb from his daughter.

"You are too rough." Mikal smacked the comb onto the palm of her hand.

"I will be as gentle with you as I am with my horse." Saul beckoned Mikal to him.

His remark brought a burst of snickering from the twins, which was muted instantly by Mikal's icy glare.

"Now sit down and stop pestering your ima." Saul placed a small cushion in front of him and pointed for his daughter to take a seat.

Mikal huffed in disgust but obeyed her father. She pitched him the comb and plopped in front of him while Saul readjusted himself on the cushion behind her.

"Now be gentle." Mikal elevated her head to a stiff and proud position and braced her back to resist the pull of the comb. "I want my hair to glisten and shine."

"Like the sweaty rump of my horse." Saul held out a long strand of her hair.

Mikal's disgust brought instant glee to the twins, reinforced from the rest of the party, including Ahinoam with a group laughter.

Mikal twisted her torso around, her fury not to be denied. "Abba, how dare you talk that way...like a common soldier."

"But I thought it was for the soldiers that you wanted to glisten and shine." Her father's face burst into mock surprise at Mikal's outrage.

"I am a princess with higher aspirations," Mikal said, and spun back around with a huff.

Merab groaned with annoyance at her sister's haughty remark, though it had succeeded in distracting her mother. She then cut her eyes at Adriel just as he was raising his head to look in her direction. It was only the second time that evening they had made direct eye contact. Merab had noticed Adriel trying to catch her eye throughout the meal after he had raised his goblet to her, but she would not look at him directly for fear of the others taking notice.

This was a perfectly spontaneous moment, and the unanticipated contact sent a jolt through Merab, causing her to drop the goat milk she just poured for her mother onto the tabletop, splashing most of the contents onto her clean robe. She felt a burst of scarlet cover her face, and she yanked a cloth rag from the table, turned her back on the crowd, and began to wipe the milk soaking into her robe. The family was absorbed in the playful exchange between her father and sister and never noticed the accident.

When Merab had done her best to wipe the spot dry, she took a deep breath and looked over her shoulder, hoping by some miracle Adriel had been struck with temporary blindness and never noticed her clumsiness. But he was looking at her, and for a moment, Merab was frozen with dread until she watched him raise his cup of wine and spill its contents down his front. In that instant, she would have wedded and bedded him if a priest could be found.

Mikal groaned as her father ran the comb through the thick strand of the hair he held in his hand.

"Princess indeed," he said. "Do not forget, you are a farmer's daughter. I will not have you thinking yourself higher than others."

"Someday I will marry, and you will want the best for me." Mikal refused to give ground. "Maybe a prince from another country since we have none in Israel."

"You will marry a nice Hebrew boy who is not afraid of hard work and able to tame a wild cat like you." Saul gave an extra hard tug on the comb.

"Ouch!" Mikal cried. She twisted around to face her father, fists drawn in a threatening pose.

Saul feigned fear, dropping the comb and raising his arms to protect himself from Mikal's wrath, uttering pleas for mercy—all for the family's continued amusement. Mikal threw herself upon her father. Those closest to the combatants scooted aside, giving the skirmish room to sprawl.

"You do not want someone to tame me." Mikal grabbed her father's left arm and pinned it behind his back. "You like me wild as wind and fire."

"Commander, have my 'wind and fire' daughter lead our next campaign!" Saul cried, a play-act of the torturing Mikal was causing him to suffer.

"The Philistines will flee in holy terror." Abner placed a small bite of bread into his father's mouth and brushed the crumbs from around his beard.

"Say I will marry a prince," Mikal demanded.

"You shall marry my horse first." Saul groaned in make-believe agony.

"A prince, Abba, for the first princess of Israel." Mikal increased the tension on her father's arm.

"I beg your pardon," Merab exclaimed. "First princess of Israel?"

No one heard her. All were enjoying the match between father and daughter. All except Adriel, and he reacted simply by leaning toward her, refocusing his piercing eyes upon her; the others were too enthralled with her sister torturing her father to be reminded that Merab, being the oldest daughter, had more claim to the title of first princess.

In reality, the family paid little attention to her, a fact of life she had come to accept. She had witnessed many of these wrestling matches between her father and sister and had, at moments, longed to throw herself into a spontaneous fray, but never found the courage to do so. Wildness came naturally to Mikal. Tameness was a quality more to Merab's liking.

She took advantage of the commotion to return Adriel's ardent gaze.

His eyes held her captive, such steady worship, plunging himself into her soul just with his eyes. She forgot her milk-stained robe. She abandoned any further need to defend her right as first princess. She was the object of another's wishful dream, and here she would remain. Not for one heartbeat did Adriel look away from Merab to catch a glimpse of her sister's one-woman takeover of the throne. The two of them indulged in their quiet, gazing reverie, ignoring the clownish mayhem raging in the room.

"My arm. I beg for mercy." Saul's pleas brought only laughter from the family.

"A simple prince, Abba, and I will release you."

"I have to fight with this arm. Please stop, I beg you."

"You know how you can stop this torture." Mikal looked to her mother when she spoke using the exact tone her mother used when responding to the complaints of her children when being justly punished for their misbehavior. Mikal was rewarded with her mother's applause for recognizing her daughter's tactic.

"A captain, then." Saul sought to have a compromise. "You shall have a captain."

"Not good enough," Mikal countered. Then she used both hands to push her father's arm farther up his back.

"You would break the arm of the king?" Saul cried, his resistance in rapid decline.

"To get what I want, yes!"

"What about the arm of your father?"

"Even quicker."

"A prince, then…a prince. I yield. I cannot bear the pain any longer."

"I knew you would come to see this clearly." Mikal released her father's arm and sprang to her feet in triumph.

The family cheered her victory, and Mikal bowed to their delighted applause. Then she knelt beside her mother who was gripping the arms of her chair and laughing harder than she had laughed for months.

"Now, Ima, we must plan the royal wedding."

"Let us find that prince first." Ahinoam patted her daughter's head as she gradually gained control of her amusement.

"Minor detail," Mikal replied with a frivolous wave of her hand. "We must design what I shall wear."

"I have always favored sackcloth." Saul sat up and dangled his limp arm before the family, hoping for their sympathy.

Mikal twisted around and waved her fists in her father's face.

"Please no more!" Saul cried, his floppy arm suddenly revived to shield him from a second assault. "I can take no more. Buy the finest material in Israel."

"You heard him, Ima." Mikal turned back to Ahinoam, but she could tell her mother was not interested in continuing the discussion of her future marriage. She placed her hand upon her forehead. "Ima, you look flushed."

"Such entertainment, how can I not be." Ahinoam dabbed the perspiration from her forehead with the sleeve of her robe. "I need something to drink."

"Merab, pour some goat's milk for your mother." Saul sprang to his feet.

Saul's disgrace at the hands of Mikal was temporary, which frustrated her. She would have preferred to have remained the center of attention a little longer. But her father was a king again—his throne and power restored.

"Dinner is over," Saul announced. "Abner and Jonathan, I want to meet with the captains, Ahiah and Eleazar, and the two prophets on the roof tonight. Summon them, and Jeush and Jarib as well. I want them at this meeting."

Mikal watched everyone spring into action and realized her performance was now over and would probably be soon forgotten. But the purpose had been served. She had distracted her mother from further questions regarding the events of the morning.

As soon as the royal family rose from their places, Merab motioned for the servants to begin removing the cushions and cups, bowls and trays from the center of the circle. She slipped over and kissed the cheek of her grandfather and Uncle Ner before they were escorted out of the room. Then the two old brothers began to shuffle toward the door with the aid of a male servant.

Merab went back to the preparation table and refilled the cup she had dropped with the goat's milk. When she moved around the table, she was stopped by Adriel when he got to his feet and stepped toward her, his hand raised. Both of them cast their eyes over the room to be sure his movement toward her had not drawn attention, but everyone was too involved in other conversations and activities to pay them any mind.

They returned to each other's gaze, and Merab felt her hand begin to tremble as she looked into his expressive, soulful eyes. From this closeness, in this light, he was more handsome than she realized. And when she saw his face flush and his mouth and tongue struggle to speak, she looked away just so he might regain the power of speech.

"Were you watching today, my lady?" he whispered. "Your brother said so."

"From the roof, my sister and me. We…I could not take my eyes off of…off of…the game." Merab took a sip of the goat milk just to calm her fluttering heart.

"I would never allow any harm to come to your brother." Adriel lowered his gaze to the floor.

"It was you I prayed would be kept from harm." Her confession caused him to raise his eyes to her, and his bright smile made her feel light-headed.

"And your brother." Adriel added a gentle tap of a finger inside the crook of her extended arm, and then traced a line down to the hand holding the cup.

"Yes, of course. My brother. Excuse me…I must…" Merab was unable to finish her thought, and she began to weave her way through the chaos of servants and family to fulfill the instruction given by her father, leaving Adriel alone. His eyes, his voice, and his fleeting gentle tracing of his finger down her forearm had completely unnerved her.

"Why are you smiling?" Mikal asked as Merab approached with the goat milk.

"Nothing. Nothing. It's nothing...I will tell you later...in bed."

Her father collected the cup of goat's milk from Merab's hand, which was fortunate because if she had tried to hold it any longer, the trembling in her body would have caused her to drop the cup a second time.

Merab grabbed her sister by the arm to steady herself and turned her around just as Jonathan dashed up and kissed her on the cheek.

"Thank you, Sister. The meal was delicious...and it may be my last." Jonathan cast his eyes toward their father. "Pray for me."

Before Merab could respond, Jonathan spun around and marched toward the front door, waving for Adriel to follow him. Merab cast a final look in Adriel's direction as he paused before following her brother out the door. Adriel smiled and gave a slight nod of his head. Merab dug her fingers into her sister's arm as she exchanged smiles with Adriel before he disappeared from their sight.

"You talked to him; I know you spoke with him." Mikal pulled Merab's fingers out of her flesh. "What did he say to you?"

"I made a fool of myself. He touched my arm. Tonight, in bed. I will tell you." Merab pulled away from Mikal, returning to the preparation table, a flutter of energy ran through her, part joy, part anxiety.

This was not just some fantasy of hers. This romantic feeling was not hers alone but was shared by Adriel. She knew this instinctively, and now in this moment she realized this feeling that rushed through her was a joyful ache she prayed would never drain from her heart.

Saul knelt down and held the cup to Ahinoam's lips. "Go straight to bed."

Ahinoam drained the contents of the cup, gasping after her final swallow. She leaned back in her chair, and Saul dabbed away the milk foam from her upper lip.

"After your meeting tonight, come to bed." Ahinoam sighed. "No matter the time. I want you beside me tonight."

"I do not want to wake you if you are asleep."

"Wake me." She placed her hand on the side of his face.

Saul kissed her hand, then leaned forward and kissed her damp forehead before he rose to his feet. He turned to see Malki and Ishvi looking at him.

"Are you boys tired? Your day has been a long one."

They both responded with assurances that sleep was the last thing they needed.

"Then I want you to stand guard tonight at the base of the stairs leading up to the roof and not let anyone pass. I want a private word with your brother and Abner before the others join us. Can you do that for me?"

Neither boy bothered with a verbal answer but spun on their heels and bolted out the front door. Had anyone been in their path they would have been plowed over.

Saul paced on the rooftop; his hands clasped behind his back. He paused at the gate at the top of the stairs and looked below to see Jarib talking to the twins. All those he had summoned were gathered at the bottom of the stairs waiting to be allowed up to the roof to join him. His sons were standing on the steps, remaining vigilant in obeying their father's command.

"Sire." Jarib took a step between Malki and Ishvi to see if the king required him.

"A moment, Jarib, please." Saul raised his hand then moved away from the gate.

Saul glanced over at Jonathan and Abner leaning against the ledge on the backside of the house. The two of them had their backs to Saul and were looking out into the blackness at the open field and surrounding hills where the army conducted its military exercises. They spoke quietly while Saul ambled along the circumference of the roof, slowly making his way in their direction. He paused behind a large potted plant and withdrew his sword, then he crept toward his son and cousin without ever drawing their attention until he was close enough to overhear them speak.

"How long had you and Adriel practiced that routine?" Abner spoke softly.

"Weeks. The hardest part was catching the stones in my sling. The pass-and-catch still needs work to be consistent. Carrying a bag full of stones into battle is cumbersome. I want to be able to sling on the run and not stop to reload. I want to…"

Saul had listened to enough. He raised the blade of his sword and brought it down between their shoulders. Both of them jerked back in response. He found the look of shock on both of their faces amusing. "Some warriors you are. I could have lopped off both your heads."

"Where did you get that sword?" Abner struggled to regain his composure after this sneak attack.

"You know the story, Cousin. I was a newborn when the Philistines sacked the city of Shiloh and captured the Ark. Father fought in that war, and some Levite gave him this sword as his reward for telling Eli, the high priest, that his sons were slain in battle. My father always believed his message killed the old man. Words are powerful, he told me. In the chaos of retreat, he never again saw the Levite who gave him this sword."

"No, no, I mean now," Abner said. "Where did you get the sword just now?"

"I keep it hidden." Saul began to wave the blade in tiny circles between his son and cousin. "All this time I have yet to stain this blade with human blood; a couple of oxen felt its fine cut. And thanks to your leadership, our army did so well against Nahash, it remained attached to my side."

"May the king never have to stain his sword with human blood," Abner said.

"I doubt I will be so blessed, but one can hope," Saul said. "I keep the blade sharp though, just in case."

"I wish our army had such fine weapons, Abba," Jonathan said.

Saul was not fooled by his son's compliment of his sword. He had both Abner and Jonathan slightly off-kilter and wanted them to regret that their actions today had brought on his anger.

"Those men today, trying to kill my son and his armor bearer, who were they?"

"Some of the best in our ranks."

"Send them home, Abner. You are fortunate I do not demand their heads."

"You cannot be serious." Abner was startled by the king's harsh judgment. "They were only performing as ordered."

"As ordered? As ordered by whom?" Saul did not bother waiting for a reply. "Not my orders. And who designed this little exhibition I watched from my roof this morning? Who gave these men permission to threaten the life of my son, the prince of Israel, the heir to my throne?"

Abner turned away, but Saul was not deterred by his cousin's silence and began to forcefully tap his shoulder with the flat side of his sword until Abner became rigid. When Abner swung around, Saul could see the anger at this demeaning treatment rushing through his body.

"It was I, Abba," Jonathan divulged. "I designed the contest with Adriel."

"You designed that match?" Saul was dumbfounded by his son's admission.

"Yes. Adriel and I had been practicing for weeks, away from the camp, away from anyone watching us. We decided we needed to test our skills in a real-life situation, not some standard training exercise."

"It was definitely not a standard training exercise. And what if one of those arrows or spears had hit its mark?"

"I would not be standing before you now."

"Point well stated." Saul raised his voice, and then he turned back to Abner. "And you ordered those men to aim at my son."

"No, Abba. I am responsible for that as well," Jonathan said, again quick to come to Abner's defense, which only irritated Saul. "I instructed the archers and spearmen to aim to disable."

"Disable. Disable." Saul repeated the word trying to comprehend it. "Just try and imagine me presenting your 'disabled' body to your mother if they had succeeded."

Saul let his sword drift from between Abner and Jonathan, downward to his feet as though a sudden weakness had taken him.

"You could not have used blunted heads on those spears and replaced the sharp tips of the arrows with balls of cloth?" Saul asked.

"Do you expect the Philistines to use such weapons against us, Abba?"

Saul's eyes turned glassy as he imagined carrying the lifeless body of his son from the field. "Disable. Disable. Imagine that," Saul whispered to himself.

"Abba, all blame should rest on my shoulders," Jonathan said. "I know it was risky. I know it was dangerous, but had it not been for Adriel at the battle of Jabesh Gilead, you would have had to bury me then."

"But I did not have to watch your close escape from death in Jabesh Gilead. Today I had to watch. I would pluck out my eyes before I could watch you die."

"Abba, you cannot protect me forever," Jonathan spoke softly. "Jabesh Gilead taught me a lesson—be the aggressor, keep moving, keep forcing the attack, do not let the enemy surprise you; you surprise them."

"I was surprised today. Yes, you surprised me today." Saul heaved a deep breath from his lungs and a calmness was restored to his heart. "And we agree to keep your mother from ever finding out. Yes?"

"Agreed. I never told her that Adriel saved my life at Jabesh Gilead."

Saul could see the relief on his son's face that he was no longer angry at him.

"I would rather face a contingent of blood-thirsty Philistines than your mother's anguish." Saul strapped his sword around his waist. "You two may have been lulled into a false belief that you had gotten by without a stern rebuke for your stunt this morning. It was good that you left quickly on your spying mission. I might not have been so merciful had I found you in the stables."

Abner and Jonathan looked at each other, their somber faces turned grim at the near-miss of Saul's dire consequence had he caught them in the barn.

"Tell me where you hide your sword," Abner said.

"A king must have some secrets." Saul smiled with sly enjoyment, and he patted his cousin's shoulder where a chaffed red mark remained. He knew Abner wanted to change the subject, and he provided a gentle pat to replace any sting his cousin felt.

Saul began to saunter around the roof in a wide circle. If anyone would change the topic, it would be him. "Why is it that no blacksmiths can be found in Israel who can forge weapons for us?" He looked back at Abner and Jonathan and enjoyed seeing their surprised expressions at his abrupt shift in demeanor.

Abner was quick to answer. "For years the Philistines have successfully kept a firm hand over our tribes by not allowing us to fashion our own weapons, and then forcing us to pay nearly a shekel just to sharpen our farming equipment."

"A mattock and a sickle are poor weapons against a sword or spear no matter how fine a point," Saul said.

"Wielding a plowshare in battle strikes our enemies with amusement, not fear," added Abner. "We train with sticks and rocks, farm implements, homemade bows, arrows, and spears, and now the weapons plundered from the Ammonites."

"And all these years Israel has been unable to respond to the oppression of the Philistines," Saul mused.

"All these years we have not had a king to unite us," Jonathan said.

Saul paused to look at Jonathan. Every severe emotion he felt throughout the day regarding his son had now evaporated. All that remained was pride.

"The Philistines believe we have no spine," Abner said.

"Our victory over the Ammonites will not alter their perception," added Jonathan.

"Perhaps it is time we took some initiative to change their perception." Saul was feeling a surge of confidence, and he stepped back to enjoy watching the eyes of his cousin and son widen. "Jonathan, you said something that inspired me."

"What is that, Abba?"

"You said the battle at Jabesh taught you to be the aggressor, keep moving, keep forcing the attack, do not let the enemy surprise you, you surprise them. Is that right?"

"That was my experience."

"Abner, would you fetch the others. I want the chieftains to hear your report of what you found at Geba, and then I think we plot some strategy."

"Yes, my lord." Abner smiled at his cousin, and then moved briskly toward the gate at the top of the stairs.

Saul took this brief moment alone with Jonathan, placing his hands upon his son's firm shoulders. "You were magnificent today, but if anything had happened to you…" Saul was overcome and choked off his words.

"Nothing did happen, Abba." Jonathan rocked on his toes. "Such feelings are useless now."

"Useless. Useless, he says." Saul could tell his distress made his son uncomfortable, and so he began to pull his emotions together. He gave Jonathan a gentle smack on his cheek. "You have a son one day and then tell me my feelings are useless."

Saul pulled back the curtain to his bedroom and peeked around the edge. He saw Ahinoam lying on her side with a large cushion propped against her back. The flame in the clay lamp sputtered. The oil was running low. She would have extinguished the flame when she was ready to sleep, but she had kept it burning for him.

He hated seeing her in this condition. She never had this much trouble carrying any of the other children, and though all were excited at the promise of a new family member, he was ready for it to end. He wanted his wife back. He needed his wife. He needed her attention and care. He needed a queen to help him be a king. No one else provided him with such assurance. No one else inspired him to such valor. No one else could complete him.

Saul was reluctant to wake her but chose to honor her request. He wanted to sleep beside her as much as she wanted him nearby. He let the curtain fall back into place and sat at the foot of the bed, reaching under the blanket until he found a bare foot. He stretched out her leg and began to massage her calf until she gradually came awake.

"What time of night is it?" Ahinoam's voice was groggy with sleep.

"Nearly dawn. The eastern sky was beginning to glow as I came down from the roof." Saul continued rubbing Ahinoam's swollen leg.

"You were on the roof this whole time?" She raised her head slightly off the pillow, a look of surprise on her face to find the night had gone and Saul was just now coming to bed. "Move the pillow. Lie down beside me." Ahinoam elbowed the cushion behind her back.

Saul returned her leg beneath the cover. He stood and let his outer robe fall to the floor, then crawled into bed, replacing the cushion with his body against his wife's back. She took his arm and draped it over her side, then whispered something, but Saul could not make out the words she spoke. He raised his head to ask her to repeat what she had said but heard a gentle snore instead. Before closing his eyes, he prayed for this baby to be born soon. His soul could feel the faint stirring of apprehension and he needed this woman by his side to help make the future not so fearful.

Chapter 10

BEFORE MAKING THE STEEP ASCENT UP THE TREACHEROUS "Tooth of the Rock" pass, Jonathan bent down to tighten the leather straps of his sandals around his ankles. They needed to be secure. He had to be sure-footed to make the difficult ascent and rapid descent of this sheer path. And he needed to wait for Adriel to join him. Jonathan had run ahead up the path while Adriel had waited below to be sure no one was following them.

This precipitous trail was foot travel only. No caravans or wagons could maneuver this single-lane road. A traveler with a mount would either turn back to find a different route to his destination or be forced to dismount and guide the beast along the perilous switchbacks cut through cliffs eroding into jagged teeth. This stretch of road saw little human travel, which would work to Jonathan's advantage.

Geba was the destination point on Israel's side of the border. The Philistine military garrison on the precipice above where Jonathan stood marked the end of the territorial reach of the Philistine nation. The outpost's location on this high plateau gave the Philistines a clear view of the surrounding terrain for any suspicious activity.

Establishing secure borders with the Philistines was a constant struggle.

Their superior military strength gave them liberty to launch raiding parties on hamlets and villages, like Geba, situated along the boundary line between the two nations. With each successful raid, the Philistines moved the borders in their favor.

While Israel might not be ready for a full-scale war with her enemy, Jonathan and his father and Abner, all the tribal council and the military officers felt the professional army of Israel was ready to mount a few counterattacks of its own. The Philistines had inflicted enough damage on defenseless villages along the border and it was decided that Israel should retaliate.

After an earlier scouting trip to Geba with Abner and Adriel, Jonathan volunteered to go back to Geba for a more thorough reconnaissance of the Philistine garrison on the cliff top overlooking the village. He and Adriel had become like brothers during their training, and Jonathan would never consider such a mission without having Adriel at his side.

This army outpost represented the farthest reach of the Philistine kingdom into the region of Israel, and the Five Lords had arrogantly marked their domain with a tall, stone monument that could be seen from great distances in any direction. It would be to Israel's advantage if such a military post could be attacked and could become a point of pride for those who succeeded in destroying it.

A week earlier, Jonathan and Adriel had slipped into Geba in the middle of the night and took shelter with a family of one of the soldiers stationed with the king's army back home. Each day, Adriel and Jonathan would slip out of the village in the pitch of the early hour before dawn and remain hidden behind the rocks or the foliage of the treetops, anywhere they could best observe the garrison and watch the daily routine of the Philistine soldiers.

After a few days of observation, it was obvious the soldiers had no fear of potential danger. Rather than maintaining any proper military code of behavior, the soldiers were too preoccupied indulging their appetites and lusts with a troupe of women specializing in such pleasures. The women arrived with a supply wagon the same day Jonathan and Adriel began spying. However, to strike the outpost during the day even with the soldiers in mid-debauchery would be foolish. Drunk or sober, the

Philistines could easily repel any assault on their garrison from their vantage point.

Before leaving home on this secret mission, Abner's instruction to Jonathan had been explicit: "spy only; do not provoke or engage the enemy." Abner's stern expression and sharp voice allowed no room for nuance or misinterpretation.

Jonathan knew the commander was only looking out for his safety, but the temptation to do something daring had been too great. How could Jonathan report to Abner what he and Adriel observed from the relative safety of hiding behind rocks and trees in the valley below the garrison? What benefit would that provide? A full report required both firsthand knowledge of how many structures were built for the Philistine garrison and how many men were stationed at the outpost.

The arrival of a traveling peddler in Geba that afternoon set the circumstances in motion for Jonathan's decision to get a closer look at the Philistine garrison. The peddler entered the village with a wagon full of agricultural tools and domestic wares to sell. He also carried a message from the king's secretary for the people in the village, "Ner, father of Abner, commander of the army, has died and now rests with his fathers."

The news of a death in the royal family was being told throughout the land. The Philistines would never suspect a traveling merchant might be carrying a message for the son of the king.

When Jonathan and Adriel returned from their surveillance post that night and received the news, Jonathan paid the family the expenses incurred for sheltering them and slipped out to the stables for their horses. They led their horses out of the village and stopped to secure their saddle pads. It was then that they made the joint decision.

"You see the light of the campfire?" Jonathan directed Adriel's attention toward the firelight from the Philistine garrison above them. "From here it appears close."

"As the hawk flies, yes, but we do not have wings." Adriel acknowledged the sight, but then went back to tightening the leather girth underneath the belly of his horse.

"How long do you think it would take to get there and back on foot?"

Jonathan hated the thought of going home for his uncle's burial with so little intelligence from his first efforts at spying on the enemy.

"A shadow's quarter turn; longer if we face trouble." Adriel rested his arms over the back of his horse.

"What say we ascend the cliff road, scout the garrison, and get a full count of the soldiers?" Jonathan proposed. "Then we dash back to the horses, ride hard, and get home before sunrise." He had envisioned the plan without any thought of potential difficulty.

"And if we run into trouble?" asked Adriel.

"Then we run even faster." When Adriel did not immediately respond, Jonathan knew what his armor bearer was thinking, that others would have a differing opinion of such an operation. "I know the king and the commander would never agree to this."

"My lord, it is dangerous, but the information would be valuable."

"And this is why we must go. Are you with me, Adriel?"

"Heart and soul, my lord."

Without another word, the two of them led their horses a little distance from the village and tied them to the base of a sycamore tree off the road and out of sight. Then they quietly jogged toward the base of the cliff.

By the time Adriel caught up with Jonathan who was waiting for him where the path began its steep gradient, the high clouds blocked any light the moon and stars might have provided. The lack of light would conceal their ascent from a Philistine sentry but could work against them if they were forced to descend at breakneck speed. A loss of footing, one stumble, and the consequences could be fatal.

Adriel stood on one foot, shaking the other to make sure his sandal was secure and then shifted onto the other foot to do the same.

Jonathan offered him the water skin for a final drink, but he declined, so Jonathan dropped it behind a rock pile beside the path.

"See you at the top," Jonathan whispered.

"See you at the top," Adriel replied in the same low voice.

They each spat in their hand before they clasped them together.

Jonathan took the lead. Though the trail was steep it was not encumbered with large rocks that had to be navigated around or scaled. Jonathan could maintain a steady pace zigzagging back and forth for the entire arduous climb. The days he and Adriel spent observing at a safe distance had been put to good use. They had committed the circuitous route to memory.

There were at least a dozen switchbacks before reaching the top, but it was hard to determine how many steps it took for each change of direction or the width of the path at any given moment. This was one of the reasons Jonathan wanted to risk the effort. The familiarity of how long it took to get to the top could only be gained by actually doing the ascent and this knowledge would be useful in the future.

Jonathan reduced his speed as they approached the last turn. They needed to catch their breaths before the final ascent so as not to reach the top gasping. They pressed their backs against the cliff wall, inhaling the cool night air. When their breathing began to stabilize, they massaged their legs to keep the throbbing muscles from cramping. Out over the valley below, Jonathan pointed out a few lights still flickering in the village and the darker swathes of the surrounding hills and forests.

Jonathan led the way up the final distance, creeping slowly, carefully placing his feet to maintain silence and avoid loosening any stones that could potentially create a rockslide and give away their presence. When they reached the crest of their climb, there was a man-made rock pile stacked at the point where the path leveled off and widened out into the main road. This stone heap marked the beginning of the path's steep descent from the Philistine side into Israel's territory.

They used the rock pile for cover, raising their heads just high enough to make out the number of buildings—a barracks, a structure that appeared to be a dining hall for the soldiers to take their meals, and two smaller buildings, plus stables. There were a couple of transport wagons parked to the side of the stables, but that was all they could see from that position. A single guard warmed himself by the fire burning in a pit situated in the center of the layout. They could hear the noise of eating and drinking coming from the dining hall and shadows of human forms moving about between the barracks and the dining hall.

Jonathan pointed to the monument a short distance from where they were hiding. It was on the far side of the road directly opposite the garrison. If they could get to that position, they could use the column and its rock base for cover. So, they slipped from behind the rock pile and dashed over to the stone pillar, dropped behind the rocky base, and lay flat on the ground.

Even at this range it was impossible to count how many soldiers might be stationed at this outpost. From the sounds of raucous laughter and singing they could not determine a specific number. Only flickers of light emanated from the barracks and the dining hall. There was no light from the two smaller buildings. The wobbly shadows cast inside the two occupied buildings made it impossible to determine the number of soldiers.

"I still cannot see from this distance," Jonathan said.

"We would have to get closer." Adriel began to crawl forward, but Jonathan stopped him with a hand upon his shoulder.

"Too risky, but I say twenty, perhaps a few more," Jonathan said. "Judging from the size of the barracks, they cannot house more than twenty soldiers, and the stables are not large enough for horses beyond that number of men."

Adriel looked up and pointed to the sky. The clouds were beginning to reveal a half-moon. "We should go. If the moon breaks the clouds, we lose the cover of darkness."

When they got to their feet, Jonathan leaned against the monument and felt the pillar shift its weight in the loose soil. He pushed it again and a few of the rocks piled around the base tumbled to the ground.

"Wait," Jonathan whispered, as he began to rock the pillar loose.

"What are you doing?" Adriel looked toward the guard to see if the sentry might catch sight of Jonathan rocking the monument back and forth.

"You are going to knock this pillar over," Adriel said.

"Clever boy. I want to go home with a story to tell. Now throw your back into it."

The Philistine sentry posted for guard duty circled around the fire burning brightly in the center of the compound. He became briefly distracted by a woman who emerged from the dining hall and began to saunter toward him holding a wineskin in her hand and offering him some refreshment. She swayed her hips and lifted the hem of her robe to reveal her legs.

The guard was not amused by her antics and shouted for her to go back inside the hall. He turned away from the woman and faced the road, and in the emerging glow of the moonlight, the guard could see something that seemed incomprehensible. The ghostly light reflecting off the white stone of the monument across the road made the tall pillar appear to be in motion.

When he took a step forward to get a better look, the woman flung herself upon his back and began to devour his neck and ears with her sloppy kisses. Instead of flinging her from his back, he began to trot toward the swaying monument to see if he was truly hallucinating.

Just when Jonathan and Adriel were about to topple the monument, Jonathan noticed the guard and the laughing woman riding on his back heading toward them. He crouched down, reached into his pouch, and pulled out a stone.

"I will hold him off. It is almost down." Jonathan yanked his sling from his leather belt and dropped the stone inside the pouch.

"Do not kill him." Adriel gasped as he pushed against the pillar. "Just disable him, and hurry, I cannot do this by myself."

Jonathan's sling began to whistle above his head. He took a few steps forward, and as soon as he released the stone, the Philistine guard grunted in shock and pain and fell backward, hurling the woman from his shoulders. She tumbled into the outer rim of the fire pit, igniting her robes. The woman began to scream as she rolled on the ground trying to smother the flames of her burning clothes. The guard lay on his back gasping for the air that had been knocked out of his lungs by the stone slamming into his chest.

Jonathan knew this commotion would bring every soldier out of the buildings. He looked behind him and saw that Adriel had succeeded in pushing the monument low enough for him to run up the side and start jumping up and down on the midsection. Jonathan tucked his sling into his belt and scrambled up the monument beside Adriel. Their combined weight and physical effort toppled the monument to the ground with a loud thud. Jonathan leapt off the pillar, and when he realized that the capital top of the column had cracked and nearly broken off the main trunk, he was elated by his spontaneous prank.

When Jonathan saw the soldiers streaming out of the buildings, it was time to make good on their escape. The scene around the fire drew more drunken laughter than any humane concern for an injured comrade and a woman desperate to keep from burning alive, but Jonathan knew the moment the soldiers realized something was amiss, they would stop their revelry and begin to investigate. The wounded guard would catch his breath, the robes of the woman would be snuffed out, and a quick canvass of the area as to the cause for this chaotic scene would ensue.

Jonathan looked again at the moon and knew that they could not depend on the cover of darkness to shield them, so he and Adriel bolted for the path, leaving behind the general confusion. The clouds had parted, and the fingernail-moon and stars provided enough light for them to see the outline of the path in front of their eyes to keep them from misjudging the turns and flying off into the open, deadly space beyond the edge of the trail.

In the boredom of those long hours of surveillance, Jonathan never discussed toppling the stone symbol of Philistine power with Adriel. The prank had never occurred to him. It was a spur-of-the-moment act, and though artless in its execution, he could not wait to return home to crow to his fellow soldiers of the insult he and his armor bearer had inflicted upon the mighty Philistine nation.

Jarib stood before a brass plate attached to the center pole of his tent, putting the final touches on his wardrobe. Today the commander's father was to be buried. Since word had been sent forth of Ner's death, a steady stream of representatives from the tribes had begun to trickle into the compound with more expected before the burial that afternoon. He thought Jonathan and Adriel would be home by now. Any number of catastrophes could explain their delay, the direst scenario being the capture or death of the prince, a thought he refused to entertain.

Everyone agreed, it was a dangerous time. The land was filled with spies, bands of nomads, traitors, assassins, all desirous to make coin to capture or ambush the unsuspecting traveler. And then, of course, there were the Philistines. Israel's unremitting sworn enemy would love nothing better than to kidnap a newly minted prince, first ever in the nation of Israel—firstborn of the first king.

Jarib did not approve of sending Jonathan on this spying mission to Geba though he wisely kept this opinion to himself. His advice had not been sought, for he had not yet earned the right to interject a comment on such matters. Jarib believed that Jonathan's recent display of military skill on the training field with his armor bearer was impressive, but also revealed a rash temperament—one needing to be modified with wisdom. A miscalculation by the prince could be fatal. Jarib's firsthand experience at the hands of ruthless enemies had taught him caution. He shuddered to think what might be done to a captured prince.

It was a dangerous time.

Jarib studied his reflection in the shiny brass plate, remembering not so long ago when his face was undamaged, when there was no shriveled mess where his right eye used to be, a time when it could be said he was handsome enough to have turned a lady's head.

Until the invasion of the Ammonites, Jarib had thought his days were set in Jabesh Gilead: the son of a city father of the merchant classes who would pursue the quiet life of a scholar, and one day, have a family of his own. Then the mongrel, King Nahash, gouged out his eye, and half his

world had been plunged into darkness. Jarib knew that the fact that his
eye had been removed by a vicious attack, that his life, his family, and
his city had been unexpectedly threatened with destruction—and then
just as unexpectedly saved from annihilation—would provide a slant to
his perspective on life for the rest of his days. Caution and fear were now
a built-in first reaction for Jarib to every threatening situation. This was
what life had taught him.

He lifted his leather eye patch from the same hook that held the
reflecting brass plate and tied the straps behind his head. Once it was
secure, he adjusted the patch to be sure it covered all the dark red flesh. He
learned a cruel lesson: reality always defeats personal choice. Perhaps clear
inner vision might be of more value than perfect physical sight.

When his military escort called from outside his tent and informed him
that Jonathan and Adriel had just been seen riding into the compound,
Jarib removed the turban from his trunk and placed it snugly upon his
head. He did not bother to check his reflection again but dashed out of
his tent and raced toward the king's compound. The two soldiers assigned
to guard him had to run hard just to keep pace.

Jarib did not see Jonathan or Adriel or their horses as he drew near the
compound.

"Where have they gone?" Jarib demanded breathlessly as he lurched
to a halt before the guards posted in front of the thick gate into the
compound.

"They rode around to the stables," answered one of the sentries.

Jarib bolted away from the gate. The front entry into the compound
had not yet been opened and the walls were too high to see over, so he
could not tell if the king or any of the royal family had risen. It was best
he saw Jonathan before announcing his arrival to the king so he might
remove any potential stress within the family.

"Does the king know the prince has returned?" Jarib asked his armed
escort running beside him toward the stables, but they did not know the
answer to his question.

When Jarib reached the stables, the guards stepped aside to let him
pass.

"I need a moment alone with the prince." Jarib raised his hands for his personal guards not to follow inside the stables. "Please close the doors. No one is to disturb us."

Jarib raced down the center of the stables, looking into the stalls on both sides and calling out the name of the prince. When Jonathan stepped out of a stall at the far end, Jarib ran to him and examined him from head to toe for any injury.

"My lord, you are safely home." Jarib bent over to catch his breath, the feeling of relief flooding over him.

"Is anything the matter, Jarib? You seem anxious." Jonathan clutched the horse's bridle in one hand and placed the other upon Jarib's shoulder and squeezed it.

"Only for the safety of the prince." Jarib's breathing slowly restored. "I sent word over three days ago. I expected you home before now. I feared the worst."

"We have a story for you." Jonathan looked back at Adriel who was removing the blankets from both horses and draping them over a wood railing. "Last night we climbed the 'Tooth of the Rock' pass to the top of the cliff and toppled a sacred pillar at the Philistine outpost above Geba; broke the crown off the top of the pagan column."

If Jarib was expected to give out praise and adulation to this news from the prince regarding his exploit, he would disappoint him. Jarib's response was an intake of breath and then silence. He straightened up and felt his blood rushing through him and his face going hot. He placed his hands on top of his turban as if it were about to blow off his head.

Jarib twisted his torso from side to side and mumbled, "My lord. My lord."

Jonathan looked at Adriel as if he might be able to interpret Jarib's odd behavior, but Adriel seemed as puzzled as Jonathan by this unusual reaction.

"You were sent to Geba to spy, nothing more," Jarib said. "Did anyone see you?"

"Please, Jarib, stop twisting around like that and just talk to me," Jonathan said.

"Did you engage the Philistines?" Jarib obliged the request from

Jonathan to stop moving. He dropped his hands to his side. "Did you attack them?"

"Well, not exactly, but…"

"What do you mean, 'not exactly'?"

"No one died," Adriel said as he moved beside Jonathan.

"Did anyone see you? Anyone recognize you? Oh, my lord."

Jarib could not comprehend all the possible outcomes to Jonathan's action, but none of them were good.

"Take a deep breath." Jonathan griped Jarib's shoulders and held him at arm's length. "We did what we were asked to do, but spying is boring. When we got word of Uncle Ner's death, we did a little reenactment of Samson and the Philistines and knocked over a pagan monument before coming home. But like Adriel said, 'No one died,' so I doubt our prank will have much impact."

"My lord, I beg to differ." Jarib's body still vibrated in spite of Jonathan's grip on his shoulders. "The king and the commander will want to know about this."

"I intend to tell them immediately." Jonathan clapped Jarib's shoulders before he started to go around him.

"My lord, it is not my place to say this to you." Jarib blocked Jonathan from proceeding by moving his body in front of the prince. He knew he was taking a risk with the prince. He knew it might incur his anger, but he feared the king more than the prince. He instantly saw the startled look on the two faces in front of him but continued straight away with his advice. "It is not my place, but I urge you to wait to inform your father. We must bury your Uncle Ner. This is not the time to speak of an act of war."

"Act of war?" Jonathan's amused dismissal to Jarib's characterization of what he and Adriel had done made Jarib realize the prince did not grasp the gravity of the situation. "Who said anything about war?"

"I have said too much." Jarib bowed his head. "Please forgive me, but I beg you not to mention this until after the burial."

Jonathan gave Adriel a puzzled look and then shrugged. "Certainly, I will wait if you think it best," Jonathan replied.

Jarib breathed a sigh of relief when he could tell that Jonathan's excitement to share the story of his accomplishment was beginning to lose some steam. He could imagine the prince and his armor bearer on their ride home repeating the story and looking forward to the soldiers' awed reactions and the countless demands to repeat the story. Jarib knew the prince believed the royal family, especially his father and Abner, would cheer his exploit. Now, Jarib had delayed the joy of telling of this dramatic tale.

"For the sake of the commander, if nothing else." Jarib hoped to soothe the prince and bring his disappointment down gently. "And if it pleases my lord, I suggest you speak to no one of this. And when you do tell the king and the commander, I request that I am present and no one else. Such sensitive information should be for the smallest number of ears."

"Arrange a meeting after my uncle's burial. Adriel and I look forward to giving you all the details. Now, I need a bath."

Jarib bowed as the prince and his armor bearer hustled out of the stables. He had averted an added disruption to the burial activities that stressful morning, but Jarib knew it was only temporary. Before the day was over the king and commander would be forced to react to a circumstance not of their choosing. He knew the prince had no idea of the potential harm his toppling of the Philistine pillar could cause. While Jonathan and Adriel might think that what they had done was the stuff of legends, Jarib knew that such antics could have negative ripple effects and he hoped that it would not lead to an all-out war.

It was a dangerous time.

Chapter 11

SAUL KNELT BESIDE ABNER AND WRAPPED HIS ARMS AROUND him, pressing his broad shoulders and chest against him and holding his cousin as he wept. Abner had kept his emotions from spilling over for the entire day, but in the privacy of the moment, under the cover of darkness, on the roof of Saul's house with just his cousin by his side, Abner crumpled to his knees and bellowed like a wounded beast. Saul did not try to console but groaned as Abner groaned. He wept for his own loss, but his tears flowed in concert with the pain wracking the heart of his cousin. No one could hold the commander in such a way except Saul; cousin to cousin, but more like brother to brother.

"We knew this day would come." Abner gasped then paused to allow for breath so he could speak a simple thought. "We knew this day would come. We have been watching him leave us for months and now he is gone. He is really gone."

A fresh wave of grief flowed out of Abner, and Saul redoubled the strength of his clasp to assure his cousin that this was a moment of shared sorrow. Arm-in-arm, knee-to-knee, chest-to-chest, a moment for his soul to empty its ample heartache in the safety of an embrace.

"This is a strange feeling." Abner sniveled as he pulled back from Saul's tight hold and began wiping away the moisture on his face with his gnarled and powerful hands. "Such a strange feeling."

"What is that, Cousin?"

"I…I do not know how to say it. I have this fatherless feeling…this absence."

"I think I understand such an absence." Saul glanced away from his cousin's wan face and saw Jarib motioning from the gate at the top of the stairs. Jarib held his leather satchel and pointed to it. Jonathan and Adriel stood behind him, and Saul knew this moment of grieving was at an end. There was business that needed his attention, pressing business, or Jarib would not have insisted they meet tonight.

He dabbed his face with his sleeve and rose to his feet, and then raised his hand, signaling for Jarib to wait a moment longer. Saul reached out to his cousin. "They are here, Abner."

"I am a grown man, and I feel lost." Abner leaned heavily upon his cousin's arm. "Where is he, I wonder? Where did he go? He was right here, and now he is gone."

"I will tell Jarib we can do this another time." Saul kept his voice lowered so as not to be heard. "There is no need for this now."

"I must get on with life." Abner pulled his way to his feet with the aid of Saul's strong arm. "I hate this feeling of weakness."

Once Abner got to his feet, Saul looked into his face and Abner nodded that he was ready, so Saul motioned for the three men to join them on the roof.

Saul kept a firm grip on Abner's shoulder and motioned for his son to approach. Jonathan said nothing but hugged Abner before he sat on the long bench in front of the fire blazing inside the large, metal basin. Throughout the day, Saul had stayed close to Abner's side. Merab and Mikal had fastened onto him, one under each arm, and remained affixed for most of the day. Saul knew their support would be a great comfort to Abner; the young women were two living pillars keeping their kinsman from stumbling.

When Adriel gave his commander a sympathetic bow of his head, he sat down next to the prince. Saul motioned for Abner to sit, and then he sat down beside his cousin. Saul was not ready to speak or listen. Everyone stared silently into the crackling fire. It was a relief not to converse. It was a relief for Saul just to let his mind rest and not be required to think of something to say or respond to something spoken.

Jarib was patient, allowing his superiors to initiate the conversation, but no one was even looking as if they might talk. Their faces remained in a trance-like freeze; their eyes glassy with reflection. He did not want to be the first to speak, especially since his report would cause such angst, but as awkward as it was to break the quiet of this moment, Jarib knew the king and the commander must be made aware of this urgent matter.

Beginning at midday and right through the afternoon, Jarib had been able to keep the regular dispatches of the scouts from the king as he and the royal family went about the day greeting those who mourned Ner's death. All the leaders deferred to Jarib's request to wait, all except Beerah, from the tribe of Reuben.

"The news is too dire," Beerah had argued. "The king needs to know at once."

Jarib and Beerah had their argument away from the crowds behind the compound.

"After the high priest has made his final prayers and the family returns from laying Ner's body in the family burial cave, I will inform the king," Jarib told Beerah.

"The king will not be pleased by this," Beerah had insisted. "And I want him to know that I argued for telling him immediately, burial or no."

"He will know all things before he goes to bed tonight. I will take the king's wrath should he so react, and I will tell him of your opinion on the matter." Jarib was learning the dynamic art of dealing with all types of people in his capacity as the king's secretary.

"We know they are on the move," Beerah had said. "What we do not know is why. What has provoked the Fifth Lord to begin moving his troops? Is this just a military drill or a move to threaten us? Will the rest of the Five Lords join the exercise? We must be prepared for the worst. There are many questions to be answered."

"Which is why it is best to wait until we know all the facts, Lord Beerah. The circumstances are changing by the hour. Collect the reports brought in from the scouts regarding troop movement and bring them to me. I will present them to the king, and then I know he will summon all the tribal leaders for their counsel."

Ever the diplomat, Jarib's argument seemed to satisfy Beerah though he stomped around the compound wall out of view like a scolded child. Jarib knew the answer to at least one of Beerah's questions. He knew exactly what had provoked the Fifth Lord's troop movement, and it was the sole reason he wanted to delay telling the king. It was not out of respect for the commander and the death of his father. That was an easy and obvious excuse. Jarib's delaying tactic was solely to protect the prince for as long as possible.

But now Jarib could wait no longer. The tribal leaders were gathering in the military hall behind the family compound out of sight from the rooftop. Each leader would receive copies of the scout's reports to study and discuss while waiting for the king and the commander to join them. Jarib would share the news and do his best to soften the wrath of king and commander should it boil over. He opened his satchel and took out the reports, handing them to Abner for him to read first.

"My lord, I have kept this news from you and the commander until now, out of respect for the events of the day, but I must inform you of the Philistine troop movement along our borders and in the Jordan Valley by the Fifth Lord. We received word shortly after midday, and I have been receiving regular reports since that time."

Jarib tried not to draw attention to the fact that he noticed Jonathan's body begin to tremble, his face registering a painful realization as they all watched the harsh waves of gravity flow over Abner's face while he read the reports.

"Are you sure?" Jonathan asked, a grimace of incomprehension at the possibility of what he might have set in motion plastered on his face.

"The dispatches are in order of their arrival." Jarib ignored the prince keeping his eyes on Abner as he held up each report to the light of the fire, his eyes rapidly scanning the contents of each account. "I had the scribes make copies for the tribal leaders and captains. They are meeting now in the military hall reviewing the information."

"The troop movement is concentrated within the borders of our tribe." Abner finished reading the last dispatch and handed them all to Saul. "This is an affront to the tribe of Benjamin and to you personally, Cousin."

"But what promoted this sudden hostile act?" Saul took the dispatches from Abner but did not bother to read them. "Why should they choose now to—"

"We are not prepared for this." Abner leapt to his feet and began to pace around the fire. "Our training is insufficient. We do not yet have the equipment and weaponry to defend ourselves should the Philistines decide to launch an attack. There are only three thousand men in our standing army. The Philistines have that many chariots alone."

"These are facts we know, Abner." Saul gripped his cousin's arm and held him in place. "But why now? What promoted this action?"

Jarib saw Jonathan reach his hand toward the fire, hold it before the flames as if absorbing its warmth, and then slipped his hand inside his robe, placing it upon his chest.

"Abba, I know the reason for this action." Jonathan rose to his feet.

"My lord, there could be any number of reasons," Jarib quickly interjected, raising his hands for Jonathan to stop speaking. He would do all he could to protect the prince, to temper the reactions of his king and commander. "We should discuss all possibilities."

"Jarib, please." Jonathan removed his hand from his robe and extended it toward Jarib. "I recognize what you are trying to do."

Jarib knew Jonathan was about to confess. He could not stop him. He would not, and it was what he loved about the young man. Jonathan chose to bear the responsibility equally for bravery or for brashness. One day, when the prince would become king, Jarib would be proud to serve him as he had his father.

"Son, what is it?" Saul let the reports slip from his hand and fall to the floor. He knew instinctively whatever information was contained in those dispatches, the question of what had promoted this action was about to be answered.

He stood silent and still as it was vividly recounted, eyes latched onto his son, ears absorbing every word, his mind imagining each detail of the scene. The actions of these impulsive and ambitious young men had threatened desolation upon the tribe of Benjamin that could potentially spread to include the entire nation of Israel. It was too absurd to think a minor prank could spark a war, but this appeared to be where the situation was leading, and at a swift pace.

Saul studied Adriel. The armor bearer had not interrupted Jonathan or tried to offer details that might be less damning to the account. But he rose and stood beside the prince once he finished. This was enough for Saul to know that Adriel declared his complicity in the story. If he were to share in all the dangers of battle, he would also share in the dangers of the displeasure of his king and commander.

"You have made us a stench in the nostrils of the Philistines." Saul raised his head to the sky and took a deep breath as if he was inhaling the stench of combat and the aftermath of the coming battle. It was an honest and pure reaction to Jonathan's tale.

Saul allowed the words to linger in the minds of the five men around the fire. They all knew this day would come, sooner than anyone could have desired, but this day was inevitable. What was also obvious was that the battle of Jabesh Gilead would be horseplay in comparison to confronting the professionally trained and fully equipped army of the Philistines, especially now that Israel had initiated the first strike, a youthful joke with terrible consequences that would be borne by an entire nation.

"If I was going to receive this kind of reaction, I might have killed a few Philistines while I was at it." Jonathan began to step back, but Saul placed his hand upon his shoulder to prevent his son from feeling a creeping isolation in his soul.

"That would have been helpful." Abner was unable to hide his gruff irritation. "At least, we would have faced fewer numbers when they descend upon us like locusts."

Saul bent down and retrieved the dispatches he allowed to slip from his hand and thrust them in front of Abner's face.

"Let all Israel heed my words," Saul said, his voice a cool rumble of boldness enhancing his lack of tolerance for any dissent to his proclamation. There would be no rebuke of his firstborn, not even from his cousin, not even on the day of the burial of his cousin's father, nor would he abide any hostility toward Jonathan on any level.

Saul was decisive and lucid in his edict: "Be very clear about this—a trumpet shall sound, and all Israel shall hear that Saul, no one but Saul, king of Israel, has attacked the Philistine outpost at Geba, and that all Israel has become a stench to the Philistines. Should there be any reproach among our people for this action the blame will rest upon the shoulders of their king."

"Abba, I—"

But Saul silenced his son with a wave of his hand.

"The Philistines have hated us since our fathers crossed the Jordan River. They consider us an abomination and have tried to wipe us out. It is time to meet them with full force. These uncircumcised pagans should fear us; and if not now, then when? The time for armed conflict came sooner than expected, but it was inevitable."

Saul knew Abner was about to explode at what he considered complete folly on the part of Jonathan, but he cut him short, forcing him to take the dispatches from his hand. Saul was mindful of Abner's emotional state and did not want to upbraid him for an honest reaction to his son's recklessness. He simply took charge so as to avoid a regretful dressing-down his cousin did not need.

Once Abner snatched the documents from his fingers with a jarring grunt, Saul addressed his secretary. "Jarib, you say the captains and generals and the tribal leaders are presently holding council in the military hall and await us."

"Yes, my lord."

"All of you join them now. And summon the prophets and priests. Get them out of bed if you have to. I want them present as well. Prepare a plan. We will face the Philistines, and if all this military movement turns into battle, we will fill their nostrils with the stink of their own blood and offal. We are to be feared. We shall no longer tremble like leaves in the wind. Now go, and I will join you shortly."

All four men departed for the stairs, but after a few steps Jonathan alone paused to look back at his father.

"Abba, I—"

"Were you able to get a good look at the Philistine outpost above Geba?"

"Yes."

"And did you count the number of soldiers stationed there?"

"It was dark, but it could not be more than twenty or thirty. There were not enough buildings or tents to accommodate a greater number."

"Good. Then your report will be of value in devising our war plan."

Saul looked at Jonathan and smiled. Small detonations of burning wood crackled inside the metal basin behind them. A thousand words could be spoken between them, but they would be spoken another time, but then in time, such words may not need utterance.

"Are you coming along?" Jonathan asked.

"I must check on your grandfather." Saul nodded for Jonathan to go ahead of him. "It has been a difficult day for him."

Saul watched his son exit the rooftop gate and disappear down the stairs. He felt the chill of relief in his spine and stepped closer to the fire for warmth. He raised his eyes to the heavens and shook his head in wonder.

"He is a gift I dearly prize. Help me keep him. Help me protect him. Help me prepare him."

Saul stood inside the door of Kish's bedroom, holding a bowl of water in his hand and listening to his father's gentle snoring. He still wore his burial clothing of material in shades of black and silver and smudged with lime and spices from carrying the body of his uncle into the family cave. In the dim light of the room, his father looked as if he too was laid out for burial.

A tight corridor separated Kish's room from his brother's. In the weeks leading up to Ner's death, Kish had remained at his brother's bedside feeding him, bathing and changing his undergarments, holding cups to his lips for Ner to slurp down the water, clasping his hand when Ner became fretful and agitated as death gradually claimed its prize.

Now Kish lay asleep on his own bed unaware of Saul's quiet observation. He had not bothered to disrobe or extinguish the flame set on the small table beside his bed. He had been too exhausted. Once the family returned from the burial cave he had stumbled into bed and had immediately fallen asleep.

Saul moved to a stool beside the bed. He placed the clay bowl of water on the table and closed his eyes, listening to Kish's slow, congestive breathing and, after a moment, he and his father were breathing in rhythm. If he sat there long enough, eyes closed in peaceful inhalation, he would be asleep instantly.

When Kish cleared his throat and rolled over, Saul snapped his head up.

"Is anything the matter?" Kish wiped his moist lips with his fingers.

"No. I just brought some water. Would you like a drink?" Saul offered him the bowl.

Kish sipped some of the water then handed the bowl to his son. He sank back into the mattress, his strength drained. The elevated lines on his cheeks and forehead made his features look like a stone crag with a gray and brown patch of beard beneath it.

"I have not been to our burial cave since your mother and baby sister died. I could not go in with you." Kish rubbed his eyes, then focused them on the ceiling. "I thought I could do it, for my brother's sake, but no. It felt like two hands pressed against my chest preventing me from entering."

"I understand. There is no need to explain."

"I remember you used to get in bed with me after your mother and sister died—sleep with me. It was a comfort to us both, I think."

"It was."

"You want to get in bed now?" Kish attempted to scoot over to make room.

"Not sure I would fit, Abba. Grown a little since then."

"You have. How long ago was that, since your mother and baby sister left us?"

"Eons."

"A long time." Kish rested his arm over his forehead. "And how old am I now?"

"Eons."

"My, my. That old...too old." Kish allowed his eyes to close.

It seemed that eons were flying by as Saul sat with his father in the silence of the room. Their breathing, the distant noises from beyond the compound wall, and the small shifts of body weight were the only audible intrusions to his ear. In this calm silence it seemed possible for Saul to solve the mysteries of the world. With enough time, enough thoughtful conversation, he and his father might come to understand the life of a person from non-being to its passage into the primordial shadow land of Sheol. But there was never enough time, never enough thoughtful conversation to share.

"Your uncle and I could talk about everything under the sun. How odd for two men to lose their wives around the same time, leaving two sons to rear on their own. How odd an existence, but we found a way. We had each other, and we held nothing back from each other, not our grief or even our darkest thoughts." Kish lifted his arm from his forehead and reached for Saul. "It just came to me, have I said enough to you, my son? Have I said enough?"

"All I could ever want to hear." Saul patted Kish's arm. "Multiple times."

Their shared amusement caused Kish to choke, and he sat up and drank again from the clay bowl Saul handed to him. When he finished drinking, Saul returned the bowl to the tabletop.

"I must go meet with the tribal leaders before I go to bed."

"That seems unusual at this late hour. Everything—"

"Fine. It is all fine. They were gathered for Uncle Ner's burial, so it was a good opportunity to meet."

Kish lay back on his cushion and stared at his son. "I can tell you are lying, even with my old eyes in this dim light."

"I never could lie to you, Abba." Saul rose from his stool. "Shall I have the servants bring you something to eat?"

"When your uncle's mind began to disappear, he would talk in his sleep. Did you know that? Would not talk when he was awake but would never keep quiet after he went to sleep. Could not understand most of what he

156

said, but he kept me awake most nights with his gibberish. Words here and there about the farm, playing in the olive groves, the wild creatures we tamed and raised, our parents' names, the name of his wife, things like that he would say clearly, the rest unintelligible. And why am I telling you this? Maybe by the end of life all things can be explained with gibberish."

"You sure there is nothing I can send over for you to eat?" Saul grabbed the stool he had been sitting upon.

"Eating now would only make my heart burn and my belly rumble, and I want to sleep. I think I could sleep until I join your uncle…and your mother."

"We will not be hasty about your departure. You have a new grandchild coming."

"And I want to bounce that grandchild on my knee and tell him stories before it all turns to gibberish." Kish's voice was drowsy, his eyelids too heavy to keep open.

Saul tiptoed across the room and set the stool by the door.

"Son." His abrupt whisper prevented Saul from making his exit. "Until Yahweh puts on a human skin, the 'I Am' Father Moses spoke of will always be a great mystery. The religious sort who speak for Yahweh may be right on occasion, but never always right. What I do believe Yahweh got right was choosing you to be king."

Kish never opened his eyes to look at Saul but spoke as if talking in his sleep.

"And that is not gibberish either." Then Kish rolled over to face the wall. "Do not let the tribal leaders keep you out late."

Kish barely uttered the last words before he was taken in by deep slumber, and Saul exited the room, his heart bursting and eager to prove his father's confidence.

Chapter 12

SAMUEL STOOD OUTSIDE HIS FRONT DOOR LEANING UPON HIS walking stick. His eyes were closed as he drew the cold air into his lungs through his wide nostrils in a single, measured breath. Once he had filled his lungs, he exhaled, slow and forceful, his warm breath turning to steam once it hit the cold atmosphere. The deep, methodical breathing each morning helped to clear his brain and his walk up the hill to the Prophet's House got his heart pumping and blood flowing.

He kept his eyes closed but heard his students pouring from their sleeping quarters and milling about in the courtyard before plodding off toward the Prophet's House to begin morning studies. None of the students would disturb his morning ritual. Samuel waited, patient and calm, until he felt her hands squeeze his arm and her head come to rest on his shoulder. Only then did he open his eyes.

"Good morning." Shira patted his shoulder.

"And to you, dear one." Samuel opened his eyes to the bright morning light.

He and Shira looked over the courtyard. They had made some drastic changes. When Samuel decided to stop traveling his judicial circuit and open a school for scribes, scholars and prophets, the barns and stables in front of their house were dismantled and reassembled on the southeastern edge of their land. Those structures were replaced with new buildings: living quarters for students, a hall for meals, an outdoor worship area and a beautiful flower garden courtyard with fruit trees.

The altar Samuel set up in the grove on the hill overlooking their property sat in the space where an old storage shed had been. Samuel and Shira were both tired of the barnyard smells that came with having livestock close to the house, especially in the summer months. A small stable and corral was constructed out of sight behind the house for Shira to keep two horses and park the wagon. There was a twinge of shared wistfulness when they dismantled the stables where Samuel had spent his days writing on the second floor and the two of them had lodged for their seven days of bliss after they married. But it was short lived.

Arm-in-arm they strolled through the gardens, pausing to admire some late blossoming flora that had yet to succumb to the cold weather. They moved out of the courtyard, passed the outdoor gathering place for sacrifice and worship, and continued down the road toward the house built into the side of the hill where Shira had grown up. That was the one structure they had chosen to preserve. They had removed the interior walls and installed support beams making it into one large room for the students to gather for daily lessons.

Samuel did not want to continue to use the space in Ramah to conduct his classes. He and Shira wanted their lives to be self-contained on their property, so they turned Shira's old home into the Prophet's House. Both of them were relieved that the days of travel were over. Now the world could come to them. They both agreed that future separations would be counted in hours, not weeks or months.

"Where are you off to this morning?" Samuel asked as they ambled over to the steps leading up the hill to the Prophet's House.

"The grapes are being pressed. I am riding over to the vats."

"In the wagon," Samuel said, a combination of an admonition and a hope.

"I think I will put a bridle on Moses and ride over."

Samuel wagged his head in dismay and sighed. They had named the gelding and mare Shira kept stabled behind the house Moses and Zipporah after their two dogs of the same name had died. It was a name incarnation worth continuing.

"I am not sure." Samuel tried hard not to influence her decision with his own anxiety about her riding Moses or any horse at her age. "He can have a temper."

"As do most males." Shira gave his nose a tweak before she started backing away toward the house. "Riding keeps me young."

"I just want to keep you alive."

"Go. Your students await." Shira waved him onward to the Prophet's House, then having made her point, started her brisk walk to the stables behind their house.

Samuel knew by the speed of her departure Shira had won again, without even an argument. He had to smile at his defeat and pray Moses was in good humor.

Samuel ascended the steps and paused outside the front door to listen to his students debating the text they had been studying for the last several days. Samuel did not mind debate in its proper context—a classroom setting, among students, an attempt to unpack meaning held within sacred writing. This was the way he had learned as a boy at the Tabernacle in Shiloh when Eli, the high priest, was his teacher. All debate would come to an end at some point, he determined, or no action would be taken, no decision made, no truth established. When he swung open the door, all the students huddled around the large table ceased talking.

"The text." Samuel closed the door behind him. "Read our text from yesterday from the fifth book of the great prophet Moses. All of you read it together."

The students assembled in small groups, the smaller boys stretching their bodies on the expansive table for better viewing of the limited number of copies of the scrolls. At first, they read in discordant, staccato voices trying to find a rhythm. Samuel clapped his hands as he began his plodding march around the table, so his students paused and concentrated their voices to unite in a perfect flow with a beautiful mixture of timbre and tone according to the quality and maturity of their individual ages.

"Remember what the people of Amalek did to you along the way when you came out of Egypt. When you were along the way the people of Amalek came out and smote you while you were on your journey. They cut off all those who were lagging behind, all those who were faint and weary, and they smote them. The people of Amalek did not fear Yahweh. Therefore, it shall be when the Lord your God gives you rest from all your enemies round about in the land Yahweh is giving you for an inheritance; you shall blot out the memory of Amalek from under heaven. Do not forget."

The students did not speak or move once they had finished. Samuel came to a standstill, remaining motionless to allow the quietness in the room to settle.

"Do not forget," he whispered. "Do not forget."

He waited in the quiet for the words of the text to deepen in the boys' hearts.

"I wonder if Yahweh ever forgets." Samuel continued his way around the table. "I wonder, when man forgets, does Yahweh also forget."

He finished circling the table and made his way to the front window that looked out onto the valley below the Prophet's House. He removed the wooden insert from inside the window and a ferocious shaft of light burst into the room as if a tongue of flame had broken free of the sun and shot through the window.

The intensity forced Samuel to shield his eyes by holding up the window insert, and the students gasped at the brightness the shaft discharged into the reverent nature of their darkened sanctum. Once he adjusted his eyes, Samuel leaned the wooden insert against the wall beneath the window and placed his hands on the windowsill. He looked over the valley below and began to speak.

"The great prophet tells the story in his second book—the book of our exodus as slaves from Egypt to the land of promise—that when we were our weakest and most faint, when the vulnerable among us were too weary to travel and unable to keep pace, they chose to strike. It was when the gap between the main column and a contingent of stragglers that consisted of the elderly, women, children and infants, a few guards with inadequate weapons to defend us, it was then they launched their attack. Just like a pack of jackals seeking to separate the weakest from the herd, the Amalekites swooped down upon the weakest of our nation and began their slaughter.

"When Moses received word of the Amalekite attack, he ordered Joshua to choose some men to race back to the end of the procession and defend those stranded in the rear of the convoy. Moses then took Aaron and Hur to the top of a hill to get a view of the battle. The Amalekites were fierce enemies. They are a war-like people who appease their gods by happily offering up their children in the fires of sacrifice, their rituals of worship are nothing more than drunken orgies, and those they capture, they mutilate and enslave. They are no better than cave dwellers, like beasts that lick blood. As long as Moses held his arms in the air the battle favored Israel, but the moment Moses lowered his arms to rest, the tide turned in favor of the Amalekites. So, Moses sat down on a stone and Aaron and Hur stood on either side and held the prophet's arms in the air until Joshua defeated the Amalekite army.

"Yahweh instructed Moses to write the story on a scroll so it would be remembered, and inserting Yahweh's promise, 'I will blot out the memory of Amalek from under heaven.' And Moses built an altar and called it 'Yahweh is my Banner,' for Moses said, 'My hands were lifted up to the throne of Yahweh.' It could also be stated as 'Yahweh is my miracle,' for it was a miracle that Yahweh wrought that day."

Samuel turned from the window and looked back into the room of frozen forms all staring wide-eyed back at him unable to move or swallow, barely able to breathe. The story had the quickening effect on their young minds that Samuel desired.

"The sons and daughters of Israel must never forget." Samuel bent down to pick up the wooden enclosure. "But if they do, be assured Yahweh never forgets."

He was about to put the square wooden frame back into the window when he heard horse's hooves pounding on the road. He thought it must be Shira riding Moses out of the courtyard, giving him the reins, but when he stretched over the windowsill, he saw two riders racing toward the Prophet's House with Shira following.

Samuel squinted in disbelief to see Nathan and Gad riding sleek, proud mounts, not the old nags they rode when departing for Gibeah to serve the king. When they reached the bottom steps, they bounced off the backs of their steeds and bound up the hill. The door almost broke from its fasteners when they burst into the room frightening everyone except Samuel. He was the only one who knew who was entering at such breakneck speed, though he had no idea why. He could only imagine ominous circumstances would cause such haste.

"My lord," gasped Nathan. He began to choke from gulping too much air, and he had to bend over to keep from passing out.

"My lord!" Gad shouted, his rapid panting allowing for a few words between breaths. "The king…has departed for…Gilgal…to war against… the Philistines!"

Nathan stood up and slammed his hand down upon the shoulder of his dear friend. He wanted to deliver at least a portion of this urgent message.

"The king urgently requests my lord come to Gilgal without delay and join him and his army."

By then Shira bolted through the door and stood between the two prophets whose raspy huffing on either side of her sounded like funnels of steam.

Samuel felt the wooden insert slip through his fingers and crash onto the floor. Then he looked down and saw the splintered wood scattered around his misshapen feet.

Saul was perched atop Adara, his beautiful stallion, at the crest of the hill overlooking the plain of Jordan just outside the town of Gilgal. It was as if the sun had not set in this part of the world. The light from the fires stretching as far as he could see kept the darkness of the night from settling over the valley.

Adara pound the ground with a hoof and tried to bolt. Saul had to yank the reins to hold Adara in place. He was sure Adara was reacting to the foreboding pulsating through his own body. Under these present conditions of facing a superior army, a horse would be a swifter means of escape, not a vehicle to ride into battle. His steed saw the blazing world in front of him and the melding bodies of horse and rider shared the quickened fear in the present hour.

"Am I dreaming, Abner?" Saul cocked his head to the right to look at his commander astride his mount.

"If so, then we are dreaming the same dream." Abner shook his head, his voice restrained by the awful view of the expanding size of the enemy camp. "We are not prepared for this."

Saul rested his chest on Adara's neck. "Each night the fires grow in number." The move helped to relax Adara, though it did nothing to calm Saul's heart.

"I was reckless, Abba."

Saul looked at Jonathan who sat on his mount on the opposite side of Saul. Adriel sat next to Jonathan on his own horse. The heart of his son was too great to sluff off the guilt of his actions at the Philistine outpost. Yet it was Saul who had called for action, and he would defend his son and his people no matter the cost.

"At first the fires numbered in the hundreds, now they are impossible to count." Abner swept his arm over their view, taking in the whole plain.

"Abba, I never thought something like this could happen."

"Exactly right," Abner said, twisting around on his horse to look squarely into Jonathan's terrified eyes. "You never stopped to think."

"We must devise a plan, Commander."

Saul turned his head to Adriel. He appreciated his son's armor bearer trying to deflect some of Abner's wrath away from his master, but Saul raised his hand for Adriel to remain silent.

"The voice of reason," Abner grumbled. "Devise a plan. Oh, we have a plan. It is called desertion. All week our *brave* warriors have been slipping out of the camp. You should have devised a plan to stop the prince from his idiotic idea to attack the Philistine outpost in the first place. Then we might not have to devise a plan now."

"I did not mean to provoke a war."

"A war is what we have." Abner again waved his arm over the countless Philistine campfires blazing across the treeless expanse of ground stretched out before them. "You think your little slingshot can stop three thousand Philistine chariots with two charioteers apiece? Not to mention all their foot soldiers. I am sure they will just throw down their arms the moment they see you coming with your double slingshots spinning above your head."

Saul pulled on the reins and began backing Adara off the crest of the hill.

"This is getting us nowhere," Saul said. "We should return to camp and see if the prophet has finally arrived."

Abner spun around and slammed his heels into the sides of his horse. He was too angry to ride back with the others. He knew he would just continue to spew his ill feeling toward Jonathan for his irresponsible behavior and chose to ride back to the camp alone. Abner had a clear sense of right and wrong, foolish and sensible, and it was the rare moment when he apologized for any damage his blunt words or actions might cause another human being. The fact that Saul did not rebuke or stop him from addressing his son in such a harsh manner was a testament to the fact that he was right.

The situation was dire, perhaps even hopeless. Abner had worked hard to train the professional army, and it was much improved over the ragtag group that fought the Ammonites, but they were not yet capable of going against these odds. Abner knew it. Every soldier and tribal leader knew it, and Abner also knew it was why the few thousand soldiers they had been able to assemble at Gilgal on that first day was dwindling at a rapid pace.

Scores slipped out of the camp at night, deserting with no thought to personal dishonor or shame, hiding out in caves and ravines. Abner was sure they hoped and prayed the Philistines might get bored and go home, then these deserters could sneak back to their own homes. Abner could not blame them. His cousin the king and his kingdom would likely be crushed by this imposing Philistine army, wiped out before it had the chance to be established, and the legends would blame him, the commander.

When Saul, Jonathan, and Adriel entered the camp they saw Abner engaged in a heated argument with Gad in front of Saul's tent. Saul used it as the operational base for officers and tribal leaders where they could read together the daily reports of Philistine troop movements and try to formulate a strategy against the insurmountable odds they faced. Saul had hoped Abner would calm down during his ride back to camp, but it appeared not to have helped. He saw Jeush put a hand on Abner's shoulder to try to settle the storm, but the commander knocked it away, and then he grabbed poor Gad by his robes and lifted him off the ground.

"Abner, put Gad down at once!" Saul shouted.

Abner released his hold of Gad's robes. The terrified man dropped to the ground and began to crawl away from the menacing threat like a plump insect.

"Gad, hold." Saul tossed Adara's reins to a soldier. He dismounted and rushed over to where Gad lay trembling on the ground. "Get up, Gad. We must talk."

Saul had to reach down and lift the poor man to his feet by his arm. Once Saul had stabilized Gad on his two legs, he turned to Abner.

"What is the meaning of this, Commander?"

"The prophet still has not shown himself. How many days now have we waited?"

"How many days has it been, Gad?" Saul kept his voice calm, a counterbalance to Abner's inflamed one. "The truth now."

"My lord, this is the evening of the sixth day." Gad's hands trembled as he wiped off the particles of grime and grass from the front of his robes.

"Six days," Abner blurted. "Six days we have waited."

"Has it been six days, Gad?" asked Saul.

"Yes, my lord...this is the sixth day." Gad's body cringed like a dog expecting to be struck by its master. "The prophet instructed us to wait seven days for him to come and present the burnt offering. We have sent word daily informing the prophet of our circumstances and urging haste, but there has been no reply."

"The prophet could crawl from Ramah to our camp in less than a day with both of his legs broken. This is outrageous."

"Careful with your words, Commander." Saul placed himself between his cousin and the prophet.

Saul got no support from tribal leader or soldier for they had stepped away from the commander. They all feared the range of his wrath. Jonathan alone was courageous enough to stand next to his father as a show of support. Saul hoped his son's proximity might bring Abner back from the edge. He watched Adriel move into position next to Jonathan's side, ready to strike if anyone should threaten the prince.

"You are the king. Why do you even bother to consult the prophet?" Abner spoke almost as if it were a plea for reason, for some level of understanding why Saul felt so beholden to Samuel.

"Unity," Saul replied. He could tell his cousin's rage was beginning to plateau. "I am giving him the opportunity to join me."

"He is hostile toward you." Abner funneled his disbelief toward Saul as though his cousin could not see the obvious. "I have seen how he is with you. I have seen how you are around him. No good comes from it."

"It is strange, Abner, I know, but I have affection for the old man." Saul looked back at Gad who was beginning to regain his composure, and so Saul released his hold of him. "I would gladly have his affection in return; but, short of that, I will take his blessing, even if he might be reluctant to give it. That is all I ask. The prophet comes to our encampment, offers a sacrifice to Yahweh before we go into battle, and the men fight with greater confidence, as would I. And should we win, then the prophet might see us with a more favorable eye. We know he was opposed to Israel having a king. My hope is that inclusion will soften his opinion."

Abner looked into Saul's eyes and took a step closer, bringing his voice to a whisper to reduce the number of ears who could hear what he would say. He spoke directly into Saul's ear. "My lord, I believe the prophet looks upon you with contempt and nothing you can do will change that." Abner pulled back to see Saul's reaction.

Saul felt his eyes begin to sharpen into a raw, hurt gaze, but this did not stop Abner from continuing to speak the truth as he viewed it.

"Prophet or no, sacrifice or no, Yahweh or no, the reality is that we face overwhelming odds and are likely to die. My lord, I want an honorable death and not one that is nothing more than an assisted suicide at the hands of the Philistine army."

"I know you do not trust the prophet, but I need him," Saul said, the moisture on his tongue beginning to bubble. "I extend my hand to him for my men and for Israel. I will take his occasional appearances even if they lack any personal affection."

"You show weakness toward men." Abner's whisper turned into a hiss.

"One man, Abner. Just one man. And how can it be considered weakness if I succeed and the prophet embraces me?"

"Because the prophet can see deep into the soul of a man and exact the dark places in his character. I fear he may use this against you."

Saul flinched at Abner's words spoken without hesitation. He had not considered the prophet capable of seeing into the dark corners of his heart and reading his soul.

"What are you saying to me? What are you warning me of?" Saul pushed his cousin for clarity, at the same time, the heat began escaping through his skin and causing an unpleasant ache to shoot down to his legs.

"Do not give the prophet any opportunity to enfeeble the king in his own eyes or in the eyes of Israel. He is in Ramah. Let him stay there."

While his head was lowered slightly, Abner kept his eyes upon him.

Saul returned his cousin's gaze but felt less assured. Abner's words had begun to deflate his strength, and he felt the power drain from him, settling into the soil around his feet. A mirage of a pool formed around him, and he moved his feet as a child testing the limits and consistency of a puddle of mirrored water. Could he have been living in a dream all this time, one he had fabricated?

The victory over the Ammonites, the tribal allegiance that followed, the prophet's lukewarm and guarded endorsement of his kingship, the prospect of another child—all were plausible details contributing to his well-being over the last several months. But now, Abner's logic marked a sudden return of the dark familiar, a realigning of old fears and dreads, a return of what he had known before but in this moment appeared worse.

He felt himself shrinking before the eyes of those standing in his presence, but he resisted the urge to flee. He would defy this mental roar of his soul's intrinsic inferiority rushing around in his head. He would stand against the fear casting its shade over his heart. He existed for a purpose, and he would not yield to the encroachment of insignificance.

"The prophet has been sent for. The prophet is expected. And the prophet will be welcome when he comes," Saul said, his words spoken to reestablish his control.

"If he comes. And what if he does not?"

Saul sensed a more charitable tone coming from Abner. Perhaps his cousin had seen the toll his berating had taken.

"If after seven days, should the prophet not arrive, what will…." Abner was unable to finish his question, and Saul was not forced to give an answer, a reprieve for which he was most grateful.

"My lord, three Philistine raiding parties have struck the surrounding villages. They have hostages from Geba and hold them at the outpost in the cliffs above the town."

Saul spun around to see Beerah and his two sons holding the reins of their horses, standing several paces behind him. He had not heard them ride into camp. He had not heard anything but the beating of his heart and echoes of Abner's words. Now the full volume of external sound crashed into his ears, and he shook his head, waking from his daze. He knew he should respond but was not sure how.

"Geba, you say." Jonathan moved over to the tribal lord. "How many hostages?

"I fear the entire village was taken, my lord." Beerah turned his attention to the prince. "Other border towns in the districts of Ophrah and Shual have been torched and dead bodies scattered about."

"What do you make of this, Beerah?" Saul was now ready to hear.

"The Philistines are overconfident," Beerah answered without faltering. "They do not fear us. They slash and cut us because they do not believe we will retaliate."

"This is what happens when you squat down and do nothing," Abner mumbled low enough for Saul's ear alone.

Saul glared at Abner to silence him, but he directed his question to Beerah. "Anything else, Beerah?"

"As we were returning to the encampment on the road just south of Geba, we intercepted a man we thought might be a spy but turned out to be a resident of Geba who claimed Philistine soldiers came from the garrison on the cliff, raided the village, and took hostages. He said those villagers who escaped had been hiding in the forest. We cannot confirm this report. Night was falling and we needed to return to camp. We did not see it with our own eyes and no one of military rank has gone back to Geba since the hostile action taken against the outpost."

Saul did not believe Beerah's comment cast judgment on the toppling of the sacred pillar, just a characterization. Word had spread among the rank and file of the prince and his armor bearer's rash vandalism at the Philistine garrison. Saul was sure Beerah did not want to indicate any disapproval or reprimand of Jonathan. While Saul knew all young men were prone to rash behavior, this action by his son just happened to cause war to break out.

"This report from Geba should be confirmed," Jonathan said, not addressing Beerah. He was looking directly at Adriel.

Saul instantly sensed the hearts of his son and his armor bearer were quickening.

"Yes, my lord, I shall confirm the report." Beerah spun around ready to fulfill the prince's request for confirmation, but Saul stopped him.

"No one is to leave the encampment tonight. It is too dangerous. We need one more day, a seventh day, and after that we shall know what must be done."

When Jarib rode into camp surrounded by his security detail, Saul temporarily forgot the current predicament and rushed to where the horses had come to a halt. Jarib was not allowed to dismount and bow before the king. Saul was at his side, too eager for his message.

"The child is born? Ahinoam is well?"

"Ahinoam is well, but the child is not born, though the pains have started and the midwives have gathered. Your wife says she will deliver this child before you come home; you are not to worry. Your daughters assured me that the queen is well-attended."

"I should be with her." Saul spoke more to himself than to Jarib.

"My lord, if you think Ahinoam needs you, go to her. We can secure the camp and defend the nation."

Saul looked into the face of Abner. He had spoken to Saul with such thoughtful concern that, at first, he was not sure it was his cousin.

"I have just lost my father. I understand your need to be at her side."

"Thank you, Commander." Saul placed a hand upon his cousin's shoulder. "I will not ask that of you or our men. It was a momentary thought expressed aloud. What would I do at home except be in the way?" Saul looked at the men surrounding him who responded to the king with nods and quiet laughter. "I was not at home for any of the births of my children except for Jonathan." Saul curled his arm around his son's neck and drew him to his side. "That was enough. I gladly yield the birth of a child to the midwives." Saul's amusement allowed the group to enjoy a moment of levity.

"My lord, permission to secure the encampment," Abner said.

"Permission granted, Commander. And have Jeush take some men and leave at once for Ramah. Perhaps an armed escort might get the prophet here a little faster."

To end the day on such a chord was a small blessing for Saul. He knew what every man remaining in the camp knew deep in his heart but would never confess; those warriors who had deserted throughout the last six days were the smart ones. They might be cowards hiding in forests or inside caves surviving on berries and sips of water, but these cowards would still be alive after the Philistines attacked. Whereas the probable outcome for those who remained with him was to have their bones picked clean by the buzzard, the raven, and the jackal. Whether the prophet came on the seventh day or not, this was the last night these men would have on earth. Saul's command gave them the chance to return to their tents to contemplate the short future that lay ahead of them.

When Abner gave the command of dismissal, Jonathan and Adriel returned to their tent. Inside, they laid out the inventory of weaponry on their sleeping mats: bow and arrows, swords, slings, small knives, flints, and smooth, round stones.

"What are you going to tell the king?" asked Adriel as he examined their arsenal.

"Nothing." Jonathan grabbed a handful of stones.

They waited for the camp to be asleep before slipping out of their tent. Jonathan could see his father's tent was dark inside, but in the tent next to it, a lamp still burned.

"Walk our horses to the road," Jonathan whispered. "I will meet you there."

Adriel went behind their tent to untie their horses and lead them out of the encampment while Jonathan slipped across the yard to the tent that still had its light burning. He listened for voices before pulling back the flap, but all he heard was a light snoring. When Jonathan peeked through the tent flap, he saw Gad slumped over onto his table sound asleep. The quill Gad had been using to write with had slipped out of his limp fingers.

Jonathan quietly entered the tent, took the quill, and scribbled a note on the scroll that laid flat beneath the weight of Gad's head. When he had finished, Jonathan slipped out of the tent to join with Adriel.

Chapter 13

THE HIGH-ALTITUDE CLOUDS IN THE WESTERN SKY ABSORBED the violet and orange colors of the setting sun. With every passing moment the colors turned richer, evolving into deeper hues of red then spreading out into the grays of twilight. Saba could not concentrate as he would have liked on the improbable colors reflected on the underbellies of the clouds or how the rich reds and browns of the landscape reflected the sunset's glow. He had to get to the outpost before dark and it was now in sight.

In only a short period, Saba had gone from obscurity to national celebrity. The best thing that could have happened to him as an artist was the toppling of his monument at the garrison at Geba. Lord Namal was always itching for an excuse to declare war and this vandalism had given him the chance to scratch the itch. It was easy to blame the Hebrews and get the instant, unified support of the other lords and from the general population. Hatred toward Israel was endemic requiring little provocation to justify war.

The day after the incident at the Geba outpost, two chariots arrived at his shop. He rode with the military officer to the Temple of Baal where he was greeted by Lord Namal who was huffing with righteous indignation at this affront to his god, vowing that this national humiliation would not go unpunished. Flanked by his generals, they hustled through the huge doors of the temple to the portico. There stood Saba beside Lord Namal as he announced to the city's populace that Lord Namal and the other lords would exact revenge upon the Hebrews for the sake of the Philistine people and their gods. Then he turned and embraced Saba before the cheering crowd.

Saba did not care that he had been used as a prop for Namal's show. He had been raised from the dead. Now Aphek's art patrons, temple priests, and wealthy politicians would commission him for new creations. Perhaps Lord Namal would come to his shop like his father before him and request a full-length stone statue of Baal to reside in his palace. The famine of employment was coming to an end, and he could feel a sense of pride being restored to his soul.

Once the Philistine generals ordered troop movements, reinforcements were sent to the outpost along with word to the disgraced sergeant in command of the garrison to expect the arrival of the artist to collect the fallen monument. When the nation went to war, the military commandeered all resources deemed vital, and the first to go were horses and transport vehicles. Saba was fortunate to secure two nags and a wagon of questionable reliability. The owner of the stable recognized Saba after seeing him next to Lord Namal on the temple portico. He rented him the wagon and team for a reduced price; the first windfall Saba received for his newfound celebrity. He would toss an extra coin from his first commission into the temple treasury in appreciation for Baal's favor.

Before he departed Aphek, Saba was presented a document bearing the seal of Lord Namal, verifying his identity and stating the purpose of his mission. The document was sufficient to get him through the numerous checkpoints along the rutted, uneven highway to Geba.

When Saba pulled the wagon off the road, he noticed that the crumbling disrepair of facades of the military buildings had now been refurbished and the grounds cleaned of all debris. Even the fire pit where he had seen animal carcasses strewn about had been filled in and a new one dug behind the stables. The number of soldiers had doubled since he had last been there, all busy with preparations for an expected battle.

The horses trotted around the corral while soldiers cleaned the stables. Spears were stacked upright in orderly towers for quick access. Shields were polished and swords sharpened. Archers took target practice, firing at straw dummies hung on the side of the barracks. Two-man patrols traversed the edge of the cliff, on the lookout for signs of the enemy. There was no evidence of courtesans having ever been on the premises.

The sergeant standing in front of the stables overseeing its cleaning looked up as Saba came to a stop beside his fallen monument. He barked an order at the men, then ran across the ground and stopped beside the wagon, preventing Saba from climbing down.

"My lord, let me offer my apologies." The sergeant saluted the artist in a rapid beating of his chest with his opened right hand. "My men will help you load the sacred pillar into your wagon, and I shall assign a proper escort to see that you and the monument return safely to Aphek. I insist you sleep in my quarters tonight."

This same sergeant who greeted him when he delivered the column, intoxicated and half-naked, was now clothed and sober, with a sharpness of mind heightened by the potential for war, and most likely, Saba thought, a prospect of severe personal discipline. At one time, the sergeant may have considered his outpost at the edge of "the bowels of the earth," but, after the toppling, he found the eyes of the nation upon him, and his negligence the cause for marshaling thousands of troops from peacetime to a war footing. The loss of his rank, his job, and his head were distinct possibilities. Saba eyed the garrison. The "bowels of the earth" was never so pristine. What a difference an act of vandalism could make.

Saba had enough light to examine the damage. The capital had not completely broken away from the column, but the crack around its neck was deep enough that he decided to chisel it off and carry the monument back to Aphek in two pieces.

"I intend to cut through the neck of the pillar," Saba explained to the sergeant. "It could take some time and it is near dark. I will work through the night, so I need torchlight. At dawn, we can load the two pieces into the wagon. I want to return to Aphek as soon as possible."

By the time the sky had darkened, Saba had unpacked his tools and arranged them at his station, devoured a plate of hot food, and arranged four torches around his worksite. The sergeant saw that Saba's team of horses were fed and watered, then ordered three soldiers to stand guard around the fallen pillar while a fourth was told to assist the artist in whatever he needed. Saba could get used to this special treatment.

In the late hours of the night, Jonathan and Adriel led their horses off the road and moved quietly through the forest until they came in behind the village of Geba and hid the horses in the community stables. They went from house to house to be sure no villagers were hiding in their homes or that some Philistine soldiers had stayed behind to hold the village after taking their hostages. Geba was completely depopulated, even of all domestic animals, except for a few stray dogs gnawing on the carcass of a dead goat.

When Jonathan stood in front of the charred remains of the home of the family who had sheltered them during their spying mission, the dire consequences of his prank to topple the Philistine monument once again began to oppress his heart.

After they had fed and watered their horses, Jonathan and Adriel climbed upon the roof of the stable. From that position they could see the firelight on the cliffs above and the obscure forms of soldiers moving along its jagged edge. They watched for some time in silence. Then they spread their armaments over the rooftop.

"I am sure they have reinforced the garrison." Jonathan kept his voice low.

"That is to be expected. Do you have a plan?" asked Adriel.

"Not to get killed."

"Good plan." Adriel took a sip of water from his water pouch. He pulled the arrows from his quiver and began to test the twine securing the arrowhead to the shaft. "What if we attacked now, use the element of surprise and darkness to our advantage?"

"I would think they would be more alert at night for those very reasons and more soldiers would be on patrol." Jonathan laid out the number of rocks he had in his pouch. "I want to have clear vision. And I want the Philistines to see who is attacking them."

"If they have reinforced the garrison, there could be twice as many soldiers as before." Adriel pointed toward the cliff top.

Jonathan did not respond to Adriel. He continued to count the number of stones he had collected and tossed away those he found unacceptable. Jonathan did not want Adriel to detect the fear in his heart. He must stay focused and prepared for the task at hand.

"My lord, we could go back to camp and ask a few more to join us. There would be plenty who would volunteer."

Jonathan detected the tremors of fear in Adriel's voice that mirrored his own, but he knew that to return to the camp was out of the question.

"I would never ask anyone to be a part of this, not even you, Adriel." Jonathan bounced a stone in his hand and then rubbed his fingers over it. He judged it inferior and threw it over his shoulder. "It was my decision to knock over the sacred pillar, and here we are with the Philistines gathered against us. My father and Abner have been unable to keep our army from falling apart this week. That has been difficult to watch, especially since I am the cause. We may be defeated, but it is my intention to make the Philistines pay a price for raiding our villages and taking hostages."

Jonathan kept his voice calm and determined. He had been attentive all week. He endured the hostility of the commander with quiet resignation. He did not try to defend his actions to the other soldiers or to the tribal leaders who spoke openly against the prince. He had accepted his father's tacit disappointment. He had watched the tension between his father and the commander rise as they counted their forces each day, discovering more and more soldiers melting away into the wilderness as it became clear there was no conceivable way the army of Israel could go against the superior forces of the Philistines and win.

The anger of an entire army, even the nation, was directed toward him, and he absorbed it without complaint or by responding with antagonism against them. Whatever was to happen in the light of dawn, the moment he left the camp with Adriel, Jonathan was resolved to engage the enemy.

"I understand, my lord." Adriel rubbed his chest with the heel of his hand.

"You do not have to do this." Jonathan sensed his armor bearer might be questioning his sanity, though Adriel had not shown any hesitation or expressed any doubts in his determination. "I will not force you, and will not blame you if—"

"My lord, I am your armor bearer," Adriel interrupted. "I have sworn—"

"You did not swear to bear arms for a fool." Jonathan tapped his head with both his hands as if in question of his sanity. Both men softly chuckled. "Here is what I think, Adriel. It matters not how many Philistines are at the garrison. Whatever the number, few or many, the numbers mean nothing to Yahweh. If the Almighty acts on our behalf, we will be saved from one hundred Philistines."

Jonathan paused for Adriel to respond, perhaps to even question the reasoning behind his theology. Was it not he who had chosen to topple the monument? Was he not the cause for the marshaling of two opposing armies? Why did Jonathan feel he must rationalize his fatal prank by hoping that Yahweh might show favor toward his decision to make things right with his father, his kinsman, his fellow soldiers, and yes, the citizens of his nation? His armor bearer was patient and silent.

"My hope is to find the hostages and free them if they are still alive. So here is my plan: at dawn, I am going to stand at the base of the 'Tooth of the Rock' in full view of the Philistines. Once they see me, if they tell me to wait, I will stay until they come down the pass and capture me. But if they say, 'Come up to us,' then I will take that as a sign that Yahweh has given them into my hands, and I will make my ascent."

"Our hands," Adriel whispered.

"What did you say?" Jonathan wanted to be sure of what he heard.

"Our hands. Yahweh has given them into our hands."

"I told you, you did not have to do this. I cannot ask you to risk your life."

"You are testing Yahweh."

"Yes, I am testing Yahweh. This is my way of casting the sacred stones of the high priest. The way Yahweh chose my father to be king over anyone else."

Jonathan watched as his armor bearer gave a final inspection of all his arrows; the feathered fetching around the nock of each arrow was secure.

Adriel tested the flexibility of his bow and the strength of the cord. His sword was sharp enough to shave his face. He scooped up the arrows and dropped them into his quiver and then stood and faced the eastern mountains.

"The sky is beginning to show signs of light, my lord. If we leave now, we can be in place by the time the sun crests the mountains."

Jonathan rose and slipped his arms into a leather harness that held his sheath and sword in the middle of his back. He next strapped a belt around his waist, then attached his pouch of stones on the front of his belt. He had four slings. Two he tucked inside the belt behind his back, the other two he held in his hands.

"Adriel, do you think it is wrong of me to test Yahweh in this way?"

"My lord, whatever you have in mind, I am with you heart and soul."

His armor bearer had chosen not to question him. He had chosen loyalty instead. He had chosen trust. For Jonathan, the confidence of Adriel was an intangible asset beyond measure that bolstered his heart.

The sound of growling caught their attention. They looked down from the stable roof and saw three jackals poised on top of the village wall trying to scare the dogs away from feasting on the dead goat. They did not need the noise of a conflict between dog and jackal fighting over a carcass to draw the attention of the enemy before they were in place. Adriel loaded an arrow and bent onto one knee at the edge of the roof and drew back his bow. Jonathan put a stone in each sling and stepped behind him.

"I have the one in the middle," Adriel said as he took aim.

"On my call." Jonathan began to spin his slings on either side.

When the slings were at the height of their spin, Jonathan whispered, "now" and let fly both stones, then Adriel immediately released his arrow.

The two jackals on the outside were knocked backward off the wall by the force of the stones striking their skulls. The jackal in the middle jerked his head up at the two humans on the roof, its mouth open to yelp but instead was unexpectedly choked by a gush of blood in its throat. Its legs gave way, dropping where it stood on top of the wall.

Saba had worked through most of the night until he had separated the capital from the column without doing any more damage to the pillar. Baal had lost a portion of his headdress in the process, but Saba was pleased with how he had been able to make a fine cut. He collapsed in exhaustion a few hours before dawn with the guards still positioned at their posts. By the time he had given in to fatigue, he was no longer able to grip the hammer and chisels; he could not uncurl his fingers. He asked the soldier who had acted as his apprentice to awaken him at first light, and then he crawled into the bed of his wagon and fell asleep the instant his eyes closed.

He could not believe how his muscles ached, the intense stiffness in his back, the inflexibility of his fingers, the pounding in his head when the soldier-apprentice roused him at dawn. The explanation was simple: his body had been bent in contorted positions throughout the night as he worked around the column, and he had slept on a hard surface. He would break his fast with a bowl of last night's stew, have his guards load the two pieces into the bed, have his team of horses hitched onto the wagon's tongue, and be on the road by midmorning. If the gods looked on him with favor and war had not broken out, he could get through all the checkpoints and be back in Aphek by nightfall. Once he got his monument safely inside his shop, he would sleep for a week.

What he did not understand was the cause for all the shouting and why the soldier-apprentice was yelling at him. The young soldier craned his neck around the side slats of the wagon, looking in the direction of the cliffs and then looked back at Saba with a face of horrified panic, his skin turning a lurid color. Saba was slow to react. He could hear the intense volume of human shouting, but it was unintelligible. He raised his head slightly. He could not see through the slats of the wagon on either side of where he lay, and his view was blocked from the front by the driver's seat. He could only see the three guards who had stood faithfully all night at the back of the wagon raise their spears and start screaming as they bolted away from their positions.

Sleep instantly vanished from Saba's brain, and he sat up. When the soldier-apprentice withdrew his sword and motioned for Saba to stay in the wagon, he knew something terrible must be happening. Saba ignored the warning and scooted to the edge of the bed. Before he stood, he watched the soldier-apprentice step away from the wagon onto the road and look toward the cliffs.

Saba blinked his eyes and saw an arrow strike the soldier's throat. He dropped his sword, gripping the feathered end of the shaft as he fell backward, his lips opening and closing like the mouth of a fish. Saba threw himself out of the wagon and leapt over the column. All the pain in his body had disappeared; his mind was clear. He grabbed his hammer and chisel and crouched behind the capital.

From his position behind the monument, he had an unobstructed view of the chaos. Bodies lay strewn in the open area, most lying still, but a few attempted to crawl. Some of the soldiers rode away on horseback, racing out of the garrison onto the road toward Aphek. Two strange-looking men, one an archer, the other with sword and sling appeared to be the ones causing this mayhem.

Saba heard weeping and screams and saw a group of people bound together with rope being ordered by the sergeant from one of the smaller outbuildings. He was shocked to see two other soldiers dragging women and children and a few men out the door. He had no idea who they were or why they were being used as human shields. The sergeant drew his sword and maneuvered into the middle of the prisoners while the two Philistine soldiers got behind the huddled group, forcing them at spear point toward the two foreign fighters responsible for the slaughter of so many of their comrades.

The hostages and their captors paused in the open area between the road and the barracks. As far as Saba could tell, the sergeant and two soldiers were the last of the Philistine combatants. The rest were dead, dying, or had fled in panic. Neither the Philistines nor the two warriors advanced toward the other. The hostages were in tears and howling in fear, but when the foreign warrior holding the two slings shouted at them in their own language, the hostages became silent. The women in the group hushed the children.

There were a handful of wounded Philistines who moaned and whimpered as they lay on the ground. The slinger and his archer companion took out their swords and went from soldier to soldier, thrusting the point of their swords into each one until they no longer moved or made a sound.

At the sight of the two fighters finishing off his comrades in such a cruel way, the sergeant picked up a young girl in the middle of the group and held the blade of his sword under her neck. The terrorized young girl burst into tears. The other two soldiers were ready to thrust their spears into a hostage at the slightest provocation. The sergeant began to shout at the foreign fighters, "Our lives for theirs! Our lives for theirs!" But the two warriors did not appear to understand the sergeant's bargain. A language barrier would certainly explain this, but what Saba could not explain was the sight of the two fighters returning their swords to their sheaths and turning to walk back toward the cliff.

Saba rose to his feet and stepped over the column onto the road. At first, he thought these two fighters must be part of a nomadic band who happened to be expert in combat or just very lucky to have killed these many soldiers without so much as a scratch. They wore no uniform identifying them, just common clothes. But when the slinger had silenced the hostages, Saba knew these two must be Hebrews. The hostages began to implore the warriors to save them, and the sergeant shouted more forcefully that all of them would die if they did not comply with their demand of a life for a life.

When it happened, it happened so fast Saba mistrusted his eyesight. Pulling free of the ropes that had bound them, the women and children ran toward the two warriors who had whirled around—the archer on one knee, his empty bow still in his left hand and the slinger behind him, an empty sling dangling from each hand. The two Philistine spearmen were lying unconscious on the ground from a stone smashing into their skull.

Two male hostages each grabbed a spear from the fallen Philistine soldiers and began to drive the spear point into their chests. There was no need to exert any effort with the sergeant. He lay lifeless on the ground with the fletched end of an arrow protruding from his right eye. Within moments, life for Saba had moved beyond his control. He had no power to stop it, no words to define it, no mind to comprehend it. The world before him was chaotic, terrifying, and drenched in blood.

Then unexpectedly, everyone left alive was looking at him, pointing and shouting in his direction. It was unbelievable to Saba that these strangers were making him the center of attention. The slinger began to advance toward him, a single sling whirling above his head. Saba raised the hammer in his right hand, but it flew out of his hand with a force that was not his own. It was an outside force, a violent, hostile force, meant to disable.

Saba dropped the chisel in his other hand and pulled his damaged hand against his chest as he fell backward to the ground. The slinger continued to advance, drawing his sword from behind his back. Saba struggled along the ground in full retreat until he backed into his column and could go no farther. At least he would die beside one of his creations. At least he would die knowing his status in Aphek had been restored. At least he would die having devoted his whole life to the work he had loved.

Saba raised his arm, a reflexive action against the drawn sword, and shouted one word: "Artist!" He repeated the word a second and third time and saw the slinger hesitate, his eminent slaying on hold, and in that split second Saba extended his arm over the column, and with his good hand, began to pound the image of Baal holding the lightning bolt.

"Artist! Artist! Artist!"

Saba could not tell if the slinger understood, for he did not respond, nor did he even repeat the word Saba shouted in his native language. But Saba did perceive a gradual deflation in the slinger's killer stance as his body began to contract, the raised sword above his head in slow descent until it rested at his side.

The slinger stepped over to the column and ran his fingers over the image of Baal and then looked back at Saba. The slinger spoke the word Saba had spoken as if he was beginning to make the connection, so Saba touched the image of Baal and then tapped his chest identifying himself as the creator.

"Artist," he said, this time with pride not quaking fear as if this would be the last word he would ever utter. "Artist."

The slinger straightened his back and returned his sword inside its sheath. The slinger turned and shouted something Saba did not understand to his companion standing with the hostages. The archer warrior then spoke to the group before he trotted over to join the slinger.

The hostages dispersed immediately and began to strip the dead and enter the buildings in search for anything worth taking.

When the archer approached, the slinger pointed to Saba and then to the column and capital and spoke in their native tongue. Saba could see the eyes of the archer begin to widen as if Saba were the object of a revelation. Then he bent down and extended a hand to Saba. Saba allowed himself to be lifted to his feet and guided over to the middle of the road. Then the two foreign fighters got on either end of the column and lifted it off the ground. They grunted and huffed, muscles in their arms and legs distending in bold mounds as they struggled to place it in the wagon bed. They did the same with the capital, pushing it to the middle of the wagon next to the column, and then tied off both pieces with the rope Saba brought from his shop.

The slinger curled his bottom lip under and gave a sharp whistle. When the hostages appeared in the doorway of the barracks, arms full of blankets and clothing, he waved for them to follow, and he began to jog toward the stables.

The archer knelt down beside the soldier-apprentice lying dead in the road, removed the arrow from his throat, and stuck it beneath his arm. Then he untied the dead soldier's breastplate and tossed it aside. He cut away two strips of the dead soldier's undergarment with his knife and draped them over his shoulder. The archer warrior pointed for Saba to sit on the edge of the wagon, and when he did so, he gently took Saba's injured hand and stretched out his arm. He made a motion for Saba to open his mouth.

The archer placed the arrow between Saba's lips and motioned for him to clamp his teeth down upon the shaft. Saba did all that was asked of him. The archer began kneading Saba's injured hand with his fingers, and Saba instantly bit down on the shaft of the arrow, grunting with agony. Had he not been seated on the end of the wagon he would have crumpled to the ground. It was as if a knife had been plunged into his wrist, and everything went black.

When Saba opened his eyes, he was lying over the column, his injured hand had been wrapped in one strip of cloth and his arm was held to his side with the other strip of cloth tied over his shoulder. He carefully wiggled his fingers and was grateful to see them move, though the motion was slight and painful. Tucked inside his arm sling was a small scroll. He unrolled it and found a few Hebrew words scratched upon it. He would have it translated once he returned to Aphek. He poked the scroll back inside his sling. Next to him was a cloth pouch containing scraps of bread and chunks of pork. In his lap was a skin of water. He had a raging thirst, so he pulled the stopper from the skin with his teeth and began guzzling down the hot liquid.

After he had quenched his thirst, he realized how quiet it was, that he heard no human voices; all he heard was a light wind blowing and the snorting of horses. He placed the water skin beside the food pouch and got onto his weak legs. He cautiously peered around the slats of the wagon. No living humans were in his field of vision, not the two foreign fighters, not the hostages, only dead Philistine soldiers stripped naked, exposed to the elements.

Overhead the vultures were gathering. The anxious neighing of horses brought Saba's attention away from the vultures circling above him and directed his eyes to the opposite end of the wagon where he saw his team hitched and ready to depart. The team of horses were reacting to the scene of dead soldiers and a flock of carrion eaters, which prompted Saba with the need for them to depart.

Saba could not believe his fortune. No one would believe his story. He did not believe his story, and no matter how often he might repeat it and how faithful he might be to the truth, he knew any listener would shake their head in disbelief. And for that very reason he might never speak of this to anyone. Saba looked back at his carved image of Baal chiseled into the column. In his mind, this fleeting and terrifying moment, seeing the god of the Philistines lying frozen on his side in the wagon, lightning bolt held tightly, his headdress a jagged cut, Baal seemed such a puny god.

Chapter 14

ON THE MORNING OF THE SEVENTH DAY, SAUL HAD HIS CHAIR and tables removed from his tent and set in the opening at the entrance of the encampment bivouacked just off the southern road on the outskirts of Gilgal at the edge of the plains of the Jordan. Two of the tables were set with food and drink. The others held a splay of drawings of the local terrain and stacks of reports. Gad and Jarib sat at the smallest table, going over all the written records of the events that had transpired over the last week.

Saul met with Abner and his officers out in the open, conducting all discussions in full view of the camp. He was determined that the prophet would not see him hiding in his tent anxious and paralyzed by fear over his deteriorating army and eminent demise at the hands of the Philistines. Saul wanted the prophet to see him actively engaged in preparations for battle. And while he wanted the prophet to feel welcome and to know that his leadership and involvement was still of vital importance to him and the nation of Israel, Saul wanted to give no impression of weakness that the prophet might be tempted to justify any leftover antagonism he may harbor for having to share power with someone he initially opposed.

Saul instructed Ahiah to have his priests build the altar in the center of the camp with dried wood laid upon it and the animals penned next to it ready to be sacrificed for the prescribed offerings. This was to be a full sacrifice so the fire had to be intense and fast to consume the carcass, leaving nothing but ash. The laver for the ceremonial washings should be filled, the seven-branched lamp stand and table for the sacred bread should be set up, the incense should be wafting into the air, and Ahiah, and the priests who would aid the prophet in making the burnt offerings, should be dressed and waiting before the altar. Saul wanted everything in place and arranged. The moment the prophet arrived in the camp he was to be taken to the altar to perform the sacrifice. There was no time to spare.

Saul instructed Abner to have the remaining soldiers break camp and load all the tents and supplies onto the transport wagons with the teams of mules hitched and ready for departure. This was the seventh day. This was the day of decision. With or without the prophet, Saul wanted Abner to order his army to move out. They would make their escape or launch their own fatal offensive, but either way, they would not stay in one spot any longer and let the Philistines come in and slaughter them in their tents.

Saul dispatched Jeush the night before with a dozen men to furnish protection and to escort Samuel on their short journey from Ramah. Saul hoped this might apply some pressure on the prophet to pry him from his home and get him on the road to the encampment. If they left Ramah at dawn and pushed hard, which Jeush had been ordered to do, the contingent would arrive by midmorning. If they took an easier pace or encountered unexpected delays, they should arrive by midafternoon. If the prophet were being irascible, refusing to arrive until the last minute they would arrive by twilight when, at that point, it would be too late. Given the volatility of the situation and the prophet's opaque and fallible attitude toward him, anything could happen.

What Saul knew to be factual in the present reality was that the Philistines had assembled to destroy him, that in this week the numbers of the enemy army had multiplied to such an extent that his scouts had quit trying to report an accurate number and given over to hyperbole: "as numerous as the sand on the seashore." There also remained the fact that Saul's own forces were deserting him in droves.

But Saul waited, as he said he would, waiting the full seven days as designated by the prophet. He could do no less, and should Samuel arrive late or not show at all, Saul would have kept his word. But it was a struggle to remain calm before his men. It was a struggle to believe that the prophet would arrive on time if he arrived at all. Why had he been put in such a position when it could have been so easy for him to get here?

By midafternoon, Saul could not sit, he could not eat, he could not listen to another updated report of the Philistines' growing ranks and his own dwindling forces—down to six hundred at last report with rumors of some of his soldiers defecting to the enemy—or learn of another town and village on Israel's borders attacked by a Philistine raiding party. And most of all, he could not bear to look his cousin in the eye. He did not want to confront Abner's glare of contempt. In the turmoil of indecision, Saul paced around his chair and conference tables, anxious for any hopeful signs of the prophet and his party rumbling down the road.

This was the very place where the prophet had reaffirmed his kingship. It was here on the outskirts of Gilgal, the ground he paced upon, where the people had gathered after his victory over the Ammonites. This ground had significance. Saul was confirmed as king here, and not just any king, but the first king of Israel, and a victorious one at that. The tribes had sworn fealty to him on this ground. There were celebrations honoring him, and sacrifices made. It was a time for Israel to rejoice for this new regime.

It was here in Gilgal where the prophet had given his farewell speech before the people, passing his power over to him. It was here the prophet had appeared in public for the last time, and it was the last time king and prophet had stood face-to-face. It was on this ground Saul was given command to rule. So why should he not take strength from that affirmation? He was chosen, by Yahweh, so why could he not embrace that choice here in this moment of crisis? Be the leader that he was expected to be? Be the leader he was chosen to be, anointed to be? The leader so many in Israel believed him to be?

Still Saul had to contend with the prophet. He could not break free of the prophet, trust his own judgment, trust his own ability to make decisions. Saul never felt at ease with Samuel. He never fully believed that

Samuel was committed to him like his family or his tribe. Yes, the prophet said he would always pray for him, but Saul wanted more than prayers. He wanted more than just Samuel's student prophets relaying messages to him or acting as surrogates. He needed the presence of the prophet by his side, but if he was not going to show himself, perhaps it was time to take the bold step to break free of the prophet's hold. And what better place to take that step than here on this ground where all of Israel had proclaimed him as king? How long must he wait for this old man?

Saul marched into the middle of the road and looked south to the vanishing point on the horizon. In the brightness of the afternoon sun, there was not even the faint blurry image of a dust cloud that might indicate an envoy heading in his direction. He turned around and looked north for no reason other than he was tired of looking at the empty landscape the south offered and needed to set his eyes somewhere different. He then looked up into the blue sky. The last time he was here, with all of Israel celebrating his kingship, the prophet had caused a little cloudburst to rain all over the celebrations. In Saul's present state of mind, it seemed to him to be the prophet's way of forcing him into a perpetual subservient role. Samuel should have just slipped quietly away and allowed Saul to take over and rule.

When Saul turned back toward his camp, there was very little movement; talk was muted. Most everyone avoided eye contact with him, respecting the isolation of his position. These men were loyal. These men stood with him. These men were present when the rest of his ranks proved craven. This had become a nightmare, but in that instant, he made the decision to fight his way out of it with these men, and he marched back into the camp without even glancing one last time in the southern direction.

"Gad, the time is past for the prophet to be here," Saul stated as he reentered the encampment. He was in no mood for second-guessing.

"Yes, my lord," Gad answered, taking a step back at Saul's bold approach.

"He requested seven days. I have given him seven days, have I not?"

He and Gad both knew the answer, but Saul needed for it to be stated publicly to all who were assembled. There must be no confusion about this fact. Any deviation from this fact would be inaccurate and based on rumor. Seven days fixed. Seven days given. It was time to act.

"Yes, my lord. The length of time to wait was seven days," Gad confirmed. "And this is the seventh day."

Saul could tell by Gad's quivering face that the young prophet was fearful of the potential dire consequences of the decision Saul was about to announce. But the hour was past, long past. If the prophet and Yahweh were too indifferent to his plight, then it was time to assert himself and take matters into his own hands.

"Jarib, for seven days there has been murmuring in the camp." Saul projected strength to every pair of ears in the vicinity. He had spun away from doubt and fear and embraced the liberation of a clear mind. "What is the gist of the complaints? Speak loud-mouthed, Jarib. Do not withdraw from the truth. I want every brave soul in this camp to hear what you say."

Jarib's shocked expression made Saul smile. He knew his secretary did not want to humiliate him in front of the soldiers. Jarib rose from his seat, and when Saul motioned for him to face the whole encampment, he obeyed.

"The main point of grievance against the king is that you are not long into your crown, and you are always leading us to war."

"This is true, Jarib. I am." Saul went over and stood by his secretary. "And I am sure every one of those pigeon-hearted souls who hold to that belief presently hides in caves and thickets or has run home, too afraid to face what might lie ahead. I am thankful that our camp has been cleansed of these gutless pretenders with their short memories. It was for this reason that all of Israel cried out for a king...to fight their bloody wars for them, yet when the time comes to fight, all they do is complain and take cover. I do not want to be king to murmuring cowards. I do not want to go into battle with those who shrink to save their own skins and let someone else do the fighting.

"I have been faithful to wait the seven days required by the prophet to come and offer a sacrifice before going into battle. I have waited those seven days and beyond, and the prophet has not come. We do not know the reason for his absence. Perhaps he is ill, or his party has had some trouble along the way. As much as I would like to have the prophet's blessing before we confront our enemies and for him to be here to conduct this ceremony, the time is at hand. Ahiah, I ask you, is it against the rituals and customs of the law of the great prophet Moses for me to offer this burnt offering?"

"No, my lord," Ahiah answered. "The priestly line has no exclusive right to perform sacrifices. The fathers of families have offered the sacrifices. The chiefs of clans have offered the sacrifices. And today, the high priest and the guardian of the Ark stand with you as covering as you seek the blessing of Yahweh."

"And it is Yahweh's blessing that I seek above all else," Saul exclaimed. "It is for the favor of Yahweh that we make the sacrifice. It is to honor the Almighty that we make burnt offerings. Ahiah, choose a lamb for slaughter. Abner, have my armor brought to the altar. As soon as the sacrifice is made, I want to dress for battle."

No one could put forth that this was an impulsive act. No one could accuse Saul of being impatient. No one could suspect him of trying to usurp the authority of the prophet. The prophet should have been here to wield his authority.

The camp went into action; a fresh energy had been restored to each heart, expelling the lethargy, a unified shout of defiance crackling in the air above them. The soldiers and priests who had remained in the camp for the week had been unable to function. They had absorbed the foreboding and inaction of the king. When Saul cut himself free from the grip of fear, everyone came to life.

"My sovereign lord."

Saul turned and looked into Gad's enlarged frightened eyes, then he approached the young prophet.

"Do you think it wise…do you think…" But Gad was unable to finish.

"Your heart is torn, Gad, I know. You see the reality around us, but feel my action is a betrayal of faith. I know you would have counseled against this." Saul placed his hand upon Gad's shoulder, a gesture to bolster the young prophet not to reproach. "I know you have concerns. You are true to your master, I understand. Do not fear. All will be well, my son."

He balled his fingers into a fist and tapped Gad's arm, then scanned the encampment. "Speaking of my son, have you seen Jonathan?" When Gad did not answer, Saul looked back at him, and this time firmly grasped the spot on his shoulder he had just affirmed. "What are you not telling me?"

Gad withdrew Jonathan's note from the pocket of his robe with trembling fingers.

"I found this on my table when I awoke this morning. Shall I read, my lord?"

"Yes, please."

Gad opened the note and looked at Saul who nodded for him to begin.

"'Gad, we have gone to pay a debt. We will return once our debt is paid.'"

When Gad finished the note, he offered it to Saul, but he did not take it.

"I never saw or spoke with him after we were dismissed last night, my lord. He never woke me. I did not find the note until this morning."

"My lord," Abner called from the altar. "The high priest is ready and waiting."

Saul turned away from Gad to the priests and soldiers gathered around the altar.

"We are all in need of forgiveness, my son," Saul spoke over his shoulder before he began to walk toward the altar in the center of the camp.

Ahiah held the laver filled with sanctified water as Saul drew near. Once he dipped his hands into the golden bowl, the priests around the altar began to blow the shofar, the Honor Guard came to attention, and Eleazar held his golden spear aloft for Yahweh to bear witness.

"Cleanse me. Purify me," Saul whispered to himself as he raised his hands out of the water and held them in the air. "I must meet the Creator of heaven and earth without the prophet at my side. I look into the universe of Yahweh in search of the favor of the Almighty. I look and see nothing. I am forced to act without full awareness. Have mercy on me. From the Mercy Seat of the Almighty, O Yahweh, extend mercy."

Ahiah handed the laver to another priest and took a second bowl and a sprig of hyssop and dipped the leaves into the blood. He began to walk around the altar, splashing the blood onto the dead lamb stretched out upon the dry wood, its long tongue hanging out to one side, its eyes a glazed, dark marble. When Ahiah had finished sprinkling the altar, he dipped his finger into the lamb's blood and swiped each earlobe of the king. Then Saul took a torch from a priest and thrust it into the wood and dry grass gathered from the plains, and within seconds the whole altar was engulfed with flames. Saul went down upon his knees when Ahiah began his prayer.

"On behalf of the king, on behalf of the nation of Israel, Your chosen people, arise O Yahweh and defend us. Let not our enemies triumph. Strike them with Your great might. You are Yahweh forever and ever. Defend us against our enemies so they may terrify no more. Hear, O Israel, the Lord our God, the Lord is One."

Saul's knees and eardrums reacted to the vibrations at the same time. The tingling sensation moved into his thighs and settled in his viscera. His eardrums caught the rumbling sound in the air. There was no clear cause for the sounds he heard or the chill he was beginning to feel. There was enough activity around the altar with the uttered prayers and blaring shofars to explain what might be taking place inside him, but he was not sure.

The heat from the fire was so intense and generated enough heat that every pore in his body should have burst with perspiration, but all he felt was the dry chill of a childhood fever, and his mind began to race with a wild and frightening sharpness. He lifted his head and opened his eyes and saw Ahiah no longer facing the heavens addressing Yahweh. Instead, his eyes were gawking with an earthlier focus, but at what, Saul could not tell.

He rose to his feet and turned around. If he had the choice in that moment of going into battle alone against the entire Philistine army or face the prophet of the Almighty, he would have chosen annihilation by a pagan horde rather than looking into the eyes of the prophet. Flanked by Nathan and Jeush, Samuel approached Saul. Over their heads, Saul could see the rest of the escort he had sent to fetch the prophet remaining where they had stopped with the horses beside the prophet's wagon.

"What have you done?" Samuel's words flew out of his mouth in a gasp of shock.

Saul touched his forehead. The skin felt dry and tight. A heat rose in his skull like the inflammation of a wound that never quite heals. He was smacked by thirst and fatigue. What had he done? What had he been doing? Waiting on the prophet. Waiting for him to arrive and do what he said he was coming to do over seven days ago. It was obvious to everyone around them. Why was it not obvious to Samuel? Had not Jeush informed the prophet of the calamitous state of affairs when he went to get him? Why had the prophet asked such a ridiculous question?

Saul could choose to square off with Samuel in the presence of everyone. He would have a justifiable argument, one to knock Samuel back on his heels, but he knew Samuel would never be silent. The prophet would never be compliant. It was not within his nature to acquiesce or consider a compromise or, in this case, offer any understanding of Saul's critical predicament. The prophet did not even offer an apology or give an account for his tardiness. All he offered was an accusation in the form of a question, "What have you done?"

Jeush moved from the prophet's side to stand next to him. Saul knew Jeush was loyal; he was not the prophet's man; he was the king's man. He had discharged his orders and delivered the prophet, but Saul could not understand why it had taken so long when there had been plenty of time to complete the mission before this dreadful moment.

"I am sorry, my lord. I got him here as quickly as I could." Jeush spoke under his breath as he leaned in, and when Saul gave him an inquiring look as to why this poor timing of their arrival, Jeush just shook his head and sighed as if any explanation would defy all logic.

Gad scooted in beside Samuel. He did have the graciousness to present a kinder expression to Saul, balancing the appalled faces of Samuel and Nathan.

Abner yanked the king's helmet out of the hands of the king's armor bearer and moved in beside Saul, clutching the helmet against his chest. He did not lower it when the sun struck the bronze rim, casting its ray into the prophet's face.

With Abner and Jeush at his side, Saul felt the puncture in his heart plugged. It no longer leaked courage.

"My lord, my army was deserting me, scattering in every direction." Saul kept his voice calm and reasonable, better to pacify the prophet. "You did not come at the set time. The Philistines are mustered from here as far south as Micmash. The Philistines have me by the throat and will come against me here in Gilgal. My only hope was to implore the favor of Yahweh without you. Since you were unable to get here on time, I acted and offered the sacrifice myself."

Saul knew there was a great divide between the prophet and him. He assumed the prophet to be proud and fierce, and the prospect of a wellspring of understanding to miraculously surface—one from which they could both drink—was not likely. Saul opted for the pure state of honesty and simple truth and hoped that approach might prove a sufficient answer to the prophet's question.

"You have played the fool." Samuel kept his eyes riveted upon the culprit responsible for this situation. "You did not keep the command Yahweh gave you."

"I reached out to Yahweh myself. Is that impossible for me to do?"

"If you had obeyed Yahweh's command, then Yahweh would have confirmed your sovereignty over Israel forever."

"What are you saying? I waited the exact time you required...waited past the time, in fact." Saul gave Gad a quick glance to see if the young prophet might confirm his assertion, but his head was bowed, and Saul chose not to embroil him in this duel. "Must I wait for you every time I need to approach Yahweh? Can I not call upon the Almighty myself, or is Yahweh your God alone?"

"Because you have acted impetuously your kingdom will not endure." Samuel raised his hand and placed it upon the king's chest as a transference of blame onto the one for whom his words would indict. "Yahweh has searched out a man for Himself, a man after His own heart, and has designated him leader of His people. You removed the crown on your head by your own hand because you did not keep Yahweh's command."

Saul was confused and did not know how to react. Was he supposed to feel chastened and humiliated? What was this pronouncement? Should he fall down in fear and trembling? Was this a curse or a blessing? No one could ever know what it was like to be him, to be inside his heart. He could keep his head lowered, folding his thoughts and feelings inside a protective covering, or he could continue to illustrate his own story with his choice of actions.

He had made an individual decision by daring to reach out to Yahweh on his own without the prophet. Saul had risked contact with the God of Israel unknown to him except by myth and history and the declarations of the prophet. He knew the reason he chose to offer the sacrifice. There was no doubt in his mind of its importance to him and to his men and, he hoped, to Yahweh. He also understood that in doing so it would likely incur the wrath and judgment of the prophet, which had just been proven true. His only recourse was to allow time to determine if he was foolish for exerting some independence or if the prophet's adamant words were nothing but a self-indulgent determination of Yahweh's resolve to see him deposed.

"I gladly take off my crown." Saul lifted his crown from the top of his head and extended the diadem toward Samuel as an offering. "I never asked to be king, and now you tell me Yahweh is finished with me because I made a conscious decision to offer a sacrifice without you? No one is king forever, my lord, but I am king today, and I have an army to lead. Shall you hold this crown for safekeeping, or shall I?"

Samuel made no motion to accept the offering of the king's royal covering.

Perhaps Yahweh had a similar reaction to my burnt offering, Saul thought.

It seemed like shouting was coming from a far distance. In Saul's ears, one hot voice cried out, calling for the sovereign king, insisting the king pay heed.

Saul tore his eyes away from Samuel and saw Beerah scrambling his way through the crowd. The chieftain from the tribe of Reuben did not care who he pushed aside or who he might offend by physical force. When he reached Saul, he fell to his knees next to Gad, but Beerah was completely unaware of all those around him. His eyes and voice were for his sovereign alone.

"My lord, the Philistines are in a terrible panic!" Beerah shouted between gasps of heavy breathing. "It began in Geba when the prince and his armor bearer attacked the Philistine outpost."

"Beerah, what are you talking about?" Saul demanded.

"Listen, my lord. Listen. Hear it? Feel the ground beneath your feet?" Beerah took hold of Gad's arm as he struggled to his feet.

A hush came over the camp. At first, nothing could be heard over the searing intensity of burning flames and the bleating sheep that were spared the knife but ran back and forth inside the pen distressed at the sight of their kin roasting on the altar. Saul and the six hundred, the prophet and his two students heard nothing. But soon the silence gave way to howls of misery, to screams of terror from throats of terrified men to the deep rumble of the earth shaking as if it were about to split apart.

"That, my lord, is the clamor of self-slaughter." Beerah touched his ear, grinning like a madman. Indeed, he did appear mad with a sheen of dust and spittle and sweat coating the splotched skin of his face. "That is the sound of the panic Yahweh has inflicted upon our enemies."

"I hear it, Beerah." Saul cocked his ear in the direction of the Jordan plains. "But explain it. Jonathan attacked a Philistine outpost and this sound I hear is the result?"

Beerah still held onto Gad's arm for support. His trembling legs would give way and he would crumble to the ground if he released his hold of the young prophet's arm.

"Where to start. Where to start." Beerah rapped his skull with his knuckles as if to knock his thoughts into coherency. "My lord, I am overwhelmed by the miracle I have witnessed and the story I must tell. Sometime this morning it began in the southern plains outside of Geba and Micmash. I do not know how he did it, and cannot explain it, but I counted twenty Philistine corpses at the outpost in Geba. I have just come from there."

"And Jonathan is responsible for this?" Saul was shocked by this revelation.

"Yes, my lord, he and Adriel. I saw it with my own eyes. The outpost at Geba, twenty dead Philistines, and now the whole army of uncircumcised dogs are turning on themselves. It is the panic of Yahweh, I swear."

"Is this the debt my son spoke of?" Saul looked at Gad for his answer.

Gad responded with a quick nod and then cut his eyes to his master to be sure he had not been caught in this little conspiracy with the king, but the prophet's attention was given to Beerah.

"Midmorning, my sons and I were scouting between Mizpah and Ramah," Beerah continued. "We were concealed at the forest's edge when we spied several Philistines, both afoot and mounted, racing from the direction of Geba like frightened rabbits and heading north for their main camp. We waited for a space of time until they were a safe distance away to be sure no other soldiers were following behind before we ventured out of hiding. We were mounting our horses when we saw two riders chasing the Philistines at full speed. It looked like the prince and Adriel, but we were not sure, and remained hidden from sight.

"We rode back toward Geba, to the outpost, and on the main road my sons and I came upon a lone Philistine driving a wagon transporting a broken stone monument back to Aphek. He was unarmed, and his right hand had been bandaged and supported by a strip of cloth. When we stopped him, he removed a small scroll from his sling and handed it to me. I could not believe what I read: a script written in the hand of the prince stating, 'This man shall have safe passage. He is an artist.' The prince's sign was beneath the lettering.

"I returned the scroll to the man, and he kept pointing behind him in the direction of the Philistine garrison, so I sent my sons to ride after the prince while I rode on to Geba. I was there long enough to count the dead before heading back to our camp."

"What happened to the Philistine with the monument, this artist?" Abner asked.

"Left him on the road," Beerah replied. "On my way back from the Philistine garrison, I caught up with the melee and rode for a while along the periphery of the battle weaving in and around the forests and hill country of Ephraim. I chanced upon some of our deserters who had found their courage and come out of hiding to join the battle. My lord, I can only describe what I saw as a great human wave rolling across the plains, a wave of self-slaughter, Philistine upon Philistine, flowing beside me as I rode, leaving in its wake hundreds of the dead and dying. You are able to hear and can soon see for yourself what is happening on the other side of those hills."

Saul threw back his head and exploded with a full throat laugh that resonated over the whole camp and subdued the noise of butchery just beyond the hills. "The panic of Yahweh. The panic of Yahweh. This I must see."

Saul lifted his crown high into the air and began a slow circular spin.

"Blast the shofar and the trumpet. Let the blast rise from your bowels. Let the ground shake under our hot pursuit. Arm yourselves. Prepare your steeds. Let the king of Israel avenge himself upon his enemies."

With the sound of shofar and trumpet splitting the air, the encampment erupted with activity. The foot soldiers raced to begin forming their columns and the mounted soldiers dashed to their horses. It all happened so quickly it seemed the panic of Yahweh had shifted to their military site. Jeush rushed to prepare Saul's horse. Abner remained clutching Saul's helmet, awaiting the order to cover his head with the crown of war.

"Did you hear that, my lord?" Saul pressed the crown to his chest and gave the prophet a resolute stare. "A panic of Yahweh brought on by my son, my true and faithful son. While I stand here feeling the shame of your denunciation, my son is causing the panic of Yahweh to fall upon our enemies."

Saul brought his crown away from his chest and rubbed a finger over the raised image of the face of the wolf.

"It appears the wolf is rising, so I think I will keep my crown a little longer." Saul spoke but did not look at the prophet. He knew best to hold his pleasure in this moment to a modest level. "I will save it for my son." Saul then held the crown out to Gad. "I entrust this to you for safekeeping. Once we are victorious, I will fetch it again."

Gad's lips began to tremble, but then he quickly took the crown and pressed it into his chest. He did not look at him or Samuel. Saul knew he had forced Gad into an awkward place: the young man did not want to appear too eager to obey the king in front of his master.

As soon as Saul released his crown, Abner stepped in front of him and raised his helmet above Saul's head.

"May the strength of the king be renewed." Abner spoke while securing the helmet upon the royal head. He could smile at his cousin without fear of receiving a withering frown from the prophet. "May the king put a swift end to his enemies."

"Thank you, Commander." Saul made a last adjustment to his headgear and tied the leather thongs beneath his chin.

Jeush led Adara up to Saul. He bowed as he handed him the reins.

Saul leapt upon Adara's back and surveyed the encampment as the foot soldiers finished assembling their columns and the cavalry took formation in front of them.

"Ahiah and Eleazar, I want the sacred furnishings to follow us."

The high priest and the guardian of the Ark bowed to the king.

"This is the day of Yahweh, at least what is left of it. When night falls and we stop to rest, I want to offer sacrifices."

Saul looked down at Samuel. The old man had not moved. The flurry of activity swirling around him did not affect his firm stance. His feet remained in the location where he had planted them in front of Saul when he asked him, "What have you done?"

Perhaps the old man had not heard Saul's order to the high priest and the guardian to follow behind him and of Saul's intention to offer sacrifices to Yahweh. Saul had not initially meant this as an insult; it was a voluntary thought, unprompted by any guile. Saul almost began to invite the prophet to join him at the end of the day but decided against it. He would share this victory with those who were loyal and not with an aggrieved old man who could easily turn this good fortune against him.

Saul watched as Abner trotted on horseback along the formations of the small army, ordering them to attention and await the king's command. While Saul waited for Abner to finish his inspection and join him at his side, he watched as Nathan escorted the prophet back to his wagon. Saul did not wish him well or safe travels. He did not offer him an armed escort for his journey home. He did not speak to the prophet at all. When Abner rode his horse to a stop beside him, Saul turned to his troops.

"You hear the tumult coming from over the next hill." Saul paused for everyone to listen one last time before they moved out. "The sound of the panic of Yahweh increases with every moment the sun passes over the sky. Yahweh has turned our sure defeat into a victory, our shame into our glory. What Yahweh began, we must finish. We are few in number, but we are the mighty ones of Israel, and we must complete the rout of our enemies.

"Do not stop until nightfall. Do not collect plunder from the camp of the Philistines or strip the dead. Do not even pause to eat. Cursed be any man who eats food this day before evening comes, before I have avenged myself upon my enemies. Anyone who eats food before nightfall is under the penalty of death. Now let our enemies feel our vengeance and fall down in the dust of the earth never to rise again."

Abner raised himself from his horse and shouted to his army. "For the love of Israel! For the glory of Yahweh! For the honor of the king!"

Gad had accepted the king's crown with only a twinge of hesitation, grasping it from the king, not retreating from the offer. In the euphoria of the moment, he had forgotten where his allegiances lay. He glanced at the prophet's craggy, bearded profile. Samuel had not climbed into the wagon, but stood beside it, his eyes reflecting the altar-fire blaze on his pupils. Gad dreaded all conflict, an unlikely characteristic in a prophet, and wished to be loyal to both king and prophet, speak and sing in praise of each. The king had dared him take the crown. The prophet had assigned him to this post. He stood between the two most powerful men in the nation, men selected by Yahweh to serve and lead the chosen. By accepting the crown, might he be bridging the distance between prophet and king?

Gad watch Samuel extend his arm toward the departing king and listened to the prophet's whispered prayer, "Remember the great things Yahweh has done for you. Serve Yahweh faithfully with all your heart, and I will never cease to pray for you."

Gad wrapped his fingers around the royal symbol of Israel's sovereignty. It was to Yahweh he owed his loyalty. It was for Israel he would serve.

Chapter 15

JONATHAN LEANED AGAINST THE THICK TRUNK OF A GIANT oak tree, swatting at a curious yellow and brown-striped bee that kept diving and swooping around his head. He took his near- deflated water skin from his shoulder, held it at his waist, and waited until the bee came to hover in front of him at eye-level. With one quick swipe, Jonathan swung his water skin. The force of the motion caused him to stumble forward, and he spun around to regain his balance to see if the bee still threatened. He did not see the small creature, so he removed the plug from the skin.

As he raised the neck to his lips, he saw the bee smashed inside the folds of the skin. He scratched the remains off the leather skin with his finger and held the smeared, brownish shell up to the sunlight to examine it. He and Adriel had not eaten since the night before, nor had they slept. Exhausted and starved, Jonathan licked the messy corpse from his fingertip and allowed it to dissolve on his tongue. The faint sweet flavor surprised his taste buds and made his stomach growl. He drank the last of his water to temporarily drown his hunger pangs.

"My lord, I see the commander and the king with our army charging after the remnant of the Philistines!" Adriel shouted. "They are driving them toward the forest!"

"Good," Jonathan said, looking through the leafy branches of the tree for his armor bearer but he was too high, the foliage was too thick, and the afternoon sun was in his face. "Come down. We can wait for them here at the edge of the forest."

The thick branches started to flutter and sway as Adriel began to descend. Jonathan stepped away from the trunk to avoid falling debris and to wait for his armor bearer when an arrow flew over his head and lodged in the center of the tree just below the first branch. Jonathan dropped to the ground and crawled on his belly away from the tree, getting behind an adjacent tree where they had tied off their horses.

"Adriel, stay still!" Jonathan yelled. "We have uncircumcised company."

Jonathan heard Adriel curse as he halted his descent. From his position on the ground, Jonathan could see the swaying branches in the middle of the tree become motionless, yet he still could not pinpoint Adriel's position. If he could not see him, neither could the enemy. At the same time, Adriel could not spot for him. Even with the remaining daylight, the foliage of the tree prevented Adriel an unobstructed view of the ground.

Jonathan could wait for the others to arrive, but it goaded him that this Philistine or Philistines could take a shot at him and get away with it. His sling was not much use in the thick woods. He was no good with a bow. The expert archer was stuck up a tree. He had his sword strapped to his back and his hunting knife tied to his side. He reached into his pouch and felt only a handful of stones. He and Adriel had been too busy pursuing and killing the enemy and had not taken the time to replenish his stock. He had to make do with what he had.

"If I shout, drop down fast," Jonathan spoke softly. "Whistle if you heard me."

When Adriel acknowledged with an airy trill, Jonathan got to his feet, using the horses for cover as he loaded his sling with a stone and took out his hunting knife. He did not want to dash from tree to thicket wielding a cumbersome sword. Though it was easy to determine the exact direction from which the arrow had been shot—from deeper into the forest, certainly, a relatively clear sight-line—it annoyed Jonathan that this was the way he would have to spend the rest of the afternoon, hunting down an assassin in the middle of thickets and trees. All he wanted to do was see his father, stuff his belly with something other than the carcass of a bee, and sleep for days.

Jonathan would have to cut a wide berth through the trees in hopes of circling around behind the enemy, so he moved with speed, making as little noise as possible. This assassin could not be allowed to remain hidden in these woods, not with the impending arrival of the king. He kept the sunlight filtering through the edge of the tree line at his back. Even though the light was good, it faded the farther he crept into the trees, and he wanted his eyes adjusted to the verdant shadows.

He slipped behind a sycamore tree and paused. A constant buzzing sound drew his attention to a clearing another few steps deeper into the forest. Jonathan saw a swarm of bees moving through the branches above his head. He watched as their sinuous, floating wave brought the swarm to the forked branch of a dead tree. The bees gradually began to disappear, and he thought they must be going deeper into the forest, but after refocusing his eyes on the area of the dead branch, the contours of a nest began to come into view. He realized the swarm had gone inside a large conical-shaped nest attached to the leafless branch. He scanned the area but did not detect any human movement. The enemy was out there, but it was impossible to locate a position.

Jonathan looked back in the direction of the tree where Adriel was forced to wait. He could spend the remainder of the day stalking or waiting, so he made the snap decision and stepped out from behind the tree to wind up his sling. He reached into his pouch for a second stone in case he missed.

When he got the sling to the right speed, he released the stone and it smashed right into the nest of bees, knocking it from the branch onto the forest floor. He jumped back behind the tree to see if the plan worked. It was not long before the screaming began, and abruptly two Philistines burst through the underbrush, wildly swinging a bow and spear, and cursing their buzzing tormentors. The weapons of man had no effect on a swarm of enraged bees. The Philistines discarded their weapons and began to smack their bare skin, but then decided flight was the only way to survive, and they both made a mad dash deeper into the forest.

Jonathan waited another few moments before easing out from behind the tree. He listened in the direction of the pursuers and the pursued until the sounds of screaming and buzzing got fainter and fainter. He then moved away from the tree and slipped over to the broken nest lying on the ground. The smell of honey filling the air around the fallen nest made him weak in the knees, and he went down on all fours.

He grabbed a stick lying on the ground and began to poke the shattered nest. There were still a few bees crawling over the nest, but the desperation of hunger was too great, and he drove the blunt end of the stick into the honey oozing out of the split seam of the nest. He brought his glistening prize to his mouth and devoured it all, comb, honey, and dead bee carcasses killed by the stone. His cheeks bulged with the delight, and he thrust the stick back into the nest and scooped the second bite into his hand.

As soon as he swallowed, he licked the sweet goop from his hand and pierced the nest again with his stick. He had flushed out the Philistine assassins and gotten something to eat all with one sling of a stone. In his mind, this was the best shot of the day.

The shouting brought him back to his senses and the nourishing substance of the honey was beginning to work its energy in his body. He leapt to his feet and could see the human images streaming around and through the trees.

Adriel burst through the trees, his ears still ringing with the prince's screams. His bow was drawn, his eyes peeled for any sight of Jonathan. When he saw him, he ran up beside him, but kept his bowstring taut and his eye on the underbrush.

"I heard you scream." Adriel scanned the forest, ready to release his arrow at anything that moved.

"Not me," Jonathan said. "It was the Philistines. They scream like my sisters."

Adriel stepped past Jonathan and swept the point of his arrow over the clearing and the treetops above for any Philistine who might step out of hiding to attack.

"They are gone." Jonathan spoke while chewing a mouthful of comb and waving his sticky hand over the clearing. "Be assured."

Adriel was not assured they were free of danger in spite of the nonchalance of the prince, so he moved about the scrub brush, giving it a final sweep before he was satisfied.

"Do not step on that nest." Jonathan pointed to the nest on the ground. "There is still good honey inside."

Adriel looked at the prince. His face and beard were coated with a brown glaze, so Adriel began to relax, unlocking his knees from their bent assault pose, and releasing the nock of his arrow from the bowstring.

"Since you mentioned it, this might be as good a time as any to talk about this." Adriel did not put his arrow back inside his quiver but held it in his hand.

"Mentioned what?" Jonathan offered the honeyed end of the stick to Adriel.

Hungry as he was, Adriel declined the prince's offer. He had wanted to speak his heart to Jonathan ever since the night of the family meal, but there had been no occasion. Events and conflicts and missions and burials and military training and battle itself all kept interfering with finding the perfect moment to share his feelings regarding the prince's sister. He was not about to let a mouthful of honey stop him now.

"I love your sister." Adriel only knew to speak like the direct shot of an arrow.

"Which sister might that be?" Jonathan asked, his tongue swiping his coated lips.

"The quiet one," Adriel said, and then waited for a reaction from Jonathan, but the prince was ignoring him, gorging himself on honey. "I am just an armor bearer, I know, but I do think—"

"You are the firstborn son of a tribal lord, the best archer in the army, and my armor bearer," Jonathan interrupted. "You are qualified to marry my sister but have not told me which one. We all grew up in the same house. I do not have a quiet sister."

"Merab, my lord."

The voices coming from the edge of the woods startled Adriel, and he inserted the nock of the arrow back into the bowstring and raised the bow at the lone warrior running toward them with lance uplifted ready to hurl.

"You love her, you say, but does she love you in return?" the prince asked.

"I believe so, my lord."

The warrior was slowing down his approach, but still held his lance aloft.

"Merab is a good choice." Jonathan was unfazed by the potential danger. "Mikal would be more of a challenge. She can drive you mad. I will speak to my father."

"My lord, no, please. I do not think this is the time—"

"The prince is found!" cried the warrior. He stopped his hostile advance and lowered his spear. "You nearly got a spear in your chest."

Jeush removed his helmet. He was covered head to foot in blood and filth.

"And you an arrow in the eye." Adriel lowered his bow.

"This part of the forest is clear," Jonathan reported.

Jeush dropped his lance and helmet on the ground and started wagging his finger at the prince and his armor bearer as he walked toward them. His teeth shone white inside his smiling, dirt-encrusted face.

"Before all the young women in Israel start throwing their bodies at your feet and poets start immortalizing you with songs, I want to hear the truth of what happened at the outpost at Geba. Beerah swears you left behind over twenty dead Philistines."

"That many?" Jonathan looked surprised by the number Jeush quoted. "We were too busy killing them to stop and count." There was more honey on the end of the stick, and he offered it to Adriel. "Last bite, armor bearer. You have earned it."

Adriel reached over to pull the honeyed end of the stick to his mouth when Jeush struck out his hand in a flash and gripped Adriel by his wrist. Both the prince and Adriel were startled by Jeush's abrupt action.

Jeush looked over his shoulder to see if any fellow soldiers were drawing near, but they were too busy racing along the forest's edge securing its perimeter before the king arrived. He yanked the stick from the prince's hand and hurled it into the dense underbrush, then withdrew a soiled, sweaty cloth from beneath his breastplate and began to wipe the honey from the prince's face.

"Jeush, what are you doing?" Jonathan backed away from the forceful scrubbing.

"My lord, be still. The king will arrive soon. He must not see you like this."

"Like what?" Jonathan ripped the cloth from Jeush's hand, tossing it onto the ground. "What are you talking about?"

"Has shedding Philistine blood caused you to lose your mind?" asked Adriel.

"Listen to me, both of you." Jeush spoke with a hard edge to his tone that would accept nothing but their undivided attention. "Your father, the king and my sovereign lord, placed a ban on eating today before we broke camp to launch our attack. No one was to eat until the king had exacted revenge upon his enemies. Anyone who does so is under a curse and will be executed if caught."

"No one is allowed to eat today?" asked Jonathan with an expression of incomprehension on his face. "I cannot believe my father would say something so rash. This is a great victory given him by Yahweh. Why would Father ruin it by ordering something so foolish? There is no clear rationale. This is an impulsive act."

"Impulsive or not, no one was to eat while we pursued our enemies." Jeush gave a quick glance back at the edge of the forest to see if any of their comrades were entering. "I had to stop some of the men from slicing a hunk of mutton from a dead sheep or cutting out the liver of a calf and eating it along the way. Since it is near dark, your king has ordered us to stop and roast the livestock we have captured so we do not sin by eating anything tainted with blood. But in truth, we could not keep up the pace of slaughter because we are all starving and near faint from exhaustion."

"Jeush, my father…I cannot believe he would—" Jonathan had to raise his hand to stop Jeush from speaking in the king's defense. "If you had been able to eat along the way you could have kept killing the Philistines, is that true?"

"Yes, my lord."

"Look at my eyes, Jeush. Look how bright they are. I have only eaten a little honey and my strength has been restored. Imagine how great our victory could be had the soldiers been allowed to eat. My father has brought trouble upon the nation."

The three men snapped their heads in the direction of the forest's edge when they heard the commotion and cheers from the men.

"The king is coming." Jeush snatched the cloth from off the ground. He handed it to Jonathan for him to finish what he had started. "My lord, clean the rest of your face. I do not want to cause any harm or division between the king and the prince. Regardless of what may have been, today is a glorious victory for Israel. Please, clean your face."

"Where is my son?"

Saul's voice was unmistakable rising above the vocal adulation for his victory and for the longevity of his kingdom.

"The king is anxious to see you," Jeush spoke rapidly. "You are worthy to be his successor. And I want to live to see that day. Take the cloth, my lord."

Jonathan looked at Adriel.

"I stand with Jeush, my lord," Adriel said. "Take the cloth."

"Say nothing of this to anyone." Jeush turned away and began to trot back to greet the king, trusting the prince would do what was good for all.

Saul alone did not eat. No sooner had the sun begun to set, Saul ordered the fires built and the butchering to begin. The meat from cattle and sheep could not cook fast enough for the ravenous appetites of his men. Once the fires were blazing, the animal skins were peeled away. Then the meat was cut from the bones and thrown onto the hot stones or impaled on the ends of their spears and arrows, charbroiled just enough to burn away the blood to make it fit for human consumption and avoid offending Yahweh.

Saul alone would keep the ban from the consumption of food; he would remain pure. He sipped water from a goblet and roved through the makeshift encampment, congratulating the men as they filled their bellies with meat and drink. He wanted to discern their attitudes, read the pulse of his men to see if there was stomach for more plunder and carnage.

The sun might be setting on the day, but to his way of thinking, this panic of Yahweh brought down upon the Philistines was not over yet. He did not want the momentum to shift or the bloodlust to wane. Why constrain the drive when their enemies were on the run, and the more he discussed this option with his captains and his commander, the more the urge to continue hunting down the Philistines was building into a unanimous mindset.

Still, Saul believed he needed one more thing to help complete the process in making his decision. He needed a sign to bolster the men to keep going, so he ordered Ahiah and his priestly detail to build an altar and offer a sacrifice. This act of worship would bring clarity and focus, and it should also solidify in the minds of his loyal soldiers that their king was grateful to Yahweh for His role in their victory. While the beast was still disintegrating on the altar fire, he and Ahiah thought it a perfect time for the high priest to cast the Urim and Thummim and receive divine approval in front of all the men so there would be no question whether or not to pursue their fleeing enemies.

Once the men were assembled for the ceremony, Saul nodded for Ahiah to take his position on one side of the sacred table. The high priest held the bowl containing the two consecrated stones and waited for Saul to give his address.

"You are the pride of Israel." Saul projected his great voice so all the men could hear him as he took his place on the opposite side of the sacred table. "You are the most valiant among the sons of Israel. You did not desert in the seven days of our darkness leading up to this battle. When all looked hopeless, you remained steadfast, and today you have given your king and your nation a great victory.

"Now we have taken time to feast and restore our strength. We have presented a burnt offering to Yahweh in gratitude for this victory. And though night is upon us, our enemy is still in flight, afflicted by the panic set upon them by Yahweh. The generals and captains and the commander, and you among the ranks, have expressed a desire to fight on, so we now seek the guidance and favor of the Creator of heaven and earth."

Saul redirected his eyes away from his men to the clear sky above him.

"Yahweh, God of the universe, shall I go down after the Philistines? Will You give our enemies into the hands of Israel and to her king?"

Saul turned to Ahiah, and the high priest cast the stones upon the table.

When Saul and Ahiah looked upon the two stones they were puzzled by the result. The Urim stone lay with the blank side up. The "yes" mark was facedown. The Thummim stone had its engraved "no" side up. It was an indecisive answer.

Saul thought he phrased the question correctly. He was facing the high priest when he asked the question. Surely Yahweh approved of this method.

Ahiah retrieved the precious stones and placed them inside the bowl. He spread his fingers over the top of the bowl as if to protect the contents.

"Cast the stones a second time." Saul waved toward the bowl, and Ahiah tossed the stones across the table a second time. Again, a split response was revealed: the "yes" side of the Urim was facedown and the "no" side of the Thummim was face up.

"Yahweh does not seem to be pleased to give the king an answer," Ahiah said.

"Is this not unusual, Ahiah?"

"Most unusual, my lord. Perhaps Yahweh is displeased in some way."

"Then we must find out." An edginess began to creep into Saul's voice. "Cast the stones once more."

"May I suggest the king rephrase the question." Eleazar stepped forward and offered his golden spear to Saul as if such an object held by the royal hand might make a difference to Yahweh.

Saul took the spear and held it aloft. "If we move against our enemies throughout the night will Yahweh give us victory?" Saul waved for Ahiah to cast the stones.

The stones rattled inside the bowl and then bounced across the table and for a third time the engraved side of one stone lay next to the blank side of the other.

"What could this mean, Ahiah?" Saul was not quite frightened enough to stop the process, yet not confident enough to continue.

"My lord, dare I suggest there may be sin in the camp?" Ahiah put forth this proposition as he hastily picked up the stones to put them back into the container. He ran a finger over the engraved side of each stone, the lettering signifying light and perfection. "I have never experienced Yahweh's silence and can think of no historical precedent of such a thing coming about to any of my priestly ancestors. I offer no other explanation than there might be a concealed sin, my lord."

"Cast the lots once more," Saul instructed. "Find out if there is sin in the camp."

Ahiah hesitated not ready to confront Yahweh with such a question.

"My lord, before I cast the stones, let us consider what we are doing. Remember the sin of Achan; he broke the ban of Yahweh and stole items from the plunder of Jericho, which was devoted to the Almighty. It did not go well for Achan."

"If there is sin in the camp, I want to know about it." Saul tossed the golden spear back to Eleazar, its uselessness proven with the third cast. "If a crime has constricted my victory over the Philistines, then I must know about it. Throw the stones."

Ahiah threw the stones upon the holy table, and when they tumbled to a stop, the engraved sides of both stones faced upward. The human silence of the army abruptly elevated the natural sounds of crackling fires, neighing horses, the cold wind blowing off the desert around the gathering of men and through the trees at the forest's edge.

Saul and Ahiah looked at Yahweh's answer. At least the Almighty had given an answer; no more wondering if the Creator of heaven and earth was paying attention. Yahweh was present and Yahweh had spoken.

"My lord, I…"

"Yes, Ahiah, yes, I know." Saul did not allow the high priest to tell him what he could see for himself. He stepped from the table and pointed to the opposite side from where he stood. "Abner, you and all the generals and captains line up on that side of the sacred table. We shall find out what sin has been committed today."

"Abba, I think I should tell you—"

"Not now, Jonathan." Saul placed his hand upon Jonathan's shoulder to stop his son from joining Abner and the others. "You and I will stand opposite from the rest."

Ahiah lifted the stones from the table and held them in his open palm before he dropped them into the bowl. He faced the king and awaited his order to cast the lots. Saul knew Ahiah would not proceed on his own; he must be commanded. The consequences of this next casting of the stones would come by his authority. Saul had placed everyone in a precarious situation. The responsibility would not be shared. If the casting of the precious stones were to reveal Yahweh's disapproval, then Saul would not blame Ahiah, the high priest would only be guilty of obeying the order, not acting on his own interests.

Once Abner and the military leaders were in line, Saul pointed for Eleazar to stand beside Ahiah. He wanted a second pair of eyes to read Yahweh's revelation.

"Let it be known, as surely as Yahweh gives victory to Israel, whoever has brought sin into this camp, shall die. Even if it is my son Jonathan, he shall die."

He had spoken. The edict pronounced, it could not be retracted, and Saul could sense a collective held breath among his men. No one spoke, not even Abner, for no one could believe their ears. Saul had been impulsive to make such a statement. How could he ever find the space to go back on his word once spoken? Was he that confident of the outcome? Was he that confident that neither he nor Jonathan would be indicted?

"I and my son stand here on one side of the table. My commander and the military leaders stand opposite us. The question to Yahweh: does the sin lie with my commander and the military command? The stones, Ahiah. Cast them down."

Ahiah did as he was ordered, but he threw them quickly and the stones nearly fell off the edge of the table.

Eleazar and Ahiah moved to the end of the table and read the stones together.

"My lord, Abner and his command are cleared," Ahiah said.

Two of the captains fell to their knees and began to weep. Jeush stepped over to them, grabbed the back of their necks, and lifted them to their feet. He gave them a fierce look, which brought an end to their crying. Fear and sorrow had now replaced all elation of their victory, and it looked as though a great tragedy would be the final act to end a glorious day.

"Ahiah, cast the lot between my son and me." Saul pushed Jonathan away from him the length of his arm. The separation must be clear for the stones to speak the truth.

"My lord, are you sure this is—"

"Ahiah, do as I say. Does the sin lie with the king? Cast the stones."

Ahiah scraped the stones off the edge of the table into the bowl and raised it up. What prayer could be offered? There was no good choice, no preferred option—the king or the prince. Which one would receive intercession? It had to be a divine decision. No man could bear that burden. It must be supported by Yahweh. Ahiah upended the bowl and the stones rattled across the table with a sharp clicking noise, hard stones bouncing on hard wood, ringing out like a rebuke until they fell still and silent.

No one looked down at Yahweh's answer. Ahiah held his head aloft, his eyes closed. Eleazar kept his face pointed in the opposite direction. Abner stood with his men and would not approach the table. Saul would have to read the stones. It was he who had ordered this procedure. It was he who had established the rules. The first to behold Yahweh's reply had to be Saul.

Saul looked down at the blank sides of the Urim and Thummim. A confirmed "no." The king had not sinned. His reaction was swift. He snatched the stones off the table and squeezed them inside his hand. He could hurl them into the desert or throw them into the altar fire. He now was poignantly aware of the folly he had created and how it would end. He had been steady and stubborn to this point, but now he was undone, the blood rushing in his body, a pounding in his head like the violent beating of wings upon a pool of still water.

"My son. My son, what have you done?" Saul's voice was a raw groan.

"I broke the king's command. I broke the king's ban not to eat until he had achieved his victory."

Saul could see the resolve in the face of Jonathan. His son would not take the safer route and plead ignorance. His son would not lie as if one could lie in the face of Yahweh's disclosure. His son would not use the fact that the army of Israel considered him a hero for his bravery at the outpost in Geba nor would he play upon anyone's sympathies. His son would not use his position as the firstborn of the king or the prince of Israel to secure amnesty against the decree of the king. His son would accept the outcome the lots had cast.

"Abba, I was exhausted and starving and I ate some honey. Here I am. I am ready to die."

"May Yahweh strike me and even kill me if you do not die, Jonathan." What else could he say? And Saul let the sacred stones tumble to the ground.

It was a race between Adriel and Ahiah as to who would first get to the king, but for different reasons: Ahiah to retrieve the Urim and Thummim from the ground and Adriel to fall at the feet of the king.

"My lord, the prince knew nothing of the ban." Adriel was at the point of tears. "We were separated from the army and had no knowledge of the king's command. My sovereign lord, in your mercy, I beg you to spare the prince. But if the command must not be broken, then may I bear the penalty. I will suffer the king's judgment."

Saul looked down upon Adriel, his face buried in the earth, his hands open in supplication. Saul noticed Ahiah wiping the dirt off the stones onto his garment after retrieving them from the ground. Desperate for intercession, he shifted his gaze to Abner.

"What have I done, Cousin? What trouble I have brought upon Israel."

If Saul could have slipped away in the darkness he would. If the earth would swallow him now, he would be thankful. He would cut out his tongue if he could only take back the ban he had spoken that day.

"My lord, may it never be said the king of Israel is not just or rules with absolute fairness." Saul could see Abner locking eyes with him as he moved closer to him. "It is an honor to serve a king who favors no one, not even his own son. No one should doubt the word of the king, and all of us here today shall remain loyal for we know the king can be trusted. But I ask my lord, should Jonathan die; he who inspired the panic of Yahweh and brought about this great deliverance? May it never be.

"Not one hair from the head of the prince should fall to the ground for all that he did today with the help of Yahweh. I say to you, my lord, should the king extend his mercy and release his judgment, no man standing here, no man in Israel will fault him, for the king is an honorable man."

Saul turned his head and looked upon the sea of grimy faces, all awaiting his verdict. Abner had shown him a pathway, an escape that brought both terror and joy. It terrified him that he had so foolishly brought his son to such a brink. But now the terror gave way to profound joy that he had been given back his son. He wanted to speak, and parted his lips to do so, but he could utter no words. He just wanted to vanish and reappear at his home. He wanted the intimacy of his wife. He wanted the raucousness of his children around the fire of their hearth. He wanted the forgiveness of his son.

"My son is mine again." Saul gripped Jonathan and plunged him into his chest.

The shofars blew. The trumpets blared. The men were of one voice and one heart, and the jubilant cry rose from the camp and rolled out upon the desert, in all points and all directions, an invisible and unstoppable wave.

Dozens of hands gripped and pounded father and son, but nothing could break them from their embrace. They were deaf to the vocal elation and the physical clasp and pull of those who wanted to touch the royal pair and feel the energy of mercy and forgiveness and resurrection flow into them. Finally, it was the abrupt silence that brought Saul and Jonathan to consciousness and release.

Still gripping the shoulders of his son, Saul turned as the crowd parted. He saw Jarib, his faithful secretary, ushered toward him as if arriving from out of a dream.

Jarib did not kneel or bow. He did not salute the king or congratulate him for his victory. He cared nothing about such things. He was desperate and insistent.

"My lord, I had just arrived back in Gibeah when your daughters insisted that I return to find you. It is the queen. You must come home at once."

Chapter 16

ABNER RETURNED TO THE FAMILY COMPOUND IN GIBEAH WITH the bulk of the army as the afternoon was slipping away. He had stayed behind with the troops when Jarib brought word of complications with the queen's delivery. Saul and Jonathan left immediately with Jarib, accompanied by Adriel and an elite squad to protect the king and prince as they had to ride after nightfall. Though the Philistines had been defeated and were now scattered and hiding, the roads were too dangerous just hours after a battle. Hordes of soldiers under Abner's command begged for the privilege of being the king's escort, so he had no problem choosing his best warriors.

Before departing for home that morning, Abner ordered the military to move with haste, retracing their march over the killing fields collecting plunder abandoned during the battle and finishing off any wounded Philistine who might have survived through the night. Abner knew once the Philistines realized the army of Israel was in retreat, it was possible they might counterattack, and he was not sure he could rely on the "panic of Yahweh" to be present for a second day.

Abner left his horse at the stables and rounded the compound wall to the front gate where the guards snapped at attention as he bolted through the opened doors. Once inside the compound, Kish stopped him in the courtyard and prevented him from going into the house. The door into the house was ajar, and Abner could see light flickering and the children moving around in the common room.

"Is she alive, Uncle?" Abner craned his neck around Kish's shoulder as he tried to force his way toward the front door.

"Yes, but she is exhausted from the delivery and getting weaker. Saul asked that all but the children remain outside. There is a wet nurse present, but no one else. Jonathan comes out on occasion and gives reports. The bleeding has not stopped."

In the courtyard there was a warm fire and a table of food and drink. Abner asked a servant to heat some water so he could wash the top layer of the grime off his body and to bring him fresh clothing. If it was best for him not to go inside, then he would stand vigil with Kish in the courtyard until the danger had passed.

"When was the child born?" Abner asked.

"Just before Saul arrived home," Kish replied. "He was greeted at the door with a son barely scrubbed clean from the blood of delivery and screaming for the breast."

"A son then, with strong cry, I hope," Abner said.

"He has a fine pair of lungs," Kish replied, but with no amusement. "He appears to have come into the world healthy. It was hearing my daughter-in-law's deep moaning that I could not endure. Never have I heard such raw groans, like receiving a mortal wound every few moments. And it was relentless. The twins were terrified hearing such cries from their mother, so we left the house and walked around the compound to the back fields just to escape. When it was done, Mikal told us the boy had come into the world feet first. Not long after, Saul and Jonathan arrived. Saul has not left her side."

Merab removed a pot from the fire where the baby's soiled undergarments had been soaking in hot water. The water was too hot for her hands, so she used a long wooden spoon to stir the clothes. She watched her brothers huddled in a corner of the common room casting bird and gopher bones against the wall. Before each toss, they placed a hand over the rim of the goblet and rattled the bones inside then tossed them onto the floor, watching them bounce off the wall. They studied the bones after each throw. With each interpretation of how the bones fell, the trio would weave an elaborate story of their futures that always came to a terrible end.

"Why must every story you create come to such a violent end?" Merab asked.

"Because we are men, and men must die in battle," Ishvi said, trying his best to deepen his voice. He snatched the bones off the floor and dropped them into the goblet.

"My turn now," Malki said, reaching for the goblet.

"Just remember to keep your voices low," Merab said and pointed to their parents' bedroom. Merab wanted to be sure her brothers' fantasy games never incited them to speak above a whisper. All verbal communication was spoken with lowered voices.

Merab tested the water with her finger and found she could tolerate the temperature, so she began to scrub the baby's soiled undergarments by hand. She watched as her sister paced the common room, holding their newborn brother against her shoulder and humming a lullaby. The wet nurse lay asleep on a grass mat, resting between feedings. Merab was grateful to have found her. This child had come into the world hungry and demanded to be fed.

"Your mother would like some goat's milk."

Merab stopped scrubbing the moment she heard her father's disembodied voice speak from behind the curtain of the bed chamber. She waved to the boys to pause their game of bones to see if her father had a second request. Mikal stopped pacing the room with the child, and everyone looked at the curtain that concealed their parents' bedroom.

Whenever their father had a request, he would speak through the curtain. He never came out, and Merab was always the one who would respond. Their father did not leave their mother's side. Since he had gotten home, he had shown no interest in his newborn son. He had not held him. He had not named him. He had not looked at him or inquired after his health. Father had one purpose and focus, and that was to care for his wife.

If her mother was half-awake and seemed lucid enough, then Merab would pull back the curtain as Mikal held the baby for their mother to see before she drifted back to sleep. But most of the time it was as if the babe did not exist for either of their parents.

"And more clean towels," came the second request from behind the curtain.

Merab removed her hands from the pot and wiped them on her robe. She poured a cup of milk from the pitcher and collected some clean towels from the shelf behind the kitchen table. Mikal stepped toward the bedroom and met Merab in front of the curtain in case Mother wanted to see the baby or felt strong enough to hold him. Malki and Ishvi rose to their feet to get a better view of the bedroom as Merab pulled back the curtain, but Jonathan held them by the scruff of their necks to keep them from inching any closer and seeing more than they should see.

"I have the milk and towels, Abba. May I give them to you?" Merab asked.

"Yes."

Merab held up her hand to Mikal to stop her from coming any closer with the baby. She would appraise the situation and determine if their mother wished to see her son. There was enough stress on their mother's health to add the additional burden of seeing her newborn and not be able to hold him. When Merab pulled back the curtain, she saw her father dip a sponge into the bucket of water, squeeze out the excess, and gently dab the sponge across her mother's perspiring forehead.

Father sat on a stool beside the bed. The room had a thin cloud of incense masking the odor of two humans kept inside a small space. One lamp provided dim illumination. Merab thought of her parents as two dark shadows residing in a vault. Were this exile not self-imposed, she would consider them prisoners with limited awareness of life outside the confines of their bedroom and reliant on others to bring provision.

Merab did not step past the boundary delineated by the curtain. What happened inside that shadowy space did not require her participation.

Merab could witness activity and report on it but could not engage in it. She waited until her father came to her.

He dropped the sponge into the bucket, got up from the stool, and stepped to the curtain. A stab of pain went through Merab's heart as she watched as her father moved through the weak light and thin mist of incense like a spirit unsure of itself. The edge of the curtain served as a line separating one world from another—a line neither she nor her father would cross, for the world in which her father existed demanded his complete connection, and he did not allow Merab or any of his children to enter.

"Wait there," her father said, taking the cup of goat's milk from Merab, leaving her holding the towels.

Merab watched as he returned to the head of the mattress and placed his hand beneath her mother's neck and back, lifting her so she could take a few sips of the milk. When she was finished, he guided her head gently back onto the cushion and set the cup on the table beside the lamp. He scooted down to the middle of the bed on his knees and drew back the blanket.

When Merab saw the dark red stains of blood beneath her mother, she looked back at Mikal and shook her head, indicating now was not a good time for a viewing. Merab wanted to shut her eyes from this frightening sight, but it was impossible. She knew no healer in Israel would know what to do for her mother. Merab must bear witness, must do all she could to care for her family in this fragile moment.

She watched as her father tenderly pulled her mother's gown above her hips and removed the bloodstained towels from between her thighs and dropped them onto the floor. He next took the sponge from the bucket and washed the blood off her flesh. Then he rose and brought the bundle of soiled towels to Merab.

Saul did not want to look into his daughter's eyes. It was much easier to keep them focused on the clump of bloody cloth, but he could not release the towels. No father should give something like this to his daughter. No daughter should ever receive such an offering. It was not the sight of blood that them unable to make eye contact. It was whose blood and how much of it had been expelled and the volume of towels he had handed off to his daughter each day. It was a cruel ritual.

"Would Ima like to see the child?" Merab asked Saul as if in attempt to break the deadlock of the passing of bloody towels to her.

Saul raised his dark eyes to Merab, eyes starved of inner light but radiating a cold flame of incomprehension at the reality within his bedroom.

"No," he whispered. "Perhaps later." He took the towels from Merab then drew the curtain, shutting the two of them back inside this woeful cocoon.

Saul knelt beside the bed and set the clean towels next to Ahinoam's bare legs. He rinsed the sponge again and took a final swipe over the fresh coating of blood on her skin. He lifted one hip and spread a clean towel beneath her, then gently tucked the other towel between her thighs before pulling the hem of her gown back down around her ankles.

She had slept through the changing of dressings, but the faint cries from the baby had roused Ahinoam from her slumber.

"It is time to feed the child." Ahinoam raised her head, a bewildered look on her face as she tried to discern in the darkness exactly where she was at the moment.

"Not to worry; he is well cared for," Saul said as he stood at the side of the bed and prepared to cover her with the blanket.

Ahinoam put her hand inside the top of her gown and squeezed one of her breasts.

"I have no warmth flowing from inside my breast, no moisture around the nipple." She settled back on the cushion exhausted. "I have no milk and too much blood."

Saul placed the blanket over Ahinoam's legs. "Merab says the wet nurse has a bounty of milk."

Ahinoam cupped her weak hand beneath Saul's chin. "Climb in beside me."

"I am not sure that is a good idea." Saul pressed the cover around Ahinoam's legs.

Ahinoam tugged gently at Saul's beard, refusing to let go until he complied with her wish. So, he raised the blanket and lay down beside her and then pulled the cover over them both. He put his arm around Ahinoam, and she snuggled into his side.

"The child is well cared for, you say?" Ahinoam asked.

"Pampered beyond belief," Saul replied.

"That is good. That is good. I can go then."

"Go where, love?" Saul was puzzled by her remark. Ahinoam was in no condition to go anywhere. But he chose to ignore it and closed his weary eyes.

Saul never should have gotten into bed. He never should have allowed himself the chance to lie down and shut his eyes, a moment to release the pent-up tension that had kept him alert and animated from the moment he got home. This bedroom, confined as it was, sickly and dim as it was, foul and smothering as it was, had become all the kingdom he wanted to rule. He did not wish to rule a nation with large borders. This room was quite enough. He could be king in this room. He understood himself in this room. He knew what was required of him in this room. He had no fear in this room. He faced no adversaries.

And though he was unable to leave this room, no one was allowed in, and he found clarity in the isolation. He could make plans in this room. He could revise those plans and refine them to an order that best served his one subject. The needs of his subject could be met with ease. The routines were simple, and he found a measure of solace in bathing and feeding and dressing and massaging his one subject. This routine was liberating in its simplicity. And though this room was a sparsely inhabited world, it was all the landscape and population he desired to govern.

It was the quickness with which he woke that startled him most. It was as if he sensed the presence of something about to attack him and he woke just in time to defend himself. He ran his dry tongue over his cracked lips and looked about the room, giving his eyes a moment to adjust from the complete darkness of slumber to the dim, interior gloominess of the room. He cocked his ear but heard nothing. No voices came from beyond the curtain. No sound of any kind of activity. Perhaps he was not fully awake, but still asleep and these effects were a part of his dream. He reached for the body of his wife. He thought he remembered her nestled between his chest and arm, but she was now on her side facing the wall with her back to him.

He leaned over and placed his chin on her shoulder and whispered her name, but there was no response. He spoke it again, and again Ahinoam did not answer. Saul pressed Ahinoam onto her back. In the pale light, her features revealed drooping lines and sunken cheeks, her eyelids ajar as if half-asleep, half-awake. He gently shook her, then lifted one eyelid and saw nothing but a white ball. He shook her a second time, more forcefully, and spoke her name; his voice raised in alarm. He had never spoken to her with such a tone, never in all their years of marriage, never in anger or frustration. She had never given him cause.

He leapt out of bed, pulling away the blanket as he got onto his unsteady legs. She could not be gone. She had not asked permission to go. He never would have granted it. He looked down at her still form. The blood had pooled around her middle, soaking through the towels, and saturating her gown. The cloying scent of blood and incense and stale human decay caused a wave of nausea, and he bent over and retched.

Saul gradually became aware of muffled voices calling after him. He placed his hand against the wall and straightened up, then spun around and grabbed at the curtain, tearing it from the wooden rod. He stared into the startled faces of Merab and Jonathan, but the sudden light in the common room cut across his eyes like a knife and he ducked his head and buried his face in the crook of his arm. He stumbled out into the common room. He had finally emerged.

After days in isolation with the wife of his youth, he had emerged like a haggard and frightened beast, his beard moist and clogged with flakes of vomit. He pointed back into the room, directing Merab and Jonathan to stop looking at him in horror. He was humiliated by their shocked expressions and turned away from them. When he heard Merab howl in grief he knew the end had come.

Saul looked around the room for a culprit. Merab rushed out of the bedroom and fell into Jonathan's arms. The twins were bouncing on their toes screaming in confusion. Mikal held her hands to her shaking head, tears streaming from her eyes. Abner and Kish burst through the door and froze at the sight of such anguish. Saul determined that none of these people had driven the sword into his heart. The wet nurse sat in the corner of the room rocking the baby in her arms and shielding his exposed ear to the clamor of sorrow. There was the criminal, the murderer suckling at the breast of the wet nurse.

Saul dashed over to the woman and seized the child by his ankles, yanking him out of her arms. The baby began to scream the moment he dangled upside down above the floor, its arms batting at the air, desperate to survive. Saul grabbed a knife from off the kitchen table and reared back his arm.

"You son of Baal!" he screamed. "You murderous son of Baal!"

Saul held the struggling baby in suspension. He knew he was crazed, that his rational thought had been obliterated. He knew madness had seized him, pushing him toward this reprehensible act. And though he felt a surge of strength rush into his hand holding the blade, he could not force his arm to swing toward the child. He could not command his arm to move. He could not maintain his grip on the knife, and felt his fingers uncurl from around the handle.

He saw pairs of hands grab for the baby as it hung in the air and tear it from his clasp. And the screaming—he was surrounded by screaming, the repeated calling of his name and the pleading for him to stop. Then his howl rose above the shrieking in the room. His woeful cry, the baying howl of a cornered beast, brought the room to a standstill, and he collapsed onto the floor.

Chapter 17

GAD SAT IN HIS CHAIR STARING AT THE KING'S CROWN NES-
tled on the pillow at the head of his cot. He and Jarib had returned to
Gibeah together. Eleazar and Ahiah and their Levitical aides had accompanied the king in pursuit of the Philistines. There was no need for the
skills of a secretary or a prophet to do the business of war. Jarib had turned
around the moment they arrived and rode back to fetch the king, but
since the king and the prince had come home, Gad had not been able to
return the crown.

Everyone had been preoccupied with the well-being of the queen;
everything else had been forgotten. Gad did not seek out anyone who
could deliver the crown for him. The king had placed it into his hands,
and he would return the royal diadem to the one who had entrusted it to
him.

After Saul and the army dispersed from the encampment, Nathan
drove Samuel in his wagon back to Ramah and then returned to Gibeah
as well. On this night, consumed in a cold mist that hissed as it fell all
around the tent, Gad sat still and quiet, entranced by the patterns and
symbols and the face of the wolf of the king's crown. He ignored Nathan
who was busy packing the last of his possessions before going to bed.

There had been little conversation between them. Gad would be relieved once Nathan departed, but he did not want to confess this feeling to his lifelong friend.

"Just sleep on it tonight." Nathan placed his neatly folded prophet's robe on top of the contents of the wooden crate. "Do nothing you might regret."

"Regret," Gad whispered, shaking his head. He found Nathan's words amusing.

Nathan closed the lid of the crate and sat down on his cot. "We were born in the same month, in the same town of Bethlehem, and have gone our whole lives as if there were no shadow of difference between us. Now I see a cleft beginning to form. What has changed with you?"

"With me?" Gad sighed, willing to contemplate the question. "Too much has changed...is changing. Now I ask you, why could you not have gotten the prophet to the camp within the seven-day time period? It was so easy. You could have walked from Ramah carrying him on your back and still have gotten there before the time expired."

"You do not understand, Gad."

"What do I not understand?" Gad blurted. He could not contain his ire, and he watched Nathan lower his eyes.

"It is not just understanding the prophet. It is more than that."

"Please explain, because for seven days the king of Israel was in turmoil waiting for the prophet. The Philistines were bearing down. His own troops were deserting and still he waited, still he obeyed the prophet's command to wait for seven days and not offer the sacrifice until he arrived. Surely, he knew the urgency. The king even sent an armed escort. What was he thinking? What was he doing?"

"He was testing the king." Nathan did not lift his eyes to his friend.

Gad shot out of his chair as though he had been stung.

"Testing...testing the king?" Such a thought was so incredible to Gad that he was not sure he had heard correctly. "What has the king done? Why does he need testing?"

"Be careful, Gad. Be careful not to question the prophet's judgment."

"What about testing the prophet? Who gets to test him?" When Gad saw Nathan's eyes bulge as he looked about the tent, pointing toward the entrance, fearful someone might overhear their argument, Gad raised his hand and lowered his voice. "Sorry to have questioned his authority. He is the prophet of Yahweh. I understand that, but you were not there to see the rack and ruin of the king's heart and mind as he waited for the prophet. You never saw the agony he experienced wondering why the prophet had not come to his aid. It was as if the prophet wanted the king to fail, as if he wanted nothing more than to see the king fail."

"Gad, whose side are you on?"

"Better you should ask whose side is *he* on? Whose side does the prophet take?"

The two lifelong friends stared at each other, yet it was Gad who looked beyond the physical dimension of Nathan's personal features and recognized an imperceptible crack in their friendship that was beginning to widen. He felt as though they were both being dragged away from one another by an invisible power over which they had no control, and this break might become more than just a minor fissure in their friendship. It might become a chasm too wide to ever restore.

"The prophet requested you return to Ramah with me," Nathan spoke softly.

Gad could tell that his forceful tone had frightened his friend; his tone and the questions he asked, the doubts he expressed. Gad needed to calm his heart so that he might calm the heart of his friend.

"Perhaps if you return with me to Ramah, your wavering faith might be restored. The prophet will know what to do. The prophet can bring you back to your senses."

"My faith is not wavering. My senses do not need to be restored."

"The prophet believes that our work with the king is done, that it would be better for everyone if we kept separate paths."

Gad felt the chill of the earth in the soles of his feet and start to rise up his legs. "Does Yahweh walk a separate path from us, I wonder?" Gad sought no answer from his friend. He looked over at the crown shimmering on the pillow, reflecting the flames of the lamps. "I must return this."

The tent flaps suddenly opened and Jarib stepped inside. His turban was soaked, and streams of moisture hung in droplets on his beard. His one dark eye burned through the tears. Jarib opened and closed his mouth in heavy gasps until he spoke finally. His voice was hoarse with sorrow.

"The queue is dead."

Gad waited throughout the night in front of the king's compound. The cold mist no longer saturated the atmosphere, but he had wrapped himself in a thick goat-hair blanket to protect him from the chill. He remained seated on a stool at the edge of a small olive grove that the queen had spared when the builders cleared the area to make way for the construction beyond the compound walls. Gad kept the crown on its pillow and held it in his lap inside the blanket. He remained awake the whole time.

At one point during the night, he watched Jarib usher Ahiah through the front entrance. The high priest was followed by the women who would prepare the queen's body for burial. Another time, Jarib came from the compound to inform the guards and a small crowd of tribal leaders and military officers of the plan to bury the queen at first light. There would be no ceremony, no gathering to memorialize, no official period of mourning. The king and family would mourn in private.

Beerah offered his wagon to transport Ahinoam to the burial cave on the back of the property. Just before daylight, a team of beautiful stallions were harnessed to the wagon and led to the front of the compound. Adara was tethered to the back in case the king chose to ride instead of walk.

Gad was the only one who paid attention as Nathan rode his mule around the compound, plodding toward the road to Gibeah where he would take the main highway north to Ramah. Nathan came to a stop in front of Gad at the base of the olive tree. They had not spoken since Jarib came to the tent to tell of the queen's death. Gad had taken the king's crown and left immediately, leaving Nathan to finish his packing.

"We can be in Ramah in time for midday prayers," Nathan said. When Gad did not respond, Nathan continued, "I tossed and turned upon my cot after you left. I never did go to sleep, so I gave up and decided to leave for Ramah."

"I have not slept either." Gad looked up at his friend. He knew Nathan was waiting for him, to give him one more chance to change his mind, to say he would return, if not now, then once he had returned the crown to its rightful owner. But Gad had not changed his mind. "My place is with the king."

Nathan sighed deeply. "You know the road back to Ramah. It will always be open." Then Nathan snapped the reins on the mule and started down the road.

Gad dropped his head. He would not watch his friend depart. The break had to be clean for it to be effective, yet for Gad, it was not without pain—no regret, just pain. As best friends, they had always argued but never with the thought that any disagreement would bring them to such a moment. They were both prophets of Yahweh, but their shared path had diverged.

One would sit in judgment of the king while the other would counsel the king. Gad chose to carry out his prophetic calling in honor of Yahweh by serving Yahweh's anointed king to the best of his ability. And for the first time in his life, he felt the growing pains in his soul and a flowering of maturity. Instead of being frightened by his decision, he felt the thrill of freedom.

Gad raised the crown in the direction of the early morning light and caught the first rays reflecting off the face of the wolf. His attention was drawn to movement at the entrance to the compound as the family began to emerge. Gad scrambled to his feet. He had been seated so long with his stubby legs tucked beneath the wooden stool it took them a moment to regain the heat of blood flow before they could move forward.

He watched as Ahiah led the priests carrying Ahinoam's shrouded body out of the entrance of the compound. The high priest held a silver tray containing smoking incense that he waved over the body as the priests placed it inside the wagon. Abner and Kish and the children took their place behind the wagon. The king was the last to emerge, tall and solitary; his long arms wrapped over his chest as if he were cold and needed to hold in warmth. When Gad saw Jarib escorting the king around behind the wagon, he was finally able to force his legs to advance.

Gad could tell that Saul was caught off guard by his approach, carrying a round pillow of goat-hair bearing his crown. Saul turned to face him but kept his eyes lowered to the ground. Gad was shocked at the sight of the king's drawn, haggard countenance. The last time he had seen him was at the encampment in Gilgal when he was resilient and bold, preparing to take on the Philistines. But this face had withered almost beyond recognition into dark, hard-lined plains.

Gad dropped to his knees at the feet of the king. When Gad drew breath, he almost gagged at the odor of the king—the king's breath, his unwashed body smelled of carrion rotting in the sun.

"My sovereign lord, may the Creator of heaven and earth have mercy on the king of Israel." Gad raised the pillow and crown above his head, forcing the words through quavering lips.

Gad raised his eyes and saw Saul staring at his crown as if he did not recognize the object or was trying to place it in his memory—a gift presented to him but without any symbolic worth. It was an object of beauty but had no other meaning for him. He turned to look at his family.

"Am I still the king?" Saul asked, but no one responded, everyone too absorbed in their own anguish.

"My lord, you are Yahweh's anointed." Gad chose to answer for a family crushed by grief, for all of Israel if need be.

"Ah yes, Yahweh's anointed. Anointed by Yahweh's anointed. I remember now. You would think that was enough to make me a king." He looked at his wife's wrapped body lying inside the wagon. "But what is a king, truly, when he has no queen?"

Saul waited for an answer, but Gad did not reply. No one spoke. There was no answer that would satisfy. Saul cocked an ear toward Ahinoam as if he caught a final whisper from the queen.

"My lord, you entrusted your crown to me on the day of your great victory over the Philistines." Gad raised the crown a little higher. "I return it now to you."

"I had forgotten about my crown. I had not expected to see it again. But then, I never expected to be standing behind a wagon bearing the body of my wife."

"It is fitting for the king to wear his crown, my lord."

"You keep referring to me as 'king.' I guess it must be so." Saul looked around at the mourners. He straightened himself but kept his arms wrapped over his chest. "It must be. So, crown me, young prophet. Crown me king."

Gad was unsure what the king meant, and he looked at Jarib for guidance.

Jarib stepped over to Gad and helped him to his feet. Then he slipped his hands beneath the pillow and nodded for Gad to place the crown upon the king's head.

Gad lifted the crown off the pillow and extended his arms as far as they would go, but his reach stopped short. He got a few more inches of height by rising up onto his toes, but it still was not enough. The crown came to the king's chin, and when Saul made no motion to take the crown, Gad's arms began to tremble.

"I am sorry, my lord. I am too short to reach your noble head."

Between his upraised arms, Gad saw the king gradually stoop and his knees began to bend. Saul paused at eye-level with Gad, and he saw a sparkle of light in the king's eyes like the quick reflection of sunlight he had just seen in the face of the wolf on the front of the crown.

"I am crowned a second time." And the king sank the rest of the way to his knees.

For days after Ahinoam was buried in the family cave, Saul would not enter the house or the compound. Abner tried to lure him inside, but his cousin refused. Instead, he roamed about the fields and forests and hills surrounding the property. He slept on the ground, did not take shelter when a cold rain fell, did not ask for a change of clothes, did not build a fire to give temporary warmth. He drank little and ate less. Abner thought that if the king was going to die in this mad state, that this was his cousin's attempt to allow exposure to the elements to hasten that end.

Abner suspended all military training and gave the army leave to return to their homes. He kept a small contingent to guard the compound, but there was no threat to the security of the nation after their defeat of the Philistines, and Abner did not want the men to see their king suffering such mental deterioration. No one knew how long it would last or if Saul would ever have his wits restored, but in the meantime, Abner would not allow the grieving king to become an object of pity or scorn. While his cousin was in such a state, Abner, along with the tribal leaders and Jarib, assumed leadership of the nation.

From the roof of Saul's house, Abner would observe his cousin move about the grounds, the idle training fields, and the hills beyond, like a disembodied spirit caught in two worlds. He knew his cousin could have easily wandered off never to be seen again, but this phantom of a man would not totally break free of the bonds tethering him to the corporeal world he had always known.

When Abner could not observe the king from the rooftop, Saul's sons took turns following their father while he wandered, keeping out of sight so as not to disturb him. A small tent was set up behind the house, providing some shelter from the elements, and Abner had Merab and Mikal prepare their father's favorite dishes and left them inside the tent. He hoped this benign trap might coax his cousin back into the world of a loving family. Perhaps if this ghostly creature that was his dear cousin be lured into this tent and taste some of the familiar dishes that at one time had given him such pleasure, perhaps he might come home.

For several days the food spoiled on the plate, but eventually Saul began to nibble on what they had prepared and drank from the wineskin. A change of clothes was left and a blanket. Saul rejected the clothes, but took the blanket, and he never spent one night inside the tent. Abner did not know how to comfort Saul's children suffering a double grief, the loss of their mother and the madness of their father. One was permanent. Abner prayed the other would be only temporary.

When it was time to circumcise and name the child, Abner and Gad went out to inform the king and found Saul outside a storage shed on a hill north of the compound. Saul was sharpening the blade of a plow with a flat stone. He did not even acknowledge that he had heard or understood what Abner said and kept running the stone along the edge of the blade. Abner had Gad to accompany him to bear witness to the encounter, and they both decided that they need not force Saul to return with them.

The ceremony was held in front of the tent behind the house. The hope was that Saul might finally have an interest in his newborn son and take part in the ritual, but he kept his distance, standing under a tree watching from the hill above.

When Ahiah asked for the name of the child, Saul shouted from behind the tree, "Son of Baal! Son of Baal!" then he disappeared into the woods. The family was not sure what to do about recording this child's name after a pagan god, so Ahiah suggested Ish-bosheth, a softer variant, meaning "son of my shame," and Jarib had Ish-bosheth, written for posterity.

The following day when Abner was informed that Adara, the king's horse, was missing from the stables, there was a great consternation when the stable keepers came running into the compound. The king could not be found making his usual rounds over the property, and when the tribal leaders and the family begged Abner to order search parties, he refused.

"The king came to the stables at night and left with his horse. My cousin came to some sort of decision and acted on it. I take this as a positive sign."

"And what if it does not prove positive?" asked Jonathan. "What if he never returns to us?"

Abner had no good answer. "We are all a bit mad at present. This is my madness, to leave my cousin in peace."

Saul dismounted from Adara, threw his blanket over his shoulder, and left the horse free to graze at the entrance of the burial cave. There was enough light coming from the mouth of the cave that he did not need a torch. He had not entered since Ahinoam was buried. He had passed in front of it as he wandered about in these last days—looking inside, listening, but never entering. He dreaded the silence, dreaded beholding the lifeless flesh he had loved, loved still, wrapped in a single sheet.

He ran his hand along the rough cave wall, bracing himself. As he went deeper into the cave, the air became scented with dust and decay and the aroma of burial spices and perfumes. Over these last days of wanderings, Saul's nose had become accustomed to the musk of his own stench, and this sweetened fragrance of burial seasonings sickened him.

He paused at the iron gate and leaned against the bars to allow his stomach to settle and his eyes to adjust to the diminished light. He felt a deep chill in his bones and unfolded his blanket and wrapped it around him. He took several deep breaths, then opened the gate and went over to where Ahinoam lay upon the stone slab. He avoided looking down upon her shrouded body; he could not allow his eyes to see her face, her beautiful face that would soon disintegrate into the chill of the cave. Instead, he looked around the crypt at the dusty, rotting members of his family laid to rest on slabs of stone or inside a carved-out indention in the cave walls. Before he spoke, he relaxed the knotted muscles in his throat with a hard swallow and a deep intake of dank, thin air.

"I just came from Rainbow Cave. I waited for you, but you never came. You should have seen the rainbow. There has been rain and the water flow was high, most I can remember. The mist was so thick it was like a cloud had formed inside the cave. The rainbow was perfect. It all was perfect…except…except for…

"I have not been home since you…I have not been home. I do not want to go home. I do not want to step back into the house we built, the house we shared all these years. I do not want to see the remnants you left behind. These last days I have wandered our land thinking I might find you, listening for your voice. Sometimes I swear I catch a glimpse of you in the distance, and by the time I have gotten to where I think you are, you have vanished. I cannot blame you for not wanting to see me. I must be a terrible sight to behold…smell even worse.

"I never understood the power of sorrow until now. My dear companion, your gentle touch, your blooming flesh, your eyes and lips, your hands and voice and arms are gone, suddenly gone. They have become whispers of memory, memories that waft into sand and disappear into the earth's silent darkness. I must still have a heart because it continues to beat, but I could lie here beside you and be content to wait until it ceased."

Saul cocked his ear anxious for a whispered invitation. He allowed himself a quick glance at her cloth-bound hand to see if it patted the stone slab, a signal for him to stretch out beside her, the last gesture of invitation he remembered her giving him. Instead, he heard a faint reverberation of a voice and looked back at the entrance of the cave. There was a human shadow approaching, and Adara was snorting and pawing the ground. He turned back to address his quiet listener.

"They keep pursuing me. They keep watching and pursuing me. I wish to be left alone, but the pull to return is strong, and I am not sure what I should do. You were so constant. You steadied my heart and mind. You were a gift I thought I would never lose, and now...if I allow myself to weep, the walls of this cave would collapse in on itself."

Saul did allow himself to look upon the whole veiled body. He eased closer to the stone slab; his head suddenly cleared by a cold wind gusting from deep within the cave.

"What did you say? 'Go home,' is that what you said, 'Go home'?"

"My lord. My lord, are you inside?"

Saul turned to see Gad crouching at the entrance of the cave straining his eyes on the darkness. Saul moved away from the stone slab and paused once more.

"Are you telling me to go home?" His voice was a miserable whisper.

"My lord, are you there?"

He did not answer Gad, but he did feel a wave of strength rising from his legs and flow into his chest and arms.

"Home. So be it." Saul did not look back. He shut the iron gate behind him and marched down the center of the cave toward the entrance.

When Gad saw the king emerge from the shadows, he stumbled backward, his face stunned with wonder at the sight of this quickened one who wore soiled, ragged garments, wrapped in a tattered blanket, with a crown atop his head entangled by hairy strands of woodland crust and debris. No wonder he recoiled as if he was witness to one of the dead reentering the world of the living.

"My lord, the prophet has come and requests an audience." Gad spoke softly, and waited for a reply, but there was none.

Gad felt as if the king were studying him as though he were some curious object he had never seen before.

"My lord, what shall I tell the prophet?"

"Nothing. I can tell him myself." Saul removed the blanket wrapped around his body and tossed it aside.

When Saul started for home, he whistled over his shoulder, and Adara bobbed his head and began to trot after his master.

Gad scooped up the blanket and scrambled after Saul who was striding down the hill toward the crowd milling in front of the little tent the family had raised as a temporary shelter.

As Saul drew near, the restive movement of the people began to harden into sculptured figures. His family, the tribal leaders, the prophet's entourage accompanying him from Ramah all froze in place and stilled their breathing, waiting to appraise the present condition of his mind.

Saul came to a stop in front of the prophet who sat in a chair in front of the tent. His lips parted slightly to release a sigh and take a deep breath as he scanned the uneasy faces staring at him, especially the one whose words never fell to the ground.

Adara stopped behind him and nuzzled his back with his snout. Saul raised his hand for the stallion to stop displaying such affection, so Adara stepped back.

Gad lumbered by him and slipped beside Jarib and the rest of the family.

"My lord." Abner stepped forward, a welcome smile upon his face, and bent his knee to Saul.

The crowd followed Abner's example. Except for Samuel. He remained seated though he bowed his head in deference.

"Your wife is at rest in Sheol." Samuel spoke once he raised his head, his voice soft with feeling. "I pray Yahweh give you peace until you join her."

Saul was surprised by the prophet's comforting tone. Even if it was simply a statement of fact, the prophet did offer a prayer on his behalf. The prophet's comment brought a twinge of defiance to Saul's lips in response to the prophet's stern face.

"Whatever prayer you might offer, I accept with gratitude." Saul returned the hardness of the prophet's gaze with his own narrow glare. After the incident in Gilgal when Saul took the initiative to offer the sacrifices before going into battle and not waiting for Samuel to be present as instructed, he was now suspicious of the prophet's sincerity. The last words the prophet had spoken to him were not words of comfort or encouragement. "Yet I know you did not come from Ramah just to offer condolence."

"The Amalekites." Samuel made his announcement with a poise of confidence of his great repute and the urgency of Yahweh.

"Canaanite desert dwellers living on the plains of southern Negev," Saul replied.

"Yahweh put them under a ban for attacking the weak and vulnerable of Israel's people when Moses led our fathers out of Egypt."

"Resurrecting an old grievance," Saul remarked. "Yahweh's memory is long."

"To the thousandth generation," Samuel said.

"Yahweh wants another war? When will the Almighty get His fill of carnage?"

"When the land the Almighty gave to the chosen is cleansed of their enemies." Samuel would not be seated for his message. He would stand. "I am the one sent to anoint you king over Israel, so listen now to the message from Yahweh."

As the prophet of Yahweh rose to his feet, Saul did not step back or flinch. Instead, he took a step forward, spread his legs, and dug his feet into the ground.

"This is what the Lord Almighty says: 'I will punish the Amalekites for what they did to Israel when they waylaid them as they came from Egypt. Go and attack the Amalekites and totally destroy everything that belongs to them. Do not spare them; put to death men and women, children and infants, cattle, sheep, camels, and donkeys."

Saul did not move. He was concentrating on the details of the prophet's message and trying to imagine exactly how he might fulfill this mission; what it might look like should he unleash the wrath of Yahweh on these people. His back was straight. His chin rose in a stiff jut. He was startled at the clarity of his thinking. After all he had gone through, the recent days of grief and sorrow, his mind was surprisingly coherent.

"You hesitate," said the prophet. "Do you doubt the word of Yahweh?"

"I never doubt the word of Yahweh, my lord. But I am always surprised by it."

"How so?"

"Yahweh put the Amalekites under a ban, and I am a king under a similar ban. The last words spoken to me was that my kingdom would not endure. You said this before we attacked the Philistines on the plains of Jordan. Now am I given back the crown and made Yahweh's avenger? Shall the banned king slaughter a banned people?"

"Yahweh has given the Amalekites into your hands." Samuel offered this promise as if to help make Saul comfortable with what he had asked him to do.

"Then Yahweh has given me a bitter victory."

Saul knew the prophet had nothing more to say. He delivered his condolences, spoken the instruction of the Almighty, and was ready to depart. He turned back to his wagon with Nathan and his covey of young prophets falling in line behind him.

Saul waited until the prophet and his company were out of sight before he asked Abner to come stand before him. He spoke in a low voice, cousin to cousin, reestablishing the familial bond.

"I must look a fright." Saul moved back, allowing Abner to study him head to toe.

"You are back with us. That is all we care about." Abner bowed his head to honor his cousin, the king, restored in mind and body.

"You heard the prophet. I have a purpose now, exact Yahweh's revenge upon the Amalekites. How long do you need to muster the troops?"

"Once you give the command, only a few weeks."

"Then let the call go out. Summon the entire army. I want this to be quick and efficient. I wish to be king without going from one war to the next."

"My lord, I say this with all affection, but take a bath and put on some royal robes. I serve a king not a wandering beggar."

Saul's carved face, mask-like with grime and grease, broke into a smile, and he threw his arms around his cousin, pressing him into his chest with a rush of tender relief.

Chapter 18

SAUL STOOD IN A SPOT CALLED "THE PLACE OF LAMBS," A HIGH elevation point of the terrain in the Negev plain where sheep were brought from the wilderness pastures every season to be slaughtered. The dazzling sunlight of midday was near blinding, and Saul shaded his eyes with his forearm. He and his personnel were clumped beneath a large canopy, observing the landscape as it followed a stream down into the valley and widened into the sprawling populace of Amalek, the unwalled City of Nomads.

There was little conversation among the group. Every option had been discussed. Every detail planned. It was now a matter of carrying out the mission of Yahweh voiced by the prophet Samuel. From the shaded safety of the canopy, everyone watched as the thick lines of troops raced toward Amalek in undulating waves. Even at this distance, they all could hear the ferocious sounds of violence and death. Saul and the others waited for the sign of fire and smoke that meant the mission had turned in their favor.

The army had been positioned at this site for over a week. When they first arrived, Abner had suggested this location for Saul's encampment where he could observe. When Ahiah told him the meaning of the location, Saul found it sadistically amusing. "We shall slaughter these Amalekites like lambs," he said, before he shut himself inside his tent to brood in solitude, leaving Abner to oversee preparations for battle.

Once Saul sent word to all twelve tribes that the Amalekites had been put under the ban for their brutal attack of the sick, the weak, and the elderly Israelite stragglers when they entered the land of promise, the desire for revenge brought volunteers by the tens of thousands. A chance to render blood for blood for a crime that took place two centuries ago was opportune. Yahweh had ordained, the prophet had pronounced, and the king had summoned. The Amalekites were a brutal people, not just to other nations, but to themselves, giving over to child sacrifice, enslavement, and ritualistic torture and killing. The evil they perpetuated had gone on for generations. So, the nation of Israel could exact revenge without fear of incrimination or scarring to the national identity or the individual conscience.

Abner, Jonathan, and the military officers spent the first few days clearing out Bedouin tribes not slated for destruction in this crusade and mapping the terrain around the city of Amalek for optimum troop positioning. If there were to be no survivors, it had to be a thorough plan. Should any of the Amalekites escape the initial assault, they would have nowhere to run except up the valley to "The Place of Lambs" and into the arrows and spears of ten thousand warriors from the tribe of Judah. But two hundred-thousand-foot soldiers attacking from all sides with the mandate to annihilate the population would keep the chances of anyone getting away remote.

The prophet had assured him of victory, but Saul was despondent, as if he were dropped into the middle of a great prairie, its vast expanse devoid of any continuance of life, the sky above revealing no glimpse or hint of Yahweh. Saul felt as though he were simply the arm of Yahweh absent the Presence of Yahweh. The Ark was a visible manifestation of Yahweh's companionship, but it resided far from here in the home of a Levite.

Since the death of Ahinoam, he had not read the sacred scrolls with Gad. He knew he should resume that practice, but the death of his wife had drained him of all incentive for study of the sacred texts. His only supposed access to the Creator of the universe was through someone he did not trust, the prophet who spoke for Yahweh but also kept his distance from him.

Gad tried his best to assure Saul when such assurance was needed, but Saul could sense that Gad also felt ill-at-ease in his presence. He was severed from any tangible source to Yahweh, and it created an inner volatility. However, on the morning of the attack, Saul asked Ahiah to build an altar in the middle of the stream and slay a heifer as an offering to assuage the misgivings in his soul.

"Let the ashes and the blood of a heifer flow down this stream into this torrent bed of indiscriminate slaughter." Saul's command was bitter in this throat. "I am not accustomed to ordering the deaths of the aged and the infant."

If the sole purpose for this slaughter was revenge, then a sacrifice would signify he, at least, had contended within himself in expiation of his role in this mass execution.

Malki and Ishvi were the first to spot the plumes of black smoke rising from the city of Amalek. The twins were perched on the ledge of a rock outcropping above the canopy and bouncing on their feet in excitement. Saul had brought the twins because he knew that at home they would be at odds with their sisters and likely create mischief if left on their own.

Saul decided it was time for them to have a closer experience of war and not be kept in the back with the supply wagons or at home. He no longer had to hear their mother's concerns for their safety or worry with the notion that exposure to brutal combat might traumatize their minds. The twins were moving into manhood and such experiences had to be faced if they were ever to become proper military officers. Besides, they were a comfort to him. They loved their father, and Saul needed such adoration.

"Come down from that ledge." Saul's tone was kind, not a barked command. "I want you beside me."

The twins scrambled down the rocky incline without complaint and dashed to their father standing beneath the canopy.

"My lord, what is that?" Jarib pointed toward a strange sight of what appeared to be water from the stream reversing its course and flowing backward in their direction. "Are those people coming toward us?"

The speed with which the fires burned through the neighborhoods and settlements in and around Amalek consuming the makeshift homes and animal skin shelters could be measured in heartbeats. The fires coupled with the savagery of Saul's army were driving those terrorized Amalekites who survived the initial onslaught and funneling them into a human tidal wave. The stream became a churning torrent as the people stampeded through the water and along its banks up the valley into the waiting ambush below Saul's observation point.

Malki and Ishvi pressed their bodies against either side of their father, and each boy curled his arm around his father's waist.

"Steady," Saul said, his voice calm but firm. "Steady. You have nothing to fear. Do not avert your eyes from what you are about to see. This is not a game. This is life and death."

Carmi, leader of the tribe of Judah, stood just outside the canopy, awaiting the king's command. His eyes were focused on Saul and not on any other area of the battlefield. A spearman stood off to one side of the tribal leader with a half-dozen soldiers standing behind him pressing the end of a shofar to their lips. Saul knew Carmi would not order the spear to be thrown or the shofars blown until he gave the order.

It was impossible for Saul to number the horde of Amalekites rushing up the valley stream toward the observation post or how many might be armed combatants who could put up a fight. Saul had to be sure the bulk of the retreating citizens were caught right in the middle of the ten thousand troops hiding in the tall grasses of the plains on either side of the ravine. Close, but not too close—within a spear's throw—was the plan, and the plan was working with flawless precision.

"Hold. Hold. Hold," Saul repeated. He felt Carmi's eyes riveted upon him.

When the screams of the Amalekites became distinguishable, when the ear could differentiate between the howls of a man and the cries of a woman and the shrieks of a child, Malki loosened his hold from his father's waist and slapped his hands over his ears.

From the corner of his eye, Saul could see Malki with his palms over his ears and twisting frantically from side to side.

"Now, Carmi, hurl the spear!" Saul yelled.

"Spearman, throw!" shouted Carmi without taking his eyes off of Saul. There was still a command for the shofars.

Saul watched the spear fly through the air and dive into the middle of the stream. It was a perfect throw and a perfect marker. The stream was wide at that point and the water shallow, which exposed most of the upright shaft.

"Hold. Hold," Saul repeated, once again as the stampeding throng tumbled and splashed toward the spear.

"Abba, what are you waiting for?" Ishvi asked. He too let go of his father's waist but crept to the edge of the canopy and dropped to his knees.

When the front row of the Amalekites reached the spear marking the middle of the stream, it was the end of their retreat.

"Blow, Carmi. Blow the shofar," Saul commanded.

"Blow! Blow!" shouted Carmi, and the pitch of sound from the ram's horn pierced the air, stopping the Amalekite advance.

There was a split second between the fading echoes of the shofars and before the troops from Judah sprang from hiding in the tall grasses, when the only thing to be heard was the flowing of the stream as it rushed around and through the long line of doomed Amalekites standing in the middle of the deep ravine. In that horrible moment of fading silence, Saul looked into the stunned faces of the remnants of a people coming to terms with their fate.

Ten thousand troops were not needed to carry out this mass killing. Saul watched his warriors fight each other for position above the ravine on either side of the stream, and even then, there were not enough targets for all the arrows and spears hurled down upon the throng.

But then his attention was drawn to the Amalekites. A strange languor had come over them as they clustered in the middle of the stream looking up at their executioners. If there were those among them who could have fought back, they chose to not engage in such a futile defense. The Amalekites did not try to run. They did not try to protect themselves. They accepted the spears and arrows and stones falling down upon them in this killing rain. The bodies fell, man, woman, child, and infant still clothed in its swaddled wrap falling from a mother's limp arms, all dropping dead in the ravine and creating a fleshy dam that caused the bloody water to stop its natural course.

Saul reached out and drew Malki and Ishvi back to him. He could feel the violent tremors rushing through their small frames, and he pressed them close. He began to second-guess his decision to bring them. Maybe they were too young to witness such atrocities. This was not a standard act of warfare, so how could he explain this slaughter to his sons when he could not explain it for himself?

Saul watched from the safety of his observation point as soldiers from Judah climbed down both sides of the ravine to reclaim the weapons they used on their victims. There was no reason to waste good arrows or spears. He wondered what thoughts might be rushing through the minds of these men as they grunted and strained to remove their instruments of death from the lifeless bodies soaking in water and blood.

After such an episode, would they resolve to never repeat such a thing? Might they disavow such actions and return home to a quiet, peaceful future? Or would this experience do nothing to reform their soul, only harden it? He felt his chest and wondered if hardening had begun in his own heart. Was this really why he had been made king—to fight wars, exact revenge, wipe out whole races of people?

"My lord, the commander approaches." Carmi pointed toward Abner riding in from the valley, leading a wagon surrounded by other soldiers on horseback.

Saul welcomed the distraction from the carnage in the ravine. He pointed for Jarib to look after his sons before he stepped from underneath the canopy to meet Abner. He could see there was someone inside the wagon but could not tell who it might be. A prisoner, surely, but there were not to be any prisoners. What was Abner thinking?

The first thing Saul noticed when Abner dismounted his horse was the spotless condition of his clothes. "You did not draw your sword today, Commander?" Saul asked.

"The fires did much of the work. There was no need. Our forces were thorough."

"Losses?" Saul was more curious than concerned. He secretly hoped for some casualties among his ranks to make the massacre somewhat palatable.

"None, my lord."

"Ah." Saul heaved a sigh, not in relief upon hearing the news, but of somberness. Saul looked over the valley and saw the heavy black cloud of smoke forming over the smoldering remains of Amalek. Yahweh would see that the chosen paid no price for carrying out his command.

"And Jonathan, where is he?" Saul cupped his hand over his brow to block the glare as he scanned the valley to see if he might locate his son.

"He volunteered to lead a company of men to search out any outlying Amalekite clans not in the city. He is making a circle from Havilah to Shur and will join us at the crossroads in Carmel on our way north back home."

"He volunteered, you say."

"Yes, my lord."

"Abner, you know my son, you know his heart." Saul dropped his voice and moved closer to Abner. "Why did he volunteer for such a mission? Why did he not come back to camp and travel home with me?"

"He said nothing to me of his reasons, my lord."

"And what do you think was his reason?"

Abner hesitated and looked away and Saul knew to expect an answer he would not like. He gave his cousin the time needed to formulate his response.

"My lord, I believe he did not want to face you. He saw no honor in this mission, not like our other campaigns. But I do not know his mind on this matter."

"And what is your mind, Commander, of our mission?" Saul looked behind Abner's eyes for deep truth, hoping it might confirm his own qualms.

"My lord, I never thought I would say this, but I must agree with the prophet. The Amalekites deserved what was commanded. When a people sacrifice a child just to get rain for their crops and ensure a good harvest, then the stench of their evil has reached the heavens. It is a righteous judgment."

Saul nodded. He was alone in his misgivings then. Only Jonathan seemed to share this fellow feeling. But of this nothing could come. The righteous judgment of Yahweh and the prophet had prevailed.

"Who do we have in the wagon, Commander?" Saul pointed to the wagon.

"Come and see, my lord." Abner guided the king around the wagon.

Saul looked at the naked man kneeling inside the bed of the wagon. His wrists were bound and soaked in blood and his arms were stretched out and tied to the railings on each side. A goat-haired robe with gold and purple ribbons tied to it was tossed in the corner of the wagon with a leafy bronze circlet lying on top. The moment he saw the man, the prisoner burst into a frantic babble.

"Who is he?" asked Saul. "What is he saying?"

"I do not know, my lord, but I assume he is the king of Amalek by what he was wearing or not wearing." Abner pointed to the wardrobe in the corner of the wagon.

"Fetch Jarib," Saul ordered, and a soldier rushed to get his secretary.

"We searched the citadel before we set it on fire." Abner nodded toward the inflamed village in the valley below. "It was the largest structure in the center of the settlement so I assumed it was for their king. We found him hiding under his bed."

When Jarib appeared at the side of the wagon, the prisoner intensified his jabber.

Saul moved closer to the back edge of the wagon. "What is he saying, Jarib?"

Jarib listened for a moment before responding. "It is a Canaanite dialect, my lord. I recognize only a few words."

"Find out if he is the king and get his name." Saul was becoming disgusted by the undignified behavior of the naked man in the wagon.

"Ask about his clothes and if the bronze-leafed band is his crown," Abner added.

It could not be called a conversation, but after struggling with a few Canaanite phrases and simple words, Jarib was able to determine the man's identity.

"He says he is the king of Amalek, my lord," Jarib said.

"He is the king?" Saul asked, feeling his stomach beginning to tighten.

"Agag. Agag. Agag." The man in the wagon repeated his name as if he were a beggar hoping Saul would take pity. His eyes seemed to brighten with hope that even in his wretched state, he might be addressing someone of equal station.

"Yes, my lord. He says he is Agag, king of the Amalekites."

Agag nodded his head furiously, half-growling, half-pleading for mercy until he slumped into an exhausted silence with a final blubber.

Saul eyed Agag. The poor man's knees were chafed, his scarified chest showed pagan deities, and his long black tangled hair was braided with strands of bead and shards of animal bone. There were not supposed to be survivors. Why did he have to make this decision? Why had Abner not made this decision for him?

"Abner, why did you not skewer him while he hid under his bed?" But Abner did not respond. "This is what becomes of us all, a mewling, contemptible creature. There has been enough killing for one day. Clothe and feed him but keep him out of my sight."

Chapter 19

SHIRA SAT ON THE TOP STEP OF THE OUTSIDE STAIRS LEADING to the roof of the house, looking at Samuel stretched out beside the fire smoldering inside the metal basin, exhausted from an unexpected encounter with Yahweh. There were two plates of cold food, two goblets, and a skin of wine on a tray beside her on the step. She had worked all afternoon preparing this meal for the two of them. They were to have a quiet dinner. They were to be left alone. Nathan and the other students were free to go to Ramah if they chose, as long as they were home by nightfall, and under no circumstances were they to interrupt their master's evening with his wife.

It was Yahweh who intruded. She had sat there all night waiting for her husband to recover, and the sunlight was just beginning to appear over the mountains. She was shivering from the cold. She had not touched the food or drink. She had not slept. She had kept watch. She could hear his heavy, wet breathing. He was not asleep, that she knew. He was gathering himself, putting the fragmented pieces of his heart back together. He could not rise, and she could not approach him until he was restored. But how could he ever be restored after such an experience?

Shira was taken by surprise at Samuel's succumbing to Yahweh's unexpected intervention into their evening. She and Samuel had been enjoying a goblet of wine and a plate of figs and flatbread as they watched the sunset from the roof, then with a kiss on his cheek, she excused herself to get their supper from below while Samuel built the fire in the metal basin for warmth and light while they ate their meal.

After all these years Shira could usually read the signs leading up to an interaction between her husband and Yahweh. He became distracted and would descend deep into thought. He would not make eye contact but look off into space and bump into things. He would not respond if she attempted to speak to him. He was severed from reality and moved into his dream-self.

But tonight, the warning signs were not there. She had gone into the house, prepared the tray of food, and was carrying it up the outside stairs to rejoin the docile and pleasant husband she had left only moments before when she heard the howling. Her heart stopped. She was sure Samuel had injured himself, and she hurried up the remaining stairs only to see her husband standing before the fire rending his robe. She stood in shock, watching him tear his garment from the collar all the way down to the hem, a duet sound of ripping material and anguished cries filling the air.

This was something Shira had never before seen. She had made this robe from the best material she could buy, a favorite garment in his wardrobe, one he was so fussy about that he insisted she clean it whenever it was smudged with dirt or soiled by food stains. Now he had ripped it in half, exposing his bare chest and legs and undergarments. She could not imagine the strength it had taken to tear the material or the agitation of his mind that would cause him to ruin something he had cared for so meticulously.

Shira knew not to approach. She knew not to attempt contact. She never allowed herself to be emotionally drawn into this mysterious, dark connection her husband had with the Almighty. She knew she was not made to withstand the pull of grief Yahweh caused on one's soul. This was only for her husband, and her role was to help put her husband back together after each encounter. But what she was witnessing was more extreme than anything she had ever seen, and she feared her husband might harm himself, falling from the rooftop or stumbling into the fire if this went on unabated.

"My lady. My lady." The voice from below the stairs drew Shira's attention, and she was distracted from viewing her prostrate husband long enough to see Nathan at the bottom of the stairs standing beneath the torch secured in a receptacle on the outside wall.

Shira tried to speak but was not sure what to say. She was not sure she wanted Samuel's favorite student to see him so distraught. She was not sure herself if she wanted to watch any more of her husband's misery articulated in bestial groans and uncontrollable weeping and raspy sighs. She set the tray on the top step.

"My lady, is he—" Nathan spoke but was stopped by Shira's raised hand.

She observed Samuel a little longer, checking her impulse to expose Nathan to his master's wild antics. She finally decided it was better for Nathan to see firsthand what extreme communication with the Almighty might look like and not just be told about it.

"Come, Nathan. You must see this." Shira waved for him to join her. She did not fear being heard by her husband. Samuel was plunged into the depths of Yahweh and would not hear or even be aware that either of them existed.

Nathan bound up the stairs two at a time and stopped beside her, breathless from his exertion. Together they watched husband and master being tossed about the rooftop, his hair flying loose like a white halo around his head, his sundered garment rippling like sails as though caught in the tempest of some airstreams.

"What is this, my lady?" Nathan asked.

"This is what comes with close association with Yahweh, but never have I witnessed anything like this. This is different. He weeps. He howls. He cannot stop. This is grief. Yahweh is funneling his grief through the heart of my husband."

"Should we do something? Should we try and calm him?"

Shira would have found Nathan's remarks quaint and amusing were she not so taken by her husband's behavior.

"We do nothing. Once Yahweh departs, he will come back to me."

"I could not imagine what the master experiences in these moments," Nathan said.

"What about the other students? Where are they?"

"In their beds, though probably not asleep," Nathan replied. "We all heard the master's cries. I came to find the cause for the alarm. What should I tell them?"

"Tell them what you see. Tell them this is what you never learn from studying holy scrolls or listening to lectures or copying the sacred texts. For some, tell them this is their future. He will summon you when this is over. Now leave us."

Once Nathan left, Shira sat down on the top step to keep vigil. The night passed and the fatigue weighed heavy on her eyelids, yet she remained awake until her husband had fallen flat beside the fire and continued to weep and cry the name of Yahweh and the name of the king till there were no more words or names to speak only a steady weeping that settled finally into harsh, taxing breathing as though exhaling from deep inside a well. And with the rhythm of his breathing, Shira allowed her head to gradually drop.

The moment she felt his hand upon her shoulder she snapped her head back and gasped. He stood before her, light seeming to radiate from him; whether the source was Yahweh or the bright dawn, she could not tell nor did she care. She leapt to her feet, and he enveloped her inside the folds of his torn robe. She felt the heat from his flesh, and for the first time all night, she was warm.

"You were here all night?" Samuel asked. "You saw everything?"

"Yes," she said, and Shira could no longer constrain her tears. "Yes, I saw everything. It was terrible, frightening. I feared for your life."

"Yes. Yes." Samuel gently stroked the back of her head. "It was fearful. It was like nothing before."

"You are back though." Shira grabbed his arms and pulled herself away for a clear look into his face. "You are back with me?"

"Yes, I am back." Samuel brought her hands to his lips. "But I must go. I must go at once and find the king."

"But you must be exhausted. You need to eat and rest."

"When I return, I will gorge myself and sleep for days, but I must find the king. It is not too late. I hope and pray it is not too late. If I find him now, perhaps I can save him from himself."

"What do you mean?"

"I feel purified by Yahweh's grief and compassion. The residue of bitterness I held against the king has been washed clean from my heart. My heart is revived with a new fondness for the man I anointed. I feel an attachment I never felt, should have felt from the beginning, and I am frightened for him. If he will only obey. The king is angry that he does not understand Yahweh. I do not understand Yahweh, but he must only obey. If I can convince the king just to obey, then maybe I can save him."

"And who will save you, my love?" Shira fell back into his embrace.

"In your arms I am saved. In your arms I have always been safe."

And there they stood. And there they could have stood, ignoring time, locked inside each other's arms, one flesh, one heartbeat, one breath, except for the insistence of Yahweh. They both were biddable to the insistence of Yahweh.

Saul placed his left hand upon the chiseled replica of his hand cut into the monument. He stroked the rough surface with his extended fingers and rubbed his fleshy palm against the stony reproduction. Above the image of his hand was a carving of the face of a wolf wearing a crown, his crown. He stepped back from the pillar and paused between it and the huddle of admirers gathered for the dedication of the obelisk. The monument was framed within an arch of palm and olive branches and set on a rise outside the village of Carmel: a northern outpost in the nomadic circuits of the Amalekites now depopulated and used as a stopover base camp for the army of Israel.

"It pleases me." Saul wiped the grainy residue from his left hand onto his clothes. "I cannot believe I allowed you to talk me into agreeing to this, but I like it."

"My lord, this is your third victory," Jeush said. "One by one, you are defeating the sworn enemies of Israel."

Carmi raised his arm to the statue. "Like Joshua, my lord, the first great commander of our nation."

"You, my lord, will finish what Joshua began when he led our fathers into the land of promise," Beerah said, and he bent his knee before Saul and bowed his head.

"You hear that, Abner?" Saul's lips curled with a grin unseen by his cousin standing behind him. "I am like Joshua, the great commander."

"Yes, like Joshua." Abner agreed with the comparison without bias or disdain.

"This day must be recorded, my lord," Gad said. "We must write of these events. Israel must remember this day."

Saul agreed to erect a monument to honor himself after the bulk of the army had been dismissed and sent home. Carmi with his troops from Judah and Saul's elite band of three thousand warriors were all that remained at Carmel.

"Yes, Gad, you and Jarib see to the writing of this event, though I am not sure I want this bloody record of our history, my history, for all to read." Saul lowered his head.

The reduced military force had taken this pause in the march for home until those assigned the task of gathering the Amalekite livestock could catch up with them in Carmel. Those cattle and sheep that did not pass inspection, deemed imperfect in any way, were slaughtered. This also gave Jonathan and those under his command the time needed to complete their foray to exterminate outlying bands of Amalekites.

Saul glanced over at Jonathan standing apart from the rest of the group with his arms draped over the shoulders of his twin brothers. Jonathan, Adriel, and their volunteer fighters had returned at dusk the day before. Saul was relieved to see his son when he came to his tent to report on the success of their mission. Jonathan did not say much and made little eye contact with him. Adriel had given the report while Jonathan stared into the fire, sipped on his wine, nibbled on some roasted Amalekite beef, and would only corroborate Adriel's account of their proficiency with an occasional nod of his head.

At the end of Adriel's report, Saul gently pressed his son for any final thoughts. "The prophet should be satisfied," was all the prince offered.

Saul did not ask him to elaborate. He, like his son, did not want to dwell on the loathsome details of this crusade.

"What do you think, Son?" Saul turned to face Jonathan while he pointed to the monument behind him, and all eyes turned to the prince for his reaction.

Jonathan opened his mouth to speak, but his lips began to quiver, and he clamped his teeth over his bottom lip. Saul noticed that the twins looked up at Jonathan, but he grabbed the tops of their heads, twisted their faces away, directing them back to him.

"All who pass before this pillar will see the power and strength of the king of Israel," Jonathan said.

"Yes. Yes, they will," Saul turned away from the glare of his son. Jonathan's look forced him to tamp down a rise of self-loathing in his stomach and he cast his attention to the high priest. "Ahiah, are the altars built?"

"Yes, my lord."

"Excellent. Prepare the sacrifices. We shall cut the throats of a few Amalekite beasts, say a prayer, and make our final push for home."

Saul gave the command, but no one in the group moved to obey. Their attention had been distracted. They were no longer listening or looking at him. Their eyes were focused upon the speeding approach of the prophet's wagon.

Nathan was in the driver's seat with Samuel in the back, just the two of them, not with his usual flock of novice prophets. Nathan pulled in front of Saul and stopped.

Saul stared at Samuel; the prophet stared back. Saul waited, listening, watching Samuel for the slightest nuance of undercurrents that would be revealed, but Samuel made no effort of getting out of the wagon.

"Yahweh bless you, my lord." Saul broke the silence with an innocuous greeting. "I have carried out Yahweh's instructions."

Samuel appeared not to have heard Saul's salutation but kept looking at him in expectation. Then he lifted his head as if a distant sound caught his ear by surprise. He placed both hands on the railing across the back of the driver's seat where Nathan sat holding the reins and pulled himself to his feet. Samuel held onto the railing and swept his eyes over the encampment. When his gaze came to rest upon the stone pillar with the carved left hand of the king and the sign of his tribe, Samuel pointed to the monument and appeared as if he might speak, but then brought his hand to the side of his face and began to tap his ear with his finger.

"What is this I hear?" Samuel whispered.

Saul looked around uncertain how to respond. He instinctively knew the prophet's question did not require him to answer.

"What is this bleating of sheep in my ears? What is this lowing of cattle?"

Saul looked into Samuel's composed face and imagined him losing his balance, pitching backward out of the wagon, and falling to the ground. He was startled by how amusing he found such a thought, but he could not avoid an answer.

"My lord, the troops brought them from the Amalekites. They spared the best of the sheep and cattle to sacrifice." Saul realized mid-sentence that he felt a cool bubbling beneath his skin. He looked down at his arm and saw streams of trickling sweat. "The livestock were chosen to sacrifice to Yahweh, your God, but we destroyed the rest."

"Please." Samuel extended his opened hand toward Saul's mouth as if to prevent him from incriminating himself any more than he had. He did not want to believe what his ears had detected and what Saul had just confirmed. He did not want to believe what Yahweh had conveyed to him the night before was true. "I must tell you what Yahweh revealed to me last night."

"Tell me." Saul's weak reply indicated to Samuel that Saul's soul was eroding with every heartbeat.

Where Samuel might at one time have been tempted to manipulate his power over Saul, he knew the words he would now speak would bring him no pleasure, only rekindle the grief he had experienced the night before. He looked into the eyes of the king and saw the soul of a pitiable and frightened man—a man he desperately hoped to save—but feared that was now an impossible task. The downward spiral had begun.

The moment he recognized the sounds of the cattle and sheep, the moment Saul tried to shift the blame to his soldiers, Samuel knew all was lost. This man who had such promise, who had such clear perspective on his place in the world, was now lost. He would speak what he was compelled to speak. He would do what he came to do. Then he would leave and never return to the king. He could no longer watch what he had helped set in motion.

"At one time in your life you knew who you were. You saw yourself as small in your own eyes, humble, unworthy to be raised from your lowly station." Samuel paused to look at the monument with the king's hand and tribal symbol. "Did Yahweh not make you head of all the tribes of Israel? Did Yahweh not anoint you king over His people?"

Samuel closed his eyes and lowered his head. He did not want to look at this object of vanity or at the person it represented. "Yahweh sent you on a mission." Samuel kept his head lowered as he continued. "Yahweh said, 'Go, claim the Amalekites for me. Make war on these wicked people until you have wiped them out.'" Samuel paused again so that Yahweh's repetitive directive might ring in Saul's ear, so its cruel truth might be affirmed in Saul's heart. "Why did you not obey Yahweh? Why did you pounce on the plunder and do what is evil in the eyes of Yahweh?"

"How dare you come into my camp like this? How dare you? I did obey Yahweh. Do you reproach me because I obeyed you? How dare you? I went on the mission, this rampage Yahweh ordered, and completely destroyed the Amalekites. I captured Agag, the king, as proof of my victory, and the soldiers kept the sheep and cattle. It was the best of the plunder, not blemished spoils, but selected as first fruits to be sacrificed to Yahweh. Yahweh…your God. Are you not pleased by this, by my victory, and by my public homage to your God?"

Samuel held onto the railing of the driver's seat in his wagon and lowered himself back into his seat. He opened his eyes and looked at his hands, hands he had laid upon the king's head when he had poured the sacred oil of Yahweh upon him. These hands were now chaffed and cracked with age, gnarled and painful to flex.

"Yahweh takes little delight in sacrifice." Samuel spoke so softly that Saul leaned over the side of the wagon to be sure he heard correctly.

"Yahweh takes more delight when you obey His voice. To obey the voice of Yahweh is better than any sacrifice."

Saul gripped the small side door so hard he almost broke it off the wagon.

"I have never heard Yahweh's voice. I have only heard your voice, and your voice has brought me nothing but pain and confusion."

Samuel nodded. He expected this reaction. He expected to be blamed. Perhaps there was truth he needed to hear, but he would grapple with that possibility at another time and place. There was more to be said. He leaned forward in his seat, interlocked his knotty fingers, and lowered his head and voice.

"Rebellion is like the sin of witchcraft. Arrogance is as evil as idolatry." Samuel shook his head from side to side. Then he turned his face to Saul and looked him in the eyes. He could not say what had to be said and not face him squarely. He owed him that much…to speak truth to the king, eye to eye. "You have rejected the word of Yahweh, and now Yahweh has rejected you as king."

The pores in Saul's body became like gushing springs. He licked his chapped lips. He sucked on his tongue for the least drop of moisture. Saul could feel the tremors as though his body would crack and fragment into a thousand pieces. He looked down at his hands gripping the wagon door and saw they were bleeding. It frightened him and he let go, leaving two bloody impressions. Saul lifted his hands, impaled with splinters.

"Why did you ever anoint me?" Saul held his hands before the prophet like a pitiful beggar. "Why did Yahweh ever choose me? Just to condemn me? Just to saturate me in His bloody vendettas against some heathen people? Why does He give such terrible commands then expect mere men to carry them out? Is Yahweh so blinded by the glory of His commands that He cannot see human frailty and take pity? If He wanted me to do His bloody work, then why did He not come to me Himself? Why did He send word to me through someone who despises me?"

Saul did not want answers to his questions. He did not want to ask any more questions. He wanted to close his ears to questions, close his ears to the prophet and to his God. He wanted to close his heart and mind to any more reminders of his failures and shortcomings. If truth was spoken, then truth had its own mysterious power to kill.

Saul looked to the heavens half-expecting to be struck dead for railing against the Almighty. When that did not happen, he took a step back from the wagon. He would regain control. He would take charge and be his own master. Every heartbeat, every breath he had left, he intended to be king. If he were struck down then he would be true to himself to that final moment. He would not abdicate his crown willingly. He was no coward. It would have to be taken from him. And he would use the prophet as he perceived the prophet had used him.

The best response for now was to agree with the prophet, not make a scene, display no anger, but be a king—every inch a king. Be a king for all those who were watching: his commander, his court, his elite army, his sons, all those loyal to him. Wear a brave face for them. Make the best of this situation, perhaps even turn it in his favor.

"I have sinned, my lord." Saul spoke with no hint of antagonism. "I have violated Yahweh's command and your instructions. I was afraid of the people and gave in to them. Now I beg you, forgive my sin, and come with me, so that I may worship Yahweh. We have erected the altars and prepared the offerings."

When Saul noticed tears beginning to trickle from the prophet's eyes, he believed his mild show of contrition was working.

"I cannot do this for you." Samuel spoke with a sob in his throat. "I cannot go with you to worship. You have rejected the word of the Almighty and the Almighty has rejected you as king over Israel."

Saul thought the momentum was in his favor. He had not expected Samuel to continue this vein of rejection once he confessed his sin. Was the old man on to his ploy?

"Drive on, Nathan." Samuel spoke and then leaned back in his seat.

When Nathan snapped the reins across the backs of the horses, Saul impulsively reached for Samuel, grabbing the sleeve of the prophet's robe. The sound of the ripping material was like the gutting of a slain beast, the sharp blade cutting through flesh. Samuel's arm flew up, a single limb tossed into the air. Nathan's quick reaction to stop the wagon kept the prophet from having his arm wrenched from its socket.

The wagon moved only a short distance, but when it came to a stop, Samuel's forward motion brought him to his feet in his wagon. He twisted his body around and glowered down at Saul holding the limp fabric in his left hand. With the stripping of the sleeve all pretense between prophet and king was stripped away.

"Yahweh has torn the kingdom of Israel from you!" Samuel shouted, waving his naked arm skyward in direct connection with his God. "He will give the kingdom to another, one better than you. He who is the Strength of Israel does not lie. He who is the Eternal Presence does not change His mind. He is not a mortal in need of repentance."

Saul's lips were parted to respond but he checked himself. Viewing Samuel in his wagon, one stout finger pointing to the sky, his bare arm exposed, misshapen flesh drooping back to earth, the prophet looked not imposing, but pitiful. He stood with the limp sleeve of the prophet's robe in his hand crusted with dried blood and splinters.

There had been too many of these moments where he and Samuel faced off. Saul resolved that this would be the last time. He would make one more effort to show he could be artful in turning a bad circumstance into a favorable one.

"Yes, my lord. I have sinned." Saul folded the prophet's sleeve into squares. "But please honor me before the tribal leaders of my people and before Israel; come with me so that I may worship the Lord your God."

Saul rubbed his thumb over the fabric once he had completed the last fold, but instead of offering it back to Samuel, he tucked it inside his leather vest—a subtle power play signifying a freedom from intimidation. Saul waited patiently for Samuel to respond. The prophet could stay and worship or depart. It mattered not to Saul. He had won either way. He made his penance public, and the offer to worship with the prophet showed humility and an attempt at reconciliation, something the prophet himself never pretended to reciprocate. He may be openly slighted by Yahweh and Samuel, but before his royal court and the people of Israel, his reputation and honor would be upheld.

Samuel let his arm fall to his side. He sensed a strange vulnerability after Saul's reaction to his pronouncement that Yahweh had torn the kingdom from him. Had he spoken in haste? In the heat of this moment, had he used the ripping away of his sleeve as an illustration of Yahweh's determination to remove Saul as king? And who would Yahweh put in his place? He had hoped it would not come to this. He had envisioned the evolving circumstances would produce a different ending. Before he had departed his home, he actually believed there could be a chance for another outcome.

"I will stay and worship with you," Samuel said.

"Excellent," Saul replied and turned to his commander. "Abner, summon the troops. The prophet will worship with us."

Saul had seen that he and Samuel were positioned in the center of the wide circle of a dozen altars set in the middle of the encampment. A leader of each tribe stood in front of their assigned altar. Beside the tribal leader stood a priest, his knife drawn waiting for the high priest to give the signal to slaughter each heifer. These twelve sacrifices from the twelve tribes were to honor Yahweh and the king for the completion of their mission. Saul was dressed in full armor for this moment. Courtly robes were not the look of strength he wanted. Armor, sword, and his crown were the look of a king.

Saul grunted as Jarib tightened the straps of his breastplate. He turned to look behind him and noticed Gad holding his crown. He smiled at this young prophet, but Gad lowered his gaze to focus on the crown. Saul knew Gad did not want to display any affinity for him before his master. When Jarib stepped away after a last inspection of his armor, Samuel turned to whisper in Saul's ear.

"Where is Agag?" Samuel asked.

"You want him here for our sacrifices?" Saul was taken by surprise.

"The king of the Amalekites should bear witness to Yahweh at this sacrifice to the God of heaven and earth."

Saul was pleased by the prophet's suggestion. He barked at Abner who in turn shouted for the command to be carried out. Two soldiers broke rank and raced off to fetch Agag. Then Saul nodded for Gad to bring his crown. When Gad stood in front of him, Saul took the crown and put it upon his head. He would not display any submissive action in front of Samuel. He was king and could put on the crown himself.

"You know what the Amalekites have done to our men whenever they have captured any of them?" Samuel spoke to Saul but watched Gad exit the ring of altars to take his place among the inner circle of the royal court.

"What is that?" Saul was curious where this might lead. It was just the two of them in the middle of the loop. What could he say that would be harmful?

"They mock us." Samuel scratched the ground with the toe of his sandal. "They mock our rite of circumcision by mutilating every male who falls into their hands. If they do not destroy us in war, they try by making us childless. You have preserved a man's life who wishes to extinguish the flame of Yahweh from the face of the earth."

Saul did not detect any hint of disapproval in the prophet's tone, just a calm imparting of information, a private history tutorial, to which Saul reacted with a jest.

"We can breed faster than the Amalekites can mutilate us."

Saul signaled for the twins to draw near.

Samuel began to feel a heaviness in his heart. Altars were built and sacrifices were prepared, but this was not a holy moment. This was not to be a moment of worship. This was a sham, and he felt he had become a false prophet by pretending to approve of this sacrifice. But when Saul's twin sons approached carrying their father's sword, Samuel felt an unexpected surge of power rush through him almost as strong as what he experienced the night before on the roof of his house when Yahweh had descended upon him. The sword was the sword of Samuel's fathers, covered with

Egyptian symbols: the top rim where the bronze hilt of the sword rested was the symbol of the Aket, the sun nestled between two mountain peaks, and the Ankh, the symbol of eternal life, on the opposite side.

The sword his father had given him, the sword Samuel had offered to the Benjamite warrior to deliver the news to the high priest that his sons had been killed in battle, the sword he had last seen on the rooftop of his house the night before he had anointed this man the king of Israel.

"Your sword. Your sword." Samuel widened his eyes, his voice a raw gasp.

"A gift to my father from a Levite on the day the Philistines sacked Shiloh and captured the Ark of the Covenant," Saul answered.

"That was…" Samuel said but caught sight of Agag from the corner of his eye.

"A long time ago, yes," Saul said.

Maybe it was the smugness of Agag's face as he was ushered into the circle that set off the rage within Samuel. Agag was escorted, unfettered, robed and crowned in his Amalekite royal attire, jabbering in his native dialect apparently amused by the formation of this sacred circle and confident he was summoned to be an honored guest at this unusual gathering. There was not the slightest hint of awareness of a potential for personal harm.

The twins offered the sword to Saul, and when father and sons became distracted by Agag's noisy entrance into the circle, Samuel yanked the weapon out of their hands.

"This is the sword of my family. This is the sword of my forefathers brought out of Egypt. This is the sword my father gave me on the day of Shiloh's destruction. This is the sword I gave to your father on the day of the destruction of Shiloh."

Agag stopped mid-stride. He felt the whoosh of air as the blade swooped by his left ear, and then he turned his head to see his left arm fall to the ground. His self-satisfied expression changed to one of alarm as he looked into the eyes of his attacker.

"As your sword made women childless!" Samuel cried just before he severed Agag's right arm at the shoulder. "So will your mother be childless among women!"

Agag's eyes bulged in horror at the sight of his blood spraying over the king's twin sons as they climbed their father's rigid body like he was a tree. Samuel slammed his foot into Agag's chest, and when he fell to the ground, Agag kept his eyes on the heavens. He did not raise his head to look at his body as it trembled with each successive blow.

When Samuel finished his brutal onslaught, he brought the sword blade to the side of his own head, grabbed a fistful of his own hair, and cut it off at the base of his scalp. Then he scattered the mass of white strands over the pieces of Agag's anatomy quivering on the blood-soaked ground, raised the sword into the air, and released a howl of triumph.

PART THREE

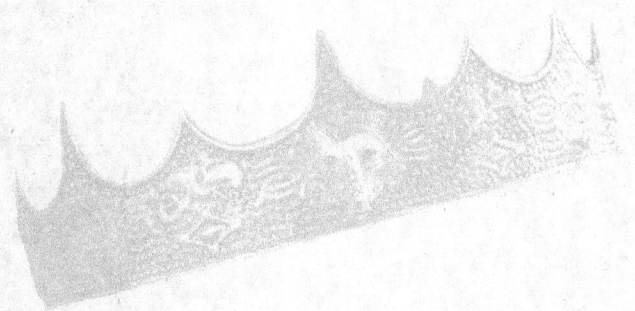

PART THREE

Chapter 20

SAMUEL SAT STARING INTO THE FIRE BURNING IN THE RAISED fireplace in the common room. The flames had not been allowed to die out since he returned home from his encounter with the king. He stared and stared; his breathing slow. He listened for the voice of Yahweh but heard only the crackle and hiss of blazing wood. His thoughts drifted back to where it began with fire and sacrifice, with burning flesh and its sweet aroma rising in the Holy Place. It had all been so simple back then, orderly and simple, no unreasonable requests by the Creator of heaven and earth. Just keep the fire burning on the altar; never let it go out. All day and all night it was to burn, a constant reminder of the special bond Israel had with the Almighty.

Since he could remember, all Samuel knew was to be faithful to that bond. He could not do otherwise. He could not envision his life without Yahweh, to reckon that Yahweh might be a creation of his imagination. He had heard the voice. He had seen the fiery persona. He had felt the divine power. Hannah, his mother, had instilled in him that he was a child of promise, a child of the vow, saturated with Yahweh's Spirit from the womb, and from the moment the altar fire in the Tabernacle illuminated his consciousness, the Presence of Yahweh devoured him.

At all times of his life, the mystery of Yahweh pulsated in and around him. At moments the grip had been gentle; at other times, it had been close to strangulation. But now he felt nothing but an absence, a slow disintegration of his soul. He had never felt so empty, absent from all connection to any form of vital life. Had Yahweh finished with him? Was this how he was going to end his life—sitting in a tub of water, staring at a fire, never again stepping outside into the light of day?

This was his fifth bath in as many days.

"I must get clean. My muscles ache. I have a chill. The hot steam clears my mind. I cannot get clean. Help scrub me clean."

He had used these reasons to justify to Shira his request for a bath each day.

However, Samuel gave Nathan no explanation for his absence at school.

"It is time you took over," was all he said to Nathan when he inquired as to when the prophet might return to the academy. "When I am able," was all he offered.

When Nathan and Samuel had arrived home late at night after their trip to see the king, Shira greeted her husband with him wrapped in nothing but a blanket and holding his family sword on his lap. Samuel was nearly dead weight. Shira and Nathan had to lift Samuel out of the wagon. When she asked about his clothes, Nathan told her they had stopped in a wooded area and buried them, including his undergarments. Nathan did not explain to Shira why there had been the need to bury the clothes. He could barely speak himself, and she could tell that Nathan's own nerves were frayed by whatever had transpired on this trip. Shira did not press him sensing the young prophet witnessed something terrible that could not be explained. He simply told Shira that he had fulfilled the desire of his master, and he was sure he would give her complete details of their story when he was able.

Shira was long accustomed to her husband's peculiar behavior, but after watching his all-night, turbulent encounter with Yahweh on the roof of their house and then seeing the state in which he returned from his visit with the king—covered in nothing but a wool blanket, shivering and groaning, his white beard and hair streaked with bloodstains, clutching the family sword that she had not seen since the days of her youth—she knew something had shifted in the universe. She knew something had occurred that might prevent her husband from ever recovering from his present mental collapse.

Samuel insisted she cover all windows, keep the front door shut, and that scraps of cloth be stuffed in the cracks to block the sunlight. No natural light, like the Holy Place of the Tabernacle, he insisted, just the light of the fire. She knew her husband needed the quiet and the darkness to listen, to heal, to reconcile the truth of his recent experience with the rawness of his heart. On one occasion during this time of no day and night—no hour singled out for any normal human activity, but a moment in the shadows of firelight while soaking in the tub—Shira was surprised when Samuel took her hand, pressing it against his cheek and repeating, "What have I done?" and "I am to blame." Her husband wept as if his tears would refill the evaporated water in his bath.

For days Samuel mumbled inarticulate phrases about the prophet Moses and the fires of Yahweh, the voice coming from inside the bush that would not burn, the Presence of "I Am" and Yahweh's inhuman expectation for Moses to lead a nation of slaves to the land of promise. Generations later, this Yahweh, this same Eternal One, had driven Samuel to grief and despair for his nation, for his king, for himself. What Shira had told her husband years ago was that she believed Yahweh needed a companion, one that not only spoke His powerful words, but a companion who would share the weight and grief of the heart of the Almighty. She never imagined that such revelations of Yahweh's heart would nearly destroy her husband.

In the end, it was Shira's singing that became the slow and steady balm for her husband's soul. She sang as she prepared meals. She sang as she bathed him. She sang at night in bed as he lay weeping softly folded into her arms. Her plaintive, whispering voice carried a soothing cure with every melody.

"Have mercy on me, O Yahweh.
Have mercy on me.
Find rest, O my soul, in Yahweh.

Find rest, in Yahweh alone.
How long will they assault me?
How long will they curse me?
How long will they try to topple me?
O Yahweh, You are my rock.
O Yahweh, You are my fortress.
I will never be shaken.
I will never be shaken."

On the sixth day, Shira rose from sleep and saw her husband sitting on a stool mesmerized once more by the flames of the fire. He was not mumbling, which was a good sign. He rocked slowly forward and back, humming one of the melodies she had sung for him; another good sign that her singing had begun to weave together the fragments of his mind. She had not yet asked for any detail of his trip and, to this point in his mending, he had not offered any. She was most curious about the plug of missing hair on the left side of his head. When she first saw the strange sight she gasped, but Samuel had not noticed her reaction. He was gone from this world, submerged inside an incomprehensible memory.

She scooted to the edge of their bed and set her bare feet upon the floor. "Would you like something to eat?" When he did not answer, she asked, "Would you like another bath? I need to go to the well for fresh water."

Samuel stopped rocking but did not take his eyes from the fire.

"I need you to cut my hair." His voice was raspy from weeping and lack of use. "All of it, down to the skin. Once you have shaved my head, I will be clean."

Shira got to her feet and began gathering what she needed to carry out her task: a pot of olive oil, a sharp knife, a bowl, some rags, and a lamp. Then she set all the items on a small table before dragging it over beside her husband. She doused the top of his head with oil and rubbed her fingers over his scalp, gently massaging the liquid into his skin. She paid careful attention to the blank spot on the side of his head, alert not to apply too much pressure with her fingers on this wound that had not yet healed. Then she took the knife and examined its sharpness in the light of the lamp.

"You are sure about this?" Shira brought the knife into his field of vision.

"Put it all in the bowl," Samuel instructed while maintaining his focus on the fire.

Shira hesitated. She had trimmed his hair when it got below the middle of his back, but this was a drastic request. For as long as she had known him, her husband's hair had been a part of his aura, an almost mystical force of strength. She had to be sure he had not spoken rashly.

Samuel took his eyes from the fireplace and looked at the sharp knife in his wife's hand. The firelight reflected off the blade. He ran a finger along the edge as if to bless it as the high priest did before cutting the throat of the sacrificial beast. Then he turned to face Shira, the first time he had looked her in the eyes since his return.

"Please," Samuel whispered, and then turned back to the fire.

There was nothing else to say. Her husband's decision was made, and she watched him vanish back into his inner world. Shira clenched the knife between her teeth and wound a portion of Samuel's dense hair in a thick strand before cutting. She repeated this process: separating a strand, twisting it into a tight coil, and slicing it with the knife. She dropped each cut strand into the bowl. With the first few cuts Shira looked to Samuel, offering to show him her handiwork, but his demeanor never altered. He kept silent, never turning to her, focused solely on the firelight. So, she continued until the remaining hair was a jagged ridgeline dangling across the base of his neck.

Before starting to shave his head, she rubbed her fingers once more over his oily scalp, then dried her hands on a piece of cloth. Beginning at his forehead and carefully working across the crown then along the back of his neck, she shaved his hair down to the roots. She cut in small rows, leaving behind lanes of bare flesh like a plowed field, then wiped the blade clean on the rags after each run. The room was quiet except for the crunch of the knife scraping across the scalp, the snap and pop of the fire, and the steady breathing of two humans.

"I have done something I have never done before. I took a human life, the life of a king," he whispered, and Shira froze the calm rhythm of shaving. She straightened her back, gasping at this news, which caused her to wince in pain at the sudden pinch to the nerves in her spine.

"Not Saul. Do not fear. Please continue," he said. He did not speak again until Shira pressed her body into his back and she resumed the gentle scraping over the top of his head with the knife.

"I do not remember much after I killed him. I can remember the night on the roof with Yahweh and leaving the next morning with Nathan. I was so hopeful that morning, hopeful that it was not too late, that I could save the king from himself. The morning was full of surprises. Once we met the king, I was shocked to hear the sounds of sheep and cattle.

"Then I discovered Saul had not obeyed Yahweh's command and had spared the best of the flocks and herds, plus the life of the king of the Amalekites. Most surprising of all was to see the sword given to me by my father in the possession of the king. It had been so long. I had forgotten I had given this heirloom to his father in the frenzy of everyone fleeing Shiloh from the pursuit of the Philistines. I had forgotten I had seen it again on our rooftop the night before I anointed Saul's head with the holy oil. I could not stop trembling when I saw the sword of my fathers.

"I confronted the king with his disobedience. I told him Yahweh was displeased and would take his kingdom from him. He made excuses for his actions, but then he appeared repentant. He asked if I would worship with him and the tribal elders and military officers. Saul begged me, but it was all for show. How could I worship Yahweh with my whole heart when I stood next to a king who had defied the command of Yahweh? Yet, I agreed to stay when all I wanted was to escape.

"I did not plan my reaction. I did not have murderous intent when I asked Saul to fetch the Amalekite king and bring him into the circle of altars. But then I saw my father's sword carried by the twin sons of the king, followed by Agag being escorted into the circle pompously acting like he was an invited guest to the ceremony. A wave of vengeance consumed me. Before I knew it, before anyone could stop me, I grabbed my father's sword and was hewing the king of the Amalekites into pieces. Something drove me to finish what the king of Israel had left undone, using the sword my ancestors brought with them from Egypt. I remember nothing else."

Samuel paused and looked around the room as if puzzled by his current location.

Shira laid her fingers upon the side of Samuel's bearded cheek and turned him to face her. His bald, oily head had streaks of red lines across the crown where she had dug the knife a little too deep. His scalp glistened in the flickering light.

"Sometimes I feel I have passed into Sheol and yet my soul is not fully awakened inside this shaded world. I feel only half present in this life and in the one to come."

"You are home, my love." Shira bent over to kiss his lips, offering proof to her husband that he had not passed over into the shades of the afterlife. "And I am done with what you asked of me."

She watched Samuel's hand hovering over the top of his head, feeling the empty, warm air just above the bare scalp before gently landing his palm and fingers upon the tender skin. He was tentative as he ran his fingers over the nubby and indented wasteland. It was a physical alteration that would require time for Shira to absorb.

"I remember one last thing," Samuel said, laying his hand in his lap and rubbing the residue of oil from his scalp into both hands. "As Nathan drove from the site, I kept hearing the king shrieking at the top of his voice. His screams rose above all the other curses and cries coming from the throng around the altars. At first, I could not make out what he was shouting, but then my ears became attuned to his words. 'I am king!' he screamed and kept screaming, 'I am king! I am king!' until fading in the distance."

Samuel rose to his feet and hobbled over to the corner of the room where the family sword was propped against the wall. He picked up the fierce looking blade and saw that it had been cleaned. He looked at Shira and she nodded.

"You should not have to clean up after my mess." His voice sounded hollow and sorrowful as he propped the sword back against the wall.

Shira set the knife on the table and began wiping her hands with a rag.

"I must confess, deep down I never wanted this to work." Samuel leaned his weary body against the wall. "This monarchy for the chosen of Israel, I could never fully embrace. It mattered not who Yahweh might have plucked from His people to be their king, my heart was never fully free of the hope to see it miscarry. Now that it has, I confess, my heart is broken. I know I had a hand in its failure."

He pushed himself off the wall and shuffled back toward his wife.

"How did the great prophet Moses do it, I wonder, lead all those people for forty years? I am too frail. I could never have done such a great task. I am too frail."

When Samuel stopped in front of her and bowed his bald head before her, Shira thought it was for her to inspect her work, but then he took her hands and brought them to his lips, kissing each finger in turn.

"I want you. I want to make love to you. I want to lie down beside you and never get up for the rest of my days. There is nothing else for me to do. Yahweh must surely be done with me as he is done with Saul. I shall spend my last days mourning the king and resting in the comfort of your strong arms."

Shira pulled her hands free from her husband's grasp and wrapped her arms around his waist, drawing him closer.

"You cannot be sure, my love." Shira kissed her husband and kissed him again. "You will always have my arms to lie in, but you cannot know the mind of Yahweh."

Shira was only speaking what Samuel himself had taught her. That as long as he lived, he must always be ready to revise whatever he might believe and whatever plans he might formulate. That once one was claimed by Yahweh there was no release even though there may be long periods of silence. That one could be overtaken by Yahweh at any time.

"Shall I remove the coverings from the windows?" Shira asked.

"Not yet. I enjoy the firelight. I feel my appetite beginning to grow, for food and for you. I feel my strength returning."

He kissed her again, and this time Shira allowed her lips to linger upon his, moistening the cracks in the flesh and softening the surfaces.

"What would you like?" she asked between kisses. "What are you hungry for?"

"Need you ask?" Their soft laughter made them loosen their grip.

"We must eat something." Shira tugged gently on Samuel's beard. "You have hardly eaten, and I too am starving."

Samuel groaned in feigned disappointment but admitted his need for food.

"Let me clean off the table first."

Samuel stopped her before she could lift the bowl of hair. "No love; that, I will do. You have done enough."

Shira went to the shelves and began to assemble fruit, cheese, and bread on a tray that would fill their empty stomachs. She paused to watch Samuel take the bowl off the table and stare at the mound of hair. It was done. The baths had cleansed his body. The shearing had removed the final residue of blood not bathed away with the constant scrubbing. The only thing left was the disposal.

"I must burn this. It is the only way to end this tainted ordeal."

Samuel took the soiled cloths Shira used to wipe clean the knife after each shaving across his head and dropped them onto the smoldering coals to build the blaze. Once the rags caught fire, he dropped the severed locks into the flames, each one a surrender of his manly strength.

Shira watched Samuel watching the fire devour each clump of hair. She saw his muscles began to tighten. His legs began to lift him. His back began to straighten. She was mistaken. He was not weakened by the shearing of his hair or of the fire devouring it. On the contrary, her husband appeared invigorated. When he dropped the last tress of his hair into the fire, he knelt down before the flames and stared into the inferno.

"Yes, Yahweh. Yes," he whispered.

Shira set the tray of food upon the table and continued silently observing Samuel kneeling in front of the fire, his face so close to the flames she thought his beard would ignite. His head glowed as if in a state of rapture. In the darkness of this room, his head appeared to radiate from an inner luminosity she had never witnessed. She made no sudden movement, but quietly sank down upon the floor to watch Samuel communicate with the flames. She embraced this moment with a smile, sensing in her heart a thickening of hallowed air as it rose from the blaze and engulfed her husband.

Chapter 21

DAVID GENTLY TUGGED THE SHEEP CLOSER TO GET A BETTER look inside its nostrils. The creature's immediate reaction was to bleat and jerk back its head. He had to grip the thick wool beneath the sheep's neck to keep it from escaping so he could finish his examination. This was an unpleasant but necessary part of the job of caring for his sheep—cleaning out the parasites in the eyes, ears, and snout on the face of each one. He dipped his rag in the pot of olive oil mixed with ashes and wiped the inside of the sheep's nose, ears, and eyes. Once he was satisfied, he released it and smiled as it raced back to the flock bleating out its complaint for this unwanted treatment.

David decided this was the last sheep of the day. He wanted to get back to composing. He picked up his rag and the oil pot and lumbered over to his campsite at the base of a large boulder and sat down on his folded bedroll underneath the branches of a spreading oak. Early on in his job as a shepherd, he learned the wisdom of keeping the sheep out of his campsite. Food sacks and skins of water were piled near the fire ring.

He reached for a water skin and filled his mouth with water. In spite of the warm temperature, it was still refreshing. He stretched his hand over the coals of the fire and felt its low warmth. He would need to gather more wood to replenish his fuel supply before it got dark, but for now he needed to get back to the song he had been working on that would just not cooperate. Lyrics and music were not coming together.

He had been roaming the high country for weeks, leading the sheep from one pasture to another. He had found this natural grazing area nestled into an open hollow surrounded by rock outcroppings and patches of scrub bushes and trees with one wide path in and out of the natural enclosure, which he had blocked off with dead-fall branches. A small pool of water fed by an underground spring bubbled out of the ground not far from where he sat, and the grass was thick and plentiful, enough to last for several days. He could sit and watch the flock and his pack-mule graze peacefully while he spent his solitary time composing.

David brushed off his garments, releasing a small cloud of dirt particles into the air and then grabbed the threadbare cloth bag with his kinnor inside. One day he would have a proper bag to carry and protect his musical instrument. One day he hoped to afford to pay an artisan to craft a fine ten-string kinnor carved from almond wood with roses engraved into the base. One day he hoped there might be a way to sing his compositions of Yahweh not just for his sheep or his family who acted indifferent to his musical talents, but for a more appreciative audience.

Perhaps there might be an opportunity to sing his songs to the musicians of the Levitical tribe. They were the only ones in Israel whose line of work was to sing, just sing. One day, perhaps. He just needed the opportunity to play in front of the right audience. He had higher aspirations than being a shepherd, living and dying in small-town Bethlehem, the youngest of ten siblings, but the bigger world he longed to experience had not yet opened itself to him. One day.

He pulled his kinnor out of his bag and examined his fingernails. They were too cracked and broken to pluck the five strings—the natural consequences of his occupation. He reached into the side pocket of his bag and took out the ram's horn plectrum and began plucking each string, loosening or tightening it as needed. Once satisfied with the sound, he strummed them all together and lowered his ear close to the pulsating strings. There was no sound like it. The harmonic vibrations of the strings created a similar reaction in his body. He leaned back against the tree and began to pluck his melody.

> "When I ponder Your heavens
> The work of Your fingers,
> And consider the moon and stars…"

He stopped and shook his head, unhappy with his choice of words.

> "Yahweh, how majestic is Your name.
> How majestic is Your name in all the earth.
> O Yahweh… O Yahweh… O… O…"

He strummed the stings madly as if erasing the words before he could start over. All of his songs swirled in his head and came out as spontaneous compositions. One day he would have the words written. One day he would find other musicians with whom he could play and compose. One day he hoped his life would consist of nothing but music.

From behind him he heard the landslide of rocks and dirt and the sound of something heavy sliding down the boulder's smooth face. He set down his kinnor, twisted around, and saw his nephew descending on his bottom down the boulder, feet forward and waving his arms.

"Uncle David, prepare to die!" Joab shouted just before he hit the ground and leapt upon David's back.

David barely had time to push his kinnor out of the way to keep it from getting smashed before his nephew slammed into his back.

Joab easily had the advantage, pushing David over onto his stomach and pinning him to the ground, pressing his full weight on his spine. He yanked one of David's legs up to his mouth and bit down hard.

"Leg of shepherd." Joab pretended to be chewing a mouthful of his uncle's leg and smacking his lips. "Tasty and delicious but needs a pinch of salt."

"Joab, wait till I get my hands on you." David squirmed on his stomach like a pinned serpent and flailing his arms, trying to knock Joab off of him.

"Sorry to interrupt your composing, Uncle." Joab took another mock bite of David's calf. "The singing shepherd…head in the stars, feet in the sheep dung. Will your new song exploit your bravery? Will the bear grow larger with each verse?"

"You will find the carcass of the bear a half-day's walk just south of here."

No one in David's family believed his story, which frustrated him to no end.

"By now the carcass of a bear cub would be devoured by the vultures, and the bones carried off by a pack of jackals."

"That bear was three times your size and weight."

"Crippled, dying, and with no claws or teeth." Joab jumped off David's back and transformed his body into his description of the bear.

David rolled over and burst out laughing at Joab's bearish antics. "Joab, you are a son of a jack mule."

"That is not a nice thing to say of your older sister, Uncle," Joab said, suddenly changed back into his human form.

David was the older of the two. David's sister had married the month he was born, and a year later, his sister gave birth to Joab.

"I did kill that bear," David said.

"If you say so." Joab turned from speaking and began to sing. "And all Israel will sing of your glory and call you the 'Bear of Judah.'"

David clamped his hands over his ears. "Stop. You will stampede the flock." He then picked up his bedroll and playfully tossed it over Joab's head. "Why are you here?"

"You will never guess who has come to Bethlehem." Joab yanked the blanket off his head. "Old buzzard-beak himself."

"What are you babbling about? Who has come to Bethlehem?"

"Not just come to Bethlehem but has come to the home of Jesse and Nitzevet, the parents of the 'Bear of Judah,' and my grandparents."

"I have no patience with you." David yanked his bedroll out of his nephew's hands and started to shake the dust from it. "Who are you talking about?"

"The prophet of Yahweh, destroyer of the Baals, slayer of pagan kings and Amalekite children, his lips always bubbling with the foam of prophesy. They say if you look into his yellow eyes, he has the power to turn you into stone."

"Samuel, the prophet and judge of Israel…at my house." David's demeanor was beginning to change from enjoying his nephew's surprise visit to one of irritation.

"And waiting patiently for your return home." Joab threw open his arms.

David scrutinized Joab's face and then burst into laughter.

"Nephew, I salute your imagination."

"Uncle, it's true. Grandfather sent me to tell you to come home immediately; the prophet of Yahweh requests an audience with you."

Joab's sober expression and unflinching delivery almost made David believe his nephew, but after a heartbeat, he knew this prankster was not to be trusted and laughed again at the absurdity of it all.

David stopped laughing the moment he saw the sheep break into a mad dash, circling the enclosure and coughing up terrified bleats. His mule raised his head and began to bray furiously.

"Do you see any cause for this, Joab?" David scanned the enclosure.

"There, on the outcropping." Joab pointed directly across the hollow. "See it?"

David squinted in the direction Joab pointed. The yellowish-brown color of his hide was so close to the hues of the rocky ledges where the creature perched that it was difficult to see. It was not until the lion opened its mouth and growled that David was able to pinpoint his exact position on the ledge. The lion appeared to be in no hurry to attack but sat on its back haunches and bobbed its head almost as if amused by the frenzy that he had created.

David grabbed his knife and stuck it between his teeth. Then he took a handful of stones and his sling while Joab scrambled up the tree branches. The sheep were racing around the enclosure. Many of them became tangled in the thorny scrub brush along the base of the rocky ledges. A few were able to leap over the dead branches David had stacked in front of the path leading in and out of the enclosure. Those few sheep may be lost forever, but he would save as many as he could.

He dropped a rock in his sling and began the mad whirling above his head. He slung the rock and it smashed into the base of the ledge several feet below the lion, whose only reaction to the inaccuracy was a bored yawn.

"You missed!" Joab shouted from the safety of the top branches.

David paid no attention to the obvious but reloaded his sling and fired again. This time it was closer to the target, smashing into the rock face just to the right of the lion. The hit was enough to get the lion off its haunches and start it leaping from perch to perch, making its way down the ledge and into the grassy enclosure.

When the lion began chasing the sheep, trying to split one away from the flock, David fired again but hit a buck, causing it to tumble and then it lay still. He could not tell if he had killed it or knocked it unconscious.

The lion succeeded in isolating a sheep from the panicked flock and quickly clamped its jaws over the lamb's woolly back. David jammed another stone inside the pouch of his sling as the lion trotted across the pasture. Just as the lion began to ascend the rocky incline, David cried out, "Yahweh!" as he released the stone. This time the shot was true. The stone flew into the back of the lion's head, causing the lion to drop the bleating lamb from its mouth as it toppled backward into the pasture growling in pain.

David dropped the sling and the last few stones and raced over to the lion stretched out upon the ground. He pulled the knife from his mouth and leapt upon the lion's back, twisting the startled lion over on top of him. The lion howled in rage, pawing the air and trying to claw its assailant. David plunged his knife into the lion's chest again and again, trying to strike the heart, and then slashed the lion's throat, severing the windpipe.

He clung to the lion until he felt the last sensation of air gasp from its lungs. Once the lion was perfectly still, David crawled out from beneath it. He got to his feet and looked at his body drenched in lion's blood. He sniffed the blood dripping from his knife. The same disturbing power after he killed the bear rushed through him, an awakened power that frightened and thrilled him, a clear passion for the kill had been kindled. He knelt down and severed the head from its body with his knife. He lifted the lion's head to the heavens and began a boisterous dance around the carcass—an untamed soul ecstatic in strength and Yahweh's deliverance.

"Yahweh is my light and my salvation.
I shall never be afraid.
Yahweh is the strength of my life.
Nothing can frighten me.
O Yahweh, You were not far off.
O Yahweh, my strength, You came quickly.
O Yahweh, You gave me strength.
O Yahweh, You delivered me.
From the lion's mouth, You delivered me."

"Uncle. Uncle." Joab could not get David's attention. He grabbed the shepherd's rod from the low branch as he climbed down from the tree and poked David with it, trying to break him from the spell of his rowdy dance.

David came to an abrupt stop and spun around, panting for breath. "Now do you believe me about the bear?"

"I believe," Joab said, eyes wide at the sight of the dead lion at his feet. "I shall always believe."

"I shall skin this lion and make a bag from its pelt for my kinnor."

"Uncle, you cannot do it now. Let me skin it for you. You must go home."

"Home?" David asked, the violent power of this moment broke its spell.

"I just told you." Joab spoke to his uncle as though he were a confused child. "Samuel, the prophet of Yahweh has come to your house. He is waiting for you. If you ride now, you should be home before dark."

"My house." David blinked rapidly as he began to reenter the present reality. "What does the prophet want?"

"You. That is all I know. You must leave now."

"What of my lion?" David looked back at its carcass.

"I will skin it for you."

"And the sheep? What about the lost sheep?"

"I shall find them. You have got to leave."

Joab untied the mule while David hastily stuffed his kinnor into its cloth bag and wrapped the lion's head in his bedroll. This he must take with him. A lion's head and a musical instrument—the tangible objects of the warrior-musician.

"Joab, I have this strange feeling that after today I will leave behind my life as a shepherd." David leapt upon the back of his mule.

"Uncle, you were born into a family of shepherds." Joab spoke with assurance as he tightened the rope that secured the bedroll with the lion's head and the bag with his kinnor. He then draped the rope over the mule's back before handing the two ends to David. "You will sire children who will be shepherds, and you will die a shepherd."

David took a deep breath, fully alert now and invigorated by the present moment. He looked into the chalky winter sky and imagined this place as a life he had lived, long past—a life that existed in the dreams of memory.

"Gut and skin my lion before you do anything else." David looked down at Joab as he tied the two ends of the rope around his waist. "Be careful not to waste any of the hide. It must be large enough to hold my kinnor."

"Yes, O Lion of Judah." Joab bowed and stepped from the mule.

David gripped the reins, kicked the mule's ribs, and began to trot around the enclosure. He waved to Joab as he guided his mule around the makeshift gate of dead branches and out of the enclosure. In the blink of an eye, he was gone. The quick heat of the presence of this shepherd-warrior-musician had evaporated. It was as if the earth had heaved its breath and shot David on a great gust toward the future.

Chapter 22

IN THE GOLDEN COLORS OF THE SUNSET, DAVID SAW THE crowd gathered in front of the house as he rode in from the foothills and onto the family property. Because of the size of the family and the steady increase in the quantity of the herds and flocks, David's father, Jesse, chose to move out of Bethlehem proper to the outskirts of the city so he could build a larger house for his offspring and expand the number of corrals and barns required to accommodate the growth in livestock. Most of David's older brothers and sisters were married and had children of their own, and the size of the family would nearly qualify them as a sub-tribe of Judah.

David recognized many of the prominent citizens of Bethlehem mingling with his brothers and sisters and their children: city elders, wealthy merchants, and revered rabbis all milled about the courtyard and outer area in front of his house. However, David did not see his parents or the famous prophet of Yahweh. He would not have recognized him anyway. He had never seen him before. Now, somewhere in this throng, was Yahweh's mouthpiece, come from Ramah for an audience with him. But why? David had done nothing to deserve this attention. Nor did he see himself as a candidate to train to become a prophet. David hoped Samuel was not here to recruit him. He wanted to be a singer.

David saw the wary looks on the faces of the crowd. They seemed unsure who he might be, dressed in the scanty, loose garments of a shepherd, his skin caked with dirt and grime from a stint in the high country, and covered with a glaze of blood. He came to a stop before the crowd. The answer to his altered appearance was inside his bedroll.

Eliab and Abinadab, his two oldest brothers, hesitantly approached David as he sat upon his mule looking at him as if he were a visitor from Sheol.

"David is that you?" asked Eliab.

"Yes. Yes. Why is everyone outside the house?"

"David, what took you so long?" Abinadab instantly began to scold the moment he recognized his voice. "And what happened to you?"

David untied the rope from around his waist. He handed his cloth bag with the kinnor to Abinadab, and then carefully began to unwrap his bedroll. With a performer's flourish, he unfurled the blanket, and out fell the head of the lion. His two brothers jumped back to avoid the head bouncing onto their clean garments, and the whole crowd gasped at the sight of the beast's head with its death-grin lying on the ground.

"Never doubt me again, brothers." David enjoyed his haughty position of looking down upon them from his mule. "Joab was a witness."

"Joab must have soiled himself," Eliab said after regaining his composure.

"The lion must have begged you to slit its throat after listening to you sing." Abinadab held up the kinnor.

"I killed it with one hand while composing with the other." David slung his leg over his mule and hopped off its back.

He grabbed the top of the lion's head and held it aloft. A few children cried out in fear and hid behind their parents, but most of the crowd reacted with awe, just as he had hoped. David enjoyed the attention. It was proof that while he might be the last born male in the house of Jesse, he was becoming, on his own merit, someone worthy of respect.

"David. David." He saw his parents pushing their way through the people.

"You are here, finally." Jesse clapped his hands, not in applause at the sight of his son's trophy, he barely noticed it, but for him to make haste. "Come inside."

"Put that thing down and come at once." David's mother, Nitzevet, waved for him to follow her.

David expected his siblings to act unimpressed with his exploit and to ridicule him for his vanity, but he did not anticipate this disinterest from his parents. They barely acknowledged the prize he held in his hand and hurried him into the house, showing embarrassment that he should be seen in public in this disheveled condition.

"Why is everyone so dressed up?" David asked when his father took him by the arm and began tugging him toward the front door.

"Inside, please. We will explain inside." Jesse motioned with his free hand.

"That thing is not coming into this house." Nitzevet pointed firmly at the lion's head swinging in David's hand. "Drop it and come inside."

David turned back and tossed the lion's head at Eliab and Abinadab, both of whom jumped out of the way before being struck.

"Take care of it," David ordered. "I want the skull and teeth."

Before he shut the door, Jesse asked the crowd to move farther out into the courtyard away from the house and to remain quiet and not disturb them.

"We shall be out soon, and then we will worship and sacrifice with the prophet," Jesse announced, and then shut the door and locked it.

It was strange enough for his father to lock the door of the house, but it was stranger for the full-sized common room to be empty of people. For as long as David had been alive, this room always bustled with his siblings, their wives and husbands, and a company of children. It was never empty and never quiet. The huge dining table in the center of the room was never clear of domestic objects or cleaned from the soil and human grime of daily family life. A tidy house was an impossible task his mother had given up years ago when the demands of ten children became overwhelming. Now, David looked across this massive table, made larger by its empty surface, and could not believe his eyes. He wondered what had changed while he had been in the high country.

Nitzevet took a pot full of water warming at the edge of the fire on the raised, stone fireplace and poured the contents into the metal basin on the table. The fire was the only source of light in the room. Normally, the windows were opened and the room was filled with oil lamps burning on shelves and stands, but the fire in the fireplace provided only a muted illumination. Nitzevet took a sponge and dipped it into the water. She squeezed out the excess water over the top of David's unkempt hair and began forcefully wiping his face and neck.

"Someone please tell me what is going on." David turned his head away, resisting every time his mother swiped the wet sponge over his skin. He was not a child any more who needed bathing from his mother.

"Hush and be still. How did you get so filthy?" His mother was undeterred by David's defiant squirming.

"We were completely surprised. No advance warning. He arrived midmorning unannounced." David's father spoke in the same soft, yet frantic tone of his mother. "He brought a heifer with him to offer a sacrifice, along with that nice young man, Nathan."

"You remember Nathan, son of Reu and Deborah. They live in town. He left home a few years ago to attend the prophet's school," Nitzevet added.

"Anyway, he asked us to join him for the sacrifice. Told us we all needed to consecrate ourselves, and—"

"Abba, why are you and Ima whispering? And why are you talking so fast?"

"Hush," Nitzevet hissed as she lifted the wide, single leather strap across his chest connected to his shepherd's breechcloth so she could scrub his shoulders.

"We have all bathed today." Jesse began picking out the caked grunge caught in the tangles of David's auburn hair and tossing the clots into the basin of water. "All of us have put on clean clothes. And then it was so strange. He asked to see your brothers, one at a time. Each one walked in front of him, and after a moment, he shook his head. He would not tell me why. He would not tell me what he was doing. He simply said none of our sons would do. Then he asked if there was another son, and here you are."

"So, the prophet is here. Joab was not lying," David whispered like his parents.

Jesse took the towel slung over his shoulder and began to dry David's hair, while Nitzevet wiped down the length of his arms and in between his fingers.

"Your fingernails are impossible." She shook her head in dismay. "Impossible."

"Never mind, Ima." David took the sponge from her trembling hand and tossed it into the basin. When he saw the blood, and dirt dissolving in the reddish, murky water, he sighed in disappointment. The evidence of his brave act would soon be tossed out into the garden. "I can finish myself." David took the towel from his father to dry his hair.

"You finish, and I will fetch your clean robe." Nitzevet turned to secure the robe but was instantly stopped.

"There is no need for clean garments. Let the boy approach."

David stood still, the power of the voice freezing the blood of his veins. He felt his chest wrapped in pain, increasing with each rapid heartbeat. He had never known what fear felt like. He had never been in a position where fear was an option. There was nothing fearful about killing the lion. It was instinct and reaction; the thought of being afraid never entered his mind. Now he was consciously aware of the sensation, and his legs began to shake. Now he knew why his parents whispered in frantic bursts and scrubbed him in violent strokes.

"But, my lord, you cannot see what he looks like in the dim light." His father spoke hoping not to offend. "He still has on his shepherd's garb. We could at least—"

"I am not concerned about his outward appearance." The voice spoke from the far, dark corner of the room. "It is the heart Yahweh looks upon."

No, Joab had not lied. The prophet was in his house. The prophet had come for him. At any moment David knew he was about to be demolished by the Almighty.

"Step forward, my son."

David saw his parents' step to the side, and he felt a chill rush through him and a sense of isolation. Cognizant of the apparitions nestled in the shadowy corner at the far end of the table, he was unable to discern their intentions. He felt unclean, that the fruitless attempt by his parents to make him presentable only made his unsanitary condition more obvious. And what was more disturbing was that this ghostly form with its foreboding voice could examine his heart. The dirt and lion grist still clogging the pores of his skin was nothing. He needed more time to scour his heart. He could not approach this specter, not like this. He was not ready. He could never be ready.

David began to creep along the side of the large, one-cubit high table used for family meals toward the disembodied voice that beckoned. His father had hired a local carpenter to build a table for the family to gather around on their cushions and eat off trays of food. David braced his knee against its solid frame as he scooted along the edge. When he was a boy, he would hide under it to escape persecution from his older brothers. Diving under it again could be an option if the phantom in the corner proved threatening.

When David reached the end of the table, his eyes had adjusted to the diffused light in the room and the prophet came into focus. He sat in his father's chair, a chair in which no one sat. Behind him stood a young man he barely remembered, clutching a jeweled ox horn in both hands. David saw Samuel gesturing for him to come closer, but he could not move his legs. He searched for the slit in the lush beard for the prophet's lips imploring him to step toward him but could not find it. The beard enveloped his face, rising upward toward the prophet's immense eyebrows. The dents and lumps in his white, bald head looked like thumbprints left by an arthritic sculptor. David ignored his nephew's warning not to look into the prophet's eyes, and when he did not turn into stone, he was able to step away from the table.

"Remove the towel from your head." Samuel pointed to the towel.

David felt like a fool. He yanked the towel off his head and tossed it on the table.

Samuel needed to be sure. He thought he had been sure when Eliab, Jesse's strapping firstborn stood in front of him, but he was wrong. *Surely*

the next son would be the one, he thought, but he had been wrong a second time, and also with the third. All the way through Jesse's sons, he had been wrong. But the last son, the youngest, not yet a man but wearing a man's clothing, smelling of a man's labor in the outdoors, his weathered and handsome features inspiring…inspiring what? Hope? Courage? Elation? Could Samuel be correct? Could he be sensing the voice of Yahweh; the affirmation of the Almighty that this ruddy lad was the one?

A sheer muscular joy began to kick through his muscles. The bitter taste of remorse at anointing Saul began to dissolve. The fear he carried with him to Bethlehem began to release its grip on his heart. And in his mind "The One" kept repeating and repeating until his lips were forced to shape the words and give them voice. Samuel leaned forward, extending his arm toward David, not to touch him, not to beckon him, but as if he was testing the heat of a fire with his hand. He then sat back, concealing the hand inside his robe. It was trembling.

"Are the other sons outside?" asked Samuel.

"Yes, my lord," Jesse replied.

"Invite them to enter, but to speak not a word; remain silent."

David dared not look at his brothers as they filed in one by one and took positions along the opposite edge of the table from where he stood. He felt their eyes staring into his skin. He knew they and their parents were just as inquisitive, just as agitated as he as to why they were gathered in a room with the only man in Israel on speaking terms with the Creator of heaven and earth. Whatever it was they were about to witness, David knew it would make his position with his brothers all the more precarious.

After Jesse closed the door, the room became still, and Samuel spoke to David. "Kneel down, my son."

David was a child again, having to be instructed in everything. He lost all self-sufficiency. He fell to his knees and fixed his eyes upon the prophet's feet and splayed toes. The moment he felt the hands of the prophet rest upon his head and begin to knead his scalp with his fingers, David dropped forward, his hands braced upon the floor.

"Nathan, anoint the boy."

David felt the liquid drip onto the top of his head and the back of his neck.

"All of it," Samuel instructed. "Empty the vessel."

David dug his fingers into the floor the moment the liquid began cascading upon his head, and his nostrils caught the scent of olive oil, myrrh, and cinnamon. He almost fainted from the pungency of the concoction. He knew this aroma would be permanently registered in his mind from this moment through the rest of his life.

"Hear, O Israel. I have made a covenant with my chosen one," the prophet began. "With my sacred oil I have anointed him. I have sworn to David, my servant. I will establish his line forever and make his throne firm through all generations. My hand will sustain him; surely my arm will strengthen him. My faithful love will be with him, and through my name, his horn will be exalted. He will call out to me, 'You are my Father, my God, the Rock, my Savior.'

"I will appoint him the most exalted of the kings of the earth. I will maintain my love to him forever and my covenant with him will never fail. His throne shall be established forever. Once for all, I have sworn by my holiness. David's throne will endure before me like the sun." Then Samuel raised his lathered hands in the air. "Hear, O Israel, the Lord our God, the Lord is One."

The oil of Yahweh's Spirit ran down David's cheeks and splashed onto the floor in small pools. He felt a cold scald on his flesh but kept his hands anchored upon the floor. And then it took him, encompassing his entire being, an infinite, purifying cure to his infected heart, an ecstasy in his body and a seizing of his spirit as this rapture raced through him faster than the flow of his blood, pouring into every nerve, every fiber, every crack of his being. When he finally lifted his hands off the floor, he felt he would be vaulted through every level in the house and burst out of the adobe roof above him.

"Yahweh, I am your servant!" David shouted as he caught himself backing into the table. "Your servant! Yahweh, your servant!"

David's eyes began to sting, and his vision blurred as his own flood of tears began to mix with the sacred oil. He felt across the surface of the table, found the towel, and vigorously began to wipe his eyes. When his sight was restored, he looked at the prophet, anticipating an explanation of what had just happened.

"Wait for Yahweh, my son." Samuel reached for the towel, took it from David's grasp, and began to wipe the oil from his hands.

"My lord, I do not understand." David cringed at the sound of his husky voice and at his boldness to question the prophet. "I am to be king…of Israel?"

"Yahweh has sought a man after His own heart and has anointed him king over His people. From now on you belong to Yahweh."

"But, my lord, I am just a shepherd. I know nothing."

"Yahweh has spoken His mind."

"Yes, my lord, but a king? I know nothing of being a king."

"Your kingdom shall be like your flock; tend it as you tend your sheep."

When Samuel finished using the towel, he gave it back to David who clutched it to his chest. Then Samuel rose to his feet and placed his hands upon David's shoulders.

"Take no step to seize the throne or try to win it," Samuel whispered. "Let the crown descend upon your head by the hand of Yahweh."

Samuel kissed each side of David's moist face and then began to shuffle toward the door with Nathan at his side.

"My lord, you will come to me again?" David asked. "You will counsel me? Be Yahweh's voice to me?"

Samuel paused and turned to David.

"There is danger for you and your family by the passing of Yahweh's Spirit to His chosen." Samuel raised a finger to his lips. "What we have done tonight has been done in secret for your safety, the safety of your family, and the stability of the kingdom. Yet, what Yahweh has spoken cannot be undone by human force. I say again, take no action of your own. Be patient, be silent, and wait upon Yahweh."

David watched as his father unlocked the door and opened it. His mother stood by his side as the prophet and Nathan paused just inside the door.

"Will you stay the night with us, my lord?" Jesse asked.

"We shall leave tonight after the sacrifice," Samuel said. "The king has spies everywhere. It is safer for us to travel under the cover of darkness."

David's father ushered Samuel and Nathan out of the door. His mother looked back inside the room. She cleared her throat, breaking the spell on David and his brothers. She waved for them to quickly exit the room and rejoin their families waiting in the courtyard.

Nitzevet was the last to leave the room. She looked back at her baby sitting on the table, his back hunched over, his face buried in the towel weeping softly. It was all she could do to keep from rushing to him and wrapping her arms around him. She knew this was too much for any of them to absorb, but she also knew in the balance of time, Yahweh's time, whether packed inside days or in fluid ages, her son would come to grasp the power of this moment and learn to shoulder the broad burdens of leadership. The thought of her son becoming the next king of Israel raised the hair on her neck.

"Are you coming, my dear?" she whispered.

"I need time, Ima. I need time."

"Of course, you do. Time is a gift. Take all you need."

When David heard the door close behind his mother, he swiftly made his way out of the common room and over to the interior steps leading to the rooftop. He raced up the flights of stairs, passing three floors of family rooms until he reached the door opening onto the roof. He went over to the backside of the house facing away from the city with a view of the mountains to the east and north. He did not wish to see or be seen by his family or the citizens of Bethlehem. He wished only to behold the firmament of Yahweh, an enormity of creation that could not contain his expanding soul. He covered his head with the oil-soaked towel and inhaled its holy air.

"O Yahweh, our Yahweh

How majestic is Your name in all the earth.
You have set Your glory above the heavens.
You ordain praise on the lips of children.
Your enemies are silenced by the praise of infants.
When I consider Your heavens,
The work of Your fingers, the moon, the stars,
Which You have set in place,
What is man that You are mindful of him;
The son of man that You care for him?
You made him a little lower than the angels.
You have crowned him with glory and honor.
O Yahweh. O Yahweh. O Yahweh.
How majestic is Your name in all the earth."

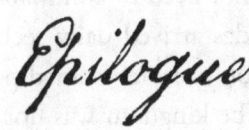

Epilogue

SAUL SAT ALONE ON HIS HIGH-BACK THRONE IN THE COR-
ner of his roof, looking out over the front of the compound and beyond.
In the darkness all he could see were shadowy outlines of buildings and
dwellings. This burst in new residents, a result of the construction sprawl
to accommodate the number of people required to serve the king, had
transformed the bare ground and woodlands of Saul's family farm. His
property had become a village for priests and military, housing for the
servants and staff under his employ. There were permanent structures for
tribal emissaries and their personnel to serve as advisors to the king as well
as represent the interests of their respective tribes. There was a constant
flow of courtiers, nobles, and subjects seeking an audience with the king.

Before he became king, Saul could count on two hands the number of
people who might travel the road to and from his house to Gibeah on any
given day. New structures had left no empty space between his compound
and Gibeah on either side of the road. Gibeah and its population of diverse
cultures had become the central city for the first king of Israel.

What had the prophet meant by saying the kingdom had been torn
from him? Saul initially thought the horrible incident in Carmel at the
circle of altars would bring his instant demise, that he would be struck

297

down before he even got home. But nothing dire happened. His soldiers re-pledged their loyalty. With each military victory his kingdom was expanding. Enemies lived in fear of him.

More and more, the prominent citizens of Israel thought it an honor to have his blessing and were increasing their tribute payments. His coffers were brimming. He did not need to commandeer sons and daughters of Israel to serve him. Hordes arrived daily seeking employment. It was a time of bounty. The nation of Israel seemed poised to dominate the land Yahweh had promised. The kingdom was not being torn from him. Just the opposite was true.

Saul concluded that the prophet just did not like him. He never had, never would. Nothing Saul had done pleased him. He had lived in dread of the irascible old man long enough. It was good to make this clean break. He had a kingdom to rule.

He gulped wine from his goblet and then refilled it. He looked at the dark contents reflecting the torchlight on its shimmering surface and tried to remember the number of times he had drained and refilled his goblet tonight. It was futile, so he took another long drink. Other than having a muddled sensation in his head, he felt no particular ill effect from his steady consumption.

He set the goblet on the table next to the folded cloth of the prophet's torn sleeve, the ram's horn that contained the oil the prophet had dripped onto his head, and the leafy, bronze crown of Agag. He brought the prophet's sleeve to his lips and dabbed the slick coating of wine from them. Then he took a small leather container from the table, removed the top and looked inside at the collection of tiny bones.

"Pagan bones," Saul mumbled. "Dry, savage bones."

He put the top back onto the container and gave it a vigorous shaking. Then he ripped the top off and tossed the bones into the corner of the roof and watched them bounce off the wall and settle on the floor.

"Little white bones." Saul addressed the multitude of bones scattered before him. He studied them intently. "You rattle and tumble and come to rest. You think you can position a man's destiny with your random formation. How can that be when I, the one who casts you against the wall, has released you?" Saul raised his arm with the empty leather cup.

"Do I not get some credit in this game? Am I not allowed some privilege in shaping the course of my destiny?"

He focused his eyes on the bleached wishbones of chickens, the pointed skulls of vultures, the torsos of gophers, the dried and withered paws and claws and tiny legs and arms of sundry creatures laid out for him to divine a future. He could spend the rest of the night studying this bony formation and remain forever baffled.

"Childish games." Saul bent over to collect the scattered bones and was startled by someone behind him clearing his throat. He leaned back against his chair but did not turn around to see the visitor.

"Commander, is that you?" Saul asked.

"Yes, my lord. We are here."

Saul did not summon them to approach, nor did he rise and cross the roof to greet them. Instead, he twisted his body and peeked around the side of the high-backed chair. Next to his cousin stood a young woman robed in a crimson colored, full-length outer cloak with a hood covering her head. Her face was lowered, and Saul could not see her features. Saul motioned to Abner for the woman to pull the hood away from her face.

"Pull back your hood, my dear," Abner whispered.

The young woman did as she was asked and pushed the hood behind her head. The dense, curly red hair wrapped around her pale face was a shock of sunlight. She kept her chin lowered. Saul tapped his chin with his finger and Abner stuck his hand under the young woman's chin to lift her head. Her beauty startled him. Even viewing her under these dimly lit conditions, Saul could see the fairness of her skin, the slender neck, and the frothiness in her eyes, smoldering in the torchlight like two glowing coals.

Though she did not look in his direction, Saul knew that she knew she was the object of his scrutiny. He was enamored by her calmness but became fully captivated when she pulled her chin away from the perch of Abner's fingers and began to turn her head from one side to the other so he might examine her profile. Then she gripped the folds of her robes and lifted the hem. She extended her right foot just enough for him to see the slender ankle and precise cut of her calf. Saul could tell by Abner's speechless expression as he watched her make this little extra effort to reveal her beauty that she had done this without his prompting. His cousin looked disappointed and shamed by her forwardness.

Saul had never looked upon another woman in such a way, not even Ahinoam. This was lust; the heated earth of his body, baking inside his clothes. He gripped the arm of the chair to keep from falling out of the seat and nodded his approval to Abner.

"You may go inside the tent," Abner said.

She let the hem of her garment fall and quietly obeyed the command.

Saul turned around in his chair, looked up into the cloudy night sky, and finally remembered to breathe. He dropped the leather cup.

Abner stepped beside the throne and picked up the leather cup.

"She has that effect on men." Abner glanced back at the tent dome of wolf skin.

Saul gradually regained control of his breathing. "What do you think of the tent Jarib had constructed for me?" Saul peeked around the throne. He was disappointed the young woman had followed Abner's instructions. But he would see her soon enough, alone, without a third party.

"The shelter will serve you well." Abner thrummed his fingers on the leather cup.

"You and the children can have the run of the house." Saul reached over and took the cup from Abner's hands. "I do not intend to go inside."

"As you wish, my lord." Abner stared down at his empty hands.

"I shall live in my tent and rule my kingdom from the rooftop. I may have the designers and builders construct me a palace. Win a few more wars; finish the job left by Joshua of cleansing the land of pagans, and the money will pour into my coffers. I will build you a palace as well, Cousin."

"That is not necessary, my lord."

"Nothing is necessary." Saul looked inside the empty cup. "What is her name?"

"Rizpah." Abner moved over to the edge of the roof and leaned his large frame over the thick, protective wall around the roof.

"Hot coal." Saul chuckled as he took a peek back at the tent. "I love the meaning of her name. Fitting, considering her ravishing, garnet hair." Then he looked back at Abner. "Have you known her, Cousin?"

"I know her family."

"Yes, but have you *known* her?"

"I know her father, Aiah. He is a spice merchant who runs a trade route from Gibeah to Hebron. He is an Edomite."

"And who would have thought such beauty would have been passed down from Father Esau's side of the family tree?" Saul mulled the thought of her ancestry. "Not quite the pure blood of the chosen people, but exceptions can be made."

"Always, my lord."

Saul looked into the back of Abner's head as he stood at the edge of the roof looking out into the night.

"I ask you again, Cousin," Saul said, leaning forward on his throne. "Have you known this woman?"

Abner did not answer the question. He kept looking out into the darkness.

"Your silence is revealing. Do you intend to keep her, make her a wife someday?"

Saul could see Abner's body began to grow taut as he dug his fingers into the lip of the ledge. His cousin straightened his body, but he did not let go of the ledge or turn around. He did not answer Saul's question.

"I assume then that is not your intention." Saul took his goblet in hand and raised it to his lips, then paused. "One final question then. Since you went to the trouble of bringing her here, may I borrow her for a while?"

Abner released his grip on the ledge and turned his profile to his cousin.

"I know what is coming, what you are about to do, and she would not be safe." Abner's voice was a soft timbre of despair. "I brought her to the king so she might live."

"That is wise of you, Cousin," Saul said, then took a sip of wine. "It is the zeal of Yahweh that I purge the nation of Israel of her enemies. To finish what our forefathers left undone when they entered the land of promise."

"Then Yahweh is bloodthirsty." Abner's blurted reply surprised Saul. "I do not understand a God who purifies a piece of geography just for His people, chosen or not."

"You were not so squeamish when it came to slaughtering the Amalekites."

"The Amalekites were cruel, attacking and killing our ancestors. The only sin of the Gibeonites was to play us for fools. Their treaty with us was self-preservation."

Saul set down his goblet and picked up Agag's bronze-leafed crown. "The moment the prophet began hacking Agag to pieces, I was set free. We slaughtered the Amalekites, and we shall continue with the native Gibeonites. The zeal of Yahweh shall inflict punishment on all His heathen, uncircumcised, enemies."

"We are breaking a treaty our forefathers made with the Gibeonites. For three and a half centuries these people have done nothing more than carry our water. They are not a threat. They are servants, nothing more."

"Take your argument to the prophet." Saul was annoyed that he should even have to mention Samuel, but then the prophet always seemed to be in permanent residence in his fractured mind like the presence of a beast he hoped to keep curled up and sleeping.

Then Saul set Agag's crown on the table, grabbed Abner's arm, and looked into his hard-edged profile. "Are Carmi and his troops in place?"

"The tribe of Judah is pleased to carry out the king's order." Abner's face was rigid, his words spoken with shame.

"The treaty the Gibeonites forged with us was based on deception." Saul loosened the grip of his fingers on Abner's muscled forearm and began rubbing it affectionately. "You are most loyal, Cousin. You are the only person in the kingdom I can trust."

"When I descend these steps there is no turning back. You may still revoke the order for Carmi and his troops to enter Gibeah and slaughter the Gibeonites."

Saul stopped rubbing Abner's arm and clamped his fingers around the muscles in a firm clasp. He looked down at Agag's crown then back at Abner who stared straight ahead, his eyes glaring at the entrance into the king's tent. Abner would not look at him. His role as king had usurped the role of cousins and the bond of family. Saul could tell that all Abner wanted to do was escape this rooftop.

"For the love of Israel. For the glory of Yahweh," Saul whispered, and then paused, hoping Abner might finish the third part of the exhortation.

"Good night, my lord." Abner pulled his arm from the grip of the king. "I will remain in my quarters until the vengeance is past."

Saul did not attempt to stop his cousin. He leaned back in his chair and listened to Abner's hasty descent of the stairs. Saul rubbed his fingers over the edge of Agag's crown and then wrapped his hand around his wine goblet. He started to lift it to his mouth but then decided against finishing its contents. No more muddling of his mind tonight. No more softening of his will. No more weakening of his body. He set down the goblet and rose from his throne.

When he took a step forward, he heard the crunch of something beneath his right foot. Saul lifted his sandal and saw the crumbs of animal bones stuck to the leather sole. He ground the bones to powder into the floor of the roof. Such childish fortune-telling would not determine his future. When the stories were written and told, he would be the determining factor for the future glory of his kingdom. He then moved toward his tent. When he reached the entrance, he peeled back the front flaps, lowered his head, and peeked inside. The young woman sat on a stool looking into the flames of a small fire. She seemed to sense his presence and raised her head in his direction and smiled.

Saul opened the tent flaps so he could move inside the shelter. The young woman rose to her feet, and when she bowed her head, cascades of red hair tumbled out from beneath her hood, adorning her face like fair red tassels. She did not flinch when Saul brought his hands to her face and lightly pushed back her covering. He could not quite believe he was looking at the young woman with desire. He could not believe his hands were trembling as he touched this stranger. He could not believe the figment of his wife who had lodged inside his heart for so long was now beginning to fade. He had to speak her name. He had to speak the name of this young woman, for once spoken, then the burial would be final. His heart would be released from the tender grip of his wife. He lifted her face and opened his lips.

"Rizpah," he whispered. "Rizpah."

HENRY O. ARNOLD

Henry O. Arnold has co-authored a work of fiction, *Hometown Favorite*, with Bill Barton, and nonfiction, *KABUL24*, with Ben Pearson. He also co-wrote and produced with Steve Taylor (director) and Ben Pearson the film *The Second Chance* starring Michael W. Smith, the screenplay for the authorized film documentary on evangelist Billy Graham, *God's Ambassador*, and the documentary film *KABUL24*, based on the book which is the story of western and Afghani hostages held captive by the Taliban for 105 days. He lives on a farm in Tennessee with his lovely wife Kay. They have two beautiful daughters married to two handsome men with three above-average grandchildren. For more information please visit: www.henryoarnold.com

ALSO BY HENRY O. ARNOLD

A Voice within the Flame
The Song of Prophets and Kings, Book One

A son of the vow. A voice for a nation.

When Israel's enemies threaten to destroy his world, it appears as though everything Samuel ever held dear may come tumbling down around him.